HARD RAIN

Janwillem van de Wetering

BALLANTINE BOOKS • NEW YORK

Library of Congress Catalog Card Number: 86-42614

ISBN 0-345-33964-9

This edition published by arrangement with Pantheon Books, a division of
Random House, Inc.

Manufactured in the United States of America

First Ballantine Books Edition: September 1987

For Nikki

\\\\\ | /////

A THUNDERCLAP PRECEDED SUDDEN HARD-DRIVING rain, blotting out the shots, two insignificant little bangs compared to the divine anger bursting forth, booming in splendor. When the rain fell, IJsbreker fell too. The rain splashed on the windowsill, into the open window on the body and the floor. Outside it lashed at the tarmac, houseboats, and parked cars, whipped trembling leaves on gigantic elms, cut into the quiet water of the canal, split myriad tiny waves that the sudden storm brushed up.

The corpse lay quietly, after a spasm that made its long legs kick and its balding head shudder. The sprawling body was lit up by lightning flashes. The city of Amsterdam, surprised by the sudden change in heavenly temper—for it had been a pristine day in spring, windless under a protective dome of clear sky —waited quietly for the rain to subside. The God-fearing citizenry of the Binnenkant, meaning "Inner Side," where bank director Martin IJsbreker resided in a luxurious, fully restored, medieval gable house, were safely home, most likely in bed, for the tiny shots cracked at 11:00 P.M. The rain was so hard that it even blocked traffic. Both quays of the Binnenkant, lit by

rustic streetlights, were devoid of movement. Nothing
stirred, except the elm's branches, begging forgive-
ness of the rain, as they tried to spring up and were
cruelly pushed down again, until four dim shapes
darted up the stone steps leading to the banker's
freshly painted front door. They slipped through the
door, which gave way willingly enough, and three of
them ran up the dark stairs. The fourth followed awkwardly, waving both arms, dragging one leg. Because
of the rolling thunder outside, exploding every few
seconds into sharp, jagged reports, accompanied by
flashes of brittle bright light, the forms could have
been demons, flushed from the inner city's drains,
eager to take over while normally forbidden territory
was stunned, and no longer aware. But demons jab-
ber, and the shadowy figures spoke, in a mixture of
Dutch and English. Two were looking down at the
body.

"Dead?" the third asked.

The fourth stumbled into the room, lurched forward, and held on to a leather couch. "Don't touch,"
the third shadow hissed. "Fingerprints, you know."

"Yes," a female voice whispered. "Give me the
gun." The barrel trembled near the corpse's face
while she waited for the thunder to rumble again.
When it came, the room shook and lightning flashed
instantaneously, adding revealing details to what had
been mere forms. No one heard the shot, not even the
girl who fired it, but there was the acrid smell of gunpowder. Her haggard face twisted. Blond hair peeped
from her hooded jacket.

"Put it in his hand."

She didn't respond to the hissed order, so her companion, a black young man, tsk'd impatiently and
knelt down too, taking the gun from her hand and
wiping it with his handkerchief, before arranging the
pistol carefully in the dead man's hand.

His mate, a curly-headed man in his late twenties,

was staring at the corpse. "Hurry," he said shrilly. "This is bad shit. Let's get out of here. Grab the loot." The fourth intruder had sat down on the couch, half turned, wiping the leather upholstery with his arm.

"Right," the black man said in English, rolling his *r*, "we know what to take, the paintings, right? And the vases? We leave the cabinet here? The cabinet is too much bother."

"The cabinet goes," the girl said. "It's a rosewood antique. The man wants it, too. He'll be outside any minute now."

"There's more junk downstairs," the curly-haired man said, "More paintings and the Peruvian stuff. We're lifting a fortune for the man."

"The pay better be good," the black man said.

"No pay. Junk for junk."

"Then the junk better be good."

"Best Nepalese," the girl whispered, "That's what he said."

"I heard that before," the black man snarled. "They'll cut the shit out of it with crap."

"Maybe we're short on choices." The curly-haired man whirled around. "What are we waiting for? Let's grab treasure."

The girl got up. "You okay, Carl? You don't have to be here. You shouldn't have come."

The young man on the couch managed, with some trouble, to stand on wobbly legs. "Yehess." He was dressed better than the others, in a clean striped shirt and spotless pressed jeans. His face, when not contorted because of the necessity to speak, was quite handsome. His recently cut hair had been combed neatly. His arms were waving wildly as he steered his body to a wall. "I'll get this puh-painting."

"Oh," the girl wailed. "The letter, I left it in the boat." She almost cried. "I'm always so *disorganized*."

"Get it," the curly-haired man snapped. "If we

don't do everything just right, we'll lose out alto-gether.''

"I feel sick, Jimmy."

He pushed her to the door. "Go. *Go!* We'll pile up the stuff, take it downstairs.''

The black man stared at the rain running down the windowsill, making a puddle on the floor. "Keep cool, man, the weather is helping out.''

"*Go!*" the curly-haired man screamed. "You too. The man'll be in the street with his truck. We'll be exposed, carrying this shit.''

"Yes, white man boss." The black man was lifting paintings off the wall.

The girl came running back, out of breath. "Here's the letter.''

The curly-haired man put the paper on a low table, placing a vase on the letter so that it wouldn't blow away. Gusts of wet wind made the letter flap. The neatly dressed young man carried a painting into the corridor. The girl followed, a vase in each hand. "Go away, Carl, you really shouldn't be here.''

"The muh-man asked me too.''

"That's all right," the curly-haired man said, switching to Dutch with an American accent. "Go down. Go home. We'll tell him you were in on it. You'll get your share.''

"Kuh-keep it.''

The girl kissed his cheek.

"I can do suh-something." He staggered back into the room.

"No," the girl said. "Go. We don't want you in jail.''

The rain stopped as suddenly as it had begun, but thunder still rolled over the city. The young man car-ried paintings as the others lugged the rosewood cabi-net down the stairs. A truck engine rumbled outside. The driver stayed in the truck cab while the four rob-bers loaded paintings and vases in a frantic hurry.

They banged the vehicle's side when they were done. The girl and the curly-haired man ran off. The black man looked around.

"Coming to the boat? The man'll be there later."

"Noho. Tuh-tomorrow." The young man stumbled away, trying to stay on the narrow sidewalk.

"Shame," a neatly dressed middle-aged woman said, safe behind her folded umbrella, warding him off with its sharp point. "A nice young man like you."

"Sssshame, ma'am?"

"Yes, you're dead drunk."

"Just sssspahastic."

"I'm sorry," the woman said, dropping her umbrella, staring into his face. "I *am* sorry."

The young man shuffled on, jerking his shoulders, twisting his head, throwing out his arms.

"DON'T TAKE A DUTCH PAPER," THE COMMISSARIS'S wife said as the stewardess came by. "When you do, we're back. Now we're still in Vienna."

"For the cartoons?" the commissaris said. He took the paper.

"Since when do you read cartoons?" his wife asked. "Oh, didn't we have a lovely holiday? Don't you feel rested?"

The commissaris grunted as he scanned the headlines.

"Do you, Jan?"

"I feel dehydrated," the commissaris said. "All those medicinal steam baths dried out my legs. And I'm overstuffed. The cooking was too rich."

"You drank too much," his wife said. "Your brother and you are a bad combination. He brings out the worst in you."

"I bring out the best in him," the commissaris said. "But even his best is a bit boring."

"I wish you wouldn't drink," his wife said, and to the stewardess, "No, thank you, we won't have any."

6

"I'll have a gin and tonic," the commissaris* growled, and read, "Martin IJsbreker? That must be Peter IJsbreker's son. Yes, here it is, a director of the Banque du Crédit. But I know Martin."

"So do I," said his wife. "What did he do? Wasn't he involved in that nasty business of the Society for Help Abroad?"

"Thank you," the commissaris said to the stewardess. "Martin shot himself."

"Ach," his wife said. "Wasn't Martin divorced some years back? He had such a nice wife."

"Halba took care of it," the commissaris said, and folded the paper. "I'm glad I didn't have to go. A self-inflicted pistol shot finished Martin off. Your health."

"Your health," his wife said. "I wish you would drink beer."

The commissaris drank. "There's just as much alcohol in a bottle of beer as in a glass of gin, I keep telling you that. I wish you'd stop harping, my dear; even with my brother I didn't overindulge."

"You had four last night, Jan, two when I wasn't looking."

"Two," the commissaris said. "If you weren't looking, you didn't see the other two."

"I peeked," his wife said. "I'm sorry about Martin, even if I haven't met him since he was a boy, but Fleur talks about him from time to time."

"I didn't know you were seeing the baroness, Katrien."

"We meet in the supermarket sometimes, and have tea afterward. Fleur has gotten very fat."

The commissaris smiled.

"Of course, Fleur was always kind of pudgy," his wife said, "but you liked that, didn't you?"

"That was a hundred years ago."

---

* The ranks of the Dutch Municipal Police are, in descending order, chief constable, commissaris, chief inspector, inspector, adjutant, sergeant, constable first class, constable.

"Don't gulp your drink, Jan. I know all about you two, even if you won't admit it."

"What's there to admit?" He looked at her over his gold-rimmed spectacles. "You were still engaged to Willem Fernandus at the time. I was free, wasn't I?"

"You were about to be engaged to Fleur."

"Was I? So how come she married Willem?"

"Because you married me. Fleur would have preferred you, she told me so herself."

The commissaris mused, tinkling the ice in his drink.

"And Fernandus made Fleur very unhappy. He isn't even paying alimony anymore, now that Huip is over twenty-one, but she must have money, she always wears something new."

"Fleur inherited shares in the bank too," the commissaris said. "Fernandus must have gotten hold of them. The bank is doing well. It has all the Society's business, of course."

The stewardess took his glass. "Another one, sir?"

"No, thank you, dear." He looked back at his wife. "That bank is more evil than ever now. It sits right in the pleasure quarter. Fernandus is probably banking for the drug dealers too."

"You think that's why IJsbreker got shot?"

"Suicide." The commissaris put his hand on the paper. "According to what it says here, Chief Inspector Halba already closed the case."

"I don't like Halba, Jan, he has shifty eyes."

"He was good in narcotics, so I was told, Katrien. His promotion was due to that. His transfer to the Murder Brigade, too."

"Do you like Chief Inspector Halba?"

"No," the commissaris said, "but I don't know him too well yet. You were right, I shouldn't have looked at that paper. The other news is bad, too. Three dead junkies in a houseboat." He shook his small head. "I know that sort of thing shouldn't upset us anymore, but I'll never get used to it. Halba refuses to work on dead junkies. He claims they aren't worth the trouble —good riddance and so forth. I don't agree."

"You work on them?"

"If I can, Katrien, but this lot died of an overdose, with the needles in their arms. so what can we do? If they kill themselves . . . "

"Fleur says that her son Huip Fernandus is a druggie too," his wife said, "but he only uses the soft stuff. Huip is a musician, Fleur says. Musicians are often on drugs, aren't they?"

"I don't know," the commissaris said. "I haven't seen statistics. You know, in a way I'm glad young IJsbreker shot himself while I was away. Now I won't have to see his employer, Willem Fernandus. Halba probably saw the big boss. The chief inspector must have been busy. He made front-page news, too, something about a German terrorist shot in a telephone booth. One of our men got wounded."

"Badly?"

"The detective is in the hospital," the commissaris said, "not in intensive care."

"Oh my," his wife said. "Not Sergeant de Gier, I hope, he's such a daredevil. Does the article give a name?"

"No," the commissaris said. "It won't be de Gier, for the sergeant had to go north, to supply testimony for the court on that murder case we had earlier this year. Adjutant Grijpstra took his girlfriend to do some camping. Cardozo is on holiday, too—in Spain, I believe."

"Jan," his wife said, "didn't your father have shares in that Banque du Crédit, too? You didn't inherit part of the bank, I hope."

The commissaris looked out of the window. "Black clouds over Holland. The paper said there have been thunderstorms and hard rain. We didn't miss much, Katrien. No, Dad sold his shares. There were four shareholders then, Fernandus Senior, Willem's father, who was president then, Baron de la Faille—that's Fleur's father—IJsbreker Senior, and Dad. Old Fernandus was the evil genius. Dad sold out to his partners—at a loss, I believe.''

''I thought your dad and Willem Fernandus's father were close?''

''Because they married wives who were related.'' The commissaris frowned. ''My mother is Willem's mother's distant cousin. Twice removed, maybe.''

''Willem and you are family?'' his wife gasped. ''I never knew that.''

''Too far to mention,'' the commissaris said. ''Willem didn't harp on the subject, either. We disliked each other.''

''And you went to the same schools. You even studied together.''

''Law,'' the commissaris said. ''I studied the articles and Willem studied the holes between the articles. He was always like that. Even in kindergarten he found an illegal way to the teacher's lap. Willem''— the commissaris stared solemnly at his wife—''is the most deliberately evil man I ever had the misfortune to know.''

His wife giggled.

''What's funny?'' the commissaris asked. ''Is evil funny?''

''What was Willem doing on the teacher's lap?''

''Feeling her breasts, of course.'' The commissaris took off his spectacles and polished them with the tip of his silk tie. ''Pretending to slide off Miss Bakker's lap and then grabbing hold. Willem was never very subtle. That time he got slapped.''

''How old was Willem then?''

''We were both four. I used to sit on Miss Bakker's lap, and Willem got jealous. The teacher had pet mice, in a terrarium with a wheel. We could look at them doing their tricks for two minutes, if we asked. There was a clock above the terrarium, and we were supposed to time ourselves." The commissaris grinned. "When I see a mouse now, I still think about that stupid clock. Crazy education. You're supposed to learn, and all you do is pick up useless associations."

"So how did Willem get you off that woman's lap? Was she beautiful, Jan?"

"A goddess," the commissaris said. "There was a rocking horse in kindergarten, and whenever I rode it I fantasized that I was saving Miss Bakker from dragons, or from the principal of the school, whom she married later. I really lost out then."

"Willem got her before the principal?"

"Willem lied," the commisaris said. "Miss Bakker had to step out a minute, and I wanted to see the mice, so Willem said, 'Go ahead, she won't be back for a while.' Of course she came back straightaway and Willem pointed at me. Willem knew she'd only be a minute. I had to stand in the corner for half an hour."

"And you never got back on her lap?"

"No. It got worse from then on. You have no idea what Willem would do. Later, when I got good at gymnastics, there was a girl we both liked. I would do my best to impress her. Willem never bothered about gymnastics. There was an exhibition, and just before it was my turn, he tripped me on the stairs. I hurt my ankle and had to drop out."

"Willem got the girl?"

"He took her to the party," the commissaris said. "It took me forever to find out how truly evil Willem was. I always excused him. He would come over to the house, we'd play together, we studied too—or rather, I'd study and he'd copy my notes, or borrow them and never give them back. And then, at law school, we shared a holiday in Paris. Willem had a car by then."

"Another love story?" the commissaris's wife asked. "You lost again? You got *me*, you know. I

didn't really like Willem. I was very pleased you se-
duced me when we went out sailing that day, in his
brother Ernst's boat."

"Katrien," the commissaris said softly, "will you
admit it now? You wanted Ernst Fernandus. Go on,
let's have it out at last. That was thirty-five years ago.
You can be honest, we're all old dodderers by now."

"Maybe," his wife said. "It was such a lovely day
and Willem had been rude again and you asked me to
your room afterward and I knew I shouldn't go, but
you said it was just for coffee, and then it was kind of
stuffy in your room and you said there was no need to
be overdressed."

"Ernst looked like Tarzan," the commissaris said.
"Tarzan with a golden beard. He'd had his first poetry
published by then. He owned that wonderful sailboat.
Ernst was everything a romantic girl could wish for.
Every time he looked at you, you squeaked."

She took his hand. "I squeaked a lot in those days.
I was a silly girl. You know who got Ernst that night?
Fleur. Willem went home by himself, on two wheels
in his stupid car. Wasn't he pathetic? And you got me.
It was the first time for me. Now tell me what hap-
pened in Paris."

"Yes," the commissaris said. "maybe I won that
time. And maybe I won in Paris, too, but that's a bad
tale. You sure you want to hear it?"

She squeezed his hand. "Yes. Keep talking, Jan,
the plane is going down, I never like it when airplanes
land."

"We went dancing on the Champs Elysées," the
commissaris said, "and I met a girl. Jacqueline, she
was called. A pretty girl. Her father had a small grocery in the Fourteenth District. I wrote her phone
number down, intending to call her the next day—she
was going to show me a museum, I think—but when I
woke up in the hotel, Willem had taken the piece of
paper from my jacket. He wasn't there. He had

phoned her, saying I was unwell, and taken her for a ride in the Bois de Boulogne. A motorcar was very special in those days. I didn't see much of Willem for the rest of the week, because he kept taking Jacqueline out. It turned out that she was rather old-fashioned and he couldn't get close to her unless he met her parents. Then she still wouldn't give in, so Willem said he'd marry her."

"Are we about to land now?" his wife asked.

"Not yet."

"Tell me when I can open my eyes."

"Willem got her pregnant," the commissaris said. "He lost interest at once. That was about a year later. Before then Willem kept driving up and down to Paris. Jacqueline was really a rather lovely girl. He brought her up to Amsterdam a few times, to impress all of us —and to annoy me, of course."

"Are we landing?"

"Now," the commissaris said. "Open your eyes. We're safe. Do you want to hear the rest of it?"

"So Willem has a child in Paris?"

"He killed it."

"An abortion?"

"Much worse," the commissaris said. "He tried to kill Jacqueline. We had become philosophers by then, and Willem was reading Nietzsche. I didn't care too much for Nietzsche, but even so, the man made some good points. I won't bore you with the argument, but Willem and I somehow agreed that all morals were nonsense. Morals were merely rehashed tribal laws, and enlightened souls such as ourselves didn't have to bother with good and evil. We could do as we liked. I agreed in theory—maybe I still do—but I insisted that we should never hurt others."

"You've hurt me many times, Jan."

He patted her shoulder. "Yes, but that was in spite of my good intentions. I didn't put rat poison in your porridge because I'd made you pregnant, did I, now?"

"Oh, Jan, did Willem do that to the poor girl?"

"He certainly did," the commissaris said, waiting for impatient passengers to file out of the plane. "And mostly to prove a point. You see what I'm getting at?"

"No, Jan. Shouldn't we get out?"

They walked through the airport's main building, arm in arm, a small, dapper old man with a slight limp, and a tall, silver-haired, dignified woman. "Katrien," the commissaris said, "don't you see? Willem wanted to show me how ruthless he was. He set me up. We were playing snooker one evening in the university café and he told me that Jacqueline would die that very night and there was nothing I could do to stop it. Willem had done his homework for once. A medical student gave him literature on arsenic. Jacqueline was the only member of her family who liked to eat porridge. Willem put the rat poison in a container she kept in the kitchen. He was supposed to be the future son-in-law and was free to wander about her parents' house. They trusted him; they didn't know their daughter was pregnant. Then Jacqueline got ill."

"Willem intended her to lose the baby?"

"He intended her to die, Katrien."

"Did she?"

"No. I took the train to Paris that same night and found Jacqueline in very poor shape indeed. The family doctor didn't know what was wrong. The poor girl was dying by then. I told the doctor about the poison. She was rushed to the hospital and her stomach was pumped. She lost the baby but regained her health."

"And the police?"

"I was questioned," the commissaris said. "They wrote to Willem and ordered him to visit them, but he never did. There was no proof. The police had a weak case."

They were waiting for the luggage. "So you won, Jan."

"Yes," the commissaris said, "and I broke with

Willem. From then on, I only saw him during class. Willem didn't go to too many lectures, but we graduated at the same time."

"There are our bags," his wife said. "You missed them."

"They'll come around again."

"Did Willem graduate cum laude too?"

"No," the commissaris said, "but he became an attorney, and in due course replaced his father as president and main shareholder of the Banque du Crédit. He set up that Society for Help Abroad, which exploits illegal gambling clubs and drug joints for the young."

"And keeps the profits," the commissaris's wife said. "I read that long magazine article to you about the Society. The gambling clubs are brothels, too. The journalist said he could prove that. Why don't you close the Society down?"

The commissaris grabbed the bags. "I can't. Willem operates in a hole in the law. Nonprofit societies are protected. It's not my department, either. His bank is bad, too, and again outside my reach."

"Fleur has a half-brother," his wife said. "Bart. We met Bart once. Baron Bart de la Faille. Maybe he has shares too."

"All I remember is a little boy," the commissaris said, "a spoiled little brat, a late child by old de la Faille's second wife. She died of cancer. Watch the luggage, please, I'll go and find a cart."

"And young IJsbreker must have had some shares," his wife said when he came back, "and he's dead." She walked ahead of her cart-pushing husband and called a cab. "Through the park, please," the commissaris told the driver.

"Could you drive slowly?" the commissaris's wife asked. "We always enjoy the park so much, especially in the spring."

"Turtle will be waiting for you in the garden," she

said as she leaned into her husband's arm. "Look at the tall poplars, Jan, and the fresh leaves on the maples." The commissaris didn't answer. "Jan? Don't think of bad Willem. You're a good man with an excellent reputation. Everybody thinks highly of you. The children are doing well. I love you. Please enjoy the park."

"Yes," the commissaris said. "Nice."

"You won, Jan."

"Yes." His small hand tapped her shoulder.

"So enjoy."

A heron sailed majestically across the road. "Yes," the commissaris said. "I do." He leaned over and kissed his wife's cheek.

‖‖ 3 ‖‖

"MORNING," SERGEANT DE GIER SAID CHEERFULLY. He was a tall, wide-shouldered man, sprawled behind a dented metal desk in the far corner of a gray room. "Had a good holiday?"

The heavyset adjutant, looking even more portly in his three-piece dark blue suit, bought a size too large to accommodate his not-too-well-distributed bulk, lumbered on.

"Hello?" de Gier asked. "Remember me? Your assistant of the last ten years or more?"

"Bah," Adjutant Grijpstra said. He turned, walked back to the door, and pushed the latch shut. He walked over to de Gier's desk and turned on his heel.

"No," de Gier said. "Please. The last time that door was replaced, I had to pay half the cost. No, Adjutant."

"Ha!" Adjutant Grijpstra shouted. His hand slid under his jacket and was back at once. A silver line linked his hand and the door. A stiletto trembled in the door's plywood.

"One day you'll be sorry," de Gier said. "Your knife's point penetrates the wood by three inches. Someone might get seriously hurt."

Someone was rattling the door's handle.

"Just a minute," Grijpstra shouted. He walked back to the door and pulled back the latch.

A young man, dressed in a rumpled corduroy suit, his small face topped by unruly wavy hair, stumbled into the room, holding his chest with both hands. He moaned and doubled up before his legs gave way.

"See?" de Gier said. "In Cardozo's case there's no big loss—he can easily be replaced—but you might hit Jane, the loveliest member of our force, or Miss Antoinette, the commissaris's new secretary. I haven't had time to convince her yet."

"Stop spoiling my practice," Grijpstra said, dropping his weight heavily into a swivel chair. "Besides, I usually aim high."

"Convince Miss Antoinette of what?" Cardozo asked, picking himself up.

"Of my harmlessness," Sergeant de Gier said, smiling. "She thinks I want a permanent relationship, but I'll never interfere with her freedom, of course. All I'm hoping for is just a few hours of shared warmth."

"After she pays for the meal," Grijpstra rumbled. "No."

"No what?" de Gier asked. "If I pay for the meal I have a hold on her. She'll feel she owes me. I don't mind owing her. I'm prepared to be as humble as she likes a man to be."

"No, I didn't have a good holiday," Grijpstra said. "Campgrounds are too noisy, and we were washed out in the end. Nellie lost her tent. First it was pressed down by all the water and then it blew away. Best thing that happened. I went home and rested for a week."

"Did you take Nellie to your house?" Cardozo asked.

"Of course not," Grijpstra said.

"Really," de Gier said, stretching. As his arms reached up, the butt of his oversize pistol was visible under his stylish jacket. "You mean Nellie still doesn't know your wife is gone? Why are you keeping up that farce?"

"Suppose my wife comes back?" Grijpstra asked. "Two women in my small, comfortable, empty, white-washed home?"

"I thought your divorce went through," Cardozo said from behind the wobbly little table that served him as a desk.

"She might just come back," Grijpstra said. "You never know. And if I took Nellie home for a week, she might just stay. Nellie has her own hotel. My wife lives in a huge villa with her sister in the country. I don't move in with them, do I?" He frowned furiously. "And what is it to you?"

"Why do you feel threatened, Adjutant?" De Gier asked. "Your wife left you because she doesn't like you. Nellie loves her freedom above all. All women do, these days. Why couldn't you extend a normal courtesy to a fellow human being, regardless of sex? A lonely woman who just lost her tent and who has only one week of her hard-earned holiday left before she has to return to the daily grind of running an over-crowded hotel singlehanded?"

Grijpstra rummaged in the drawer of his desk. He found a cigar, bit off the tip, and spat it into the waste-paper basket. "So what else is new? You two been busy? Any business? Can we get out of my private life?"

Cardozo watched the adjutant's slender knife. "You're getting better, Adjutant—you're hitting the door now."

"I hit what I intend to hit," Grijpstra said.

"How come you never tell us beforehand what you're aiming at?" Cardozo asked.

"Ah," Grijpstra said. "Answer that yourself." He turned his chair around. "Sergeant, report."

"Dead banker," de Gier said. "Suicide. I saw a

report signed by Halba and Adjutant Guldemeester. Being up north, I wasn't in on that. Three dead junkies, overdosed on pure heroin in a houseboat at the Binnenkant. Guldemeester checked that out, too. A German terrorist got shot. Big trouble at Headquarters here, but that's internal politics, of course. You don't care for politics, do you now?''

"No," Grijpstra said. "Anyone have the file with the daily reports?"

De Gier got up and presented the adjutant with a sheaf of dog-eared pink paper held by a transparent plastic cover. "It's all in here."

Grijpstra leafed through the file. "The dead banker lived at the Binnenkant? The junkies' boat was berthed in the Binnenkant canal?"

"Yes, I saw that." De Gier crossed his long legs on his desk. "Same location. The houseboat happens to be just opposite the banker's home. I asked Adjutant Guldemeester, but he claims the two incidents are unrelated."

"What's with politics?" Cardozo asked. "*I* care. Any interesting gossip?"

De Gier leaned back as far as his creaky chair allowed. "A carton of weaponry was lifted from the ballistics room. Our two pathologists are at war with each other. It seems that half the charwomen keeping this place clean are illegal aliens. Coins have been filched from the coffee machines. Several attractive female prisoners have a way of being taken out of their cells at night by unspecified personnel."

Grijpstra looked up from the file. "That isn't gossip, that's fact."

"The gossip is that changes for the better are now due, Adjutant." De Gier's large brown eyes twinkled. "Some colleagues are saying so. There's leakage to the press. Journalists are writing up our mess. There was a lengthy editorial in Saturday's paper that wondered why so few crimes are solved and why highly placed officers keep being issued with new expensive cars. It also mentioned the new chief constable and his apparent failure to deal with ineptitude and gross corruption."

"The chief constable just sits around," Cardozo said. "Chief Inspector Halba sneaks around. Adjutant Guldemeester helps him sneak."

"Four corpses." Grijpstra closed the file and shook it. "So that houseboat where the junkies died is opposite the house where the banker lived? Did you see the other complaint referring to the Binnenkant?"

"The helpless old lady?" de Gier asked. "Saying some musicians are drumming her out of her home? I've seen that complaint before. Doesn't she live at number 20?"

Grijpstra pushed himself free of his chair and walked over to the opposite wall. His stubby finger prodded at the city's map. "Number 20 should be just behind the houseboat where the junkies died. Old ladies don't sleep well, they like sitting at their windows late at night. The night the banker died was the night the big thunderstorm broke. Maybe the old lady watched the spectacle from her apartment. The report says she lives upstairs and the musicians make their racket in the lower part of the house. If she lives upstairs, she can look over the houseboat and see the banker's house across the water. Maybe she noticed something unusual. She could even have heard the shot. The corpse was found near a front window."

"Near an open front window," de Gier said. "The hapless banker could have been watching the bad weather, too. All that thunder reminded him of gunfire. He looked for his gun."

"For his Walther PPK pistol, according to the report," Cardozo said. "Expensive. An appropriate weapon for an influential man to have around."

"An illegal weapon," Grijpstra said. He walked back to his desk. He picked up the file and pointed it

accusingly at de Gier. "And the junkies just happened
to die on their boat across the street? The very same
night?"

"You know, Adjutant," de Gier said gently, "this
is not our case. Besides, it's closed."

Grijpstra dropped the file and pounded it softly with
both fists. "The report is too brief. Is the commissaris
back yet?"

"You wouldn't suggest," de Gier said, "that a case
closed by colleagues should be reopened, would you
now?"

Cardozo brought out his notebook. "It's the junkies
that get me. Do you know that I had a junkie visit me
here? An American who said he lived in a houseboat
on the Binnenkant? His name was Jimmy. One of the
dead is called James T. Floyd in the report. Isn't
'Jimmy' short for 'James'?"

"Ask de Gier," Grijpstra said. "Our intellectual
sergeant knows all about everything. He even reads
French literature."

"Sergeant?" Cardozo asked.

De Gier nodded.

Cardozo checked his notes. "Jimmy called here a
month ago. Pity the file doesn't give physical descrip-
tions." He reached for his telephone and dialed. "Mr.
Jacobs? How're you doing? You're not? I'm sorry. Is
that right? You don't want to be doing? That's okay,
then. Listen, a question, Mr. Jacobs. You have a dead
young man there, an American, James T. Floyd of
Berkeley, California, it should say so on the tag on his
toe. I want to know what he looks like. Sure, I'll
wait." Cardozo held his hand over the phone's mouthpiece. "Yagh! I can hear Jacobs pull the metal box out
of the fridge." He dropped his hand off the receiver.
"Tall? Long blond hair? Missing front teeth? Thank
you, Mr. Jacobs, that's what I wanted to hear." Cardozo replaced the phone.

"You're acquainted with the deceased," Grijpstra said. "That's nice."

Cardozo grimaced sadly. "Yes, Jimmy came to tell me about some planned murder. That's what I like about specialization. We're the Murder Brigade, so if a visitor says 'murder,' he's sent to us. Pity I didn't believe him at the time."

Grijpstra pounded his desk with more force. "Dead junkies on a boat. Dead banker in a house across from the boat. Dead junkie, when still alive, comes here to gab about murder. Adjutant Guldemeester says there's no connection. Chief Inspector Halba diagnoses one case as suicide and the other as an overdose. Bah!"

"Constable?" de Gier said. "Why didn't we get to hear about Jimmy?"

"I forgot," Cardozo said. "We were working on the Frisian case. Lots of odd birds drop in here from time to time. Odd crazy birds. We chase them away. You're lucky I made a note. He was in here two minutes before he fell off his chair. Wanted heroin in exchange for information."

"But subject mentioned murder. Did he mention anything else?"

Cardozo shrugged. "A murder that was planned. He would tell me all about it in exchange for junk. The informer was ill. A scarecrow, a sight. If this Jimmy turns out to be the dead James T. Floyd, I won't be surprised."

"What happened after the subject fell off his chair?" Grijpstra asked.

"I picked him up," Cardozo said, "walked him down the stairs, and pushed him into the street. Standard instructions. Sick junkies aren't taken to hospitals anymore, since treatment is usually refused by the medical staff. Waste of time and trouble."

"He must have said something more," de Gier said. "A lot of words fit into two minutes."

Cardozo read from his notes. "Subject claims to study Chinese literature at the University of California in Berkeley. He had taken a year off to visit magical Amsterdam."

De Gier gestured enthusiastically. "We could check, you know. There are enough details. I could send a teletype message to all stations. Most junkies are known to some cop or other. Jimmy probably dealt junk, too. The Alien Department might know of him as well. You think he really was a student, Cardozo?"

"Maybe," Cardozo said. "Subject must be intelligent, for he spoke passably good Dutch, learned within a year. He could have been well off once, a refined-looking wreck."

"Missing teeth," de Gier said. "A fight?"

"Junk does that to them." Cardozo shifted his papers around absentmindedly. "Pity I didn't follow up."

"You could have reported subject to Narcotics," de Gier said.

"Waste of time, Sergeant. Narcotics used to be Chief Inspector Halba's show. At Narcotics, nobody has time to listen."

"Halba had already been transferred to the Murder Brigade by then."

"And he hadn't been replaced," Cardozo said. "That department wasn't functioning. It functions a little bit now. Chief Inspector Rood is supposed to be in charge again."

Grijpstra sighed. "Nothing much has changed. Isn't it great to be back at work? Sergeant, it's your turn to buy me coffee at the café of my choice. The commissaris isn't back yet, I take it. You didn't answer my question just now."

De Gier dialed. "Miss Antoinette? It's me. Has the chief shown up yet, or is he still in his Austrian sulfur bath? Miss Antoinette? Remember my suggestion? I'm sorry if I made my intentions too clear, perhaps, but if I don't we'll never get anywhere together. Since you're so shy, I mean, and since I'm shy, too. This afternoon? Thank you very much.''

"During working hours?" Cardozo asked. "Are you out of your mind? That's all we need. You'll be suspended for sure. There's a whole list of complaints against you as it is.''

"The commissaris is due back this afternoon," de Gier said. "I know about the complaints. Halba was waving the list at me. Dangerous driving and Lord knows what. Balderdash, mostly. Adjutant? Did you read what the file says about the German terrorist? There's more trouble there.''

"Colleagues killed the fellow, didn't they?" Cardozo asked. "In a telephone booth. I saw it in the paper on the way back from Spain. Chief Inspector Halba was in charge of the hunt.''

"He wasn't really," de Gier said. "Chief Inspector Rood prepared the case, traced the suspect, did everything. Halba stepped in at the last moment. There's news value in such an arrest. Halba is a fool. He placed detectives around the booth. When suspect started shooting, colleagues had to return his fire, and since there were cops on all sides, someone was bound to get hurt.''

Grijpstra groaned.

"See what happens if we aren't around?" Cardozo asked. "By the way, I heard some talk in the canteen just now. Informers tell us that both Halba and Guldemeester seem to be having a good time at local night spots.''

"I know," de Gier said. "Small town. Bad news travels fast.''

"You heard about the chief constable as well?"

"Out on the tiles too?" de Gier asked.

"Extramarital trouble. A blonde photo model he shows off in his Porsche.''

"Forget the coffee," Grijpstra said, and stomped

over to the door. He yanked his knife out of the wood. "I'm going out alone."

Cardozo looked up when the door banged behind Grijpstra. "What's with him?"

"Holidays never agree with the adjutant," de Gier said. "He probably feels he's been missing out. He turns his back a moment, and four corpses are strewn about in the same location." De Gier picked up a pair of drumsticks from Grijpstra's desk and stroked a cymbal that formed part of a set of battered percussion instruments wedged between a filing cabinet and the window. "What do you think, colleague? Something smelly about the banker's death, maybe?"

Cardozo pouted. "I never trust you when you call me 'colleague.' "

De Gier tried a roll on the big drum. "Answer the question."

"Maybe," Cardozo said. "Suicide is pretty easy to prove."

"Easy to disprove, too." De Gier scratched the snare drum with both sticks. "Pity Grijpstra hasn't been playing lately. Too much on his mind. All our troubles are getting him down. Silly, really. Troubles are exciting."

"You haven't been playing either," Cardozo said. "You two let me down. I only joined the department to listen to your compositions. Variations on a Bach theme adapted for snare drum and piccolo. That used to make me happy."

De Gier hit the side of the drum, alternating sharp raps with more scratching of cymbals. He whistled some high notes. "Was that the theme?"

"Yeh," Cardozo said, "it gets sad later. First you build up a good strong rhythm and then suddenly there are all these moody notes."

"Better wait for Grijpstra to come back, then." De Gier dropped the sticks. "I'm much too cheerful on my own. Come along, colleague." He opened the door. "After you."

"Where to?"

"There's a shortage of officers this morning," de Gier said. "Lead me to a café of my choice. It's your turn to pay. I won't do any work until the commissaris returns this afternoon and hands out orders."

⫼ 4 ⫽

THE COMMISSARIS, LIMPING THROUGH AN ENDLESS corridor on the top floor of the Police Headquarters Building, wondered whether anyone remembered that he could have been chief constable himself. When honors are turned down, they're usually forgotten. Many of the officers he had gotten close to in some way had retired during the last few years. The previous chief constable was a good older friend who was asked by the mayor to sound out the commissaris about the offered promotion. The commissaris hadn't given a reason for his refusal then, for he was talking to an officer he was asked to replace. To say that the job wasn't interesting enough might have sounded impolite. A chief constable doesn't hunt; a chief of detectives does. The commissaris preferred to remain out in the open. He found the door he was looking for, and knocked. A green light flashed on.

"Had a good holiday?" the chief constable asked. "Care to sit down? Coffee, perhaps?"

"No, thank you, sir, I haven't been to my office yet."

The commissaris looked at his superior, finding the man hard to define. Polite, smooth, well-dressed, of course, no characteristics that stood out. Maybe that was why he had climbed so high in little time. "To float upward because of lack of weight," the commissaris's father had been fond of saying when he discussed the careers of others. Perhaps. He had to be careful, the commissaris told himself. Jealousy always makes judgment murky.

"Whatever happened during your absence has been properly taken care of," the chief constable said. "Did you hear about the terrorist? That came off rather well."

"There was a victim on our side?" the commissaris asked.

"Unfortunately." The chief constable nodded sadly. "Not a life-threatening wound, but in the face, I'm afraid. Plastic surgery will be required."

"Anyone I know?"

"I forget his name. A young detective."

"Ah," the commissaris said. "See you later, sir."

He undertook the long walk back to the elevator, thinking that he should perhaps be using his cane again. The cane was too conspicuous, however. It might alert the authorities to his infirmity. The rheumatism was improving somewhat lately. The Austrian baths didn't help, of course, but his wife always had such a good time in Bad Gastein. She liked fashionable resorts. And the commissaris was supposed to like calling on his retired brother who lived peacefully in a luxurious chalet in the Austrian Alps. They would invariably discuss old times. The commissaris preferred discussing new times, but there weren't any for his older brother. Reminiscences. The commissaris scowled. Would he be analyzing the past too, soon? His retirement crept closer every day. He still enjoyed the present.

A uniformed officer walked by, saluting politely. "Glad to have you back, sir."

"Yes," said the commissaris. He stopped and turned. "Halba?"

The officer stopped and turned.

"I was reading the paper in the plane this morning. Seems you've been quite busy. Do you have time to see me later this afternoon? Bring me up to date?"

"Certainly, sir," Chief Inspector Halba said. "Will sometime around five be in order? The mayor wants to see me this afternoon, about the terrorists. Bit of a celebration. That's why I'm in uniform. The press is invited. Perhaps you might care to come, too."

"Awfully kind," the commissaris mumbled. "But not really, I think. Haven't seen my men yet, you know. Are they all back now?"

Halba's eyes glinted behind his rimless glasses. "Haven't seen them sir. They don't like to report to my office. I was meaning to mention that to you. Sergeant de Gier especially seems to be rather, ah, 'self-willed' is the word? I realize I'm new to the brigade, but a bit of respect for rank . . ."

"Quite," the commissaris said. "See you at five then, Halba. My regards to the mayor."

In the elevator down, the commissaris realized who Halba reminded him of. Memories of the war had flashed back. The commissaris, then a junior police officer unwilling to cooperate with the German occupation forces, had been jailed for a good while. He was rightly suspected of being a member of the resistance. Being somewhat skilled in the art of interrogation himself, he had managed to plead innocence, but one of the Gestapo officers didn't give up. *Herr Leutnant* visited his prey daily in a dank cell. The German officer had all furniture removed from his prisoner's quarters and the floor flooded with an inch of dirty water. The prisoner was given a bit of bread each day and nothing to drink, so he drank from the floor. He also lay on the floor. His rheumatism started up during that painful period. Physically, the German from the past and the chief inspector from the present had little in common, but there was something about the way they both talked, showing their front teeth when they smiled. Yes, the commissaris thought grimly, two smart rodents, each from a different species.

He reached his office. His secretary was already there and put herself in his way. Surprised, the commissaris extended a hand. She pecked him on the cheek.

"Miss Antoinette," the commissaris exclaimed, feeling the small moist spot her lips had left.

She smiled. "You can kiss me too." She bent down.

"Modern times," the commissaris grumbled.

"Mere politeness," Miss Antoinette said. "Working relationships have changed, you know. Go on, sir, it doesn't hurt."

He kissed her cheek quickly and escaped behind his desk.

"You don't find me distasteful?" Miss Antoinette asked.

The commissaris shook his head energetically.

"Don't I look like your wife?"

The commissaris thought.

"I do," Miss Antoinette said. "When she came here and when we walked downstairs together, the doorman thought I was her daughter."

"You're the same size," the commissaris agreed. He gave in and smiled. "I like your new outfit. Very businesslike, yet charming."

She turned around. "I bought it because I wanted to fit in. You have such a distinguished office. Did you notice I polished your desk and the cupboard? Don't the lions that support your table shine? All your furniture is sixteenth-century oak, isn't it?"

"The plants look good too," the commissaris said. "You must have taken good care of them. Have you seen Adjutant Grijpstra and the sergeant?"

"They were inquiring after you, sir. The sergeant is a nuisance."

The commissaris reached for the silver thermos flask on his desk. Miss Antoinette was quicker. "I'll pour your coffee, sir, It's special. I bought beans and ground them myself."

"Delicious," the commissaris said. "You're spoiling me, dear. The sergeant is after you?"

"He makes advances."

"You want me to speak to him? I thought he was still enamored of Constable First Class Jane."

"Jane says he's good," Miss Antoinette said. "Aren't you going to Chief Inspector Halba's press party this afternoon?"

The commissaris shook his head. "How's the wounded detective doing?"

She filled his cup again. "The poor man's jawbone is completely smashed. There's a lot of talk about the incident, sir. The men say Chief Inspector Rood should have been allowed to finish the case, and that Halba botched the arrest. He put in so many men that the suspect became suspicious."

The commissaris grinned. "A suspicious suspect?"

She blushed. "Am I not saying it right? I was only trying to phrase my report correctly, but I'm not really a policewoman, of course. I only type."

"I'm sorry," the commissaris said. "Go on, dear. I'm very interested. Suspect opened fire?"

"With a fully automatic weapon," Miss Antoinette said. "An Uzi, I believe. He had hidden it under his jacket. Then we—well, the cops I mean—started shooting back and a police bullet hit a detective behind the telephone booth. Sloppy strategy, the men are saying."

"So it seems," the commissaris said. "Halba, eh?"

"Nasty man," Miss Antoinette said. "He keeps bothering me too. I'm complaining now, sir. The sergeant I don't really mind."

"Yes," the commissaris sighed. "Halba is a present I think I could do without. I wish he had stayed with Narcotics. He was doing well there, I hear. Murder requires a different approach altogether."

"You should hear what the girls at Narcotics have to say about Halba, sir."

The commissaris waved a small hand. "Yes, dear, but that's just talk. I heard something too. Narcotics is slippery ground, a lot of money is involved. There are informers to be paid off, rival gangs to be played against each other. Halba would fit well into that scene. What interests me is why he would apply for a transfer to my deparment."

"Yes," Miss Antoinette said briskly.

"You're interested too?"

"Maybe I know."

"You do?" the commissaris asked. "Well, then, tell me."

"He's after your job, sir. Commissaris ranks higher than chief inspector, doesn't it?"

The commissaris sipped his coffee. "Well, he'll have to wait."

"Maybe he won't, sir." Miss Antoinette walked to the door. "Anything else? Can I send in Grijpstra and de Gier?"

"Yes. Please do."

The commissaris thought Miss Antoinette had attractive hips, and an even more attractive way of swinging them when she suddenly turned. He opened the file she had placed next to his cup, and grunted irritably as he read.

There was a knock on the door. "Yes?" His assistants walked in, in order of rank.

"Well," the commissaris said twenty minutes later, when the three of them were looking at a map that de Gier had unrolled on the paneled wall. "Reopen two closed cases? Are you sure now, Adjutant? Won't we be stepping on long toes?"

"But you are interested, sir," Grijpstra said. "Especially as you're sort of personally involved."

"You knew the dead banker," de Gier said. "How was that now? Martin IJsbreker's father and your father were partners?"

"I don't think Martin was born then," the commissaris said. "All this goes back a long way, Sergeant. There were four partners in the Banque du Crédit, but my father backed out. That left three. IJsbreker Senior, Baron de la Faille, and old Mr. Fernandus. I knew them all, since we moved in the same circles. Willem, old Mr. Fernandus's son, went to school with me."

"But you aren't friends with Willem Fernandus, the bank's current president, anymore?"

"Please," the commissaris said. "I don't even greet Willem when we meet in the street. That bank's reputation has gone down even further, Sergeant. Fernandus has been in a lot of scandals. His practice as an attorney is infamous, as you know if you've been reading the papers."

"The Society for Help Abroad?" Grijpstra asked.

"Started by Willem Fernandus," the commissaris said, "and very likely linked with his bank. That bank has never had a good aura about it; that's why my father got rid of his shares. It only has one office, situated fairly close to the prostitution quarter. The bank reputedly helped the German occupation. Fernandus was a double agent who somehow managed to jump clear when the war was over."

"Willem Fernandus," Grijsptra said, "not his dad."

"Yes, Willem," the commissaris said. "Let me see now. I think my father and the others all had equal shares. My father sold out, and old Fernandus may then have had half. Willem inherited half of that, so he only got a quarter, but his brother Ernst was never interested in business, so Willem may effectively control Ernst's shares as well. Then Willem married the Baroness de la Faille, whom I also know; she's an old lady now, and divorced. Fleur's share probably went to Willem. But Fleur only inherited half of her father's stake, for he married again and had a son. The son I met once, when he was still a child. I wonder how young Bart fits in now."

"And then there was IJsbreker Senior," Grijpstra said. "Father of the subject who shot himself. The report says IJsbreker Senior was a banker, so maybe he ran the bank. Willem Fernandus doesn't run the Banque du Crédit, sir?"

"Willem is the president, Adjutant. He probably doesn't handle the day-to-day business, because he's still an attorney with an office on Prince Hendrik Quay, quite an impressive building."

"With nasty-looking gargoyles sitting on the steps," de Gier said. "I pass that place often. The mansion has recently been restored. The gable was sandblasted and all the ornaments repaired."

"We could find out," the commissaris said. "Prince Hendrik Quay is only a stone's throw from the Binnenkant, where IJsbreker Junior lived and died. The Banque du Crédit is also on the quay, two blocks east of Willem's office."

"A stone's throw away from a houseboat where Adjutant Guldemeester found three dead junkies," Grijpstra said.

"So you were saying." The commissaris shook the thermos flask. "Maybe we can squeeze three small cups out of this smart invention. Miss Antoinette has been improving things here. Oh, by the way, Sergeant, you find my secretary to your liking?"

"Sir?" de Gier asked.

The commissaris found two more cups. "Yes."

De Gier scratched his buttock. "Well . . . eh . . . sort of cool. Not very responsive."

"Ah," the commissaris said. "You're answering

the question behind my question. So Cardozo actually met one of the junkies. Adjutant, when you have a minute, I'd like you to check the reports from ballistics and pathology on Martin IJsbreker. I don't imagine there has been a proper autopsy on the junkies, but you might find something there too. Pathology must have checked on the overdose supposition. And you, Sergeant, send a routine message to all personnel about the American student of Chinese, saying that we'd welcome any data at all. Subject interests me because of the information he didn't give after all.''

"Would you like us to visit the premises where IJsbreker died?'' de Gier asked.

"Yes, tonight, maybe.'' The commissaris rubbed his hands together enthusiastically. "I'd like to come along. We'll need a key. Maybe Guldemeester has the IJsbreker key.''

"Adjutant Guldemeester won't like this, sir.''

"No?'' the commissaris asked. "No. Perhaps you're right. So you'd better see him straightaway, Sergeant. Yes, I think that would be best.''

"He might refuse, sir.''

"Then bring him in here, Sergeant.''

Grijpstra laughed.

The commissaris frowned. "You're not enjoying the discomfort of a colleague, I hope.''

"No,'' Grijsptra said. "I was thinking of Guldemeester's birthday party, earlier this year. De Gier and Cardozo were invited, too. Bit of a disaster that was.''

"Ah?''

Grijpstra looked at de Gier. "Leave me out of it,'' de Gier said. "I had a terrible time.''

"Let's hear this,'' the commissaris said. "Or shouldn't I?''

De Gier sat down on the edge of a chair. "May I tell it, sir? Grijpstra will exaggerate. Have you met Guldemeester's wife, Celine?''

"Perhaps I have, Sergeant. Pretty? Long blond hair?"

"A most attractive young lady," Grijpstra said.

"Guldemeester must be your age, Adjutant. Fifty or so?"

"Celine is around thirty," de Gier said. "They haven't been married long, and they won't be married long, either, I would guess. Guldemeester likes to drink—as we all do, of course—but I felt rather uncomfortable, so I only had a few."

The commissaris looked at Grijpstra. Grijpstra nodded.

"I hate birthday parties," de Gier said. "I don't particularly like Guldemeester, either. I should never have gone, but he invited me and I thought it would be rude to refuse."

"I always refuse," the commissaris said.

"Mrs. Guldemeester made a pass at me," de Gier said. "Everyone was quite drunk by then. Except me, as I mentioned."

"You got drunk?" the commissaris asked Grijpstra.

"Grijpstra threw up on the goats," de Gier said. "But that was afterward. Guldemeester keeps goats. Mini-goats, strange-looking specimens, from Mongolia, I believe."

"They all died," Grijpstra said.

"Probably a rare breed," the commissaris said. "Couldn't stand your treatment."

"No, no," Grijpstra said, "nothing to do with me. Some disease, it must have been. I got drunk because that household made me unhappy. De Gier and I are different that way. He won't drink when he's unhappy."

"So Mrs. Guldemeester made a pass at you, Sergeant?" the commissaris asked. "And that upset you? You should be used to that sort of thing by now."

"Our hero," Grijpstra said. "It's because of that

ridiculous mustache. It makes women curious, they want to lift it up."

"It's my high cheekbones," de Gier said. "Anyway, I didn't respond, so Celine stripped on the table."

"She *what*?" asked the commissaris.

"She did, sir," Grijpstra said. "Cardozo liked that. He gave her the idea. He kept talking about how he would like to infiltrate that nightclub, or gambling joint, or whatever one would like to call it, that belongs to the Society for Help Abroad and gets written up in the papers a lot. Best striptease in town. Guldemeester said he'd been there several times in the line of duty and the the show was truly excellent. Meanwhile, his wife had been making up to the sergeant, who just sat there and called her 'ma'am' and—"

"Well, what did she expect?" de Gier asked. "She is Guldemeester's wife."

"More, probably," the commissaris said. "Perhaps she expected more. Go on, Adjutant, you've made me curious."

"Well, sir," Grijpstra said, "so Celine said that Cardozo could see a striptease right then and there, but she kept looking at de Gier."

"Then what happened?"

"We went home," de Gier said. "After Grijpstra threw up on the goats."

"Oh," the commissaris said, "so Mrs. Guldemeester didn't really perform?"

"She did," de Gier said. "It took forever, too. She must have practiced. She had special music for her act. 'Pyramid' by the Modern Jazz Quartet. You know the piece? It takes quite a while."

"Good composition," Grijpstra said. "We should try that sometime. Some very tricky passages, though; maybe you won't be able to follow."

"No," de Gier said. "I'll be thinking of that party again."

"From what I hear," the commissaris said, "the experience might have had some pleasant aspects. De Gier, you've been here from time to time while we were away. Have you heard anything about reorganization at Headquarters here?"

"I hope there won't be," Grijpstra said. "Reorganization makes the mess worse."

"There'll be an investigation, sir," de Gier said. "State detectives have been called in by the mayor. They're supposed to concentrate on corruption and on cases that have been recently handled in an unprofessional way."

"I hope they won't ask for my cooperation," the commissaris said. "I wouldn't like to intrigue against colleagues."

De Gier stared at the commissaris.

"Yes, Sergeant?"

"No, sir." De Gier shook his head. "I was just thinking. Anything else you have in mind? I'd like to send that message off and see what Halba and Guldemeester have done, exactly. Shall we meet here tonight?"

"I'll meet you at Martin IJsbreker's house," the commissaris said. "At seven. No, make that eight. I'd like to look around the area a bit first, I think."

⦀⦀⦀ 5 ⦀⦀⦀

"VERY NICE," ADJUTANT GRIJPSTRA SAID. "BEAU-tiful, in fact. Lovely example of Golden Age architecture." The adjutant stood solidly at the extreme edge of the quay, his head tilted to obtain an optimal view. De Gier leaned against a tree. Together they observed a slender four-story gable built up out of varnished bricks, holding tall windows in bright white frames. A seagull had just landed on the gable's tip and was silhouetted sharply against the sky, which was still sparkling blue, but tinged with the first hue of coming darkness.

"Got the key?" de Gier asked.

"Sure," Grijpstra said. "He wouldn't give it, of course. Wanted to know why and so forth. Colleague Guldemeester can be quite awkward when pressed."

"So you had to press him, eh?"

"Leaned on him with my full weight," Grijpstra said. "Threatened and cajoled. Still had to find the key myself, in the end." Grijpstra lowered his head. "You know Guldemeester is a squirrel? He must keep a hundred ballpoints in his desk, filched from everywhere. He had a hundred keys, too."

"So how do you know you got the right one?"

Grijpstra held up the key. "Labeled. See? Gulde-meester just stood there while I searched his desk. Wouldn't play at all."

"Did you see his notes, too?"

"No notes," Grijpstra said. "No gun. Remember that carton filled with weapons that disappeared from Ballistics, the one you told me about?"

"No," de Gier said. "Not our gun. You mean the Walther PPK that IJsbreker shot himself with went out in the missing carton?"

Grijpstra nodded. "Lifted by a Turkish charwoman, or so they claim at Ballistics. It's all hushed up. The chief constable doesn't want the papers to know. There was a dismantled machine pistol in that carton, too, and a couple of Magnums. Weapons taken from a Turkish drug-running gang. There's a thought that the Turks pushed some of their women into Headquarters to retrieve the guns."

De Gier was still admiring the gable. "Cops sell guns, too. My neighbor bought a pistol from a con-stable who stopped him for drunken driving. As it would be his second conviction, the sucker paid a small fortune in cash and the cop took pity and threw in the gun. My neighbor told me about it when I asked him to take care of my cat. I had to stay overnight up north."

"Makes you proud of your profession," Grijpstra said. "So, no gun to check with the bullet in IJsbrek-er's head. Did you see the pathologists?"

"That was another negative," de Gier said. "Notice how the entire gable was rebuilt, not just patched up somehow, as you usually see in a restoration. Must have cost a pretty penny. I wonder if IJsbreker owned the house."

"We can check with the Registry of Deeds tomor-row." Grijpstra walked around parked cars. "The Banque du Crédit may own the place. If IJsbreker has shares in the bank, he may have wanted to avoid prop-

erty tax. No businessman in his right mind owns anything in his own name anymore. Personal property is
mere weight these days. All you want is to have the
use of the stuff.''

"At no cost," de Gier agreed. "Borrowed interest-
free wealth that will last until one's death. In IJsbreker's case, death came rather early. Want to hear something?''

De Gier produced a small cassette recorder and held
it near Grijpstra's ear. He clicked its switch. "Hello,"
a rich baritone voice said, "this is Martin IJsbreker's
answering machine. Please leave a message. I'd just
love to have your message. I'll answer as soon as I
can. Wait for the beep.''

Grijpstra looked surprised. "When did you get
this?''

De Gier pocketed the little machine. "Just now.
IJsbreker's phone is still connected. Doesn't he sound
jolly?''

"A good powerful voice," Grijpstra agreed. "Arrogant, strident, authoritative, I would say. Not depressed at all. Perhaps the tape is old. Maybe he has
been using it for years.''

"Old tapes are usually scratchy." De Gier turned
away from the house. "I say there's a hint here that
IJsbreker was in no way depressed. Let's cross the
bridge and have a look at that houseboat where the
junkies were found. I'll tell you about the pathologists
on the way.''

De Gier stopped on the bridge linking the two quays
that framed the canal. Some little boys were paddling
an old canoe along. They wore folded paper hats, and
the boy in the bow waved a wooden sword, ordering
his crew onward. His thin shouts were drowned in the
rumble of a heavy diesel engine propelling a cargo
vessel along. Its bow wave made the canoe bob
jerkily. The boys screamed with joy. "I used to do
that," de Gier said.

"You still do that," Grijpstra said. "That's your trouble. We aren't playing games, you know."

"That's *your* trouble." De Gier patted Grijpstra's shoulder. "You won't see the fun. Did you read that bit in the paper about a whole new cluster of galaxies that some wise-ass discovered? A billion new worlds to choose from? Anything you can imagine will be out there, any game you can possibly play."

"Can't get there," Grijpstra said, "and if I could, it would be serious too. Self-centered beings breaking reasonable rules. I don't care whether they're small and green. It'll be the same horror, endlessly repeated, with types like me running about forever, hopelessly trying to restore order."

"What's hopeless?" de Gier asked. He pointed down. "See that? A fish. Big fish."

Grijpstra peered. "You're putting me on. That water is polluted."

"Carp or something," de Gier shouted. "I saw him whopping his tail. Look! Another one."

"My fishing rod broke," Grijpstra said. "I won't get another one. They're too expensive now."

"And yesterday," de Gier said triumphantly, "there was a great crested grebe in front of the Hôtel l'Europe. There used to be only garbage there. A grebe, I tell you."

"Bird?" Grijpstra asked.

"With a tuft on his head."

Grijpstra pushed his bulk off the bridge's railing and moved on slowly. "It's still shit, Sergeant. The whole thing is shit. We're losing."

"To lose," de Gier said cheerfully, striding along. "Not a bad idea either. Anarchy would be fun. With my back to the wall." De Gier stopped and gestured. "The enemy everywhere, in relentless pursuit of good guys like you and me. Superbly armed, they hunt us down, but you and I melt into the shadows. We live furtively on catfood."

"Why catfood?" Grijpstra asked.

"That's all we could find in the deserted supermarket," de Gier whispered.

"You've been going to the movies again."

"Okay," de Gier said. "The catfood came from a movie. Or was it dogfood? I forget now. But the lone warrior seemed to enjoy it, licking his fingers and all, and he had this great car, and some nice-looking woman got raped, they showed that quite well. I think he saved some others from the bad guys and then raced off again." De Gier prodded Grijpstra's belly. "You know, maybe you're right, you shouldn't be in on this. You're too slow and sad. We'll have you killed in the adventure's beginning. You're just dead weight, but I'm sorry to be rid of you. You can see it on my face." De Gier stared sadly, looking down at Grijpstra's corpse. He sat down on his haunches. His hands felt through the air.

"What're you doing?" Grijpstra asked. "Leave my body alone."

"You may have something of value," de Gier said. "Some shells for my shotgun. I'm alone now and could use your knife."

"You wouldn't last a minute on your own," Grijpstra said.

De Gier straightened up. "You sure you want to be in on this? I've a feeling the present situation doesn't agree with you. My fantasies aren't as far out as you think. The present may prove me right."

"Tell me the negative about the pathologists," Grijpstra said.

"Weird tale, Adjutant. There's no autopsy report at all, nor will there ever be. The doctor who did the job won't talk, and the other can't substantiate what he claims to have seen. There were two bullets in IJsbreker's head, against one cartridge found on the floor."

Grijpstra thought. He raised a hand and declaimed,

"The dead banker struggled to his feet and shot himself again."

"Two bullets," de Gier said. "But only one hole. The hole was in the middle of IJsbreker's forehead."

"That's against statistics," Grijpstra said. "People shoot themselves through the temple or the mouth or, once in a while, between the eyes. Not through the forehead as a rule."

"Two .22-caliber bullets."

"The missing gun was a .22," Grijpstra said. "The fellow at Ballistics remembered. The empty cartridge ejected by the pistol was .22, too. But if two bullets penetrated the same hole, an automatic weapon was used, capable of producing extremely rapid fire. A Walther PPK is only semiautomatic. Admittedly, the trigger is set finely so that shots can be fired at minimal intervals, but even so, the second bullet would cause a second hole. I say an assault rifle was used, either American or Russian, and IJsbreker was shot from there somewhere." He pointed at the north quay.

"From across the water, Adjutant?"

"Sure," Grijpstra said. "Remember the report? IJsbreker was found in front of an open window on the third floor. From where we were standing just now, opposite from here, on the south quay, we had to tilt our heads back even to *see* the third floor. A shot from that position would have been too tricky. If two bullets made one hole, the weapon must have been extraordinarily steady. The rifle was set on a tripod, I say. You're sure there were two bullets?"

"One got lost," de Gier said. "That's why the chief pathologist is so upset. They gave him IJsbreker's corpse late in the day, and he rushed the job. Apparently everything went wrong. The other pathologist was bitching at him. The electric saw he uses for opening up skulls broke down. Our doctor threw up his hands in despair and went home, halfway through the job, leaving the two bullets he found in IJsbreker's head near the edge of the table. One of the illegal alien charwomen came in early the next day and cleaned the floor, perhaps inadvertently sweeping away one bullet that must have rolled off the table."

"The chief won't sign a report that states one bullet was lost."

"He won't even talk to me," de Gier said. "The other guy, the one who isn't paid as well and isn't responsible for the department, talked, but that's only because he likes to make trouble for his chief. He won't make a statement under oath either."

"Anarchy," Grijpstra said.

De Gier lifted a leg and skipped halfway around the adjutant. "See, lawlessness on both sides is already with us. Isn't this fun? We can perhaps imagine a solution, but we can never make it stick."

"So we give up," Grijpstra said, "because of foul play. I think both gun and bullet were lost on purpose."

De Gier skipped back. "If you give up, I'll go alone. I'll fight foul too. Now that the whole organization is in a shambles, new possibilities arise. There should be a good fight in here somewhere. It'll be a change. I've been trained too nicely. I'm tired of bowing and scraping on the judo mat. Let me kick them in the balls for once."

"No," Grijpstra said, "I'll keep you straight. Where are we so far?"

"You," de Gier said, "had just placed a crack shot behind a tripod bearing an assault rifle of American or Russian make. Why? Because of the caliber of the bullets?"

"Yes." Grijpstra looked around. "Modern rifles are small caliber. American rifles are stolen from army barracks, and Russian rifles are handed out free to terrorists. Where did our killer position himself? On the roof of that houseboat?"

"That's the houseboat where the dead junkies were

found," de Gier said. "Anyone standing on the boat's roof is in full view. It was bad weather that night. Raining cats and dogs. It's hard to make a good shot when you're being pelted with pets."

"So the killer was indoors, maybe?" Grijpstra asked. "In the house behind the boat? At number 20, where the old lady is being drummed out by musicians? Hey!"

Grijpstra scratched his short, stubby hair with both hands. "This is confusing. I don't want an old lady in my theory as yet. Didn't you say that you had read her complaint several times in the general file? I never saw the earlier versions."

"That's because you always look for big stuff," de Gier said. "Little bits of information are interesting too. Here is this old lady who keeps dragging herself to the local police station because ruffians want her to vacate her home—"

"The report didn't say that," Grijpstra said.

"Reports don't present conclusions, Adjutant. They try to feed us facts. Why would musicians drum an old lady out of her upstairs apartment?"

"They want the whole house?"

"Of course," de Gier said patiently. "They live downstairs and want the upstairs too. This area still has a bit of controlled rents. That old lady will never move unless you drag her out by the hair. Anarchy is not yet complete. The citizens keep up appearances. They would object to old ladies being publicly abused."

"So the ruffians drum." Grijpstra was still scratching his head. "Aren't we making this too complicated? We still have three dead junkies to fit into the theory. Forget the old lady."

"You brought her up, remember? Her location is of interest because the killer may have placed his weapon in her building."

"Hold it," Grijpstra said. "Some order here. Drumming goes all ways. Noise spreads sideways, too. Why didn't the other neighbors complain?''

De Gier pushed Grijpstra ahead of him, and they walked off the bridge and along the northern quay. ''Behold.''

''Yes,'' Grijpstra said thoughtfully. ''Empty house on the left, empty house on the right. No one there to complain on either side. *Now* I see. This area is close to the growing red-light district. Aha.''

''Simple, right?'' de Gier asked. ''Happens all the time. This will be some new sex club or gambling joint, or a hotel for hanky-panky. The old lady is in the way. If she moves out, there will be three houses available, nicely arranged. Knock the inside walls out, call the interior decorators, install strobe lights and sunken whirlpool baths, bring in the band.''

''The band is already there.'' De Gier stepped up on the sidewalk and looked into the windows of the downstairs apartment. ''Look at those drums.''

''Better than ours,'' Grijpstra said. ''There's a good-quality guitar, too. See the staircase? The musicians have the second floor, too, which leaves the third and fourth floors for the old lady. There are two front doors, so each apartment has its own entrance.''

''So the rifle was fired from the second floor?'' de Gier asked. ''Drummer and guitar player are suspects. We're doing well, Adjutant. We've got this thing almost licked.''

''You sure?''

''You don't think so?''

''I'm not too bright,'' Grijpstra said. ''What we've come up with is pure conjecture. I still have the missing pistol, and the bullet that maybe got swept away, and Halba's and Guldemeester's verdict of suicide, and Guldemeester refusing to hand over the key, and this small detail of the three dead junkies, and then one of them seeing Cardozo a while ago and babbling about murder before fading away.''

"It'll all fit in," de Gier said. "Care to check out the boat? We might need a warrant, but the door is probably open."

Together they contemplated the houseboat's state of disrepair. Once a sturdy steel vessel used for transport of the city's waste, it had been topped by a superstructure built of discarded boards painted in a garish variety of colors. Broken furniture had been pushed up front, perhaps in an attempt to arrange a sun deck. Ripped plastic bags containing indefinable mush were heaped in the stern. A stovepipe, stained with soot, hung at an angle across the cabin's roof. The gangway consisted of overlapping strips hacked out of soggy particle board.

"Palace of pipe dreams," Grijpstra said.

De Gier read the boat's name. *Rhinoceros of Doubt*.

"Don't get it," Grijpstra said. "Do you?"

De Gier read the name again, stenciled fairly neatly on the vessel's side. "Not yet. Check the gangway. If it carries your weight, it may support mine, too."

The boat's interior was damp and dark. "There you are," the commissaris said. "I thought you'd show up here." His old-fashioned shantung suit made a patch of light in the long narrow cabin. The commissaris sat on a rocking chair that creaked slightly as he moved.

"Hello, sir." Grijpstra dropped his hand, which had gone halfway toward the gun in his armpit. De Gier, legs slightly apart, hands dangling, relaxed.

"Just me," the commissaris said. "I've been here awhile, wondering a bit. Rather an unpleasant atmosphere here, don't you think? Can you feel it?"

Grijpstra sniffed, and de Gier moved about slowly. "Yes," de Gier said. "Death. Decay. Fear, too, I imagine."

Grijpstra cursed. His foot had kicked a doll's head that rolled about, staring in all directions with one curious eye, winking slyly with the other.

"Evil?" the commissaris said. "The inhabitants

sold their souls to the drug's genie?'' He pointed at a low bed in the middle of the cabin, covered with rags. ''That's where they must have been found—three promising young people who became shadows of themselves. Notice any inconsistencies? Not everything here is bad. There's still some live thought about, showing up as the remnants of a different activity, perhaps.''

''These?'' de Gier asked, studying framed examples of Chinese calligraphy hanging on a wall, each representing a single character drawn in strong brushstrokes.

Grijpstra mumbled, ''Well done.''

''One black junkie, one female, and Mr. Jimmy Floyd, student of Chinese,'' de Gier said. ''These must have belonged to him.''

''What's this?'' Grijpstra asked. De Gier looked round. Grijpstra pointed out his find, a head of a rhinoceros, hung like a trophy above the commissaris's chair, an expressive shape assembled from odd bits of wood, fitted craftily together. De Gier went over to study the object close up.

''Fascinating visualization,'' the commissaris said, still comfortable in his rocking chair. ''A completed puzzle assembled from random parts. The artist had a good eye, don't you think?''

De Gier's eyes had become more accustomed to the dim light filtering through the cabin's single small window. ''The colors are good too, sir.'' He admired the long sharp horn, slightly curved upward, of a light orange color that contrasted strikingly with the various grays of the head's gnarled cheeks and forehead. ''A rather strong image.''

''Of doubt?'' the commissaris asked. He got up, holding on to the sergeant's arm. ''Strange. A well-made piece of what I would classify as modern primitive art, dominating a miserable floating shack. Artful creativity suspended in terminal negativity. We'll

have to figure out the contrast sometime soon. Shall
we leave? All this moisture in the air makes me feel
my legs."

De Gier held his arm around the commissaris's
shoulders while he steered the frail old man along the
ramshackle gangway. "This boat is a danger to the
city's health," the commissaris said. "You can alert
the Water Police when you're near a phone. They
should drag it away forthwith. Adjutant, would you
mind bringing the rhino's head along? We'll hold on to
the sculpture for the time being; maybe it'll turn out
to be a clue. Lock it in the trunk of your car."

While the commissaris and the sergeant waited for
the adjutant to return from the car, parked in an alley
farther along, de Gier reported. The commissaris
looked at the giant carp below the bridge. "Amazing,
Sergeant."

"Alleged deliberate loss of evidence," de Gier con-
cluded brightly. "There may be witnesses, however,
and we could still work on possible suspects. I daresay
we can still find some."

"It's the Japanese," the commissaris said. "I can't
understand why they're getting such a bad press in the
West. We should be grateful to those dexterous peo
ple."

"Japanese suspects, sir?"

"You too?" the commissaris asked. "Why should
we blame their diligence for our woes?" He smiled as
the mouth of a large fish broke the surface and
smacked its shiny fat lips. "I'll have to bring some
bread next time we're here. That carp wants to be fed.
No, Sergeant, I think we should see the Japanese as
our benefactors. Now that they're taking over the
world's industry and our factories are slowly grinding
to a stop, pollution here is bound to decrease dramat-
ically. You see the signs everywhere. Nature is coming back. We can breathe fresh air and truly enjoy
ourselves again."

"Were you listening to me at all?" de Gier asked.

"Yes," the commissaris said. "Most of what you said had come to me while I was indulging in a little reverie in that unfortunate floating coffin, but your old lady is new. Her presence may open up a new avenue, I think. And I'm glad you mentioned the musicians who have been bothering her. We're badly in need of suspects, don't you agree?"

"You want Grijpstra and me to go after them, sir?"

The commissaris was absorbed in the spectacle of the carp again. De Gier cleared his throat. "What?" the commissaris asked. "Right, no, Sergeant, just to go after them won't be good enough. Catch them at their infernal drumming. Trying to chase an old woman out of her home seems a fiendish offense. If you can catch them at that perfidious activity, you have a better hold. Don't even mention IJsbreker's death for now. With skillful treatment, our suspects might trip themselves up."

"The downstairs apartment was empty just now, sir."

"Try tomorrow." The commissaris looked at the alley. "There's the adjutant. That rhino's head inspired me, Sergeant, I spent a long time looking at it when I was in the boat. Odd to see such good work mixed up in such a foul mess."

Grijpstra joined them and together the three men walked to IJsbreker's mansion. De Gier played his cassette recorder on the way. The commissaris nodded when the machine clicked off. "Why did you phone IJsbreker's number?"

"I thought there might be someone in the house," de Gier said. "A girlfriend, perhaps. We could have questioned her."

"Didn't you say IJsbreker was divorced, sir?" Grijpstra asked.

"So my wife heard," the commissaris said. "I haven't seen Martin in years. We should talk with his ex-wife; perhaps she was still in contact with her husband.''

IJsbreker spoke again from de Gier's cassette.

''Doesn't sound at all like the voice of a man who is about to shoot himself,'' the commissaris said. ''The possibility of murder is shaping up nicely, I would say.''

''A multiple murder,'' Grijpstra said.

The commissaris lightly touched the adjutant's arm. ''But we have no indications yet that the bodies are connected. You're referring to the junkies, Adjutant?''

Grijpstra pointed at the houseboat. ''In sight of IJsbreker's house? Three simultaneous overdoses? It happened the same night?''

''Nah,'' de Gier said. ''The shots weren't fired from that boat. It's too low. IJsbreker got hit on the third story of his house. You mean that the junkies might have been witnesses and had to be removed?''

''I don't know what I mean yet,'' Grijpstra said.

''If we keep looking,'' the commissaris said, ''we'll find some meaning soon, but perhaps we're not supposed to look. I do get that impression.''

IIIII 6 IIIII

"Ah, Chief Inspector," the commissaris said the next morning. "Had a good press party? I haven't seen the *Courier* yet. Are the journalists pleased with your elimination of that German terrorist?"

Halba, looking shabby even though his suit appeared to be brand new, stood uncomfortably on the commissaris's splendid Persian rug.

"Please sit down." The commissaris dialed. "Miss Antoinette, could you bring in that elegant thermos flask? I have a visitor." He smiled at Halba. "If you please, Miss Antoinette?" The commissaris replaced his phone. "Got to say that now. The ladies around here are getting stronger on proper etiquette."

"Bitches," Halba said, almost inaudibly. His thin lips curved. "Yes, quite. I'm sorry I didn't show up yesterday, but the mayor was in a rather boisterous mood. Took us to a pub close to City Hall and kept us there until the wee hours."

Miss Antoinette came in and poured coffee. She passed Halba's cup. "Mr. Halba, the bank phoned again. Your wife called, too. Some trouble about your credit card, the man at the bank said. He insisted that you call him as soon as possible, and your wife

54

seemed very upset. The problem is insufficient funds, I believe."

The chief inspector's left eye twitched. "Yes, I will take care of the matter." Miss Antoinette swiveled her hips triumphantly as she swung her tight body through the door.

The commissaris's eyebrows were still raised as he addressed his visitor again. "Uh. Yes. There was something that has escaped me for the moment." He stared at his hands, spread neatly on his desk. "Ah, I've got it again. Your colleague Rood telephoned just now. About his man in the hospital. Poor fellow isn't doing at all well. But how did that melee with the German go, exactly? It's still unclear to me. The terrorist was shot dead in a telephone booth?"

"Very tricky," Halba said, "I'm still amazed we didn't have more trouble. Terrorists are really exceedingly hard to handle. We found him because a woman who rents rooms alerted us, saying she had a German-speaking guest who had dropped several cartridges between his bed and the wall. She let us in when the fellow was out. The woman said the German was always telephoning from a booth further along in the street, although there was a phone in her hall. We found several clips that fit an Uzi machine gun, hidden between the German's shirts in a drawer. Since we couldn't find the gun, we assumed that subject was carrying the weapon about. The short-barreled version of the Uzi can be easily hidden under a jacket. The woman's description of her guest fitted one sent to us by the West German police of a well-known terrorist."

"Were you in charge of the initial investigation?" the commissaris asked.

"No, Rood was," Halba said. "Rood located the suspect in the street, but hadn't made the arrest, so I took over. Rood is mostly Narcotics now, and since I was then in charge of the Murder Brigade—"

"You murdered the suspect," the commissaris said, "and the investigation, according to Rood. Chief Inspector Rood had planned to follow the suspect to detect possible ramifications. We're after the entire terrorist organization, after all. Couldn't you have waited with the arrest?"

Halba recrossed his legs, leaned his arms on the sides of his chair, and tried to make his fingertips meet in a self-contained gesture. His hands slipped apart. "I thought a delay would be too dangerous in this particular case. Terrorists plant bombs that go off in public places. The sooner we catch them, the better public order is served."

"Just gun the fellow down?" the commissaris asked. "If the German had been followed, he might have led us to his friends. We could have tapped the phone in that booth. Wouldn't it have been better if you had placed your men in such a way that there was a minimal risk of hitting each other?"

Halba shook his head. "The detective who was hurt had no business being behind the booth. Police activity often involves danger. We all take chances from time to time."

"We do have arrest teams, Chief Inspector. Military Police squads that have been endlessly trained for just such occasions."

"There was no time," Halba said. "One has to make quick decisions in a crisis." He lit a cigarette. "Are you initiating an inquiry into the matter?"

"I might mention the matter to the chief constable," the commissaris said. "I never like it when one of our men is hurt."

"The chief constable was at the party, too, last night," Halba said. "I was under the impression that Henri approved of the way I acted."

The commissaris opened a file. "Miss Antoinette gathered all available information relating to another matter I wanted to see you about, the IJsbreker case.

I'm missing the pathology report. Ballistics hasn't come up with anything either, and it seems that important evidence has been mislaid."

Halba sighed. "That matter has been fully discussed with the chief constable. The missing carton is the subject of a secret internal investigation. Have you seen the corpses yet?"

The commissaris shook his head.

"If you take the trouble to see IJsbreker's corpse," Halba said, "you'll note a discoloration of the face due to gunpowder, proving that the pistol's barrel was pressed against IJsbreker's head when the shot was fired. We definitely have a suicide here."

"One hole in the forehead," the commissaris said, "and two bullets in the head. The pathologist is delaying handing in his report."

"One bullet supposedly got lost." Halba scratched his chin. "That leaves one bullet again. The only real bullet, as far as I'm concerned. Perhaps you should ask Guldemeester what happened; it's really his case."

"Adjutant Guldemeester called in today," the commissaris said. "He's taking the day off. You signed all the reports, I believe. You weren't at IJsbreker's house at all?"

"Only briefly." Halba's fingers kneaded his chin furiously. "I have no reason to doubt Guldemeester's statements. The adjutant's a very experienced colleague. Everything fitted exactly. Powder burns on the head, a letter on the table, typed and signed. *I've done this myself, things got to be too much, sorry if anyone is inconvenienced,* that sort of thing. Guldemeester checked the signature with papers at the bank."

The commissaris flicked his lighter and looked at the flame.

"Cigarette?" Halba asked, offering his pack.

"Hmm?" The commissaris put the lighter back in his pocket. "Oh no, thank you. I'm cutting down. No smoking in the morning. You know, Chief Inspector, I never trust typed suicide notes. People who work in offices are known to sign blank paper at times, because they're off somewhere and don't want to wait for the secretary to write what they dictate.''

Halba stubbed out his cigarette with excessive force. ''IJsbreker was emotionally disturbed. Guldemeester talked to the bank's vice-president, a Baron de la Faille. The baron stated that his chief had shown signs of obvious mental stress for some time.''

''Doesn't de la Faille replace his ex-superior?'' the commissaris asked. ''Couldn't there be a motive there?''

Halba touched the tip of his nose. ''You wouldn't be jumping to conclusions, now? Guldemeester visited the bank too, and was told that it belongs to Willem Fernandus, the attorney, who lives farther up Prince Hendrick Quay. He called on Mr. Fernandus too, who wasn't at all sure who would replace the Banque du Crédit's dead director.''

''Let's see now,'' the commissaris said. ''Missing gun, missing bullet. A typed note. Ah yes. I'm reopening this case, Halba, after due deliberation, of course, so I went over to IJsbreker's house last night. Adjutant Guldemeester was good enough to give Grijpstra the key. Did you notice that at least ten paintings had been taken down from the mansion's walls? The discolored areas were quite obvious, I thought. A cabinet must have been removed too. I saw a curved outline on the wall that indicated its shape. Display cabinets often have curved tops.''

''No,'' Halba said. ''As I keep saying, I rushed in and out. We were busy with the terrorist that day, a more pressing matter. Guldemeester handled the whole case by himself. I'm sure there's an explanation. Perhaps the objects were moved after the adjutant visited the house. Perhaps the heirs . . .''

The commissaris shook his head. ''No. The front

door was still sealed when we came. Do you often do that, Chief Inspector? Sign reports describing events and situations you haven't properly observed?"

Halba glanced at his watch. "Not normally, but as I keep explaining, there was a crisis at the time. I have to go now; there's a meeting of staff members in a few minutes. Are you coming too?"

"I think I'll skip it for once," the commissaris said.

Halba walked quickly to the door. He paused with the doorknob in his hand. "Yes?" the commissaris asked.

"I don't like this at all," Halba said sharply. "I hope you know what you are doing."

"I think I do," the commissaris said. He smiled when the door clicked shut. "And I *do* rather like this." The commissaris took a watering can off a shelf and casually watered the profusion of flowering plants on his windowsills before looking at his watch. "There. That should give him enough time," he said. He dialed a number, listened, broke the connection, and dialed again. "Miss Antoinette? I just phoned Guldemeester's home, but the line is engaged. Would you keep trying for me? Please? If you can't get through, I'd like you to pinpoint his address on a map. I believe that the adjutant lives a few miles out of town."

⫼ 7 ⫼

IN THE DETECTIVES' OFFICE THE PHONE RANG, JIN-
gling on and on, cutting off now and then, and starting
up again. De Gier, coming back from the canteen,
where he'd listened to dismal conversation on the subject of State Detection's threatened investigation—
nobody thought it would do more than cause further
useless trouble—picked up the phone. "Homicide,"
he said pleasantly.

"Sergeant de Gier?" a muffled voice whispered.

"Yes?"

"Prince's Island," the voice said. "The Ancient's
Café, in an hour." The voice was replaced by a me-
chanical hum.

"Yes?" Grijpstra asked from the door, seeing de
Gier shaking the phone.

"Karate," de Gier said. "He and his co-demon are
onto something. Now what? I only want to work on
that dead banker. Do we allow ourselves to be side-
tracked again? Karate and Ketchup have messed us
up before."

Grijpstra sat on his desk, carefully peeling the plastic off a cigar. "In interesting ways. I could do with a
laugh."

"What's with you?" de Gier asked. "You like the ordinary. You're a stodgy, slow, unimaginative member of the petrified old guard. Let's stick to our parts. I'm the one who's out for adventure. I wouldn't mind adventure now, but there were the corpses at the Binnenkant, and we should do some work. Have you seen IJsbreker's body yet?"

"Sure." Grijpstra licked his cigar. "I thought you were on your way down too. Did you chicken out again? I've seen worse bodies. A somewhat seedy but well-dressed gent, rather bald on top, a bit pudgy all over, due to soft living, of course. Remember the ladies' underwear we found in the leather couch at his house? And the traces of cocaine on the glass coffee table? According to Mr. Jacobs, there was a faint smell of perfume when they put IJsbreker in the fridge. The pathologist came down and had another look too."

"The one who talks?" de Gier asked. "Or his disgruntled chief?"

Grijpstra nodded. "The one who talks. There were powder burns on the corpse's face. The pathologist mentioned advanced cirrhosis of the liver. A hard-drinking man in his late forties, our banker was. Did drugs too—cocaine; his nose is a mess. No heroin—we found no needle marks anywhere. He could have smoked it, of course."

"So you want the case closed again?"

Grijpstra grinned at the sergeant's suddenly stooped shoulders. "Why? Because of the powder burns? So someone fired a blank in his face. It's been done before. Subject is shot from a distance and then the scene is changed so it appears he has been shot from close by." The adjutant raised a lecturing finger. "We're now assuming murder, and therefore premeditation. Why was IJsbreker shot during a thunderstorm with hard rain? That storm was predicted, very handy for covering up the sound of a shot. If I had paid attention in that campground, I could have saved Nellie's tent."

De Gier smiled.

"Good," Grijpstra said. "That's my boy. I might have despaired too, if there hadn't been two bullets."

De Gier looked grim again. "Only one, Adjutant. The other one is hearsay."

"Hearsay from a disinterested party." Grijpstra lit his cigar and sucked contentedly. "The pathologist who talks has no motive for hampering our job."

"Except getting his boss in trouble," de Gier said. "Our two doctors are rivals who like to trip each other up. The one underneath wants to climb on top. He imagines a nonexistent bullet and spreads the rumor all over the building. The authorities will begin to question the integrity of the top doctor. The top doctor has always been a hard man to work with. Uncooperative, right? Now he loses a bullet and he won't sign a report."

Grijpstra studied the tip of his cigar. "Too far-fetched. There must have been two bullets. Everybody expected just one. One suicide, one gun, one bullet. The second bullet is almost surreal. There's nothing special about the assistant pathologist; he's your regular pseudo-intellectual, badly qualified, sniveling, backbiting corporate slave." Grijpstra took a deep breath, but forgot to take the cigar out of his mouth. He coughed through the cloud of smoke billowing from his cigar. "The fool is quite incapable of imagining the surreal."

"You don't like the man?" de Gier asked. "Okay. Two bullets. Want to come to Prince's Island with me? Dally with demons?"

"Why do you always drive on the tramway tracks?" Grijpstra yelled in the car.

"Quicker," de Gier yelled back.

"Slippery," Grijpstra protested.

The car, obeying de Gier's pressure on the accelerator, screamed out of a bad swerve. "You know," de Gier yelled, ignoring the traffic lights of a busy crossing and forcing the aging Volkswagen through a crack between a bus and a truck, "we could be lucky. I sent out that message to all stations. James T. Floyd? Student of Chinese? Remember? The guy who fell off his chair?"

Grijpstra tried to stub out his cigar, but the car's jerky movements kept making him miss the ashtray. He threw the butt out the window, but a sudden change of direction make the car catch the cigar again. Grijpstra grabbed it and burned his hand. "Aaaah!" There was a bicycle ahead now, very much in the way. De Gier missed it.

De Gier slowed down, looking for a parking place. "That cyclist shouldn't have been on the tracks. Tracks are for trams."

"We aren't a tram."

"And for emergencies," de Gier said.

"We aren't an emergency."

"We're a continuous emergency," de Gier said pleasantly, after he'd parked the car and was strolling next to Grijpstra through narrow alleys. "That's why I joined the police. We're supposed to break rules so that others may learn to obey them. We drive faster in superb vehicles, we apply violence with our superguns, we think more freely with our superior cerebral equipment, we violate restrictive taboos with our boundless insight into the limitations of morality, we . . ."

De Gier's strident tenor passed Grijpstra by. The adjutant had absorbed the timeless peace of the antiquity of his surroundings, expressed in the polished cobblestones underfoot, the rows of delicate little houses, each with slight variations in gable design, and the harmonious way the tall windows flanked inset doors. Ahead, a small white bridge curved gracefully upward, and a cluster of floating, bright-feathered ducks, quacking conversationally, produced pleasant reflections in the water of the moat under the bridge.

"Yes," the adjutant said.

"You agree?" De Gier looked down at his peaceful companion, plodding at his side.

"I could give it up," Grijpstra said. "You heard all that muttering in the building this morning? Our colleagues are worried about their job security again. Stupid jobs prop them up. They think the coming investigation may kick them out. I think I would welcome a good kick. I would fly forever—around here, for instance. Why be part of a repetitive rigamarole that keeps you going around in circles? I know"— Grijpstra gestured forgivingly—"that I'm not really an artist yet. Take that painting I'm working on now. I haven't found the right green, but here"—his hand swept toward the moat underneath, its water reflecting the delicate green shades of mossy waterwalls— "given my freedom . . . and I think I would take up some drumming again." The bridge's chains creaked, and Grijpstra put a hand behind his ear. "Hear that? I could re-create that sound on a cymbal, work it into a composition of my own . . ."

"Yes," de Gier said.

Grijpstra looked up. "I'm glad you hear it too. Now listen to the seagulls. There's something in their cry that you could play on your flute."

"Not a bad move, eh?" de Gier asked, resting his hand on the adjutant's shoulder. "Sending that general message out? We need information on those dead junkies. So far we have nothing but their proximity to another corpse, but if we can trace this Jimmy and find out how his routine could have crossed the banker's path . . . Here's the café."

A vague shape stirred behind the worn counter as de Gier held the door open to facilitate the adjutant's ponderous entry. Two other shapes straightened up in the semidarkness of the room. The barman shuffled close.

"Morning," Grijpstra said benevolently. "Still this side of death, Bert?"

"Oh, yes." The old man grinned, showing his toothless gums. "Looking on, you know. Jenever, gents?"

"Good idea," Grijpstra said. "I prefer an early start. A good beginning may last until deep in the night." Grijpstra and de Gier carried their glasses to the far table. Two young men in jeans and leather jackets got up and shook hands.

"Ketchup," Grijpstra said.

"Karate," said de Gier. "It was you on the phone?"

"Hello," the detectives whispered, looking over their shoulders.

"Cloak-and-dagger again?" de Gier asked. "That's all right. Want us to whisper too? Let's have the reason for your call, colleagues."

"Jimmy the junkie," Karate said. "We know everything, but you shouldn't send out inquiries like that on the open circuit. We're under surveillance. The charge is innocence. We're the last innocents in our entire district."

"And phones are out altogether now," Ketchup said. "All phones are tapped by State Detection."

"And State Detection isn't innocent, either," Karate said. "They're the other side too." His polished fingernails shone in the sparse light of the pub. His made-up eyes gleamed.

"Gay?" de Gier asked.

Ketchup's hennaed hair gleamed too. "We're promoted now. Our rules prescribe the gay disguise. If one doesn't want to draw attention to oneself, one looks like this."

"My dear," Grijpstra said, "gays don't look like that anymore. Haven't you been told?"

Ketchup offered his tobacco pouch. De Gier rolled a cigarette, having trouble with hard green particles that broke through the paper. "Dope," Karate said. "Here, let me do it. Part of our new I.D. If we aren't stoned, the bad guys aren't supposed to believe in us. We're doped all the time. So are the State Detection cops. We caught two the other night. They were gliding around in their convertible Corvette. We drive an old Camaro, wax polished of course, but not quite the same thing. State Detection is special. So we arrested them on a charge of dealing and they had to tell us all. We're buddies now. They told us about your phones."

"You're first," Ketchup said. "An honor, in a way. The Corvette is supposed to follow your commissaris, but since your chief hardly moves, the state cops hang out in this part of town. More amusing."

"Not good," Grijpstra said. "This jenever is excellent, however. Your health, Sergeant." He looked at Karate. "Did you tell them that what they are doing is not good? They should go after Halba, and the chief constable himself. They're our worst. Gambling debts and blonde dollies. And after Adjutant Guldemeester. And most of Narcotics. The Gambling Department. The Aliens Branch. *We're* okay."

"No," Karate said. "Let's not be retarded, Adjutant. It's the other way round. The bad guys are winning. State Detection has gone over too. That's what the dicks said. *They're* okay, to balance things again, but they're up in the air."

"I can smoke this?" de Gier asked, studying his joint.

Ketchup lit a match. "Don't inhale too deeply or you'll fall over. This is dope provided by the state; we spread it around and make lots of friends. Rather strong. Pure pure."

"I like that," Grijpstra said. "The simile of the seesaw. Us good guys are up, the very few of us. The view is better from up here. Now what about Jimmy?"

"Zen," Karate said. "Jimmy was into Zen. We got to start with Buddhism here, or you won't follow our lead so well. Do you understand Zen?"

Grijpstra kept up one hand. Karate nodded. "You're the one. And all. And that's the sound."

"Hello?" de Gier said. "Am I still in this, too? Modern mysticism isn't quite my field. Am I missing something? Did Grijpstra give the secret sign?"

"The adjutant disposes of insight," Ketchup said. "That's what matters now, it's important."

Grijpstra put his tulip-shaped glass down. "The sound of one hand. Two hands can clap, right? They make a sound. Now one hand, simply raised, presents the sound of total stillness. I read that in the paper."

"For shit's sake," Karate said. "Now why do you spoil it? Once you start explaining, it's all gone."

"Advanced students can explain," Ketchup said, "because when it's gone it pops up again. You're not advanced yet."

"Grijpstra is advanced?" de Gier asked, sucking in dense smoke. "Then Zen can't be right. Once Grijpstra understands it, there's nothing to understand."

"You must be advanced too," Ketchup said. "Are you, Sergeant? There *is* nothing to understand."

"I've been understanding that particular aspect of the hidden creed for years," de Gier said. "I have this bed, you see, an old hospital bed, with rails on each side, that I painted gold on a rainy afternoon off. I got white sheets and blankets. There's something insightful about white and gold."

"If I hear 'insight' just once again . . ." Grijpstra said.

"Insight," de Gier said. "I get it by lying down on my very special bed, which is a gate to the forever, to the unlimited afterward, to the eternal underneath. I lie down and I sort of nap—and this is important, you can't do it with your shoes on, or even in socks—I get my toes around the bars, the bars at the foot of the bed, and then, after a while, I sort of get to be half awake, and then I know these things, like what one hand expresses." He held up one hand. "Yes?"

"Jimmy?" Grijpstra asked.

"All this insight," Karate said. "I didn't think it could be catching. That you have some of it, Sergeant, I get that in a way, but the adjutant too? I always thought the adjutant was rather a heavy type. Limited, you know?"

De Gier smoked and coughed by turns. "So he is, but there's a lot of tension on Grijpstra, and every now and then something may break through. Call it insight. You can't compare it to the commissaris's knowledge. Or it could be imitation. Maybe the adjutant repeats remarks the commissaris is good enough to make at times. If you have a master around you . . ." De Gier peered with one eye at the glowing joint. He folded his lips around it and extracted a large quantity of smoke. "A master. Someone who sees that there's nothing at all and he expresses that and you mumble after him. That isn't true insight. *I* do have some insight, because of that trick with the bed and my toes."

"Jimmy?" Grijpstra asked.

"Okay," Ketchup said. "Jimmy. We arrested suspect on a splendid day. The fellow was a dealer, he met the description. We took him to our station, but we were disappointed."

"Very small," Karate said. "Crumbs. Half-grams. Half-grams don't add up. He existed on that junkboat on the Binnenkant canal, with an expensive ladybird from exclusive The Hague—past tense, of course, they lose their veneer once the needle gets in. We met the lady too—her father is a psychiatrist, with two Volvos parked up front, and a garden with magnolia trees—she still had the highfalutin accent of The Hague. Good to lure clients in the alleys up here. Makes a bit of a change. A street hooker, no choice. The medicine is high-priced."

"The lady is dead too," de Gier said.

Karate swiped at smoke floating by. "Sergeant, that joint is too strong for you. Put it away. Yes, dead, and the black fellow too, but there were four junkies on that boat and you only have three bodies under ice. What happened to the fourth?"

"We do have four bodies," Grijpstra said. "Counting the banker. You guys know the fourth junkie?"

"Yes," Ketchup said.

"Description?"

Ketchup stood up, hunched his shoulders, crossed his arms closely on his chest, and turned his hands in. He pressed his head down on a raised shoulder. One side of his mouth sucked inward. He shuffled around the table with one knee pushed out, mumbling and stuttering.

"Spastic?" de Gier asked.

"Met subject in the boat," Ketchup said, "when we took Jimmy home and searched the vessel. There was almost nothing there. A mess, sad to see. The black fellow suffered from cramps, the lady from The Hague was starved, Jimmy spat blood, but the spastic looked fine. We didn't notice straight off that he had some physical trouble, but then subject tried to say something."

"Never saw him again?"

"No, Adjutant. We did go back once to help pick up the bodies, but the fourth fellow must have missed the onslaught."

De Gier smiled. "Keep it up. I like this fluent conversation. Do you know that I can see the space between the sounds?" He flapped his arms. "What is said here is like swans, floating high in the sky, suspended in eternal and liquid silver."

Karate pulled the joint from de Gier's mouth and squashed it in the ashtray. "Those three died of an overdose of pure heroin. I find that hard to believe, somehow. Pure heroin is never sold. Each body had a brand-new needle in an arm. The substance was checked in the laboratory. It was so strong that one injection could take a tribe of gorillas one way to heaven."

De Gier stirred coffee, plonked down by old Bert. "You see this? See how the milk turns? I read answers in the pattern. I'm understanding more and more."

"Smoke some more," Grijpstra said. "It'll increase your insight. Brand-new needles, Karate? How come? The boat people are known for their dirty equipment."

"And we found this uncut heroin," Ketchup said. "Something very wrong there, Adjutant. I say their deaths were planned by some outside agent. Subjects could never have afforded what killed them. Their place was a shambles."

"Not quite," Karate said. "Remember the rhino's head? The spastic subject had created the structure, from floating garbage picked up in the canal. That's hard to do, when you can't control your hands too well. I watched him move. He seemed to keep going where he didn't want to go."

"I've got the artwork at home," Grijpstra said, "and some framed Chinese letters. Very nice, I thought."

"The colors," de Gier said, still stirring his coffee. "I mean, colors are everywhere, they exist here too, in the coffee, but just try to take them out, and to fit them in."

"I said that just now," Grijpstra said and pushed de Gier's shoulder. "On the bridge, and I never got through to you. The greens in the canal . . ."

"Right," Karate said. "Chinese letters, I almost forgot. Listen here, Adjutant. We had handcuffed Jimmy and I didn't have my key and Ketchup had gone back to the station to look for it and then I saw the Chinese stuff. So I ask, 'What's that?' And Jimmy says he studies Chinese philosophy. I didn't believe him. Subject is dirty, has no teeth, is a bicycle thief and a pimp. He was living off what that lady brought in."

"So he studies Chinese too," Grijpstra said. "I paint."

De Gier looked up and spoke slowly, adding appropriate and expressive gestures to his words. "I play the flute. The more miserable our regular lives are, the deeper are our emotions. Beauty, whirling up from cesspools, takes on wondrous shapes, subtle shades, there is a melody that only the unhappy can hear . . ."

"Sergeant?" Grijpstra asked. "If you please? Yes, Karate?"

"So Jimmy says he made those letters himself—an impossibility; the fellow is quite gone. And the letters were beautiful. So I tell him not to bullshit so much, and what do you think? The lady from The Hague fetches some paper and a jar of ink, and he's got a brush and *schnatz whyatzh*, Jimmy throws down a Chinese phrase."

"With handcuffed hands?"

"Right," Karate said. "Swoosh. Down on the paper. No thought. Just one stroke. There it was."

"*Mu*," Ketchup said.

"Moo," repeated de Gier. "The lowing of a cow. Cows have it too. They can say it all in their one eternal sound."

"No, this is Chinese," Ketchup said. "Meaning emptiness, not-there, you know? That's Zen again. So there is nothing. And subject drew that for us, in half a second or so. He explained all and everything. By denying, you know? There's nothing going on."

"Ach," Grijpstra grunted angrily.

"Right!" Ketchup shouted, slapping the table. "I mean, he's right, the asshole, even I can see that at times, but does that mean you have to go down that far? Poison yourself in a garbage boat? Can't he arrange it a little nicer?"

Silence surrounded the table, filled with disdainful lack of acceptance.

"Nothing fits too well," Ketchup said. "I was back on the boat by then and got Jimmy's cuffs off, and we were on our way. So how about the banker? We did try to get into that, too, but your adjutant kept us out of the house. Practically kicked us down the stairs, and it was a death in our district. Chief Inspector Halba had his ratty snout into that hole too."

"Bah," Grijpstra said.

"Something wrong, right?" Karate asked. "And on the same canal we have the old woman with her eternal drumming complaint who never gets a chance to speak to our sergeant. Another matter we're not supposed to meddle with."

"Our sergeant says he'll fix it himself," Ketchup said, "but he can't find the time, because he has to sail a lot on the Vinker Lakes, with his flat-bottomed imitation antique yacht, handcrafted, worth a bagful of gold. Your Halba goes along at times, with female company hired from the motel out there."

"But our sergeant does find the time to tell us what not to do." Karate rolled a joint too. "We can't just bring in any junk. There's junk and junk. If we find it in the street we do a good job, but we can't touch anything that can be connected to the Society for Help Abroad. The Society makes our sergeant nervous."

"And the State Detection cops in their Corvette don't do anything useful, either, although they cruise in the area a lot, seeing what goes on. They're too busy investigating the commissaris."

"Aha," Grijpstra said. "You hear that, de Gier?"

De Gier smiled kindly. "I'm going to challenge the black knight, Adjutant." He punched the air with his fist. "The final day is close. Evil finally shows itself in its darkest form. There will be a black knight out there worthy of my dazzling splendor. We'll have a duel forthwith. Now that restrictions are being lifted, I can at last show my true nature. I'll battle the fiend. We'll gallop at each other, visors down, in a field at dawn.''

"Yep," Karate said, "the sergeant is right. That's just what Ketchup and I are planning. Corruption frees us. The core of the enemy is the Society for Help Abroad, and their headquarters is in our district, on Gelder Quay. We propose to attack their club, you and us. Cardozo can join. He's around already, we saw him today.''

"A duel," de Gier said. "Maybe I'll help you fellows a bit at first, but then I'll dash out alone, no longer on the commissaris's leash, not befuddled by Grijpstra, unhindered by Cardozo.''

"You come along with me," Grijpstra said, pulling de Gier off his chair and supporting him with one arm. "I'll take you home for your nap." He looked at Karate. "Cardozo is around?''

"Working," Karate said. "He came out of the Banque du Crédit, with a clerkish type. We saw them having coffee together later on, looking sneaky.''

" 'Bye, Bert," de Gier said.

The old man waved feebly from behind his counter, grinning with withered gums. "Catch 'em, Sergeant."

⫸ 8 ⫷

THE COMMISSARIS'S SILVER CITROËN SLOWLY FOL-
lowed a narrow road on a dike separating low fields
from a river. "Ah," the commissaris said, seeing a
turn-off ahead. He parked the car and looked again at
the map that lay on the passenger seat, grunting as his
finger found a wavy red line, marked by Miss Antoinette's neat arrows. The river showed up on the map
too. He had to be on the right track, close to his goal
—too close, maybe. It was still early in the day, and
Adjutant Guldemeester, cashing in on the recently in-
stituted system that encouraged policemen to take
time off rather than demand extra pay for working
overtime, might be disgruntled if he was bothered before ten in the morning. The commissaris grimaced as
he switched the engine off. This was not a pleasant
call. He suspected an official of negligence, to frame
the charge lightly. There might be more. Guldemeester's track record, never brilliant, had dipped sharply
lately. The man worked sloppily, if he worked at all.
The adjutant's life-style invited suspicion too. It was
a pity that the police department no longer welcomed
inquiries into the daily conduct of its members. The
commissaris, as he left the car, briefly rethought his

general opinion of the country's overall direction. Although he never admitted his socialist sympathies, he was ultimately in favor of a society that spread its wealth, giving to each citizen according to his needs, but the danger was idealization of the state of mind of the average person. "We are," the commissaris had said to his wife, "still egotists, forever looking out for number one. We shouldn't be, of course, but we may as well admit our ignorance. If we're not aware of our petty greed, we'll drag the whole thing down." She'd kissed him, for she thought he was cute when he held forth. Katrien is very practical, the commissaris reflected. I've got to think things out that she has known all along.

As he crossed the road, a low-slung sports car growled toward him at excessive speed. The Corvette squealed its tires as it suddenly slowed down. The driver waved him on. The commissaris dragged his painful leg to the strip of lush grass bordering the river. The car was menacing. He felt cold sweat inside the collar of his shirt, and a thin icy trickle running down his back. More proof to support his theory that socialism had taken a dangerous turn. Rob the energetic and intelligent citizens through high taxes in order to support stumbling efforts of the weaker sector of the population. All very well, but overtaxing interferes with people's sense of justice. Extreme taxation will be dodged. Hoodlums follow the example of their betters. The system corrupts, because of undeclared taxable income that has to be furtively spent. The criminal potential of the mind provides expensive and illegal pleasure. The two young men in the sports car would probably be pimps, exploiting a pleasure club, taking a break after a dark night of preying on their illegally rich clientele. Or they could be providers of unregistered labor, hiring officially unemployed energy, renting it out at a sizable profit, in cash transactions. The commissaris wondered why the Fraud

Department hadn't managed yet to apprehend the two subjects. A mere check of the car's registration would lead to a house search revealing suspicious wealth. Both men were likely to declare no income. Their club, or company, would most certainly be unable to show necessary permits. A nest of vice could be immediately ripped apart. But the Fraud Department employed men who were like Guldemeester, untidy dodderers easily persuaded to take a bribe. And who was he criticizing, anyway? the commissaris thought. He himself was in charge of Guldemeester, allowing the adjutant to get away with petty condoning of irregularities. Was there anything the commissaris could do to clean up Homicide, if a chief constable presented him with a chief inspector like Halba, a much worse example of the self-serving public servant?

Well, the commissaris thought, so much for negative thinking. There was always something he could still do. He would do it a little later.

A little honesty, the commissaris thought, might be in order. He didn't care two hoots for Guldemeester's comfort. He wanted to spend some pleasurable time at the river now.

A fisherman on a folding chair, flanked by a lanky blue heron, waiting for any small catch the man might not care to take home, nodded a greeting. The commissaris raised a hand. The graceful bird, perched on one leg, had turned sideways to make sure that there wasn't any threat to its peace of mind, and disdainfully directed its plumed head back to contemplate the river's clear water.

The commissaris, not wanting to disturb the two friends, strolled the other way until he found a small pier jutting into the river. He sat on its low flat railing and admired the clouds, fluffy and white, floating lazily above the wide landscape. He grinned. The fisherman, sitting next to an expensive and what looked like a brand-new motorcycle, of a Japanese brand, of course (bless Japanese diligence, the commissaris thought), was probably unemployed too, making use of some imagined disability (a mysterious back complaint, perhaps) so that he could spend his time on what he really cared to do. Who wants to be the slave of a smelly machine in a foul workshop, to manufacture luxuries for others? If conditions can't be changed, their possibilities can be used. Maybe, the commissaris mused, he should accept the pleasant prospect of early retirement and move to some tax-exempt island in a tropical sea, with a climate sympathetic to his rheumatic complaint, and hang out on the beach thinking sly old man's thoughts.

Suck them if you can't join them. Who said that? Halba said that. Halba was always saying things like that, in private, during brief encounters in a corridor or an elevator, never at a meeting where methods of improving the city's welfare were solemnly discussed.

The commissaris admired the river's rippling surface until sharp pangs of conscience prodded him into activity again. He ordered his unwilling legs to carry his restless mind back to the car.

He drove on slowly, trying to read numbers on fences that shielded small cottages, each surrounded by its acre of garden. He turned the wheel when he recognized Guldemeester's late-model Mercedes, parked with its front bumper pushed into a row of cedars that might have been clipped into decorative shapes once, but hadn't been bothered with for a good while. The Citroën nosed along the narrow drive leading to the house, past wavy weeds rising from flowerbeds where individual tulips and daffodils still struggled bravely. A stone gnome pushed a toy wooden wheelbarrow along, from which sprouted more weeds. The gnome, grinning inanely, didn't seem to mind.

The commissaris rang the doorbell, then knocked and shouted. Guldemeester appeared at the side of the house, holding a beer can in a dangling hand. His shoes weren't laced. Bloodshot eyes gleamed above his unshaven cheeks. "Morning."

"How are you doing, Adjutant?"

"Just taking the day off," Guldemeester said, trying to push up his slipping eyeglasses but pressing his nose instead. "I had a hard night."

"Got a minute?" the commissaris asked. "Can we sit down somewhere?"

"In the back." Guldemeester turned and walked unsteadily ahead. Behind the house, a hammock had been strung between two thin poplars rising from clusters of dying rhododendrons. Empty cans were strewn about in the tall grass. The remains of two bicycles leaned against the house.

"A beer?" Guldemeester asked.

The commissaris looked around for somewhere to sit. "No, thank you."

"I'll get a chair from the house," Guldemeester said. The commissaris followed his host into the kitchen, where a stack of dirty plates, most of them still holding remnants of food, tottered in the sink. Guldemeester dropped his can on the floor and yanked a fresh one from a carton. "Sure you don't want a beer?"

"Yes," the commissaris said. "Why don't you go back to your hammock? I'll find a chair."

He walked into a room where furniture had fallen over, newspapers and empty cigarette packs littered the floor, and the TV set was partly covered by dirty clothes. Guldemeester came in too. "Why didn't you phone? I could have tidied up."

"Your line was busy."

"Right," Guldemeester said. He stepped aside as the commissaris carried out a chair.

Back in the garden, Guldemeester raised a leg and aimed it at the hammock. His heel caught in the hammock's ropes and he toppled over backward into a bush. "Are you all right now?" the commissaris asked, untangling the adjutant's leg. "Maybe you'd better sit on the ground. Here, lean against the tree."

Guldemeester groped about for his spectacles in the grass. He poked them at his face. "Drunk, you know."

"Yes," the commissaris said. "I do get the impression that you're a bit under the weather."

Guldemeester sat up. "You ever get drunk?"

"Not so much these days," the commissaris said. "Your wife isn't with you?"

"Celine is a whore!" Guldemeester yelled. He dropped his voice after he had smiled forgivingly. "That's okay. It's her vocation. Other women become nuns. More money in proshtitution." He pointed at the house. "Helped with the payment. Freelansh work, but she's professional now. Livesh with her shishter in Amshterdam."

"I see," the commissaris said.

Guldemeester shook his head. "It didn't work out."

"No?"

The adjutant's head kept shaking. "No. She'll get her money back. I'm selling the place. Don't want the money. Maybe she needs it. Yesh?" He flailed both arms about and the beer can shot off into the bushes, trailing foam.

The commissaris retrieved the can. Guldemeester peered into its little hole. "Empty." The can fell and rolled down his leg.

"You'll be leaving this pleasant place, then?" the commissaris asked.

"Leaving the country," Guldemeester said, slumping against the poplar's trunk. "Haven't told you yet. Damn the job. Never liked it."

The commissaris nodded helpfully. "I understand."

"Going to Spain. Better out there. Nice job." The adjutant smiled craftily. "You came about the dead banker, eh?"

"Yes, Adjutant."

Guldemeester wagged a finger. "Naughty, naughty. The case ish closed."

He swept his hand edgewise through the air, cutting the top off all possible explanations.

"You didn't have too much to do with the case?" the commissaris asked.

"No." Guldemeester closed one eye. His head dropped and he raised it with some trouble, trying to focus the other eye on his visitor's face. "I'm sorry, but I'd razzer not discush the matter."

"Is that what the chief inspector told you to say?"

Guldemeester nodded solemnly. "Yesh." His head dropped on his chest. "I'd razzer not discush the chief inshpector eizzer."

"Did Halba get you the job?"

Guldemeester's eyes crossed.

"Did Halba get you that nice job in Spain?"

"I'd razzer not discush . . ."

"You should be in bed." The commissaris stepped foward. "On your feet, friend. I'll help you into the house."

"Not in the bed." Guldemeester said in a suddenly clear voice. "I sleep on the couch downstairs. The bed reminds me of Celine." He attempted to push aside dead leaves dangling in front of his face.

"Give me your hands, Adjutant." Guldemeester wasn't heavy, and the commissaris dragged him up without too much trouble.

"See that shed?" Guldemeester asked as he staggered to the house. "Built it myshelf. For the goatsh. My little friendsh. I'd let them out when I came home and they'd gambol about."

"I've got a turtle," the commissaris said.

"Good." Guldemeester patted the commissaris's arm. "Good."

"To the couch?" the commissaris asked.

They passed the staircase. Guldemeester pointed at

empty bottles lying on the steps. "All ashleep, the little fellers."

"The bottles are your friends?"

"Yes," Guldemeester said clearly again. "The goats are dead."

The adjutant, steered along by the commissaris, flopped down on the couch. The commissaris picked up Guldemeester's legs and lifted them onto the couch too. "Comfortable? Maybe you can have goats again in Spain."

"Don't know," Guldemeester said. "Should have asked him."

"Who?" the commissaris asked.

"Fernandush," Guldemeester said sleepily, turning on his side.

The chief constable was waiting at the elevator when the commissaris walked through the lobby. "Morning," the commissaris said. He looked at his watch. "Afternoon, rather." He turned away. "Maybe I should get something to eat."

"Why don't you come up to my office for a minute?" the chief constable asked. "I missed you at the meeting."

The door slid open and they both got in. Two constables stepped into the elevator too, pointing at their caps, pushed to the backs of their heads. "Good day, gentlemen." The chief constable smiled. The commissaris mentioned the unusually good weather lately. He mentioned it again when they walked through the long corridor to the chief constable's office. "Very pleasant spring, good time of the year to be about."

The chief constable indicated a chair. "You were out all morning, I couldn't reach you on the phone. Working on something?"

"The IJsbreker case," the commissaris said, shaking immaculate white cuffs from his shantung sleeves. "I think I'm getting somewhere."

"That case has been taken care of." The chief constable pushed a box of cigars across the top of his desk.

"No, thank you," the commissaris said. "Closed?"

The chief constable nodded. "We discussed the matter again this morning. There's sufficient evidence to believe that Martin IJsbreker shot himself in a despondent mood. All conditions point to a conclusive supposition."

"Maybe I will have a cigar," the commissaris said.

The chief constable waited until the commissaris's cigar burned properly. "I think the missing gun and that nonsense about a second bullet can be ignored. Powder burns on the corpse's face, the letter, testimony by employees of the Banque du Crédit—we have more than enough to stop wasting time and turn to something else."

"To what, sir?" the commissaris asked.

"To the terrorists. There may be others about."

"Halba can work on the terrorists," the commissaris said airily. "He already had one shot. You approved of his method, I hear."

The chief constable's fingers drummed on his desk. "I'm serious. The IJsbreker case is closed."

The commissaris got up. "Well, that's that, then. I'll be off to lunch." He walked to the door.

"Commissaris?"

"Sir?" The commissaris looked over his shoulder.

"What will you work on now?"

The commissaris stopped and turned. "Oh, there's always something. The old lady, I think."

"Which old lady would that be?"

"The old lady who is being drummed out of her cozy apartment, sir."

"I'm not familiar with that complaint," the chief constable said, waving cigar smoke away.

"It's in the daily file, sir, several times in fact."

"I thought you were in charge of Homicide?"

"A drumstick," the commissaris said, "could be a dangerous weapon."

The chief constable nodded. "I didn't know." He smiled. "But then I've never been a member of the Murder Brigade. By the way, my name is Henri, I should have mentioned that before."

"I know, sir," the commissaris said. "Chief Inspector Halba told me so the other day." He hesitated. "Am I excused?"

The chief constable looked away. "Yes."

\\\\\\ **9** /////

"YES, MRS. JONGS," DE GIER SAID INTO HIS PHONE, "this is the police . . . about your complaint . . . No, dear, this is Headquarters, not your local station."

He listened. "No, dear, I'm not kidding."

He listened for quite a while. "Terrible. Absolutely, Mrs. Jongs. Tell me . . . just a minute now . . . yes . . . Would you perhaps keep a bucket around the kitchen?"

"Couldn't this be arranged a little more simply?" Grijpstra asked when de Gier finally hung up.

"No," de Gier said. "You didn't want to phone, so we'll do it my way. She wouldn't believe me at first. Listen carefully now, this is the plan. We meet in the garage here tonight at seven sharp. I'll come earlier to make sure that the van, overalls, tools, and whatnot are ready. You arrange the availability of a couple of cells."

"There are never any cells available," Grijpstra said. "The new jails we keep hearing about will be ready within five years. Can't we put this off till then?"

"Get cells, Adjutant." De Gier pounded his desk. "I don't care how you do it. Grant a rapist an all-night

84

walk through the park. It's Thursday, so the stores will be open until ten. Let a few shoplifters off so that they can keep in practice."

Grijpstra had cleaned his pistol and was trying to insert the clip.

"Other way around?" de Gier asked.

"Right." Grijpstra frowned as the clip clicked into place. "Thank you. I'll never get used to the new model."

"Please remember that the Walther P5 has no safety device."

"Really?" Grijpstra slid the clip out again and pushed cartridges into its open end.

"You'll kill someone," de Gier said. "Nontechnical types like you shouldn't be issued guns."

Grijpstra slipped the pistol into his shoulder holster.

"You'll shoot *me*," de Gier said, "But it doesn't matter. Death is the final and greatest adventure of them all. May it come swiftly, by the hand of a friend."

"I'm not really your friend," Grijpstra said gently. "Fate has pushed us together. I've never cared for your company much. You're everything I detest. Your slightest action irritates me intensely. Even if you don't do anything at all, I can't stand having you around." He sighed. "I'll be much better off without you."

De Gier sat at the edge of his desk, smiling down on Grijpstra. "So why did you pick me up just now? I could still be on my bed, enjoying the final vapors of the forbidden weed, twirling my toes, listening to the meaningful purr of Tabriz, upside down in my arm, rowing her legs, assuring me of her love by a tickle of her tail."

"Sergeant?" Grijpstra asked pleasantly.

"Yes?" De Gier crossed his long legs and turned his head a little so that he could see his profile in the mirror across the room. He adjusted his silk scarf.

"Why don't you smoke dope all the time?" Grijpstra asked. "You never buy it. You never take any home when it comes your way. You like dope, don't you?"

"Hmmm?" de Gier asked, still looking into the mirror.

"Won't you please tell me?" Grijpstra asked kindly.

"No," de Gier said pleasantly. "No, I most definitely won't. Why should I explain my inconsistencies to you? You would never understand. You don't see the beauty of deliberate, exceptional behavior. You're programmed to blindly follow whatever common sense prescribes. You're common, Adjutant. You're the average personified. You obediently trot along your predestined path. I detest you too, you and everything you stand for . . ." He looked at the door.

Cardozo came running in and froze in his tracks. "I'm sorry."

"For what?" Grijpstra asked.

"For interrupting," Cardozo said. "I'll go. I hate it when the two of you go into this lovey-smiley act. It makes me feel left out. I know I'm the odd man out here, and that you only tolerate me because I'm handy for running errands, but usually I can put up with being abused. Not when you're like this."

"You're too sensitive," de Gier said. "What makes you think we were being harmonious just now?"

"My sensitivity." Cardozo brought out his dogeared notebook. "I'll be quick and leave. I checked with the Registry of Deeds. The house IJsbreker died in belongs to the Society for Help Abroad. I checked with the Registry's computer and got a list of all Society property. Binnenkant numbers 18, 20, and 22 belong to the Society too. Number 20, the middle building, was only purchased last month. That side of the street is still rent-controlled, so Mrs. Jongs can only be thrown out if she doesn't send in her monthly check; even then the process might take a year."

"So she has to go voluntarily," Grijpstra said.

"And she won't," Cardozo said. "The Society might offer her money, of course, but drumming is cheaper."

"Good," de Gier said, "but that isn't all you did today. What else can you tell us?"

"I met Miss Antoinette in the corridor just now," Cardozo said. "She's all worried. The commissaris had her look up the registration number of a Corvette. It belongs to State Detection."

"Driven by men in leather jackets?" de Gier asked.

"I don't know."

"Driven by men in leather jackets," Grijpstra said. "Does that surprise us?"

"What else, Constable?" De Gier asked. "Come out with it. You were having coffee with a clerk. Why?"

"This is what else," Cardozo said, emptying the contents of a small paper bag on his table. Two plastic beetles, each two inches long, sprawled on their backs. He picked them up and wound their mechanisms by turning tiny plastic knobs on their bellies. He placed the beetles facing each other and watched their slow approach. The beetles whirred as they walked; as soon as their front legs touched, they stood up and began to maul each other with toothed jaws. Cardozo pulled his toys apart and made them repeat the performance. "So the investigation has started up," Cardozo said pensively, "and the State is concentrating on the commissaris first. What does that mean?"

"More misery," Grijpstra said.

"Joy," de Gier said. "Pure joy. Ultimate liberty. I always suspected that evil would one day try to catch us from all sides. We're the only good guys left and no longer restricted by what others may think of us. Any decent cop we ever knew has either left the force or gotten himself transferred well away from Amsterdam. Even the old chief constable bowed his patriarchal head when the bad guys started shoving. Only the commissaris . . .''

"And Chief Inspector Rood," Grijpstra said. "Don't exaggerate."

"And Constable-Detectives Ketchup and Karate, maybe," de Gier said.

"Ketchup and Karate mean well?" Cardozo asked. "I've been wondering lately. I saw them just now driving a punky Camaro, with eyeshadow up to their ears."

"They're crazy," Grijpstra said. "Which makes them useful. They don't think very constructively, either, which is an asset again."

"Muddled," de Gier said. "They haven't developed enough yet to be crazy. The commissaris is truly crazy." He made his swivel chair go through a full turn. "Do you know that that is my main fear? That the commissaris isn't really crazy, but merely another good guy? A multiplied Grijpstra?"

"I don't think so," Grijpstra said. "I think he's truly crazy. I've never liked the commissaris either. He isn't serious, he has that funny way of darting around, you can't grab hold of his motives."

"So the leather jackets are trailing the chief?" Cardozo asked. "Would they go after me too? They'd have to do it on roller skates. I'm riding a bicycle again. The garage took my car back, some restriction in the budget."

"So who is the clerk?" Grijpstra asked.

"I won't tell." Cardozo rewound his beetles. "I haven't worked this out yet. All in due time."

De Gier walked to the door. Grijpstra got up heavily and approached Cardozo by sidling along the wall. "Hey," Cardozo said.

"I've been rightfully accused of being an emergency," de Gier said. "Whoever said that saw deep into my soul. That I've restrained myself a little so far was because normality still threatened me somewhat."

"Cardozo," growled Grijpstra. "Who is that clerk?"

De Gier moved closer to Cardozo too. "But the situation has changed. Even the State is against us now. I can forget my last scruples. I can finally have a good time. I could, for instance"—he quickly grabbed Cardozo by the throat—"kill someone."

"Cardozo," growled Grijpstra, pulling back his fist.

"Okay," Cardozo said.

"There's a good chap," de Gier said, stepping back. "Tell you what, I'll get the coffee, even if it is your turn again. Don't say anything until I'm back."

Grijpstra dialed. "Miss Antoinette? Did the commissaris see who was driving the Corvette that bothered him?"

"Thugs?" Grijpstra asked. "A description, please?"

He nodded. "That's what I wanted to hear. Leather jackets. Could I speak to the commissaris himself now?"

"A visitor? . . . Who? . . . thank you." Grijpstra hung up.

"Who?" Cardozo asked.

De Gier came back with the coffee on a tray.

"Willem Fernandus," Grijpstra said, "the infamous attorney, the evil genius behind the society that fouls up the city, is in the commissaris's office right now."

"Great," de Gier said. "I hope he's there at our invitation. We have the enemy on a string." De Gier dangled an invisible string from his free hand. He suddenly jerked it, forcing a diminutive Fernandus to face him at eye level. "Hop. There you are. Hello."

"The commissaris has no enemies," Grijpstra said. "I like to think that he's too essentially polite ever to become angry with anyone."

"He doesn't care enough to be concerned," de Gier said. He smiled at Cardozo. "Enough sugar? Not too much milk? I stirred twice. To your liking, I hope?"

"A little too sweet," Cardozo said. "Could do with more milk. Otherwise it's just right."

"Too strong." Grijpstra put down his cup. "You'll never learn. Didn't the commissaris tell us that he and Fernandus go back a long way?"

"And that they don't talk to each other anymore," de Gier said. "Surprising. Very. Do we have a hint of humanity here? I'm not sure I like that."

"My brother Samuel got me a free ticket to this play the other day," Cardozo said. "Being eternally unemployed, Samuel finds things to do. It's amateur theatrics now. The play was about Tibetan holy men, calling themselves 'mountain lions,' who have been chased off their mountaintops by Chinese economists. It was called *The Mangy Dog*. The point seemed to be that when a mountain lion comes down to the village, the common people take him to be some other kind of stray dog."

"Is that so?" Grijpstra asked. "I'm glad you told us."

"I get it," de Gier said, "but nobody ever chased the commissaris into our lowly spheres. If he is here, he'll be here by his own choice."

"Would you care to light the incense, Cardozo?" Grijpstra asked. "And dust the floor, perhaps? It's time for us to prostrate ourselves."

"Go ahead," de Gier said. "Ridicule what you can't understand as yet. See if you can drag us mountain lions through the mud."

"Us," Grijpstra said.

"Got to go now," Cardozo said, tiptoeing away from his desk. "I'm busy. 'Bye."

De Gier jumped up and rushed to the door. Grijpstra drank his coffee. De Gier came back. "Couldn't catch him, eh?" Grijpstra asked. "You're getting old. Go home and take another nap. I'll see you in the courtyard at seven sharp."

⫶⫶⫶ 10 ⫶⫶⫶

"BUT I'M NOT," FERNANDUS SAID, WAVING HIS small fat hands excitedly. "No, I'm not at all what you imply. What has gotten into you? Look at me. I'm Willem. Wimpy, to you. We went to kindergarten together. We looked at goddamn *mice*. We were pals."

"No," the commissaris said.

Fernandus, dressed in a well-made but inconspicuous suit that was, to the trained observer of status symbols, easily discernible as very high-priced, flashed a golden smile, highlighted by his perfectly repaired canines. His recently permanented silver curls waved as his hands gestured more eloquently. "Jan. Why keep carrying all this old anger? I came here with pleasure. I was looking forward to meeting you after all these years."

"You came here," the commissaris said, "because you were told to come by a uniformed constable. If you hadn't come, I would have signed a warrant. You're a material witness in a murder case."

Fernandus held on to his smile. "You look neat, you look like the very symbol of authority. Do you know you would make an impressive judge?"

The commissaris smiled noncommitally.

"Yes," Fernandus said, "I can see it now. You developed well. As was to be expected, of course. Just look at you." He sketched the commissaris's outline in the air. "A neat little old aristocrat, framed by flowering begonias, looking innocent enough behind that impressively sculptured desk. But don't"—Fernandus raised a hand—"let anyone underestimate your ferocious power when you suspect injustice in the land. Now what murder might you be referring to, Jan?"

The commissaris took his time, lighting a cigar. "You're here to receive fair warning."

Fernandus's hand shot out. "I'll have a cigar too."

"Fair warning," the commissaris said. "You chose the evil path, Willem. How do you find it? Easy?"

Fernandus slumped back. "There we go again. Our last discussion was over thirty years ago. I didn't agree with you then and I disagree with you now. I chose the convenient, realistic path."

The commissaris, with a delicate old-mannish gesture, tipped ash off his cigar. "I chose the good path. I don't find it easy, that's why I ask."

"I stopped smoking a year ago." Fernandus said. "I've just decided I will break my habit of nonindulgence. You did that to me. You're the tempter. How can you be good?"

The commissaris bent forward. "No, really, tell me, are you having an easy time at being bad?"

"Cigar," Fernandus said.

The commissaris shook his head. "No friendliness. I became your enemy when you were killing Jacqueline by putting poison in her porridge. You can buy cigars in our canteen. One floor down."

"Fuck you," Willem said quietly.

"You suggested that before," the commissaris said quietly.

Fernandus grinned. "That's forty-five years ago. We *will* delve into the past. To answer your question, no, I don't find it easy to pursue my path. Sure, later on it gets easier. We get sly with age, and once you get the thing going, it gains momentum by itself; you must have experienced that in your career, too."

The commissaris nodded. "But you did have troubles."

"I still have troubles," Fernandus said, "but I take care of them better."

"As in Martin IJsbreker's case?"

Fernandus sighed. "I saw that coming."

"Of course you saw that coming," the commissaris said. "You saw it coming when the constable knocked on the impressive sculptured door of your million-guilder* mansion."

Willem waved the figure away. "Multiply that by two."

The commissaris showed his yellowish teeth. "Martin ran your bank. Did he acquire too much power? Or did he merely have his hand in the till? Did he help run the Society too? More pilfering there?"

"Questions, questions." Fernandus got up and walked over to the commissaris's desk. The commissaris quickly pocketed his cigar case. Fernandus sat down again. "I won't put up with your arrogant prying. I don't have to answer. I'm not a material witness. I was nowhere near Martin's house when he died."

"You ordered the killing," the commissaris said. "Look at you. You appear to me as the archetype of organized crime. You could be cast as the boss in any of a dozen gangster movies. You've got a slimy, self-satisfied expression that somehow mixes well with the false father image that attracts your misguided assistants' loyalty. Does a true father chop down his erring son?"

Fernandus giggled. "I never understood where you

---

* A Dutch guilder equals about thirty-eight cents in U.S. currency.

picked up those biblical ideas. Your parents weren't Christian."

"The collective unconscious," the commissaris said. "We all draw from its symbols. It happens to be Christian on this side of the world. If we were living in the East, you'd accuse me of quoting the Diamond Sutra."

"I'm glad you've kept up on your reading." Fernandus got up. "I'll be right back." He paused at the door. "Provided you admit that I'm here of my own free will. For old times' sake. Yes?"

The commissaris considered. Fernandus waited.

"You're here of your own free will," the commissaris said.

Fernandus came back. "Your canteen only sells cheap brands. I asked your charming secretary to go out and get me some good ones."

"Sit down," the commissaris said. "You think you're here for old times' sake? You're really here to be warned: you'd better face that, Willem. I'm going to get you. I'm trying to fight fair, so I thought you ought to know."

Fernandus laughed. "I always got you before. Remember Miss Bakker's sexy lap?"

"You were talking about watching mice together just now," the commissaris said. "Those mice dethroned me. That was the only purpose you ever saw in those mice. Remember how you sailed through school by copying my homework?"

"Of course I do," Fernandus said. "But you broke off the fight. I thought you'd given in. You were the weaker of us, Jannie. I really thought you saw that when we split up."

"You know," the commissaris said softly, "I never saw it that way. I still think we are of equal strength, but when the same quantities of energy are applied to the good and the bad, the good will eventually win."

Miss Antoinette came in. "Thank you," Fernandus

said, "you're wonderful." He turned around. "You're beautiful, too. My good friend here should be very happy that he secured your cooperation. Are *you* happy here?"

Miss Antoinette blushed. "Yes, sir, I am."

Fernandus gave her his card. "Maybe you'd be happier elsewhere. If you ever, for whatever reason, would consider a change, I'd advise you to come and see me at once. The pay would be, eh, let's see now, I don't want to make rash promises . . ." He looked at the floor, then continued, "The pay would be at least ten times what you earn here."

Miss Antoinette stared.

"Yes," Fernandus said, turning back to the commissaris. "Where were we, Jan?"

"Thank you, dear," the commissaris said to Miss Antoinette.

Fernandus felt his pockets. "I'll need a light."

Miss Antoinette brought him a side table with an ashtray and a box of matches. "Thank you, dear," Fernandus said.

"You're welcome."

Miss Antoinette left the room.

"Hah," Fernandus said as he lit his cigar. "That's better. I should never have given it up. All this talk of lung cancer and having your legs amputated . . . why live in fear? We'll all die of something. How's your health?"

"Rheumatism in the legs," the commissaris said. "I got that when you were partying with the SS."

Fernandus waved his cigar about. "Collecting information that I passed on at the right time. I would have been knighted for it if the newspapers hadn't made that stink a while ago. Were you in on that?"

The commissaris shook his head. Fernandus looked at the door. "A very attractive woman, Jan. I hope you didn't think I was trying to steal her away from you."

"Me?" The commissaris looked surprised.

Fernandus shrugged. "You'll lose her anyway."

"How so?"

"Because *I* will get *you*." Fernandus addressed the tip of his cigar. "That's why I'm really here. To warn you not to warn me. You have no idea what forces I can call into the field. You'll be smashed before you get started."

"I've already gotten started," the commissaris said. "Surely you've learned by now that weariness is a warrior's best weapon. Aren't you just a trifle cocky, Willem?"

Fernandus hit his knee. "Turn that around. Who's bluffing whom? You are the one who's in a weak position." Fernandus snorted. "Look at you, even physically you're in bad health. I hear about you from time to time; you're always off on some sort of sick leave. Whatever energy you may think you can apply, you'll have to draw from the State. The State is out of energy these days. The police, like any other corrective office that represents the ailing government now, malfunctions."

The commissaris tapped his desk blotter with a letter opener, a small model of a bayonet. "Don't underestimate your opponent, Willem. My brigade still works."

"Does it now?" Fernandus leaned back in his chair. "Key officers retire ahead of time, or get transferred to quiet pastures, and are replaced by nincompoops. You're the last of the Mohicans, Jan. Your tribe is dying out."

"Wimpy, Wimpy . . ." The commissaris shook his head.

Fernandus bounced up. "If your brigade functions, how come all that evidence got lost?"

"You're referring to the gun?"

"Of course I'm referring to the gun."

"Now," the commissaris said, "which gun might

you be referring to? The Walther PPK pistol that fired a blank in Martin IJsbreker's face, or the automatic rifle you had set up across the road? By the way, Willem"—the commissaris smiled—"you should instruct your marksman to read his instrument's instructions. Those rifles can be set for single shots."

Fernandus looked about the room, grinning at the oil portrait of a seventeenth-century constabulary officer, dressed in a black velvet jacket with a high lace collar, holding an ancient pistol. Fernandus pointed. "That dignitary looks like you—twice your size, of course, but your arrogance matches his shortsighted stupidity quite well." Fernandus dropped his hand. "I tell you, Jan, maybe that captain wielded more power with that muzzle-loading handpiece of his than you do now, I don't care how much modern might you may be able to command. It won't take much to bring you down."

"I didn't," the commissaris said, "invite you to come here to listen to your bragging. I'm warning you. If you give in now, you'll save yourself considerable trouble."

Fernandus puffed on his cigar. "And how should I give in?"

The commissaris balanced his letter opener on his finger. "Close your bank, dismantle your phony tax-free Society, and admit to having committed at least one crime that's serious enough to have you locked up for three years. We're both old men now. Three years will do."

Fernandus nodded. "As I suspected. This *is* a personal matter." He imitated the commissaris's high voice. "We're *both* old men."

The commissaris shook his head. "I don't follow."

Fernandus blew a perfect smoke ring.

"Are you saying I'm personally interested in bringing about your downfall?" the commissaris asked. "I assure you I'm not."

"You are," Fernandus said. "Let that go for the moment. How do you propose to attack? Before I give in, I should see how serious my situation is. You did say *fair* warning earlier on, I believe."

The commissaris put his letter opener down. "Hold it, Willem. Why should I be personally interested? Because of Martin IJsbreker's death? Admittedly I knew Martin, but I never liked the boy that much. Besides, he was on your side. Martin had shares in your pernicious bank. He directed the damned thing. He must have been active in the Society too. Crooks kill crooks, what is that to me? Maybe I'm interested in the junkies. Three young people who could have amounted to something. You abused them first, squashed them later."

"How's that, Jan?" Fernandus studied his cigar.

The commissaris straightened up. "Very well. I visualize a three-pronged attack on your dungeon of filth. The Tax Inspection Office will raid your bank, and my colleagues will rip your Society apart while I concentrate on the murders. That IJsbreker didn't commit suicide is proved by a vase."

"Ah," Fernandus said. "A vase. Interesting. What vase?"

"A Peruvian vase," the commissaris said. "A valuable piece of Inca art. I saw that vase used as a paperweight to hold IJsbreker's so-called suicide note down. Allow me to digress for a moment. You will remember that Martin showed some artistic talent as a youth. He won prizes at school. We all liked to think that he would be famous one day."

"He wasn't that good, Jan."

"But Martin IJsbreker was artistically inclined."

Fernandus nodded. "Maybe so."

"So he became a collector of art," the commissaris said. "Through you, Martin got himself into the money business. He combined money and art. Martin

privately owned at least ten valuable paintings that
you had removed."

"I did?"

"Yes," the commissaris said, "and there were also
quite a few vases stolen from IJsbreker's house. I saw
their imprints in the dust, on a number of shelves all
over the house. But one was left, used as a paperweight. What does that prove?"

"Prove?" Fernandus said. "It proves nothing."

"Oh, yes," the commissaris said, "it proves that
the thieves you employed were sloppy. Unprofessional. Hired to do a one-shot deal. Expendables. You
had them paid in heroin, strong heroin that killed them
off the very same night."

"That's your attack?" Fernandus asked. "Really,
Jan. Based on a vague supposition?"

"Not so vague, Willem, and certainly not when I
follow up further. Once I connect the junkies to the
middleman employed by you, and once I work on that
middleman a bit . . . The artworks are still around,
and can therefore be traced. You intend to sell them
off at auctions so that the cash IJsbreker pilfered from
your bank comes back to you. There are links, and I'll
find them one by one. Meanwhile, you'll be arrested
on tax-evasion charges. You won't be able to interfere
while some spineless lackey, presently employed by
your organization, squeals."

"No?" Fernandus asked.

"No," the commissaris said. "You'll gradually waft
away. It won't even take long. Very soon you'll have
nothing to fade into except—happily for you—death.
Give in now and you'll suffer less. That's why I said
that we're both old men now. Why go in for an all-out
fight? It just means unnecessary fatigue."

"Can I say something now?" Fernandus asked,
happily waving his cigar.

"Go ahead."

"If you feel old, Jan, it's because you *want* to feel

old. I can see your self-inflicted age. Now look at me. I've gotten stronger with age. Do you have any idea how much money I control these days? Any idea what that money can buy?"

The commissaris picked up his letter opener again. "Egotism is supposed to decrease with age." He felt his leg. "Ouch. We're getting rain again. I can feel it. Willem, at our age we should be mostly concerned about the welfare of others, rather than our own. What do you care about your personal wealth now?"

Fernandus puffed up his cheeks before exhaling with force. "Your altruism tires me. Besides, it isn't true, you don't give a fly's fart about others either. Are you in pain?"

The commissaris kept rubbing his legs.

"Get yourself pensioned off, Jan. If you don't, I'll have you kicked out of office." Fernandus moved his shiny boot. "And I do mean *kicked*. Katrien won't like your shameful defeat spread all over the *Courier*'s front page. How is Katrien?"

"We're doing well together," the commissaris said. "How's Fleur?"

Fernandus pulled back his foot. "Don't rightly know. Haven't seen her for a while. When I do, she whines."

"You're not taking care of Fleur?"

"Fleur has always been a dead loss. I got sick of dragging her about."

"I see." The commissaris made the letter opener reflect a ray of sunlight. "So you got rid of her, like you got rid of Martin. Strip them of their belongings first, eh?"

"Of course," Fernandus said. "Property always ends up in the hands of those who can handle wealth. Fleur cost me more than her shares in the bank were worth. I got them out of her when we divorced. IJsbreker's shares I bought from his wife."

"IJsbreker wasn't divorced?"

Fernandus laughed. "You didn't know? Here I'm giving you free information. Do you see now that you're bluffing? No, Martin and his wife, Trudy, still had hopes of getting together one day. She's in Rotterdam now, staying at her parents' house. My accountant figured out the worth of Martin's shares, and she was pleased to sell them to me."

"Not at their real worth."

"What's real worth?" Fernandus asked. "With present taxation, no business shows the profits it makes. Most gains are paid out in benefits. Martin had benefits because he was an officer of the bank. Why should I pass those along to truant Trudy?"

"But Martin's wife has kids, they need education."

"Bah," Fernandus said. "One dropped out of college and the other should have graduated from high school years ago. Two more helpless brats that socialism can take care of. Martin's boys are as useless as the junkies you're crying about. Be realistic, Jan. Drugs are part of the present, as slavery was a hundred years ago."

"Disgusting," the commissaris said softly.

"I agree," Fernandus said. "You started this meeting off by calling me evil. I've always been the bad guy in your eyes, from the moment I pushed you off Miss Bakker's lap, but all I have ever done is see things as they are. You think I enjoy looking at filthy young people wandering about, breaking into my Daimler at night? Human garbage that stinks up the streets of this fair city? Our forefathers didn't enjoy the smell of slave ships, either, but a lot of the money that went into the splendid architecture that makes up our town today was made from the slave trade. The helpless will be exploited. Look at the extremes today, Russia and America—do you see any essential difference? Only the elite lives well. I'm part of the elite. So are you, in a small way. If you hadn't been so wishy-washy, you would have stayed with me and done a lot better."

"You wouldn't, by any chance," the commissaris asked, "have helped to finance the manufacture of poison gas used in the death camps, would you now?"

"Don't think so." Fernandus flicked some ash off his leg. "Might have, of course. The bank invested in German chemical shares before war broke out. In the first war, the Banque du Crédit financed the Fokker airplanes that did so well in the Luftwaffe. Your grandfather owned part of the bank then. There must have been profits, and some of them have paid for that nice house you live in on Queen's Lane."

"Dad sold his shares, Willem."

"To my dad," Fernandus grinned. "Proves my theory that idealism weakens your position. It's the curse of your family. If you held those shares now, you'd have a grip on me." He got up and walked about the room. "Can I go, or am I officially detained? I've got things to do."

"If you go now," the commissaris said, "I'll put more force into my attack. You'll topple within two weeks."

"You'll be back on Miss Bakker's lap?" Fernandus asked on his way to the door. "Is that what you're after?" He put his hand on the knob. "You won't be, Jan. I'm not joking, either." He turned as he opened the door. "I'll put you in the corner of the classroom again, with a pointed hat on your head. Back off now, and maybe I'll let you be. Give you a rest so that you can still totter about a bit. What do you say? Deal?"

The commissaris's small head was illuminated by late-afternoon sunlight that made the entire room shine. The flowering plants on the windowsills added a profusion of bright color. Fernandus retreated into the shadow of the corridor.

||

WHEN ADJUTANT GRIJPSTRA MARCHED INTO THE Headquarters courtyard at 7:00 P.M. sharp, a mustachioed athletic plumber, dressed in sky-blue overalls, started up a cream-colored van proclaiming on both side panels that the sturdy vehicle belonged to Jansma & Son, plumbers since 1949. The van rumbled up and stopped.

"Get in, Dad," the younger Jansma shouted. "You can change in the back."

Adjutant Grijpstra clambered into the vehicle. "Switch your engine off—I don't want to bang about in here. Where are my overalls?"

"On top of the toolbox, Dad."

There were muffled remarks. "Too large . . . can't get my gun in . . . too tight . . . what is this thing . . . zipper? . . . zipper got stuck . . . stupid . . . must be an easier way."

The younger Jansma waited peacefully. "All done?"

The older Jansma fell into the passenger's seat. "Drive easy, now. Stay away from the tram rails."

Young Jansma eased the van into traffic. "Yes, Dad."

"I'm not your father," Old Jansma said.

"Just for now," Young Jansma said. "How's the painting? Were the bones I found you of any use at all?"

"Got them all in." Old Jansma bounced uncomfortably on his hard seat. "The ducks' skeletons are acceptable now. Floating nicely in the slosh, but the background's still wrong. Whoa. You passed the house."

"Yes, Dad." Young Jansma backed up the van, turning the unwieldy vehicle cleverly until it almost touched the curb. He grabbed the toolbox and bounded down to the sidewalk.

A fat, pimply young man opened a window on the first floor. "You better get to it."

"To what?" Old Jansma asked, lowering himself ponderously from the van's cabin.

"To the filthy fluids," the fat young man shouted. "Dripping through our ceilings. The old woman upstairs leaks."

"Would you be paying our bill?" Old Jansma asked. "No? Then shut your mouth, young sir."

Young Jansma, lugging tools and assorted tubes, joined his elder. He studied the young man's face. "Would that be venereal?"

"What?" the fat young man shouted.

"Your facial moonscape," Young Jansma said. "Maybe you should cover it with ointment. Or wear a mask."

"You see," Old Jansma said, "you don't see yourself. Others do. You might save us having to look at you."

The window banged shut. Young Jansma rang the doorbell. The door creaked open and the Jansmas looked up a narrow bare staircase. A little old lady peered down from the landing on the third floor.

"Mrs. Jongs?"

"You the plumbers? Come up quickly. The sink . . ."

The Jansmas climbed the stairs. "You're the cops?" the old woman whispered loudly, holding bony fingers behind her ear to catch the answer.

"At your service, ma'am." Old Jansma briefly held a gnarled little claw protruding from the woman's well-worn shawl.

Mrs. Jongs led the way to her kitchen. "I empties out the bucket six times." She cackled. "Ain't they complaining downstairs? They're banging on my door just now, but I don't open for nobody but the fuzz. Heehee."

"Now," Old Jansma said. "My partner will clean up all these puddles nicely, and you and I will have a little talk. What are your nasty neighbors' names, dear?"

Mrs. Jongs found a mop. "I does it."

"No, dear." Old Jansma grabbed the mop and handed it to Young Jansma. "Do a good job, son."

"The fat fellow downstairs is Huip Fernandus," Mrs. Jongs explained in her tiny front room. "His friend is Heul. My, ain't they wicked? Heul ain't home now, he's out shopping, be back in a minute. Buying fancy cans. They can't cook, you know. Coffee? I got it ready. Never thinks you would really come, but I makes the coffee anyways."

Young Jansma came into the room. "I filled up two buckets and emptied them into your sink. So four buckets of water went down there. Got them good and angry. Fine job, ma'am. Nice start. We'll finish the job."

Mrs. Jongs poured coffee into cracked mugs. She pointed at the wall. "See that? Them three round spots? Know what that is? That's where my mother's plates is hanging. Breaks on the floor. Comes off the wall because of them noises." She opened the window and looked at the van. "You Jansma and Son?"

"Can we drop the act now?" Young Jansma asked.

Old Jansma touched Mrs. Jongs's dried-out hand again. "Adjutant Grijpstra, ma'am, assisted by Sergeant de Gier."

"They're good plates," Mrs. Jongs said. "Antiques, they call them now. Handpainted, with flowers, all different. Bob wants to sell them, but they're my mother's. Bob needs some cash then, I ain't bringing in so much no more. But the plates're my mother's."

"Bob?" Grijpstra asked.

"My husband dies of the shakes. Bob sees lizards. They crawls so, he says. First they are snakes but then they got handsies and footsies. Bob tells me all about them lizards. And he is shaking and trembling and moaning and groaning. 'Get the lizards, Annie,' but I never sees them so much."

"You see them a little?" de Gier asked.

"No. Just to please Bob. I ain't really seeing nothing. They's big." Mrs. Jongs held her hand about a foot from the ground. "With tongues. They sticks their tongues in Bob's mouth."

Grijpstra's foot felt nails sticking up out of the floorboards. He stamped them down with his heel. "It's them noises what does that," Mrs. Jongs said. "I got a hammer, but the handle breaks."

"The noises come every night?" Grijpstra asked.

Mrs. Jongs's permanent wave danced across bare patches of skull as she nodded eagerly. "Them noises."

"Tonight again?" de Gier asked.

"For sure." Mrs. Jongs peered around a curtain. "There's Heul, on the bridge, see? Boy with the paper shopping bags? When they eats here, they makes them noises later."

Grijpstra sidled up to the window. "Male subject. Tall. Thin. Punk hairstyle, dyed orange. In his early twenties. Something on his T-shirt. Can't see what from here."

De Gier, hiding behind the curtain in the other window, looked too. "Picture of whale under an atomic cloud. I've seen those shirts before. The slogan says, 'Nuke the Baby Whales.' "

"That's in foreign?" Mrs. Jongs asked.

"American," de Gier said.

The folds in Mrs. Jongs's face crinkled. Her false teeth clacked excitedly. "Americans are good guys. Yanks. Remember?" She looked away from de Gier. "You don't." Her claw pushed Grijpstra's shoulder. "*You* do. When they rides into town? On them shiny tanks? Chasing the bad Jerries? Ain't that a sight?" She pointed at the shawl knotted around her waist. "I has a little Yank later. Wants him to ride out of me, all glorious-like, but he drops. Can't hold him no more. The Jerries gives me the sickies." Her dentures clicked even faster. "Then Bob gets me, me and the other girlies, but Bob marries me. Have to work for the favor. And then them lizards come . . . and then the old-age cash every month . . . but it ain't much, the old-age cash. And now them noises."

"We'll get the noises," Grijpstra said.

"Can't pay you nohow," Mrs. Jongs said. "I always pays, but then I gets so old so they laughs at me, can't work them when they laughs."

"In a little while we leave," Grijpstra said. "Then we slip back again. We'll catch the noises."

"Don't leave." Mrs. Jongs tried to put her cup on the table, but it slipped from her hand. De Gier caught the cup. "I'm afeared of the noises. Nobody comes now. Cahcarl would come but now the boat is gone. The water fuzz takes the boat this morning. The junkies are dead, I sees the other fuzz carry them out. And there"—she pointed across the street—"Himself's dead too. Himself was my TV. Got no TV myself. I has one but they takes it. Leaves the door open and Jimmy gets it. Or the black one. Not the lady, the lady she don't steal from me.''

"You knew the junkies well?'' de Gier asked.

Mrs. Jongs nodded. "But they need cash when they get sick. Oh, do they ever get so sick. They get shakes too, but the lizards don't get to them. Them junks sneeze too much.''

"Cahcarl didn't take the TV?'' Grijpstra asked.

"No. He don't get sick.''

"And the other cops didn't carry Cahcarl from the boat?''

"No.''

"Mrs. Jongs?'' de Gier asked. He got up and twisted his arms while he walked slowly through the room, dragging a leg. His head rested on his shoulder. "Mmmmissusss Johngsss?''

"Yep,'' Mrs. Jongs said. "That's Cahcarl. He's called Carl, really, but he stutters so. When you ask for his name he says 'Cahcarl,' so we call him that. That ain't nice.''

"And he didn't live on the boat?'' de Gier asked. "This Cahcarl?''

"He lives at the Overtoom,'' Mrs. Jongs said. "Don't know no number.'' She opened a cupboard. "See? Cahcarl makes that. That's Mouse.''

"Looks more like a dog,'' Grijpstra said.

"Yes.'' Mrs. Jongs shivered in her shawl. "My dog. Mouse, I calls him. A truck squashes Mouse. He's getting old, he can't see no more. Don't hear so good either. So Cahcarl makes Mouse again for me. I keeps him in the cupboard, away from them noises.''

The image was put together from scraps of trash wood, connected with cotterpins and screws. It had a rope tail, and bottlecaps for eyes.

"You like Mouse?'' Mrs. Jongs asked.

De Gier smiled. "Yes. A chihuahua, was he?''

"Oh yes.'' Mrs. Jongs put Mouse back into the cupboard. "Dear little doggie. Cahcarl likes Mouse too.

Takes him for walks, but that day I takes him and Mouse goes away. Cahcarl cries. Then he makes him again. Looks just right."

"We better go," Grijpstra said.

"Don't go." Mrs. Jongs took the adjutant's arm. "I got them fears."

"But if we don't go, the boys downstairs won't make the noises. We've got to hear them first. Look here, Mrs. Jongs," Grijpstra said, stroking Mrs. Jongs's hunched shoulder, "we'll be right back."

"We'll only be gone a minute," de Gier said. "I'll go down with the adjutant. We'll get into the van, and I'll slip right back into the house. The adjutant will come back later. Don't worry, Mrs. Jongs."

"Stay here. Them noises . . ."

"Don't worry." De Gier followed Grijpstra downstairs. The van started up and pulled away from the sidewalk. De Gier leaped out of the cab and into Mrs. Jongs's street door, and pulled it shut behind him. He sneaked up the stairs. "Here I am."

"Good," Mrs. Jongs whispered.

"They never saw me come back," de Gier said. "We'll just sit here awhile. They can't hear us if we don't move."

Mrs. Jongs held her finger in front of her lips. "Right," de Gier whispered. He pulled a portophone from the trouser pocket of his overalls. "You hear me?"

The portophone crackled.

"Hello?" de Gier said.

"Give me a minute," the portophone replied. "Got to park this thing. It's big, can't find a space."

"Done," the portophone said two minutes later. "I'm walking on Prince Hendrik Quay now, turning into an alley north, ready to come into the Binnenkant. Okay?"

De Gier peeped around the curtain. "Okay, they

must be inside. Stay close to the wall. You're coming in from the east?"

"Never know where's east," the portophone grumbled. "I'm coming from the right side. I won't pass their windows. Open the door."

De Gier slipped into the corridor and pulled the rope that followed the stair railing down to the door's lock.

"More coffee?" Mrs. Jongs whispered when Grijpstra, no longer in his overalls, tiptoed into the room.

They raised their cups. Mrs. Jongs sat on a straight chair, Grijpstra and de Gier on a sagging couch.

"Tell us about Himself across the road," de Gier said, "who replaced your TV. Can you see that far?"

Mrs. Jongs opened the cupboard again and showed him a pair of dented brass binoculars. "Bob looks through them at me and the other girls, when we work down in the street. They're sharp."

"Nice guy?" Grijpstra asked. "Your Bob?"

"No," Mrs. Jongs said. Her dentures snapped shut.

"But the lizards got him," de Gier said.

Mrs. Jongs passed him the binoculars. "I always tries to shoo them out."

De Gier trained the binoculars on IJsbreker's house. "What did you see there, Mrs. Jongs?"

She cackled and clapped her claws.

"Nice?"

"Oh yes," Mrs. Jongs said. "Nice underwears. I never have none. Just regular blue cotton pants I has. Bob saves on clothes." She pointed across quays and canal. "Them stockings and them panties, bras and all, and they takes that off, and Himself with the champagne, and the sniffies."

"Sniffies?" Grijpstra asked.

"Off the table," Mrs. Jongs said. "All of them on their knees."

"Good times, Mrs. Jongs?"

"Oh yes, the sniffies makes it last. On and on and

on. For hours. Three of them sometimes, and Himself, busy with everything, he has two hands."

"I see."

"So does I," Mrs. Jongs said. "I sees it all. For hours."

"But you didn't see Himself die?"

"That's the thunder night," Mrs. Jongs said. "First them noises and then the thunder too, and me with the fears."

"Did you see the paintings in Himself's house?"

"They takes them," Mrs. Jongs said.

"Who, Mrs. Jongs?" De Gier's nostrils quivered.

"The junkies?" Grijpstra asked patiently.

She nodded. "Must have. They takes everything. Jimmy must have took my TV. The black guy gets my bag, in the street. But the cops here don't see nothing."

"And Cahcarl helped rob Himself?"

She shook her head. "Not him. Cahcarl never gets sick. The others do, then they need the cash. Oh, that poor lady, she comes here and I makes coffee but she always stays cold and then she goes into the alleys and hustles again. The lady takes Himself's paintings."

"You saw her take IJsbreker's paintings?"

"No. She must have, though. And Jimmy, and the black guy too."

"Not Cahcarl?" De Gier's eyes shone.

"No." Mrs. Jongs held her head to the side, looking at de Gier.

"Yes?" de Gier asked.

"You got Bob's eyes."

"Aha," Grijpstra said.

"I fight," de Gier said, trying to shake himself from Mrs. Jongs's steady gaze, "in the light."

"The lizards gets Bob," Mrs. Jongs said, "them lizards with them scratchy hands."

DZJAAWOOHOOo-ooo . . .

De Gier fell into threadbare cushions on the couch,

covering up his ears. Mrs. Jongs's chair jumped off the floor. Grijpstra rose slowly. The floor seemed to come up. The nails that Grijpstra had pounded back into the floorboards popped their heads free again. Amplified guitar jangles tore at the walls and the ceiling. Drums banged and rumbled, making the windows rattle. Mouse danced in the cupboard, delicately, on spindly wooden legs. Pots and pans clanged in the kitchen. De Gier thought he saw Bob's lizards, scratching on glass surfaces with long bony nails. Their fiery tongues asped through his mouth into his brain. He staggered to the door, pushing Grijpstra ahead of him. Together they tumbled through the corridor and slid down steep stairs into the street, still holding their ears. De Gier tore his gun free and banged the butt on the door leading to the downstairs apartment. Grijpstra leaned against the bell. The cacophony was less loud in the street. It stopped just before the door gave way. The fat youth whom they had seen before gaped at them. His heavy-lidded eyes seemed glazed.

Grijpstra pushed young Fernandus aside. De Gier ran inside. A tall young man tried to stop him. De Gier ran the obstacle down, yanked him up again, turned him around, pushed him into a wall, forcibly pulled his arms together behind his back, and clipped his wrists together with handcuffs.

Grijpstra thumped young Fernandus in the belly. "You're under arrest." He slapped his face. "Turn round."

"What?" mumbled Fernandus, his face pushed against the wall. A second pair of handcuffs snapped shut.

Grijpstra faced de Gier, breathing deeply. Heul turned around. De Gier pulled back his fist. "That's enough," Grijpstra shouted. "Don't, Sergeant." De Gier's fist trembled and dropped.

"It's all right," Grijpstra said. "You got him." He

closed the door behind him with a careless kick of his heel. "Lead the way, boys."

Fernandus and Heul stumbled into the room.

"Sit down."

"What?" Fernandus snarled. "What's this for? That's breaking and entering. You got a warrant?"

"My father is on the City Council," Heul squeaked. "Huip's dad is an attorney. You can't treat us like this."

"Police," Grijpstra said. He looked around the room. "All this gear is confiscated. You've been harassing a helpless old lady."

"She poured water on us," Fernandus said. "You told her to do that? *That's* harassment. You're illegal. I want to phone Dad."

"I'll get the van," de Gier said. "We'll throw all that stuff in." He walked around the room. "Where do these wires go?"

"Up," Grijpstra said. "Check them out."

De Gier ran out of the room and up the stairs. He came back in a moment. "They've got loudspeakers screwed against Mrs. Jongs's floor. Nice charge, Adjutant. We can prove intent."

"Let's prove more," Grijpstra said, pushing the fat young man back into his chair. "What's your full name?"

"Huip Fernandus, my father is Willem Fernandus. He'll have your ass for this."

"Let's see some dope," de Gier said. "You're both full of pot. Huip, give us the dope or we'll tear the place apart."

"I want to see your warrant," Heul squeaked. "We've got rights. My father is on the City Council."

Grijpstra unfolded a paper and held it in front of Heul's eyes. "Okay. Where's the dope?"

"There's the phone," de Gier said. "Go ahead." He picked up the receiver. "Here."

Young Fernandus dialed slowly.

"Busy," Huip Fernandus said. "Let me try again."

"Phone my dad," Heul squeaked.

Huip dialed again. De Gier held the phone to Huip's ear. "No answer."

"They're out," Heul said. "I forgot."

De Gier put the phone back. "Pity."

Grijpstra picked up the guitar and smashed it against the wall. "No dope in the guitar?"

"Willful damage," Huip Fernandus yelled.

"Accidents will happen," de Gier said. "I'm sorry."

"Now," Grijpstra said, "what next? The drums? I don't really like to destroy drums. Shall I try the amplifiers first?"

"Wait," de Gier said. "Over there, that floorboard is loose. Stamp on this side. Over here. Go on."

Grijpstra stamped on the floor. The opposite end of the board flew up.

"Well packed," de Gier said, squatting down, lifting plastic bags from the hole under the board. "Hashish. That's nice. Pound bags?"

"Five bags," Grijpstra said. "We'll have that."

De Gier picked up two pairs of ear protectors. "You bastards. Got these on while you made your racket, eh?" He yelled into Heul's ear. "You hear me?"

Grijpstra shook his head. "He's crying." He yelled into Fernandus's ear. "What's he crying for?"

Fernandus held up his cuffed hands. "Hold it."

"Let's get the van," Grijpstra said. "We'll have you strip-searched at Headquarters. Find a little coke, maybe. Let's see your arms now. You boys inject too?"

"Hold it," Fernandus said. "You're overexcited. Good music does that to lower minds. We've seen it before. Drives the audience wild. Okay, calm down. We don't want trouble. Take the dope. Keep it. There's some money there. Money is good stuff. We'll lose this time. Sometimes a man has to take a loss. Right, Heul?"

Heul nodded, swallowing sobs.

"We'll take the speakers down," Fernandus said. "We'll practice nicely from now on. Got to practice. We're musicians. We play for the Society for Help Abroad. We help feed the foreign poor."

"You don't want trouble with the Society," Heul whimpered bravely. "That's big shit. You want your ass kicked, cop?"

The bell rang.

De Gier opened the front door. "Why, hello," a young man in a leather jacket said, standing next to what appeared to be his twin brother. "Just as we thought. A little trouble? Got it all fixed?"

"All fixed," de Gier said. "Your Camaro's double-parked. Better get the clunker out."

"We thought we might be able to help," the twin said. "Supply some assistance to colleagues?"

"We've got it all tied up."

"What did you get, Sergeant?"

"Two and a half ki's of hash, valuable musical instruments, partly damaged now, two suspects, harassment."

"That's good. Busy night. We saw Cardozo calling on his clerkish friend. In Mad Nun's Alley. He's there now. Number 13, a boarded-up shack." The leather-jacketed young man kept his voice low. "Do you think *he* needs any help?"

"No," de Gier said. "Not now."

"You may not be able to hold the suspects," the twin whispered. "Better beat them up. You're fighting rough now. This is our district, we'll back you up."

"Thanks," de Gier said. " 'Bye. Your car is double-parked."

"It's all right," de Gier said when he got back into the room. "I'll get the van. Be right back."

"Hold it." Fernandus waved his chained hands. "We'll find you some cash."

De Gier softly thumped Fernandus's head while he looked at Heul. "I'll phone your dad myself tonight and raise a reporter. A councilman's son in big trouble looks nice in print. What else can we put in? Been making any kiddie movies lately?"

"Good stuff," Fernandus said. "Care to see our specialties for celibate priests? We'll throw in some videos for voyeurs. Quit kidding, asshole. Let's make a deal."

"Good." Grijpstra grinned. "We'll put in bribery too."

De Gier backed up the van and opened the side door. Grijpstra pushed the suspects into the car. Fernandus stumbled over the toolbox and fell, dragging Heul down too.

"Oops," Grijpstra said from behind the wheel.

Heul whined and Fernandus cursed when de Gier lifted the electronic equipment into the van.

"Could we have some quiet back there?" Grijpstra asked.

De Gier threw in the remains of the guitar and the set of drums. The skin of the big drum broke.

"Ooooh," Huip Fernandus moaned. "Ooooh."

"What was that now?" De Gier asked.

"Oooooh," Fernandus said, "we'll get you for this, cop."

De Gier slid the side door forward and jumped on the passenger seat. Huip Fernandus climbed across what was left of the drums. He spoke into de Gier's ear. "We'll get old rattlehead too, plug up her leak."

⁙ 12 ⁙

THE RAIN STRUCK AGAIN. THE COMMISSARIS, DRIV-
ing to Headquarters, felt as though he were in a one-
man submarine, looking out on an aquatic world.
Streetcars glided past his car like gleaming whales,
and hundreds of cyclists in their shining plastic coats
darting about everywhere could be a shoal of herring.
The Citroën's windshield wipers, set at double speed,
swooshed helplessly as the rain drove against the
windshield. Traffic lights flashed ahead, the eyes of
some luminous water beast; telephone wires broken
by the storm dangled like the tentacles of a giant jel-
lyfish. The commissaris persisted, guessing at directions, and finally managed to slither through the gates
of the police courtyard. He left the car and splashed
through puddles, in galoshes his wife had thoughtfully
provided, and thankfully made his way through the
building's revolving doors. A uniformed guard saluted
inside. "Sir?"

"And a merry morning to you too," the commissaris said kindly, trying to ignore the cold drops leak-
ing into his collar.

"Chief constable wants to see you, sir."

"I think I'll have coffee first," the commissaris said, pressing the elevator's button.

"And there's some other geezer too. Your rank, sir. State Detection."

"Two geezers, meeting head on."

"Didn't mean that, sir." The guard grinned. "If you need assistance, sir . . ."

"What would you do?" the commissaris inquired.

The guard considered possibilities, holding his hand against the elevator's electric eye. "Trip him up on the stairs? An accident?"

The commissaris smiled. "We'll try diplomacy first."

The guard stepped back. "Good luck, sir, enjoy your coffee. Take your time. I haven't seen you yet."

Miss Antoinette served the coffee. "Well, what did you think of my old friend Fernandus, yesterday?" the commissaris asked. "Did his generous offer lead you into temptation?"

Miss Antoinette blushed.

"Ten times the pay?" the commissaris asked. "High-priced leisure supplied at irregular hours? A variety of interesting men?"

"I'd like to see the Society's club," Miss Antoinette said. "It was designed by Flaubert, the famous interior architect. He's going to do the mayor's room too, in the new City Hall building."

"You like Flaubert's work?"

"Oh, yes," Miss Antoinette said. "I went to his exhibition in the Municipal Museum, they had all the photographs and some maquettes."

"Of the Society's whorehouse too?" The commissaris studied, holding his head a little to the side, Miss Antoinette's figure. "You would look irresistible in a split skirt."

"More coffee, sir?"

The commissaris held out his cup. Miss Antoinette

poured from the silver thermos flask. Their heads came close. "You mean up to the hairline, sir?"

The commissaris dropped his cup. "Miss Antoinette!"

She brought a sponge and cleaned up his desk.

"Really, Miss Antoinette, what a disgusting thing to say."

"I shocked you," Miss Antoinette said triumphantly. "Weren't you trying to shock me?"

The commissaris cleared his throat.

"You were," Miss Antoinette said, "but we have equality now. Women can be disgusting too. I've been practicing. I've thought of the most horrid things to say. You want to hear some?"

"No." The commissaris carefully checked his cup for cracks.

Miss Antoinette put her hands on her hips. "Maybe I'd like to be a whore sometimes. Whores have a lot of fun. Just a few evenings a week. Beats watching boring television."

"But, Miss Antoinette . . ."

"Yes? Here you are, sir, please don't drop your cup again."

"But you're beautiful," the commissaris said. "We all hunger after you, you don't have to watch TV by yourself."

"You too, sir?"

The commissaris raised a protesting hand. "I don't watch TV."

"No, hunger after me?"

"Ah, well . . ."

"So?"

"Well . . ." the commissaris said. "A figure of speech. I'm an old man, dear."

"And unavailable. I would love to watch TV with you." Miss Antoinette noisily blew her nose.

"Dear?" the commissaris asked softly.

"Yes," she said through her handkerchief, "I know

I'm blushing. So you don't watch TV and you have a lovely wife."

"Sergeant de Gier hungers too," the commissaris said.

The phone rang. Miss Antoinette picked it up. "Yes?" She handed it over. "The chief constable, sir."

"Right," the commissaris said into the phone. "I'll be over in a minute."

"You're in trouble," Miss Antoinette said when the commissaris broke the connection. "He phoned before. There are rumors all over the building. I didn't want to tell you before you had your coffee."

The commissaris rubbed his hands.

"You like trouble, don't you?" Miss Antoinette asked.

"This sort of trouble I can deal with," the commissaris said.

"You can't deal with mine?"

He was about to walk past her, but turned and gently held her arm. "No, dear. I'm sorry. I've never understood women very well. You wouldn't really like to work in Fernandus's palace? Did you say that to annoy me?"

"Yes." She was ready to dive behind her handkerchief again.

The commissaris hesitated, then wandered off to the door. She walked ahead and held it open for him. "Good luck, sir."

He shook his head. "No. Maybe I want bad luck. Things have to turn against me now, dear. Maybe it'll be the only way I can work this."

Her hand touched his. "Well, then, I wish you bad luck, sir."

"Yes . . . yes. Thank you, dear." He tried to forget the uncomfortable interlude with Miss Antoinette as he painfully climbed the steps, choosing discomfort rather than the elevator's speed. He needed a little time to reflect. Did he know now what he was up to, or was he allowing subconscious urges to decide his course of action? He was shaking his head as he entered the chief constable's room.

"There you are," the chief constable said. "Good. I was just beginning to worry. Please meet a colleague, Commissaris Voort of Central Detection's head office in The Hague, who has been looking forward to meeting you." The commissaris shook hands with a wide-chested man who bent over him. Voort wore a blue blazer and light gray slacks. A golden clip fastened his necktie to a spotless white shirt. The commissaris noted that the clip was shaped like an anchor. "How-dedo," Voort rumbled. The commissaris mumbled his response, "Vrawah," meaning, possibly, "very well."

"Now then," the chief constable said. "How about some coffee first? No? In that case, let's come straight to the point."

"Corruption," rumbled Voort. "Rumors. Unpleasant. Start straight at the top, called in by the mayor. You've heard, I'm sure."

"Flattered," the commissaris said. "Very. I'm the top now? You've already dealt with the chief constable here?"

"No," the chief constable said. "I'm of no interest to Paul Voort."

Voort nodded invitingly at the commissaris. "Paul."

"Aha," the commissaris said. He looked at the chief constable. "No interest in your doings, or non-doings, perhaps?"

The chief constable shook his head, trying to hold on to his welcoming smile. "No, you see, I've only been recently transferred to Amsterdam, but you've served here all your life. A formality, of course. We all have to play the game, isn't that right, Paul?"

"Absolutely, Henri," Commissaris Voort rumbled.

"I see." The commissaris nodded helpfully. He

began to get up. "Well, we met. Good luck with your investigation. I have some work to do."

"No." Voort put both his hands up, palms toward the commissaris. "No. Sorry, old chap. Got to do this properly, you know? Full reports and whatnot." He thought. "And so forth. The whole caboodle. You're off duty for a while. Bit of a holiday." He closed his eyes and chuckled.

"Is something funny?" the commissaris asked.

"In a way," the chief constable said. "We all have to play the game. In your case, it shouldn't take more than a week or so. The first part of the investigation" —he looked at Voort—"is financial, am I right?"

Voort nodded briskly. "Absolutely, that's the proper procedure, I always like to work this way. I have some pointed questions here." He brought out a notebook and poised his ballpoint. "Income?"

The commissaris mentioned a figure.

Voort wrote it down, then crossed it out. "Impossible, you should earn at least double that."

"Twelve times my monthly check," the commissaris said.

Voort nodded and wrote. "All right, you were deducting taxation."

"Half my income is taxed away?" The commissaris shook his head. "Incredible, doesn't leave much, does it now?"

"You do have a free car," Voort said accusingly. "What's it worth?"

The commissaris shook his head. "The car is mine. The car the police bought had to be repaired after my recent investigations up north. I had some criticism from the administration about costs, so I replaced it at my own expense."

"Hah," Voort said, noting the fact down. "A new Citroën, I believe. You paid cash? Where did you get the cash?"

"I wrote a check," the commissaris said.

"You can prove that?" Voort raised an eyebrow. "The car wasn't a present?"

"Maybe my wife paid for the car," the commissaris said. "I don't remember now. Yes, perhaps she did. She has savings. Always investing in this and that. Likes to dabble in the stock market, Katrien does. Very clever, I'm always amazed. Wait a minute." He scratched his nose. "I may have used my own check after all, I can sign on both accounts. She too, of course. Or did Katrien pay now? Because I paid for her fur coat two years ago? Why do you ask?"

"This is no good," Voort said, crossing out what he had written so far.

The commissaris smiled. "Shall we try your next question?"

Voort turned a page. "Mortgage. Do you have your house mortgaged?"

The commissaris's smile widened. "You'll have to ask Katrien. The house is in her name. You see, that's because of my affairs."

"Affairs?" Voort asked loudly. "With women, you mean? *Other* women?"

"I could explain," the commissaris said.

"Please." Voort narrowed his eyes. "Please do."

"I *could* have affairs," the commissaris said. "My wife and I discussed that possibility many years ago. If I had these possible affairs, she would ask me to leave the house. I can't be asked to leave my own house, so I had the title transferred to her name." The commissaris crossed his legs and studied his well-polished shoe, which moved jerkily at knee height. "Of course, she could have affairs too, in which case I would not ask her to leave the house. Hmmm." He studied his shoe again, as if its rhythmical half-turns surprised him. "Couldn't ask her to leave her own house. Don't you find the ramifications within the concept of marriage complicated, Mr. . . . uh . . ."

"Voort," Voort rumbled. "Paul, to you, if you like. I don't bother with marriage anymore."

The commissaris's pale blue eyes concentrated on the copper buttons of Voort's blazer. He suddenly slapped his forehead. "Paul Voort, the yachtsman, how silly of me! You have this wealthy lady friend who keeps you in boats. Won a prize crossing the Channel, didn't you? And you lost it again because of foul play? What a shame. Poor fellow."

The chief constable spoke loudly. "Now, please."

"Just read it in the paper," the commissaris said to Voort. "I'm not professionally interested. You'd have to commit murder for that, and in Amsterdam, of course." He smiled. "You can operate nationwide? How very convenient for you."

"Let's get back to what we're supposed to be doing here," the chief constable said, waving at Voort, who showed signs of wanting to say something. "So you don't have affairs."

"No," the commissaris said. "But I could, maybe. You know what men are like, especially when they are a little older. How old are you now?"

The chief constable shrugged impatiently. "My age is not under discussion here."

The commissaris adjusted his glasses and peered intently at the chief constable's face. "Early fifties, I would say. That's when we lose confidence, but we gain it at the same time, if we do well in our careers. I know I was sorely tempted at your age. I was thinking, 'Suppose this beautiful blonde photo model comes along, in a Porsche . . .' " He took his spectacles off and pointed them at the chief constable. "You like Porsches, don't you?"

"Just another type of car," the chief constable said.

"Don't know that for sure," the commissaris said. "No, there's perhaps a special glamour there. To me, the Porsche has a female shape. Now suppose that type of car is driven by a luscious human female and I could ask her to ride me around town, do a few night spots, show her off a bit. Say she admits to a tendency to love older, powerful men—and we are powerful in a way, highly placed police officers do wield a certain clout—yes, I might be tempted. Wouldn't you?"

"Excuse me," Voort said.

"You're excused." The commissaris waved invitingly. "Next question, please."

"Has your house been remodeled?" Voort asked in a threatening bass voice.

"Oh boy," the commissaris said. "Oh boy. You got me there. I do believe it was. Windows painted, ceilings fixed up, water pipes ripped out of the walls and replaced, a new porch in the back. Katrien thought I didn't notice."

"But you paid for the repairs?"

"Not that I know of." The commissaris replaced his spectacles, taking his time. "No, sir. It was meant as a surprise, you see, so I think I was only supposed to notice when the job was done. Bills would surprise me ahead of time. But there won't be any bills, I'm sure."

"Because someone is presenting you with surprises?" Voort rumbled.

"I think it's Katrien again," the commissaris said, "paying in cash. You know that all—well, let's say most—workers in the building trades are unemployed these days. So they're on welfare. Welfare doesn't pay for their cars and other necessities. So they work anyway, for cash. You don't deal with these problems in The Hague?"

"But where does your wife get the cash?"

"I wonder," the commissaris said. "She has private investments, as I said. You could ask her. Can you ask her?"

"I certainly can," Voort said, peering at his notebook.

"Yes, but does she have to answer?" The commissaris shook his head. "I'm in murder myself, and you're now investigating fraud, but I rather think the same rules apply. You need a serious suspicion. Wouldn't you have to convince a public prosecutor first? You might possibly need some proof before I could be ordered to show my private papers. It isn't as if Katrien and I are flaunting our vast wealth. I do think I could afford to buy a car and have my house remodeled on my after-tax salary—once in a good while, of course, and it has been a while since I spent money on such necessities. And Katrien, well, she did inherit a bit from her parents. Only daughter, you know. Let's have the next question."

"Second house," Voort rumbled.

"Yes," the commissaris said, "I own a vacation home."

"Where?"

"Suppose I won't tell you," the commissaris said. "Do I have to tell you?"

Voort poked his pen at a gold-capped front tooth.

"I don't have to tell you," the commissaris said. "Same thing again. You need a serious suspicion, then you can drag me to a judge. If I still refuse, you could charge me with hiding evidence. This is a game, isn't it?" He looked at the chief constable. "You said that just now. Let's see if State Detection can locate my summer cottage. Might not be so easy. Houses are registered by town. There are a lot of towns in the country." The commissaris rearranged his legs and examined his other shoe. "I could give you a clue. It isn't really a house, it's more like a small trailer, or rather it was when I last saw it. I haven't been there for a while. Katrien wants to sell it. You could ask Katrien, of course, but there we go again—she doesn't have to answer you. May I use the phone?"

The chief constable pushed his phone across the desk.

The commissaris dialed, waited, and then spoke. "Katrien? Listen, this is fun. There's a colleague from

Central Detection here who has all these questions. About how much money we have, and so forth. It's all a game. Like they play in The Hague. Government games? You've heard of those? . . . What's that?" The commissaris looked at Voort. "No, he isn't nasty, just nosy, you might say, but I say that we don't have to answer his questions . . . You agree? . . . Good. Yes. I will be careful, dearest. Even if it's a game. Good-bye." He put the phone down. "So I'm off duty for a while?"

"With pay," the chief constable said. "Like an extra holiday, but I thought you might not like that. If you cooperate with the investigation, your discomfort won't last too long."

"Oh, I don't know," the commissaris said. "I daresay I could find something to do with my spare time. Something useful, even." He clapped his hands. "Yes."

"You're not being helpful," Voort rumbled. "Not at all. I'm still prepared to work in a friendly way."

"No, no," the commissaris said. "I insist. Each game has its rules. Let's pretend we're sworn enemies, colleague. I'll be as tricky as I can be. Dodge your questions, trip you up where I can, and, of course, I expect the same from you. Let's play cops-and-cops. Cops-and-robbers I know by now, but this variation is new to me. Let's match wits." He pushed himself out of his chair. "You must excuse me. I'm off duty now. May I still spend time in my office, or is that out too?"

"I would like you to be within reach," Voort said.

"I'll be around," the commissaris said. "I might be home from time to time. Give me a ring whenever you like."

The chief constable walked to the door. "Please. I didn't expect this sort of behavior from you. Do be serious."

The commissaris frowned. "I'll try. That's part of the game? We pretend the investigation matters?"

"There are penalties," Voort rumbled.

"Such as?" The commissaris stood opposite Voort's seat.

Voort sneered. "Lack of sympathy when I do turn something up might mean a dishonorable discharge."

"Very well," the commissaris said. "All right, do a good job, you two. No mercy. Let's have a good game. What if I win?"

The chief constable stood in front of the door. His lips trembled and his eyes bulged. "You won't, I swear you won't. Not after this."

The commissaris turned his back to Voort. "The Porsche?" he whispered loudly. "The blonde photo model? My insinuations didn't upset you, I hope?" The commissaris stepped closer, smiling up at his much taller opponent. "Don't get nervous this early in the game."

The chief constable stepped aside. "Get out."

" 'Bye," the commissaris said. He didn't look around when the door banged behind him.

"Well?" Miss Antoinette asked when he came back to his room.

"I'm off duty." He switched on the faucet of a small basin in the corner of the room, and beckoned her close.

"Oh, no," Miss Antoinette quavered. "I don't want to lose you."

"Just for a little while." He nodded. "So far, so good. Look after Halba for me."

"That miserable man?"

"Only a little," the commissaris said. "Keep an eye on the chief constable too, and on Paul Voort, my colleague from State Detection." He pocketed the case of cigars that she had picked up from his desk. "Thank you, dear." He took his gun from the drawer of his desk and locked it away in the safe hidden by the gold-framed portrait of the antique constabulary officer. "Won't need that, I think. Wouldn't do to shoot anyone when I'm off duty. Now, dear, you might have some time off every now and then, with me not here. We could meet." He pointed at a map of Amsterdam. "Here, I'll show you. Over there."

"On the—"

He put his hand to his lips. "Right. Do you know how to get there?"

"Yes."

He held her by the hand and walked back to the running faucet.

"Every morning at ten? If you can't make that, at four in the afternoon will be fine. You might be followed. Can't have that. Put on a bright raincoat, then take it off somewhere. Change trams."

"Yes." She smiled. "Yes, sir."

"You can trust Grijpstra, de Gier, and Cardozo," the commissaris said. "No one else. If you're followed too much you can reach me by letter at the café on the island, or you can talk to my wife. She goes shopping after lunch. Meet her in the grocery store around the corner from my house."

"How exciting," Miss Antoinette said. "I love it."

"It won't be at ten times your regular pay," the commissaris said sadly.

"But can I wear a split skirt?"

The commissaris took his time washing his hands.

"Please? I'd like to be a vamp for a good cause."

"We'll see."

"Please?"

"All right, all right." The commissaris looked around the room, nodding at the begonias and the potted palm next to his desk.

"You will be back here?"

He sighed. "Yes, dear. I think I will, but this will test my talents. I may be a babbling wreck when I come back. My habits are strong by now." He shook his head. "To reverse them . . ."

She kissed his cheek. "Be ruthless. We'll all help."

"Yes." He opened the door. "See you, Miss Antoinette."

⁗ 13 ⁗

"THIS IS MRS. JONGS," THE COMMISSARIS'S WIFE said. "She'll be staying with us for a while. Remember? Adjutant Grijpstra phoned late last night, saying that he might bring a guest?"

"I heard all about your predicament, Mrs. Jongs," the commissaris said, shaking the old woman's hand gently. "I hope you'll be comfortable here."

Mrs. Jongs rattled her dentures. "I don't bother you?"

"Not at all." He touched her stooped shoulder. "Our pleasure entirely." He smiled at the worried look on Mrs. Jongs's crinkled face. "We'll soon have you home again. In the meantime, please enjoy your stay with us."

"I cooks," Mrs. Jongs said, "and I cleans."

"We're cooking now," the commissaris's wife said. "Your favorite lunch. Veal ragout and rice. Mrs. Jongs is tossing the salad. She has been talking to Turtle in the garden."

"Good turtle," Mrs. Jongs said. She picked up an object from the hat rack in the hallway. "I brought Mouse."

"Isn't he wonderful?" the commissaris's wife

asked. "Mouse is Mrs. Jongs's pet. De Gier thought she might be lonely without him. He and Grijpstra are waiting for you in your study."

"He ain't real," Mrs. Jongs said. "Real Mouse squashes under a truck. Cahcarl copies Mouse. Good, ain't he now?"

The commissaris admired the wooden dog. "Excellent animal, Mrs. Jongs. Cahcarl, eh? Friend of yours?"

"Oh, yes," Mrs. Jongs said, "oh, yes."

The commissaris climbed the stairs, impatiently pulling his right leg along. "The pain isn't worse, is it?" his wife asked. "Please, Jan, don't strain yourself now. You were so relaxed after Bad Gastein."

"Bah," the commissaris said from halfway up the stairs. "I feel better now."

Grijpstra and de Gier stood up as he entered his study. "Sorry, sir," Grijpstra said, "but Huip Fernandus and Heul have been released already, due to shortage of cells, and we can't have them harming the old dame."

"Your wife said it's all right," de Gier said. "I thought of taking Mrs. Jongs to my apartment, but, as subject is rather nervous and may need care . . ."

"Yes. Yes, Sergeant." The commissaris checked his watch. "Twelve o'clock seems slow coming today. I would like my first cigar of the day now. So tell me more. I'm sorry I was so abrupt on the phone last night, but I'm almost sure my line is tapped. Let's have a full report."

De Gier spoke for a while.

"I see," the commissaris said. "That's good. A full frontal attack on Fernandus's fortress, resulting in the arrest of his son and confiscation of valuable instruments and a fair quantity of soft drugs. The initiative is ours this time. Isn't it pleasant to go all out? Do sit down, Sergeant. No, Grijpstra, that's my seat. Try the rocking chair, it's comfortable too. What's our gain so far?''

"Harassment of a helpless old lady," Grijpstra said. "That's about all the charge boils down to, but the prosecutor was impressed. It was the details in our report that got to him. Loudspeakers screwed against Mrs. Jongs's floor, the broken antique plates, the suspects mentioning their important fathers. I had a photo crew over this morning; the pictures they came up with are nice and sharp. We even have the shards of the plates. Mrs. Jongs had been trying to glue them together."

"The hashish won't stick," de Gier said. "It was found in a building belonging to the Society, with free access to all members. Suspects claim they didn't know they had two and a half kilos under the floor. The bribery attempt is no good either. They're both first offenders."

"Did you get Heul's father to Headquarters?" the commissaris asked. "Heul Senior is a prominent member of the Socialist Party."

Grijpstra grinned. "Yes, sir, and he was interviewed by a reporter. Kowsky of the *Courier,* best man we could find."

"That'll be front-page news, then." The commissaris nodded. "Heul Senior has helped to subsidize the Society. Thanks to him, we have all these canteens in town that sell drugs to the young." He shook his head. "Silliest system I've ever heard about. We drug our own youth at a tax-free profit that supposedly goes to the needy abroad but is retained here to finance luxuries for the rich. And we *subsidize* the stupidity out of our wages. How did Councilman Heul take the confrontation?"

"Smoothly," de Gier said. "He took Kowsky over to the Society's club for a drink afterward."

"That wasn't so clever." The commissaris checked his watch again. "Kowsky will write that visit up too.

He'd rather be in with us or he won't get nice news. Is it in the paper yet?''

De Gier shook his head. "I phoned Kowsky this morning. He got very drunk at the club. Tomorrow, maybe.''

"Hmm," Grijpstra said.

"You don't trust Kowsky, Adjutant?''

"No, sir.''

"Is there anyone you trust?" de Gier asked.

Grijpstra was busy lighting a cigar. The commissaris looked at his watch again. "You can trust me," the commissaris said lightly. "I'm a good guy. I'm ready to admit that now. I find myself very committed to our present cause. Too much, perhaps.''

"How so, sir?" de Gier asked.

"Well . . ." The commissaris hesitated. He pointed to the ceiling. "I always fancied myself to be up there, Sergeant. Floating, you might say, free from any petty cause whatever.''

"Detached?" Grijpstra asked, looking at a photograph of the commissaris as a young uniformed police officer, riding a horse.

"I don't like that word anymore," the commissaris said, "and I don't like the way you say it, either, Adjutant. But you're right. So, let's see. A fine for Huip and Heul, they lose their musical instruments and electronic equipment, and they'll maybe get a few weeks suspended. The courts are still holding up. I'm glad our judges are appointed for life at maximal pay. To keep them out of temptation helps during a bad period such as we're having these days. I'm interested in Mrs. Jongs now. She saw IJsbreker's frequent partying and she connects the junkies to the disappearance of the dead man's treasure. A definite lead there.''

"Yes," de Gier said.

"Very flimsy," Grijpstra said. "While the photographers were busy in her house, I asked around the neighborhood. Mrs. Jongs is known as one of the local loonies. Her pimpish husband must have beaten a lot of sense out of her. It wouldn't do to drag her into court.''

''A lead for us, I mean,'' the commissaris said. ''So far, we've only thought up a connection, but now we have someone from the area who confirms that the unfortunate girl and her afflicted friends were guilty of breaking and entering before. Who is Cahcarl?''

''The fourth junkie,'' Grijpstra said, ''who is not on heroin, and therefore did not die of an overdose.''

''The maker of Mouse.'' The commissaris checked his watch again. ''Ha. Five more minutes. So our spastic stutterer created the rhino's head. Did you notice the similarity in technique? You have the head, Grijpstra, maybe you can bring it here sometime. Those two artworks link the suspect to his dead friends and to Mrs. Jongs. You haven't seen the artist yet?''

''The Overtoom is a long street,'' de Gier said. ''We don't have a number. I wanted to go there now and make some inquiries in the stores. Cahcarl must be very noticeable. Do we arrest subject when we find him, sir?''

''No.'' The commissaris put his tin of cigars on his lap and held his hand poised over it. ''No, we have to think of Halba too. I won't have the chief inspector interrogating any of our suspects in this case.''

''That boy is in danger,'' Grijpstra said. ''They killed his associates. Cahcarl must know where the loot from IJsbreker's house went and who supplied the lethal heroin that paid for the theft.''

''I'd like to get to know Cahcarl,'' the commissaris said. ''Bring him over here. Katrien likes to take care of the weak. She has taken care of me for forty years. Ha!'' He lit a cigar, closed his eyes, and sucked smoke luxuriously. ''Ha.''

"How long will you keep this up, sir?" de Gier asked.

The commissaris smiled. "An excellent cigar indeed. What's that, Sergeant? Oh, I see. I'll be good in the mornings and bad in the afternoons and evenings. Symbolic, don't you think? Now, I have some news for you, I've been released from my duties for the duration of an investigation that centers on my career."

Grijpstra coughed. De Gier reached over and slapped Grijpstra's back. "They started on *you*?" Grijpstra asked between coughs.

"Of course," the commissaris said, daintily waving his cigar about. "I never expected otherwise. Once types like Halba become powerful in the force, types like me have to go. But this present activity suits me, Adjutant. When the law is twisted, I can't do much legally."

"Heh heh," de Gier said. "I've been waiting for this."

"Easy," Grijpstra said.

"Yes, easy, Sergeant." The commissaris nodded. "You aren't off the leash yet. We'll lengthen the rope but you'll still be pulled up short if you want to practice the martial arts too much."

"Heh heh." De Gier put his hands on his knees and smiled at Grijpstra.

"No," Grijpstra said.

"Released from my duties," the commissaris said. "Isn't 'release' a lovely expression? I still have duties, of course, but I can define them myself now. My self-inflicted duty now is the destruction of the Society for Help Abroad. Adjutant? What do we do next?"

"Lean on Heul," Grijpstra said. "He's the weakest link in their chain. I had a good look at Heul last night. If we can get him away from Huip Fernandus, Heul might confess to having supplied the dope to the junkies. We could waive that and have him implicate young Fernandus. Fernandus is tougher, but if we break him we have the leader's only son."

"They aren't weak enough yet," de Gier said. "Let's raid the club first. Illegally, of course."

"There you go already," Grijpstra said.

"Don't you want us to go?" de Gier asked the commissaris. "Karate and Ketchup would like to be in on the raid. Their sergeant is bought by the Society, so they can only hunt the Society's competition. This sergeant owns a high-priced sailboat on the Vinker Lakes. That's where the motel is."

"The motel," the commissaris said. "That would be the private country club where all rooms are continuously reserved for Society members? That muckraking magazine my wife cherishes mentioned the motel."

"The motel is protected by the local police," de Gier said. "We can raid it later."

"Raid," Grijpstra grunted. "What raid? You mean we burn the place down? Have charred bodies on our hands? Are you crazy?"

De Gier dropped his voice to a persuasive level. "Just rob the club a little, Adjutant. Annoy the opposition. Show them they aren't as safe as they'd like to be. They can't officially complain, for the reporters would swoop down and write about their illegal activities. Two illegals cancel each other out."

"Sir?" Grijpstra asked.

"Yes, Adjutant." The commissaris looked over Grijpstra's head. "I was thinking about Karate and Ketchup. Courageous little daredevils, are they not? They've been promoted to detectives, I hear. Can we trust them, do you think?"

"Grijpstra doesn't trust anybody," de Gier said.

Grijpstra scratched his badly shaven chin. "We could use them a little. They've been helpful so far. Pointed out that you're followed by a State Detection

Corvette. Karate and Ketchup have got good eyes. Told us about Cardozo, too."

"Cardozo?" the commissaris asked. "Yes, de Gier mentioned that just now. Cardozo seems to be out on his own somewhere. Did you go to that address in Mad Nun's Alley?"

"Not yet, sir," de Gier said. "I think Cardozo wants to impress us. He'll show up in his own time."

"We could use an inside contact in the club," Grijpstra said.

"Oh, my," the commissaris said. "Oh, my."

"You've got someone in mind, sir?"

The commissaris looked at de Gier. "Oh, dear. Another decision. I have to consider morals again. Should I ask Katrien?"

"Beg pardon, sir?"

"Never mind," the commissaris said. "I'll work this out. Why don't you try and get hold of Cahcarl, meanwhile? Even if we can't use him as a witness, it'll worry Fernandus once he knows that Cahcarl is in our custody. I think I'd like to talk to subject. Just pick him up and bring him over. He could enjoy protective custody at my place too. What do you think?"

"Then what, sir?"

"Then you take a break," the commissaris said. "Drive along the Amstel River a bit. Check with me later. Stay away from the phone. If I'm not home, I'll pick up messages at Bert's place on the island." He got up. "Away with you now."

ⅢⅢ 14 ⅢⅢ

"How?" de Gier asked. "By being the police. We can find anybody."

"Shuhure," Carl said, beckoning the adjutant and the sergeant into his loft. "If they're spahastic."

"Okay," Grijpstra said. "It was easy, Mrs. Jongs gave us the name of your street. We just asked around the neighborhood. Nice place you have here."

Carl lived in the top-floor loft of a large old house; the loft had its own front door and a steep staircase unbroken by landings. De Gier wandered about the vast space, weaving his way through the statuary that showed up everywhere. "You've been busy. This is great stuff."

"How's Mrs. Johongs?" Carl asked, leaning against a full-sized standing lion that growled near the door. The structure, looking fairly realistic, had been made from slabs, probably leftovers from sawn logs. The animal appeared to smile and had raised its tufted tail in a gesture of jolly eagerness.

"Mrs. Jongs is fine," Grijpstra said. "You may meet her a little later. She's staying with our chief."

"You're aharresting me?" Carl asked.

"No," de Gier said. "We'd like you to come with

us, though. Maybe you should take some clothes. We believe you're in danger and would like to ensure your safety."

"Amazing," Grijpstra said, looking at a row of large insect heads, displayed on a wall like hunting trophies. "This must be a mosquito. What are those wavy things coming from the eyes?"

"Not eyeyes," Carl said. "The eyeyes are on top and the si-hides of the hehead, those things are an . . . an . . ." He was bending sideways, contorting his mouth, his elbows jerked backwards, but the word still wouldn't come out.

"Antennae?" Grijpstra asked. "I see. Most expressive. This is some collection."

Carl, dressed in spotless jeans and a short-sleeved striped shirt, took the adjutant to the back of the room, where a microscope had been set on a table painted a meticulous white. A glass box held some dead moths. Carl held up a large magnifying glass. "Vehery beautiful."

"You catch them?"

"The spihider does." Carl pointed at an open window covered with cobwebs. He produced a pair of tweezers and took out a dead fly, steadying his hand with the other. "I hahaven't made a flyhy yet."

De Gier was looking at another table, covered with carpenter's tools, jars of nails, and a pot of glue bubbling on a hot plate. Heaps of broken boards, twigs and dried stalks, odd-shaped rocks and pebbles, flanked the table. "How do you get all this stuff?"

"I fihind it," Carl said. "Keeheeps me busy."

"You on welfare?"

"Noho."

"But you don't do regular work," Grijpstra said.

"This isn't reh-reh-reh . . . gular work?"

"Yeah, sure," Grijpstra said, "this is expressive stuff, really. I envy you your talent." He looked around the huge room again and concentrated on the

skeleton of a horse assembled out of material that was
probably charred plywood, remnants of a gutted building, perhaps, cut to size by a saber saw; the cadaver-
ous animal seemed to prance in high spirits. The
adjutant smiled widely and encompassed all the sculptures and other artful displays in a sweep of his arm.
"This is something else again, but you don't make
money on it, do you?"

"I dohon't neeheed to."

De Gier brought out a pack of tobacco and offered
it to Carl. "Noho thanks, my hahands tremble." Carl
found a packet of cigarettes among his tools and lit
one. "My fahather sends money."

"That's nice," Grijpstra said.

"Noho," Carl said. "Dahad never comes here. Because I'm spahastic."

"And your mother?"

"Noho, she's a Buhuddhist."

"The compassion of the Buddha?" de Gier asked.

"Noho," Carl said. "She lihives in a coh-coh-
comm . . ."

"Commune?"

Carl nodded gratefully. "Vehery hoholy." He
frowned furiously. "Fuhuck her."

De Gier admired a huge bird, swooping down from
the ceiling, with wings made out of black garbage bags
and a long beak twisted from sharp wires. "That's my
mohother," Carl said. "My fahather's over there."
De Gier walked over to the indicated corner. He
stepped back when he saw a human figure sitting on a
chair.

"Shit," de Gier said. "Look at this, Adjutant."
Grijpstra ambled over. "Shit," Grijpstra agreed. Carl
had outdone himself. The other figures all had a sur-
realistic touch—they were funny in a way, even the
leering spider and beetle faces, even the bird of prey
—but the sitting man, reading a newspaper, was horribly plain and ordinary, wearing a real suit, shirt, and

tie. The meticulously sculptured wooden body implied, in its attitude, a complete self-centeredness, accentuated by the arrogantly tilted head that peered at columns of figures from deeply recessed eyes. The paper was the *Financial Times* and there was a satisfied sneer on the man's thin mouth; evidently the shares he owned had done well that day. The suit, tailor-made out of superior tweed material, fitted the figure perfectly. "I tohook the suhuit," Carl said. "Dahad had thrown it out. Shoehoes too. Everything."

De Gier felt the gold wristwatch. "Did he throw out his watch too?"

Carl smiled. "I stohole it, he's gohot soho many."

"What does your dad do?" Grijpstra asked.

"Sehells oil to Sohouth Africa."

"You've got friends, Carl?"

Carl turned toward de Gier, twisting his mouth. "Fuhuck friends."

"But you were friendly with Jimmy, and the black dude, and the lady."

Carl shrugged.

"So why did you hang out with them?"

Carl wandered away, his arms swinging awkwardly, his feet pointed toward each other. "You loved the lady?" Grijpstra asked gently.

Carl stopped and turned slowly, and his arms, the hands twisted inward, jerked up. "Sohome. Jimmy was okay. The black duhude muhmugged me, that's hohow we met. I foho . . . foh . . . "

"Followed him?"

"Right. Becauhause of the papers in my wallet. Wahanted them back."

"And so you met the lady?"

"Right."

"But your friends are all dead now," Grijpstra said. "Didn't you get some junk too? In pay for the robbery? Whoever gave that to you meant to kill. That's why we're here.''

"To ahaharrest me?"

De Gier was rolling another cigarette. "No, Carl, you have to believe us. You're not under arrest. If you don't want to cooperate, we'll leave you be, but we found you easily enough and so can they. I mean Heul and young Fernandus, the guys who were trying to pester Mrs. Jongs out of her house. There are probably others. IJsbreker was shot—he never committed suicide, we know that now. I think you know it too. You're not charged with any crime, but we think you can lead us to the killer.''

Carl was looking through his magnifying glass at the dead fly.

"We'll take you to a private home," Grijpstra said. "Mrs. Jongs is there already. We believe her to be in danger too.''

Carl looked around. "Mayhaybe you're the kihillers.''

De Gier put his police card on the table. Carl read it. "Mayhaybe you're poholice killers.''

"Police killers," Grijpstra said, still looking at Carl's father scrutinizing the *Financial Times*. "You think a cop shot the banker?''

"Dohon't know fohor shuhure.''

"Weren't you in IJsbreker's house?''

"Wohon't say.''

"So you were," de Gier said. "We thought you weren't. Did you want to help the lady? Where did the paintings and vases go?''

"Dohon't know.''

Grijpstra studied a wolf's head about to chomp down on a fluffy toy bunny that was peering innocently from between its captor's ferocious fangs. "This is fantastic. We should get you an exhibition somewhere. The Museum of Modern Art would be interested, I think. Doesn't the commissaris know the director there?'' He looked at Carl. ''The commissaris likes your work. He's seen the rhino's head and Mouse. Those pieces are safe.''

''The comm . . . comm . . .''

Grijpstra mentioned the commissaris's name.

''Hah,'' Carl said.

''You've heard of our chief? You'll be staying at his house, in Queen's Lane, not far from here. That's where Mrs. Jongs is now.''

''The commissaris has a nice wife,'' de Gier said, ''but she doesn't care for art. The adjutant here paints. She hangs his painting in dark corners. They're sort of gruesome.''

''You payhaint?'' Carl asked Grijpstra. ''What?''

''I'm not very good,'' Grijpstra said. ''A Sunday dabbler. I'm always mixing up the wrong colors. Like now, I'm doing this waterscape, it needs canal greens. The ducks are all right, I've got the ducks drawn in.''

''The ducks haven't got any flesh on their faces,'' de Gier said.

''I got the ducks right,'' Grijpstra said, ''but I need this pale green for the water and I can't mix it.''

''Greeheens?'' Carl asked. ''I got some.'' He led Grijpstra to a shelf holding an array of jam jars, each filled with dried shredded plants. ''Seehee the frog there?'' The frog, assembled from scrap wood, had been sprinkled with green dust.

''That stays on?'' Grijpstra asked. ''Do you glue it?''

''Yehes.''

Grijpstra picked up the frog gingerly.

''Why not?'' de Gier asked. ''You can fish up some water weeds, dry them, and glue them on. You can do anything you like.''

''Perhaps,'' Grijpstra said slowly. ''Yes, that might be an idea.''

Carl smiled. ''You're welcohome.''

"Yes." Grijpstra touched Carl's shoulder. "Thanks."

"We'll be going, then," de Gier said. "Please come along. If you don't like it at the commissaris's house, we'll bring you back. Okay?"

"Yehes," Carl said.

\\\\\\ 15 \\\\\\

"So far, so good," Grijpstra said while de Gier turned the Volkswagen into a lane leading to the Amstel River. "Carl liked the commissaris's wife, don't you think?"

"I thought Mrs. Jongs and he did a great hug," de Gier said. "I like unlikely hugs. I find them inspiring. The half-burned horse he had up in his loft was inspiring too. That's the horse the knight rides into heaven, when he has smashed the other knight on the field at dawn, after a long and exhausting duel. I'm looking forward to that final feat."

"We did that right," Grijpstra said. "You think we're getting better, Sergeant? Dealing with a genius who uses a body that's almost completely out of whack? I noticed that I kept wanting to talk to Carl as if he were retarded, even though the fellow is more intelligent than the two of us put together."

De Gier glanced at his rearview mirror. "Would you mind leaving me out of your equation? Did you notice we're being followed? No? Who did notice?"

"You," Grijpstra said. "My heartfelt congratulations. Very clever of you, especially as you're the only one who can look at the rearview mirror."

The car reached the dike. De Gier checked the mirror again. "Two bearded types in comic hats, driving a Daimler. Are we being honored with a State Detection escort too? Don't they have regular vehicles in The Hague? Did you see that Corvette parked in front of the commissaris's house?"

The Daimler flashed past them, low and sleek, the smooth hum of its powerful engine controlled by a chrome-plated angel stretching its wings on the radiator cap.

"Classy car," Grijpstra said. "Why do they pass us if they're following us? Nobody follows us. You're getting nervous again."

De Gier laughed carelessly. "Me, nervous? I wouldn't know the meaning of the word. White knights have no nerves. They did follow us, because I didn't take the regular route from the city to the river, but a scenic roundabout, deliberately chosen while continually aware of anything going on around us. And the Daimler kept following."

"What are we doing on this road?" Grijpstra asked. "Get off it. I want to drive on the dike, contemplating river water."

"I chose this road too," de Gier said. "I feel adventure here. It may lead to an ancient castle. A noble lady waits for us on the ramparts. She is dressed only in a veil. She waits for me, but she won't take off the veil until I have slain the black knight."

"Do turn around," Grijpstra said. "I have bad nerves, and your knightly talk jangles them. This road is a dead end, and I want to watch ducks."

The Volkswagen bounced as it hit a pothole. "Hold it," Grijpstra said. "Stop." He reached for the microphone under the dashboard. "Headquarters? This is . . ." He held the microphone in front of de Gier's face.

"Two-sixteen," de Gier said.

"I'm listening," a young female voice said.

"Amstel Dike, maybe three kilometers south of the city line, an abandoned truck with a cargo of what looks like sheets of tarpaper, stuck in the soft shoulder. I'll read you the license number. Looks like the truck is ready to slide into the moat. Nobody around the vehicle. Please alert the local police."

"Can we go again?" de Gier asked when the message had been repeated and acknowledged.

Grijpstra nodded. "Find some ducks."

The Volkswagen was still on the country road and had begun to turn onto the dike when the Daimler, parked just behind a curve, started and approached the Volkswagen at speed, coming from the left. De Gier, knowing he had the right-of-way, accelerated. The Daimler accelerated too. Grijpstra shouted. The Volkswagen hit the Daimler broadside and began to crumple. Grijpstra's head shot forward and broke the windshield. The steering wheel pressed hard into de Gier's chest. The heavy Daimler, carried by the Volkswagen's momentum, steered to the left but managed to shake the little car off. The Volkswagen hobbled on, crossed the dike, nosed into the opposite shoulder, and was held by a poplar. Grijpstra's head snapped back. The skin of his forehead was sliced in three places and began to fold over.

I'm looking into Grijpstra's head, de Gier thought. How revealing to be able to look into another man's head. He reached into his pocket to find a handkerchief that might serve as a bandage. He leaned over, trying his other pocket.

The door on the sergeant's side opened and he fell out of the car. He fell through the grass growing at the side of the road, into a steep tunnel with living walls. The walls consisted of lizards, embracing each other. As he kept falling, or floating, he saw the lizards let go of each other and wave cheerfully at him. They stuttered amusing bits of wisdom that he instantaneously and fully understood and immediately forgot. The diminutive reptiles sang, with sirenlike voices. Blue lights revolved in their bright eyes. They suddenly grew much larger but only two were left, dressed in white coats, like grocers' assistants; they picked him up and carried him into a large biscuit tin. One sat next to de Gier, a kindly lizard hiding behind a black beard that, after the biscuit tin had begun to move and finally stopped again, must have been lost somehow, but the black color remained, although the lizard now seemed to be female. Her voice was remarkable, and she used it in a jazz song that de Gier defined as mathematically correct. The biscuit tin was lifted off his prostrate body but he kept moving, through a corridor. De Gier wanted to tell the lizards to please stop changing all the time; he appreciated the way in which they tried to keep him amused, but he had never cared much for nurses.

So the lizard was a real nurse. De Gier accepted reality again, with some misgivings, and inquired where Grijpstra might be.

"In the other bed," the black nurse said. "Don't sit up now. Your ribs are broken."

"Grijpstra?" de Gier asked.

"Now remember this good," Grijpstra said. "There was a woman at the side of the river, with a hairbun on her fat face. I'll be forgetting that hairbun in a minute. The bun called the ambulance. And there were two state cops, don't forget the cops either. Their uniforms are different, but they're still cops. And there was only one hairy type in the Daimler, the *green* Daimler, you got that?"

"What about the lizards?" de Gier asked.

Grijpstra didn't react.

"Lizards," de Gier said.

"I think they were more like cops," Grijpstra said. "Lizards have no hairbuns on their fat faces either. I don't think lizards have hair at all. Where are you? On the field at dawn again? There weren't any knights, either.''

"Right," de Gier said. "The black knight. How could I forget? He came in early, dealing the first blow. That's what they do, black knights. Sneaky assholes.''

"You didn't have the right-of-way," Grijpstra said.

"No?" de Gier asked. "*No?* Any vehicle coming from the right has the right-of-way. I passed my sergeant's exam. That was one of the lead questions. I was leading, Adjutant.''

Two State Police officers came into the room, talking softly, for the nurse held a long, slender black finger in front of her sensuous pink lips. "You didn't have the right-of-way," the officers told de Gier. "That side road was marked, on the tarmac. A white line. White letters. Stop. That's what the letters said.''

"Never saw that," de Gier said. "And neither did you. You were in the tunnel, pretending to be lizards. I did see what you were doing there. Embracing on work time. Okay. I won't report that.''

"No," the officers said. "But we *will* report that you crossed lines and letters and caused a bad accident.''

"Okay," de Gier said. "Crawl into some pimp's mouth so that he can't beat up that nice old lady anymore. What is it to me? This is naptime anyway.''

The nurse brought breakfast.

"That was quick," de Gier said. "I was just sliding off into my nap. Would you mind switching off the sun?''

"You were talking and snoring all night," Grijpstra said. "No wonder Constable Jane doesn't want a steady relationship with the likes of you.''

"Let her marry the likes," de Gier said. "I got some knighting to do.''

The nurse closed the curtains.

"Is your head closed up again?" de Gier asked. "I

looked into it yesterday. You got a porterhouse steak in your head."

"They pushed it back," Grijpstra said. "Are you in pain?"

"Only when I breathe," de Gier said.

The nurse fed him his breakfast. She was still black. She also still had a mathematical jazz voice. She was humming a breakfast song. De Gier liked the melody but the words were kind of silly, as they often are in music. The lizards shuffled through his chest, in tunnels, but they didn't seem to like the tunnels, for they kept digging new ones.

"Ouch," de Gier said.

"I'll inject some painkiller," the nurse sang. "Won't hurt at all. Here. Hah."

De Gier floated off, on waves of pain.

⫿⫿ 16 ⫿⫿

"THERE YOU ARE," CHIEF INSPECTOR HALBA shouted when he saw Cardozo bicycling out of the hospital's yard. "Come here."

"Yes?" Cardozo said, putting a foot on the ground.

"Where have you been, Constable? Several notes were placed on your desk, ordering you to report to my office."

"Haven't seen my desk for a while," Cardozo said.

"So where were you? You know that the commissaris has been temporarily relieved of his duties and that I'm in charge of the brigade?"

"You?" Cardozo asked, drying his face with his handkerchief and huddling further down in his threadbare raincoat. "Terrible weather, don't you think? Why you?"

"Why not me, Constable?"

Cardozo shrugged. "Oh, well, it's logical, perhaps, with the way things are going. I'm not on duty, I don't have to report anywhere."

Halba gaped.

"Holidays," Cardozo said. "I had a lot of overtime saved up, and this is my brother's bicycle—the one

you had issued to me fell apart. I left it with the other
garbage in the Headquarters yard. 'Bye now.''

"Wait!" Halba shouted.

"Yes?" Cardozo put his foot on the ground again.

"Until when are you on holiday?"

"Until our case is cracked," Cardozo said. "And
you with it. I don't work under you.''

"Constable," Halba said slowly, "I don't accept
your insolence. I'll be applying for your transfer to the
Traffic Department.''

Cardozo shook raindrops off his unruly hair. "No,
I'll resign first. My uncle Ezra wants me to take over
his market stall.''

Cardozo pedaled off. A Citroën drew up next to
Halba's BMW. The commissaris got out. "Ah. Morning, Chief Inspector. How're my men doing?''

"Market stall," Halba sneered. "He'll need a license for that. It'll be withheld. Insurrection of the
slaves, indeed. Won't have it, you know.''

"Who's the slave?" the commissaris asked.

Halba pointed to Cardozo, bicycling through the
hospital's gate. "He's planning to work a stall in the
street market, says he won't serve under me. I tell
you, that case is closed.''

"Cardozo's case?" the commissaris said, putting up
an umbrella. "Isn't this rain a bother?''

"IJsbreker's,'' Halba snarled. "You're all working
on IJsbreker still. You're defying orders.''

"Let's go into the building," the commissaris said.
"Or have you come out just now? How are Grijpstra
and de Gier doing?''

"Hah," Halba said as they entered the hospital.
"How do you know they're here? They're not supposed to leave their beds.''

"Birdies," the commissaris said, "do fly by my ear,
transmitting information. Have you ever noticed,
Chief Inspector, how many birds there are in this city?

At any given location you can count at least nine species. Crows, seagulls, herons . . ."

Halba asked for the room number at the counter. They got into the elevator together. ". . . sparrows, starlings, terns . . ."

"Please," the chief inspector said.

". . . thrushes . . ."

"You'll lose out on this caper."

". . . goldfinches . . ."

"You may think you're a wily old bird yourself."

". . . and canaries," the commissaris said. "They sing, you know. Lovely songs. Meaningful, too. What would we ever do without canaries, eh, Halba?"

Halba steamed behind the commissaris as the old man limped along, swinging a silver-knobbed bamboo cane. "Here we are."

"Sir," Grijpstra said, "you shouldn't have put yourself out. It's just a scratch."

"I looked into his head," de Gier said. "He's got a lot of meat in there. Never thought I'd see the meat in the adjutant's head."

"And you, Sergeant?"

"I can walk," de Gier said. "I tried just now. I smoked in the lavatory. I'm quite comfortable, thank you, sir."

"Morning," Chief Inspector Halba said.

Grijpstra nodded, holding on to his bandaged head. "We can't have visitors," de Gier said. "Just family. We're seriously wounded."

"Glad to hear that," Halba said. "I'll be brief. You, Adjutant, will be on extended sick leave from now on. Your accident was discussed this morning with this hospital's surgeon and the chief constable. In view of your age and general condition, aggravated by your present wounds, you're ordered to stay away from Headquarters for at least a month."

"That's nice," Grijpstra said. "Thank you."

"You're very welcome." Halba turned to de Gier.

"And you, Sergeant, are suspended. You have a record of dangerous driving and the State Police officers who investigated your accident yesterday say that you failed to grant the right-of-way to an oncoming vehicle."

"Without pay?" de Gier asked.

"I've suggested that, Sergeant. You will be staying home to reflect on your reckless attitude. When you're readmitted to the force, you will be on probation for a year."

"Heheh," de Gier said. He held on to his chest. "Ouch."

The commissaris pointed to the door. " 'Bye, Chief Inspector."

"He *would* bang the door," Grijpstra said, holding his head.

The commissaris sat down, taking out his tin of cigars. "I can't smoke here?" He looked at his watch. "It's a quarter after twelve already."

The nurse came in. She glanced at the commissaris. "No smoking here."

"We're fine, nurse," Grijpstra said. "We would like a half hour to discuss business with our chief."

"No business," the nurse said.

"Just chitchat." The commissaris smiled at the nurse. The nurse smiled back.

"She's beautiful," the commissaris said when the nurse had left. "I shouldn't say this because it's a racial slur, but I privately think that beautiful black women are more beautiful than beautiful white women. Anyone care for a cigar?"

"Please," Grijpstra said.

"If you don't mind," de Gier said.

They smoked peacefully for a while.

"You were set up?" the commissaris asked. "Do you have a description of the other car?"

"No number," de Gier said. "It was a green Daimler, 1976. Pretty silly to use an uncommon car. Maybe it was just an accident. The driver and his companion were young men, bearded types, they wore duckbilled caps.''

"Maybe it's fashionable for the enemy to use uncommon cars," Grijpstra said. "State Detection drives a Corvette.''

The commissaris got up and looked out the window. "The Corvette is in the yard here now. I spoke to the driver earlier on, introducing myself. If they're going to follow me about everywhere, we may as well get acquainted. The driver is a sergeant, made up to resemble a gay person, like his assisting constable-detective. He told me they like to drive confiscated cars supplied by the drug trade in The Hague. So a Daimler got you?" The commissaris closed his eyes. "A Daimler, eh?"

"I'd like to check that intersection," de Gier said. "I never saw a stop sign painted on the road. I'm usually quite alert.''

"Heyho," the commissaris said. "Willem Fernandus was complaining that junkies break into his Daimler. Maybe Cardozo can find out the color of the Daimler that Fernandus drives. I saw Cardozo at the gate just now. How is he?"

"Secretive," Grijpstra said. "I asked the nurse to phone Miss Antoinette. She must have told Cardozo we were here. He kindly looked us up but he still won't say what he is working on. Did you see Miss Antoinette this morning, sir?"

"I certainly did," the commissaris said. He tried to blow a smoke ring. "Fernandus can blow smoke rings. I've never been able to do that. It's because Fernandus has a naturally pouting mouth, I suppose. An elderly cherub, damn the fellow. Miss Antoinette . . .''

"Yes?" de Gier asked. "Yes?"

The commissaris shook his head. "I don't know. I'll never understand women, Sergeant. Are they naturally promiscuous, as we are? Have I been misinformed? I always thought that women have a, uh, natural tendency to, uh, purity."

"No," de Gier said.

"Yes," the commissaris said, "but your opinion doesn't count, Sergeant. You have a, uh, natural charisma that seems to attract female favors."

Grijpstra struggled into a sitting position, carefully holding on to his head. "So have you, sir."

"No, no," the commissaris said.

"I think the adjutant is right," de Gier said. "Perhaps you think along Victorian lines, sir. Grijpstra and I took that evening course on guilt. The pychologist postulated that older men have guilt feelings toward women, because they think they abuse female purity out of their power position. Since the sexual revolution, guilt in men has considerably diminished, but that may have been too late for you."

"I think," Grijpstra said, "that Miss Antoinette would just love to be promiscuous. She's lonely. She might even take me on, if I offered steady company, but first she'd have her fling with macho men."

"Like me?" de Gier asked. "She won't fling with me."

"You joke with her," Grijpstra said. "That's insulting. You've been getting into a flirtatious attitude that won't get you anywhere with refined types like Miss Antoinette."

"Refined?" the commissaris asked. "If only you knew what she has been suggesting."

"What?" de Gier asked. "What?"

The commissaris sighed. "She wants to be our inside contact at the Society for Help Abroad's club."

"Ah," Grijpstra said. "What's wrong with that? That'll be her fling."

"But don't you see?" the commissaris asked. "That means that Fernandus . . ."

Grijpstra puffed on his cigar. De Gier tried to wriggle into a more comfortable position.

"You think I'm jealous?" the commissaris asked.

"Maybe I could kill Fernandus," de Gier said. "He's a bad guy for sure, but he would be too easy to push over. Little old fat fellow, I hear. I need a matched type. A proper adversary."

"Do you think I'm jealous?" the commissaris asked. "I probably am. Katrien says I am." He smiled shyly. "Katrien was engaged to Willem Fernandus. And now I want him to stay away from my secretary too?"

"Maybe Miss Antoinette can make a deal," Grijpstra said. "Try the club out for a few evenings and take on only who she likes. We do want information. We can't just bluster into the joint and take potluck. Halba might be there and warn the others off. Those places usually have bodyguards serving as waiters. We could be thrown out before we're properly in."

"You think I'm too much involved in this case?" the commissaris asked. "Admittedly, I know the enemy personally, but Willem does run a bad show, to the detriment of the city. It's my duty to stamp him out."

De Gier chuckled and clutched his chest again. "Halba has no idea that he's doing me the ultimate favor. I'm no longer a cop. I could beat him up now without the slightest qualm, but then he isn't the right opponent, either. A lazy lout on the judo mat, always claiming some injury to get out of a good fight. The chief inspector's not a very good shot, either. Do I really want his scalp?"

The nurse came in. She glared at the commissaris. "What is this?" She waved at the smoke and opened all the windows. "You'll have to leave." She snatched the cigars out of Grijpstra's and de Gier's mouths.

"Nurse?" the commissaris asked.

"Yes? You have to leave at once."

"Nurse?" the commissaris asked. "Please. I have

a serious problem. About women, I mean. Can I ask you a question?''

She looked down at him, impeccable in her starched spotless uniform. ''Ask away.''

''Are you married, nurse? Betrothed, perhaps?''

''I'm free.''

''Now,'' the commissaris said, ''if you had the opportunity to dally with wealthy and handsome men— different ones, I mean, a few evenings, for no more than a week, and, please excuse me, this is a theoretical question, it's that I don't understand the female mind very well, you see—would you accept such an offer?''

''I'm available,'' the nurse said.

''Available,'' the commissaris said. ''I see.''

''Our chief means,'' Grijpstra said, ''would you work in an elegant sex club for a little while, for a good cause.''

''What good cause? Money?''

''More than that,'' de Gier said. ''You'd get paid, but you'd help do away with some nasty stuff that has been bothering the city.''

''Sure,'' the nurse said, ''but I work nights this week. How about next week?''

''We already have an applicant,'' the commissaris said, ''but I'm not sure we should accept her services. The unfortunate idea seems rather immoral to me.''

''Sex is not immoral,'' the nurse said. ''Now, if you please, I've got to air this room.''

The commissaris left, shaking his head, tapping the linoleum floor with his cane.

''You're Murder Brigade detectives, aren't you?'' the nurse asked. ''That young fellow who was here just now told me. Aren't you supposed to be special?''

''The sergeant is.'' Grijpstra raised an accusing hand. ''He drives lone vehicles through the wasteland. He sits in dead trees and eats catfood from rusted cans. If you ever get raped, and then killed by a dart from a crossbow, he'll avenge your disheveled corpse.''

''I will,'' de Gier said, showing his strong teeth, arranging his thick curls, brushing up his full mustache, breathing in to show the smooth curves of his pectoral muscles. ''Ouch.''

''Poor thing,'' the nurse said. ''And you drive through a stop sign.'' She tucked in de Gier's sheets. ''Rest now. Gather strength. Let me know when you're ready, and I'll get myself raped. I saw that movie too.'' She tucked Grijpstra in next. ''You should both have a nap now. Shall I sing you to sleep?''

''Dear nurse,'' de Gier whispered. ''Chant to me, let me fade away into your voice.''

The nurse hummed a lilting little song.

''Dear nurse,'' Grijpstra whispered.

She sang on; the lullaby, in the melodious language of the Surinam blacks, filled the room with soft, deep-throated tones that reached around the patients' painful bodies, smoothed their worn nerves, caressed their minds.

The nurse tiptoed out of the room. The adjutant and the sergeant smiled in their sleep.

⁗ 17 ⁗

Mrs. Cardozo, a short, wide woman with the same curly hair as her son Simon, but rather more tidily arranged, pressed the polished brass bell on an imposing iron gate. The gate guarded a raked pebble path leading to a low building adorned with turrets at each corner. Each turret carried a spire, and each spire supported a Star of David. A camera attached to one of the gateposts began to whir and swivel while a metallic voice spoke from the other post.

"Yes?"

"Sarah Cardozo to see the consul," Mrs. Cardozo said briskly.

"It's the Sabbath," the metallic voice said. "Sarah Sarah go away. Do come back some other day."

Mrs. Cardozo rang the bell again.

"You don't speak Yiddish?" the gatepost asked.

"Shabbish the shabbash," Mrs. Cardozo said, "let me in or I'll climb the gate."

"You'll be electrocuted," the voice said. "Who are your bodyguards?"

The camera whirred more energetically and increased its arc so that it could take in Mrs. Cardozo's companions. She pointed to her right. "My son

Simon, Mr. Rosenblatt." She pointed to her left. "My houseguest, Izzy Sanders, an Israeli like yourself. Now let us in." She shook her umbrella at the camera. "I don't like today's climate."

"How do you know my name?" the little loudspeaker asked.

"We met before," Mrs. Cardozo said. "I gave you money. I'm the chairperson of the Committee for Trees in the Desert."

The gate clicked open. Mrs. Cardozo pushed it with the point of her umbrella and marched in. Two swarthy young men bounded from the building's front door at the end of the path and blocked the way. They said Shalom and ordered Simon and Izzy to raise their hands and turn around.

"*Shalom*," Mrs. Cardozo said. "It means 'peace,' so be peaceful with us."

"What do you have under your arm?" asked the young man who was frisking Cardozo.

"My gun," Cardozo said. "You can take it out. I'm a policeman, my card is in the breast pocket of my jacket. You can take the card out too."

The young man read the card and put it back. "You can have the gun again when you leave."

"You won't feel me," Mrs. Cardozo said, "but you can look in my bag." She snapped the bag closed again. "We come in peace, on a matter of life."

"Or death," said an elderly man with an unkempt beard. He walked down the steps leading to the front door. "Some visitors wish us death. We take precautions. I'm sorry they're rude." Mr. Rosenblatt's wide shoulders slumped and his long spine curved forward, but the sadness of his physical bearing was belied by a sparkle in his slanting Slavic eyes above strong cheekbones. He offered Mrs. Cardozo his arm.

Cardozo bounced up the steps, Izzy slouching behind him. The consul spoke to Izzy in Hebrew. Izzy had trouble formulating his hesitant answer.

"A deserter?" Rosenblatt asked in Dutch.

"I'll explain everything," Mrs. Cardozo said. "I remember there's a room in this building, with chairs to sit on. It's time for a glass of beet juice, it seems to me. All in good time."

"Time," the consul said, as he guided his visitors into a large back room, mostly furnished with computer gear, placed haphazardly on plastic-topped tables, "I don't really have, due to being at war forever."

"No!" Izzy tore at his tousled hair with both hands. "No more war, please," he shouted. "Stop it. At once."

"We are a little crazy today?" the consul asked.

Izzy glanced at a computer screen, then covered his eyes. His shoulders shook.

"Izzy is a good boy," Mrs. Cardozo said. "He went to school with my son Samuel. I knew him well. Izzy is an idealist and became an Israeli and fought in your wars."

"Our wars," the consul said.

"No," Mrs. Cardozo said. "Maybe the first few, but you can't go on exchanging eyes for eyes, teeth for teeth. Exchange hearts instead."

"They have none, Mrs. Cardozo."

"Maybe we tore them out?"

"You preach love at me?" the consul asked. "Let's hear about love. Where is this love?"

"Here," Mrs. Cardozo said, touching her breast, "I brought you some today, you can plant it in your desert."

"What do I give in return?" the consul asked. "Thank you for your love. Now what do you want?"

"A letter," Mrs. Cardozo said. "For Izzy here. He needs papers. He can't hide forever. He works a lousy job and lives in a hole in the wall. Stop chasing him. Izzy stays in my house now, but he needs more than chicken soup and noodles. Give him back his identity."

"Talk to me, Izzy," the consul said. "Tell me what happened. You gave up the good fight?"

"It wasn't a good fight," Izzy said. "In the beginning, maybe it was. They shot at me first, so I wanted to shoot back and the colonel leaped ahead, shouting, 'Follow me.' The sand was all around us, the biblical sand, and I saw Moses and Aaron leading us on, to the Promised Land for us Chosen People. All the bullets whining past us and into the colonel were fired by the wicked Pharaoh, who had whipped us because we couldn't build the pyramids fast enough. I placed my machine on the colonel and his body sheltered me, and my bullets brought the charging SS men down, and the guard who sprinkled gasoline on my grandfather's beard and then struck a match."

"Oh, yes," the consul said. "I did that in Warsaw, but the corpse I hid behind was my older brother, and my rifle malfunctioned. I had to scurry away like a rat in a sewer."

"That's how Izzy was living here, when my policeman son Simon found him," Mrs. Cardozo said.

"We have better rifles now," the consul said. "Good machinery helps. Our airplanes strike anywhere. It's not good, but it's better."

"Machines!" wailed Izzy, looking around the room.

"Izzy tells us he had shellshock," Cardozo said, "after the battles. He fired a bazooka into a tent."

"The kids that came running out," Izzy whispered, "were afire, like my grandfather's beard."

"Then Izzy got transferred," Cardozo said.

"That was worse," Izzy said slowly. "The flying machines informed my machine and I helped to compute the data and my machine programmed drones and the drones zoomed over the desert and were killing kids again. The kids were dots on my screen. My machine penetrated into the enemy's machines and

made them turn around and kill more kids, and set the
old men's beards afire. *I* did that." Izzy pulled franti-
cally at his tie.

"So Izzy came back here," Mrs. Cardozo said.
"Now he has no papers. He lives in fear. I can't cure
him unless you help."

Mr. Rosenblatt buried his fingers in his beard.

"You have a beard too," Cardozo said kindly.

The consul nodded. "My beard flows in freedom.
I'll defend yours for you. So Izzy no longer is a freedom fighter?" He looked at Izzy. "Please give me
your full name and army number."

The consul fingered one of his keyboards. "Let's
see what we know." The Teletype clicked. It kept
clicking after Mr. Rosenblatt stopped touching his
keys. He read the answer that lit up on the screen.
"Yes, that's right, we are looking for you, but we may
have found you already. Let me try something else."
He moved his hands to another set of keys. The screen
came alive again. The consul looked at Izzy. "Eze-
chial Sanders? Illegally employed by the Banque du
Crédit? Residing in Mad Nun's Alley?"

"Yes," Izzy whispered.

"We can't arrest you here," Mr. Rosenblatt said
sadly. "It would be better for you if you gave yourself
up. I'll have you flown back to Tel Aviv and you can
explain your reasons to the court. If you had battle
fatigue before, you'll probably be forgiven and your
guilt will take wing and fly back to hell."

"There's nothing to forgive," Mrs. Cardozo said.
"Izzy fought the wrong fight. You won your wars,
now treat the enemy with respect."

"It's not so easy," Mr. Rosenblatt said. "There are
rules. Izzy broke them. He also betrayed us. The Banque du Crédit finances surreptitious activity, buys illegal oil, lends the profit to the enemy, helps them to
buy more arms."

"You won't give Izzy a letter to the Dutch authorities." Mrs. Cardozo asked, "so that he can apply for a passport here again and live a useful life?"

"No," Mr. Rosenblatt said.

"Mother?" Cardozo said. "There's a nice garden outside. Take Izzy for a walk. Let me talk to Mr. Rosenblatt for a minute."

"You see," the consul said, "I can't just give. There's no end to giving. We'll give it all away and I'll be behind my brother's corpse again, in a Warsaw alley, and my rifle won't work, the rifle we gave money away for so that a crook could make a profit."

"Exactly," Cardozo said. "Mother, please take Izzy for a walk."

"Come along, Izzy," Mrs. Cardozo said. "I saw some weeds in the garden, we'll go and pull them out, for free, as our gift."

"Now," the consul said to Cardozo. "You're a policeman? How did you meet with Izzy?"

"I agree with you," Cardozo said. "I fight the good fight too. My department now battles the Banque du Crédit. I met Izzy there. He has changed, but I recognized him as my brother Samuel's friend. I thought I could use Izzy."

"You don't want to save him?"

"My mother will save Izzy," Cardozo said. "She flies in heaven. I grovel in the dust."

Mr. Rosenblatt read his screen. "We were aware that Izzy worked at the Banque du Crédit, but didn't worry too much. Izzy got to the bank through the drug trade. He must have met other Israeli deserters who have started coffee shops here and sell hashish and marijuana. Their accounts are with the Banque du Crédit. Izzy has good computer training. The bank must have hired him without papers because that way he would owe them. They have a grip on him because they could give him away to us."

"So remove Izzy's fear," Cardozo said. "Then he can help me better."

"To do what?" the consul asked.

"To bring the bank down."

Mr. Rosenblatt pressed buttons. The screen faded and then filled up again. "The Banque du Crédit is owned by Willem Fernandus. Fernandus also runs that phony Society for Help Abroad that controls the semiofficial canteens that are set up by the city to keep unemployed youths off the street. The canteens sell drugs. The drugs are partly Arab. There's a lot of money made and it certainly does not go to the needy abroad. The Society also exploits a sex club and brothel that caters to the high and mighty."

"A mess," Cardozo said.

"Run by powerful men," the consul said. "Here are more names. Baron Bart de la Faille, Martin IJsbreker."

"IJsbreker is dead."

"Yes," the consul said. "I have that here too. A suicide."

"With two bullets?" Cardozo asked.

"I see." The consul smiled at Cardozo. "What department are you with?"

"Homicide," Cardozo said.

"Isn't there some reorganization scheduled at your Headquarters?" The consul switched off the screen. "I hear your commissaris was relieved of his duties."

"And I'm on vacation," Cardozo said, "and the adjutant and the sergeant who work directly under the commissaris are respectively on sick leave and suspended without pay. The team is complete and active. We have other support."

The consul scratched his beard. "What's your rank?"

"Detective constable first class."

"Not so high," the consul said.

"The commissaris is under surveillance," Cardozo said. "He doesn't know about my angle yet. I want to surprise him. Could you look at your screen again?"

"What do you want to know?"

"How good Izzy is with computers."

"I just checked that," the consul said. "Lieutenant Sanders was second in charge of a mobile center that broke into the enemy's communications. Izzy must be very good."

"Write that letter," Cardozo said. "It's a small thing. You have the authority to clear him."

"Why was IJsbreker shot?" the consul asked.

"I think Fernandus wanted him out of the way," Cardozo said. "There was a struggle for power. Three junkies were killed, after they removed IJsbreker's wealth."

"So they're that ruthless?" The consul got up and looked out the window. "Your mother is weeding our garden in the rain."

"What is Izzy doing?"

"He's being useless," the consul said. "Sitting on a rock. Talking to himself."

"A letter from you will uncrazy him," Cardozo said. "Then he'll be useful again. That bank is an enemy fortress; we can blow it up."

"My specialty," the consul said. "I blew up a lot of buildings. I got shellshock too, and was transferred to diplomacy. I saw a dead Arab who looked just like my Warsaw brother. The Arab was killed by a device that I placed."

"We'll do all the work cleanly," Cardozo said, "for mutual profit. Just write the letter."

"What if you went away?" the consul asked, "you and your dear mother?"

"And Izzy?" Cardozo asked.

The consul's lips became a pink nipple that pushed itself from the gray curls of his beard.

"The kiss of compassion?" Cardozo asked. "All is forgiven and forgotten?"

"Forgive we don't," the consul said.

"All right," Cardozo said, "forgetting is fine too."

He pointed at the files strewn about on the tables. You have quite an administration here. In administrations, much is forgotten. Forget your charges."

"Well?" Mrs. Cardozo asked in the garden.

"It's okay," Cardozo said.

"He said that?"

"He did not say that," Cardozo said. "And he has lost something now, his administration is a shambles."

"What?" Izzy asked.

"His charges against you, it seems," Cardozo said. "When I left he had stopped looking. Apply for your Dutch passport. I don't think this consulate will object."

⫸ 18 ⫷

"Is she beautiful?" the commissaris's wife asked, watching how her husband arranged his new pale blue tie, standing very straight in front of the full-length mirror in the hallway.

"Yes," the commissaris said.

"Whowho?" asked Carl, swaying his unbalanced body into the hall. "That's a nice tiehie."

Mrs. Jongs dragged the vacuum cleaner behind her. "Bob also sees other women. He has three at home, and me, I'm his wife."

"Who?" the commissaris's wife asked. "I thought your womanizing was over now. All this gallumphing about is getting you into trouble, Jan. You need a much stricter routine. I wish you could go back to work."

"She's part of my work," the commissaris said. "She's my secret agent and she's young and beautiful, so I put on my new tie."

"Secret agent indeed," his wife said, brushing his sleeves. "And I polished your shoes. Is she the secretary you're sending to the whorehouse?"

"Where are my car keys?" the commissaris asked.

"I've got to go. I'll be late. I had them here on the table."

His wife patted his pockets. The keys rattled. "Here they are. You're seeing Miss Antoinette?"

"She has volunteered for the job," the commissaris said. "We've discussed my relationship with Miss Antoinette at length, Katrien. I never sent the poor girl anywhere. It's Willem again, *he* made the immoral suggestion."

"But she's doing it for you," his wife said, buttoning his jacket. "That's the part I don't like. I wish you would understand women a little better."

"We does it all for them and they never understands," Mrs. Jongs said. "Can I clean here now? Carl, is this yours?" With the vacuum cleaner's snout she touched scraps of wood stacked in a corner of the hall. "That's Tuhurtle," Carl said, "me and the co-hommm . . ." He waved his hand furiously, trying to trip the word off his jaw.

"We found the pieces together," the commissaris said. "Last night when we were out for a walk. Don't you like the head, Mrs. Jongs? The State Detection sergeant found that for us. He came along, he can't drive his car in the park. It's a champagne cork."

"That's Tuhurtle's foohoot," Carl said, "the other cohork is his heahead, the one with the meh-metal still on."

" 'Bye," the commissaris said. His wife followed him to the door. He kissed her cheek. "I'm not a dirty old man."

She kissed him back. "I know, Jan, but it isn't fair. Older women can never find lovers, and all that old men have to do is put out a hand." The commissaris put out his hand. She held it between hers. He retrieved it gently. " 'Bye, Katrien, got to go now."

He walked to his car. The Corvette parked across the road started up. The commissaris waved at the driver. He got into the Citroën and wound the window down, waiting for the Corvette to make a U-turn and come alongside. "Morning," the commissaris said. The sergeant's companion sat up straight, rather awkwardly, for the Corvette's seats were luxuriously tipped back. "Morning, sir."

"I don't want you two to know where I'm going today," the commissaris said, "so I thought of a special trick. We'll have some fun, okay? See if you can catch me. Back up a little, please, so I can get out of here."

The Corvette backed away obediently. The commissaris maneuvered the Citroën out of its tight parking place and swung the large car into traffic. He drove as far as the Rijksmuseum without doing anything spectacular, the Corvette following close behind. The commissaris grinned into his rearview mirror and said, "Now." Cyclists were all around him, heading straight for the gateway through the museum's main building reserved for two-wheeled traffic only. The commissaris switched on his left-turn indicator, swerved a little to the left, turned the wheel back, then made the car jump dead ahead. The Corvette followed, forcing protesting cyclists to the side. "Very well," the commissaris said. "Thought this was it, did you? Tried to lose you and I failed? Good. Now watch this." He turned right and drove parallel to the center lane reserved for trams. A tram appeared and slowed down for the tram stop. The commissaris slowed too, staying abreast of the tram. Passengers filed in and out. The tram's doors would close any moment now. "Hurrah!" the commissaris shouted, and stopped, shifted his car into neutral, and pulled on the emergency brake. He jumped out of the Citroën and into the tram. The tram closed its automatic doors and clanged its bell. The traffic light ahead had changed to green. The commissaris looked back and grinned. The Corvette was blocked by the stationary Citroën. The State Detection constable, resplendent in his polished leather suit and hennaed hair, had left the Corvette and was running after the tram. The commissaris waved. The tram turned left and made use of its clear lane to accelerate.

The commissaris left the tram at the next stop and waved a cab down. "Prince's Island."

"Sir," the cabdriver said, and put up the flag that activated his meter. The commissaris checked his watch. Five to ten. Too early to smoke cigars, a little too late for his meeting with Miss Antoinette. She would wait.

She got up as he walked into the café, hardly limping; perhaps the sudden leap from car to tram had disturbed the pattern of his usual morning pains. "Dear," Miss Antoinette said, "I did so worry about you."

The commissaris nodded to the skeletal barman. "Morning, Bert."

Miss Antoinette skipped up to the bar, displaying a long perfect leg through a split in her tight skirt. "A jenever, please, nice and cold, and a vodka and tonic with ice for me." She carried the drinks back, put them down, and whirled on the gleaming floorboards. "Do you like my outfit? Aren't I realistically wicked now? Like the short skirt? Don't you just love the low blouse?" She bent down.

The commissaris looked away. "Splendid, dear."

"Do look," she whispered. "The bra is transparent. Willem bought me lots of clothes yesterday, it took forever trying them on. Do you think this is my true self?"

The commissaris looked. He coughed discreetly. "Most attractive."

She bobbed her head. "You like my hair too?"

"Wonderful." The commissaris raised his glass. "Your health. Should you be drinking in the morning?"

"I can do anything now," she said breathlessly, "I

am a spy. I bring you information. Nobody followed me here. Willem trusts me." She pouted. "I don't know whether the news is so good."

The commissaris sipped his drink, shuddering at the impact of alcohol dissolving into his blood. "News is neutral, dear, it can be used either way. First tell me what you had to do to gain Willem's trust."

She laughed. "So easy. Men are vain. I flattered him. I said he impressed me, that I had heard so much about him, that my work with you was boring, that I wanted to see his gorgeous club. He came and picked me up."

"Did Willem drive his Daimler?" the commissaris asked. "A large low green car?"

"A Daimler?" Miss Antoinette asked. "I think it was a Rolls-Royce, old-fashioned, square and black, with a uniformed driver."

"Yes," the commissaris said. "You liked that? Then what did you have to do?"

Miss Antoinette thoughtfully tinkled the ice in her glass. "Oh, nothing much. I thought it would be like that book *O*. Have you heard about Lady O? The beautiful young lady who surrenders to evil? And the evil men pick her up in a Rolls-Royce and she has to take her panties off and swear she will never wear them again, and she has to sit on the cold leather seat? I love that story, but Willem just talked about what I would be earning. Ten times my police pay, and in cash, tax-free. He gave me a lot of money straight off."

"There are no free lunches," the commissaris said. "He put his hook in you. Did Willem take you to his brothel?"

"Later," Miss Antoinette said. "First he took me to his home. He has such a beautiful antique house. I'm staying there now. Do you know he collects rare works of art? And that he has wines a hundred years old?"

"You drank old wine," the commissaris said. "What were you wearing?"

"My office suit with the starched blouse. I wanted to look demure. Willem is stealing me from you. I wanted to look like your property."

"You're not my property," the commissaris said.

"I still am," Miss Antoinette said, "but Willem doesn't know. I had to call him Willem and he calls me Toine. You want to call me Toine too?"

"No," the commissaris said. "We have a formal relationship, Miss Antoinette."

She touched his leg under the table. "We do? In my new role?" She tried a low giggle that came out well. "I'm a vamp. I vamped Willem. It was really quite easy. I don't even have to work in the Society's club and he keeps promising things. We're going to stay at some castle in Spain and I get to fly to Calcutta."

"What's in Calcutta?" the commissaris asked. "That's one of the hellholes of the earth. Smuggling, maybe?"

She bent toward the commissaris again. "Yes, isn't that exciting? Willem says he can deal with the customs here, but first he has to take care of you. He's really scared of you, you know. That's the bad news. He wants you out of the way."

"But I am," the commissaris said.

"He doesn't trust you," Miss Antoinette said. "He believes you're still active, but he isn't sure. I think he'll try to kill you if he feels you haven't given up."

The commissaris grinned. "And the castle in Spain? That must be Ten Haaf's place. Have you heard about Ten Haaf?"

She shook her head. "Shall I ask?"

"No," the commissaris said. "Don't solicit any information. Ten Haaf fancies himself a master criminal, now retired. Willem and I knew him when we were still students. Another silly man. I think Guldemeester went to Marbella."

"Marbella? Isn't that on the south coast of Spain?"

"The land of the happy," the commissaris said. "The happy and the bored."

Her hand was on his knee again. "You should be careful. Willem said that accidents will happen. Grijpstra and de Gier already had an accident. How are they now?"

"They'll be up and about in a few days," the commissaris said. "Meanwhile, I'll wait. So Willem's nervous, is he? Fear will make him stumble."

"You still plan to raid the club?" Miss Antoinette asked. "Please don't destroy the building, it's so beautiful in there. Day after tomorrow might be good. Fernandus will take me to his other club, at the Vinker Lakes, I haven't been there yet. This other man will take care of the place here, a baron."

"De la Faille?"

"Yes, I met him. He hasn't met any of you yet, so he won't be suspicious."

"Bart met me," the commissaris said, "but he was still a boy then. I could change my appearance somewhat. You think the club will be busy then?"

"Yes," Miss Antoinette said. "I heard Fernandus and de la Faille talk. De la Faille looks like de Gier—he's tall and handsome and sporty and better-mannered than the sergeant, and has the same mustache but darker, and I think he's gay."

"My dear," the commissaris said, "since when is de Gier gay?"

"De la Faille is very gay," Miss Antoinette said. "I felt it in the way Willem introduced me to him. Willem acted as if de la Faille were harmless. Willem is possessive, don't you think?"

"Did Willem . . . " The commissaris studied his drink. " . . . eh, possess you?"

"Yesterday, a little," Miss Antoinette said, "after we had bought the clothes. He bought me other clothes too, sort of old-fashioned, with a high lace collar and a long skirt, and I had to walk around his bedroom and take them off again and he called me 'Miss' and was kind of silly. I don't know what Willem was getting at. He behaved like a little boy."

"Oh, dear," the commissaris said.

"Maybe he's too old to do much," Miss Antoinette said. "Are you too old?"

"Absolutely," the commissaris said. "Miss Antoinette, I'm too old."

"Even to do a little?"

"Too old to do absolutely anything."

"Well," she said, "you could watch."

"Bert," the commissaris shouted, "more alcohol, please." Bert shuffled over and made the jenever jug's silver spout tinkle.

"You don't want to watch?" Miss Antoinette asked.

The commissaris swallowed and shuddered. "You and Willem?"

"Just me?"

"No." The commissaris took out his tin of cigars, looked at it briefly, and put it back in his pocket.

"I have this book of photographs," Miss Antoinette said. "They show men who watch women in expensive hotel rooms. The women sit or stand around, or they lie on antique beds, all calm and relaxed, and the men watch them. The men are always dressed. Sometimes they have their backs to the women but then they look into mirrors, very elegant mirrors, with gold frames, and there are flowers in the room, roses, and the men smoke long cigars and drink cognac, maybe."

The commissaris drank his spiced gin.

"I don't think watching is very fatiguing," Miss Antoinette said, "but it could be exciting, don't you agree? Watch and be watched? You in your nice suit. I like your tie."

"Oh, dear," the commissaris said. "Katrien bought me this tie. You should be careful with your fantasies, dear. Celine Guldemeester had fantasies too. Living them out might not be as harmless as she thought."

"Yes." She released his knee. "I forgot. I met Celine at the club."

"Is she happy now?" the commissaris asked.

"She was a bit drunk." Miss Antoinette giggled. "Like I am now. I don't like being drunk, but just a little is fun. I wish I could be drunk like this all the time. Celine kept talking about de Gier. She just *loves* de Gier."

"Yes," the commissaris said.

"*I* don't love de Gier."

"No?" the commissaris said. "Why not? Most women seem to like de Gier."

"He's too healthy," Miss Antoinette said. "Healthy men are always so stupid. I only like handicapped men. I don't like men who can do anything they want to do. They don't need me."

"Is that why you like old men?"

"Willem needs me." Miss Antoinette smiled.

"You don't love Willem," the commissaris said. "That's impossible." He looked fierce. "So what else did you and Willem do?"

"Well . . ." Miss Antoinette pursed her moist lips and pushed a lock of hair away from her eye. "Not much. When I still had the dress on, he sat on my lap, which was awkward, for he's rather heavy. He kissed me a bit and caressed me, sort of. Rather sneakily, I thought." Her shoulders trembled above the low blouse. "Willem is very sneaky."

"Yes," the commissaris said.

"Would you be sneaky if you sat on my lap? You're not heavy."

"No," the commissaris said. "Not if I was aware that you didn't like that type of activity. Bert? Could I have another, if you please?"

"I didn't altogether dislike it," Miss Antoinette

said. "I'm sometimes sneaky myself. And then we had a bath."

"Together?"

"Yes." She laughed. "In a sunken tub. Enormous, black marble, and the water swirled, and we were both admirals and we had fleets of nutshells."

The commissaris looked around. Bert had poured the jenever but seemed now lost in thought. "I'll get it." Miss Antoinette pranced past the commissaris. She came back. "You didn't look. I walk differently now. Willem likes that. I sway."

"Willem can look," the commissaris said. "What else happened, dear? Never mind the sex, I think I can visualize that part of your encounter well enough. Any information I can use?"

"At the club," Miss Antoinette said, "Willem and that silly baron who looks just like de Gier talked about a man called Ryder. I met Ryder too. A big fat guy who looks like a frog. Ronnie Ryder."

"The fellow who owns all the clothing stores?"

"Yes," Miss Antoinette said. "Willem explained it to me later, when we were nutshell admirals. I let him win. You've got to make waves, and when a nutshell capsizes, you've lost it."

"Yes," the commissaris said. "I know, but Willem cheats. He throws water in your eyes and then he quickly sinks a few."

"How do you know?" Miss Antoinette said. "Amazing, he kept doing that to me too. But that Ryder fellow cheats too. It seems that Ryder had lost a lot of money when his cheating went wrong, and Willem's bank took over the debts, but all the goods in the stores belong to Willem now. The baron is arranging sales in all the stores and races around to empty the registers, and Ryder doesn't want that."

"Well-known gambit," the commissaris said. "They'll collect all the cash, which is more than whatever Ryder owes the bank now. He'll go bankrupt anyway, and Willem makes a cool million."

"Yes, but Ryder got wise to that. Ryder and Willem were supposed to be close friends, but Ryder knows now that they're shaking him down, so he hired some lawyers and they got quite a bit of cash back for him. Some contract trouble, Willem said. But he still wants the money and now pretends that he and Ronnie are friends again so that Ronnie will come to the club and lose the money at roulette. He's coming every night and they keep allowing him to win. So far, that is."

The commissaris nodded. "Another old trick. When is Ronnie going to lose the lot?"

"Next week, I think," Miss Antoinette said. "I'll let you know. Maybe that's when you should raid the club."

"Yes," the commissaris said. "Exactly. Thank you."

She tittered. "All the money will be on the table. They don't have chips in the club. All the gambling is for cash. It'll be a fortune."

The commissaris checked his watch. "Not yet." He looked again. "No, my watch is slow, I think." He lit a cigar.

Miss Antoinette's slender fingers touched his hand. "Do you know what Celine asked me? If I had left you as well. Celine has a crush on you too."

"On de Gier," the commissaris said.

Miss Antoinette bent farther toward him. "That's physical. The part she really loves de Gier took from you." She pulled a lipstick and a mirror from her handbag and busied herself for a while. She looked up. "And Celine feels she has betrayed that part by working for Fernandus. She wants support. If I betrayed you too, she doesn't have to feel too bad." Miss Antoinette dropped her mirror back into her bag. She smiled happily at the commissaris. "But I'm still yours."

"Exaggerations," the commissaris said. "You project more onto me than I could ever be worth. Your father died young?"

"My father is a fool," Miss Antoinette said briskly. "He only believes in work. Dad bores me. I won't even go to his birthday parties anymore." She smiled. "He's not manly."

The commissaris looked furiously at his cigar. "No, dear. De Gier is a real man, he shoots bull's-eyes only, has a black belt in judo, rides motorcycles and whatnot. I never achieved anything in the manly field. I'm just sly." He threw ash from his cigar. "And self-centered. Why can't you see that?"

"If"—Miss Antoinette raised a finger—"*if* you were sly, there would be a purpose to your slyness. You use whatever comes up and you always use it right." Her hand was on his again. "You fascinate us."

"Tell Katrien," the commissaris said. He grinned. "Now if *she* would say that." He thought. "Well, she has said it at times." He tipped his cigar carefully into the ashtray. "So Celine likes de Gier?"

"If you ask me," Miss Antoinette said, "Celine joined the Society's club on the chance that de Gier might visit there. She couldn't get him at her home. De Gier is too straitlaced for that, but if he happened to stray into the club she could catch him."

Bert shuffled close, holding the jug. The commissaris held his hand above his glass.

Miss Antoinette laughed. "That Willem. What a pity you weren't there to see it. When he sat on my lap? And was fondling my breasts? You know what he said?"

The commissaris coughed. She waited. "What did he say, dear?" the commissaris said between coughs.

"*If Jannie could see me now*." Miss Antoinette was laughing again. "Don't you think that's crazy?"

⁗ 19 ⁗

"Always sohomething," Carl said, trying to bend a ragged shingle, "never mahade a tuhurtle's shehell before."

The commissaris held up the turtle. "Sit still, friend, you're supposed to be a model."

"You can puhut him dohown," Carl said, squatting on the commissaris's back porch. Mrs. Jongs, standing behind the two men, cleaned windows. The commissaris's wife called from inside the house. "Jan, Adjutant Grijpstra is here."

"Hello, Adjutant," the commissaris said, beckoning Grijpstra toward the porch. "How's the head? Still plastered up?"

"He showed me just now," the commissaris's wife said. "There's a big red gash underneath the bandage, with stitches. Poor Grijpstra. I wish de Gier wouldn't drive so recklessly."

"I'm fine, sir." Grijpstra sat down on the bamboo chair that Mrs. Jongs had brought out. "Hello, Mrs. Jongs. Hello, Carl."

"I'm mahaking Tuhurtle," Carl said. "It's nehever eaheasy."

"Turtle has a lot of character," the commissaris

182

said. "Look at the head, Grijpstra." Grijpstra gingerly held the little structure, squinting through half glasses that he extracted from his breast pocket with a flourish. "This is good. What did you use, Carl? Bits of shell on a cork?"

"Carl just broke up a mussel shell," the commissaris's wife said. "Clever, eh? Glued all the little pieces together differently. The shiny parts are the inside of the shell and the gleamy eyes are bits of a toffee wrapper he found in the street."

"Looks just like Turtle's face," Grijpstra said. "Better. Turtle can look pretty silly at times, but his head is kind of thoughtful."

"Carl managed to portray the essence of Turtle's deeper being," the commissaris said. "I envy you chaps your artistry. How are your ducks doing, Grijpstra?"

"Yes," Grijpstra said. "I went home before I came here. Remembering them from the hospital wasn't so good. I thought I had mucked the ducks up, but there's some promise there, if only I could catch that green background. And if I do, the thing probably still needs work. May I borrow your car, sir?"

"Oh, yes," the commissaris's wife said to her husband. "Your car. I forgot to tell you yesterday. Some real strange-looking hulk brought the car back. He was wearing an earring and his lips were made up. He said he found your car near the museum, with the engine still running. Forgot all about that. You and your gallivanting about town all day. You give me bad dreams."

"I had a dream too," the commissaris said. "Something nasty was trying to drown me in a black bath, but I met Carl down there, who was making water sculptures, and Mrs. Jongs . . ." He looked away. "Well, never mind Mrs. Jongs."

"I dreams too," Mrs. Jongs said, squirting a blue

liquid on the windows behind the porch. "About Bob's lizards. They helps me out. Bob ain't so nice."

"Wahater scuh . . . scuhulptures?" Carl asked, picking up the shingle, which kept slipping from his fingers.

The commissaris's wife caressed Carl's hair. "You're so clever, dear." She stared at her husband. "I'm sure you can make water sculptures too."

"How come State Detection got your car?" Grijpstra asked.

"I was waiting at a traffic light," the commissaris said, "and it just wouldn't change. There was a tram standing next to me, so I left my car and hopped into the tram. The State cops must have happened to come along and they found my car. Very kind of them to bring it back."

"I see," Grijpstra said.

"And how's the sergeant?" the commissaris asked.

"Home," Grijpstra said. "De Gier had his neighbors look after Tabriz and they phoned the hospital to say that Tabriz had been breaking jam jars in the kitchen again, so the sergeant took Nurse home to help him clean up. She has mornings off."

"Oh dear," the commissaris said. "Another intangible. I wanted the sergeant to save his energy."

"For what?" the commissaris's wife asked. "For Miss Antoinette? Because Willem isn't doing much? You think the poor thing is getting all overexcited?"

"Don't be flippant, Katrien," the commissaris said. "All of us are working on a most serious criminal case right now. I need to fit all factors in, for optimal benefit. This is very tricky, Katrien. De Gier has no business with a nurse right now."

"With a beautiful black nurse," his wife said coldly. "You told me about that attractive nurse."

"Do you have Miss Antoinette on Fernandus now, sir?" Grijpstra asked. "Does that work?"

"Too well," the commissaris said. "There are complications there that I can't fathom as yet."

"Poor Jan," his wife said. "I'm going in, I have things to do. Would you like to come in too, Mrs. Jongs, and help me with the lunch?"

"I'll pihick the sahalad," Carl said, "if Tuhurtle hasn't eaheaten it all."

"Is the commissaris going anywhere today?" a tall man asked when Grijpstra walked to the Citroën. "The constable and I are getting bored. We've been here all morning."

"Have we met?" Grijpstra asked.

"Sorry, Adjutant." The man pushed himself free of the tree he had been leaning against. "Sergeant Biersma, State Detection."

Grijpstra shook Biersma's hand. "And you know me?"

"We identified you from a photograph in our file," Biersma said.

"I don't think the commissaris is going out today," Grijpstra said. "I'm off on a little job. Why don't you and your constable come with me? Bit of a change. I'll drop you off here again. It shouldn't take long."

The sergeant whistled. The constable clambered out of the Corvette parked in front of the commissaris's house and stretched his back. "Damn that car, it's too low for me." The constable was tall too. "How are you, Adjutant? The name is Ramsau."

"We're going with the adjutant, Ramsau," the sergeant said. "Can we have lunch, Adjutant? Our treat?"

Grijpstra drove to a small café on the Amstel River, south of the city. They sat on the dock and ate smoked eel on toast. "Expensive," Grijpstra said, "but I don't mind if The Hague is paying. Why are you driving that Corvette? An oversized sportscar from unlimited lazy luxury land? I can spot that vehicle with all my senses switched off.''

"Why not?" Sergeant Biersma asked. "It's a crazy assignment anyway. Voort doesn't know his hemorrhoids from dirt in a drain. How can we ever follow a chief of detectives with half a century of experience? You know your commissaris got away again yesterday?''

Grijpstra waved the waiter down for more eel. "Tell me.''

The sergeant explained.

"Hoohoo.'' Grijpstra blew toast crumbs over the table. "Excuse me. Hoohoo.''

Constable Ramsau cleaned his face with a napkin. "It's not that funny, Adjutant. We couldn't leave the Citroën blocking traffic in a main thoroughfare, and your chief had left his key in, so I drove the car away. Then I was arrested.''

"You shouldn't have left your ID in the hotel,'' Sergeant Biersma said.

"You shouldn't have left your ID in the hotel, either,'' Constable Ramsau said. "We had to raise Commissaris Voort to get me out. The local cops thought I was some dumb fag who cruised around in a stolen car.''

"Why would they ever think that?" Grijpstra asked. "Hoohoo. Excuse me.''

"Yes?" the constable asked, flicking a sliver of eel off his cheek.

"Fashionable these days,'' Sergeant Biersma said. "All our detectives dress up as the wrong type of fags. Yours do too. We met some in town, driving a Camaro.''

"This is very tasty eel,'' Grijpstra said. "I'll have some more. How's your investigation going?''

"It isn't,'' Sergeant Biersma said. "Never thought it would. We're running after the wrong man. Commissaris Voort can't find any hidden wealth your chief would be hiding, and there isn't any, I'm sure. We can't find any Chinese."

"Ah," Grijpstra said, taking another plate of eel from the waiter, "Chinese. What do you want with Chinese?"

"Prove our charge," Constable Ramsau said. "The charge is that your chief has been paid off by the Chinese. In your last case, six Chinese got killed and there was heroin everywhere and a Frisian dealer got shot and your team never arrested the killer. So you were paid off, right?"

"Wrong," Grijpstra said. "A cop shot the dealer and then the cop fell off a roof. He wasn't even pushed. We don't arrest cops, you guys arrest cops."

"Don't we ever?" Constable Ramsau said. "I've worked on a dozen cop cases now and I haven't even touched a suspect yet. We chase the wrong cops. Maybe we should chase our chief."

"Mr. Wang," Grijpstra said. "There's a Chinese for you. He owns a restaurant in Bolsward. The commissaris likes Mr. Wang. They meet from time to time. Tell Voort to see Wang."

"Thanks," Sergeant Biersma said. "That's good. We finally came up with something. How do we know about Wang?"

"Because I told you," Grijpstra said. "You tricked me. I'm stodgy and stupid. I've got that reputation in the force."

"More eel?" Sergeant Biersma asked.

Grijpstra burped.

"No more eel," Constable Ramsau said. "A dessert? Two pounds of fat eel slithering around in half a gallon of whipped cream, and a heavy pie crust to press the mixture down?"

"No, thanks." Grijpstra stood up. "I may have a little job for you. Sergeant de Gier and I had an accident a little farther along on this dike, and we vaguely remember a woman who called an ambulance. I'd like to see her, but I don't know what house she came from. There are several houses in the area where we got hurt. We also vaguely recall a truck loaded with tarpaper stuck halfway on the dike's shoulder. We hit a heavy green car that got away, with a bearded type at the wheel, wearing a duckbilled cap. Would you help me by going from door to door? Anything you turn up will be of value."

"You will join us, of course," Sergeant Biersma said.

The waiter brought the bill. Grijpstra passed it along. "I'm on sick leave. I thought you two wanted a change. Perhaps you should take off your makeup first."

Sergeant Biersma woke Grijpstra more than an hour later. "Adjutant?"

"Yes?" Grijpstra said, struggling upright in the Citroën's backseat. "Any luck?"

The sergeant and the constable got into the car. They both held up papers. "Signed and sealed," Constable Ramsau said. "Two witnesses. Your lady and another one who lives at the corner opposite. Here you are. Nice statements."

"Read them to me," Grijpstra said. "Only the relevant parts, if you please."

" 'I saw,' " Constable Ramsau read, " 'a large, low, green car parked in front of my house. A young man in a duckbilled cap got out. He had a beard. He walked over to a truck loaded with tarpaper that was stuck in the mud. He took a sheet of tarpaper off the truck and placed it on the tarmac at the intersection of my road and the dike. I found the sheet of tarpaper the next day in the bushes at the side of the road, torn up and crumpled. It must have been swept up by the white compact that hit the large green car that afternoon and was busted up. The large green vehicle had

been waiting in front of my house and started to move
when the small white car came out of my road. The
green car was driven by another young man with a
beard and a duckbilled cap. This man was tubby; the
other, the one who put the tarpaper down, was thin. I
didn't understand what those two young men were
doing.' "

"Not so clever, this lady," Sergeant Biersma said.
"The one I found in the house opposite hers, a woman
with her hair done up in a bun, wasn't too smart,
either. She phoned for the ambulance and this is her
statement: " 'I saw a young man with a beard and a
duckbilled cap wandering around at the intersection. I
couldn't see what he was doing. I wasn't paying much
attention, as I was busy keeping house. I did see him
bend over, doing something or other in the street, and
his hat fell off. He had orange hair, cut in the shape of
a narrow brush. Then he put on his hat again.' "

"Thank you," Grijpstra said.

"Suspect covered the stop sign on the road with a
sheet of tarpaper," Sergeant Biersma said. "You
therefore didn't see the marks, and since you were
coming from the right, you assumed you had the right-
of-way. The green car placed itself in your way delib
erately. The punk who dragged the tarpaper about
knew you would be hitting the green car from the
right, so he stayed out of the vehicle to avoid getting
hurt himself. The punk must have been picked up by
his mate later on. That's an attempted-murder charge.
Do you recognize suspects from these witnesses' de-
scriptions?"

"The paper-dragger is called Heul," Grijpstra said.
"The driver of the car is probably Huip Fernandus.
The car, a Daimler, belongs to his father, Willem Fernandus. Sergeant de Gier and I arrested young Fernandus and Heul on a charge of harassing a helpless
old lady, and they must have taken their revenge."

Sergeant Biersma whistled. "Isn't Willem Fernandus the attorney who runs the Society the papers have been going on about?''

"The very same man.''

"Some shit,'' Constable Ramsau said. "Tell us more.''

Grijpstra explained.

"And you're working on that IJsbreker case now?'' Sergeant Biersma asked. "Sick leave and all? Your commissaris too, even if he is relieved of his duties, and this Sergeant de Gier who got suspended without pay?''

"We could be,'' Grijpstra said. "So could a few others. But you wouldn't be too interested in our attempt to clean up this city. You're working against us.''

"I think we could be interested,'' Constable Ramsau said. "Don't you think so, Sergeant?''

"Hoohoo.''

The sergeant and the constable ducked.

"Why are you so nervous?'' Grijpstra asked. "I just laughed a little. You? *You* would be interested in bothering dangerous criminals? You might get hurt. You're slick, sleazy government types from The Hague.'' He gave Sergeant Biersma the Citroën's keys. "You can drive back, I'm still a little tired. You have no idea who we're up against. Remember IJsbreker? He got shot. Remember the junkies I told you about? They got injected to death. We have two witnesses staying in the commissaris's house, where they can be protected.'' He pointed at the bandage on his forehead. "See what happened to me? Sergeant de Gier has two cracked ribs.''

"So?'' Sergeant Biersma asked.

"So you want to stay out of this,'' Grijpstra said, settling back in the luxurious upholstery of the Citroën. He closed his eyes.

The Citroën turned quietly and followed the dike back to Amsterdam, gliding easily through tight

curves on its wide radial tires. Downy clouds hugged
hazy fields. A windmill turned slowly, pushed by a
soft breeze. A heavily loaded barge trailed lazily behind a tugboat, hardly turning its engine because of
the current pushing it along. Ducks, quacking contentedly, glided by.

"Adjutant?" Sergeant Biersma asked. "How could
we be of help?"

Constable Ramsau looked around, waiting for an
answer. Grijpstra slept peacefully, burbling moistly
through parted fat lips.

⫸ 20 ⫷

De Gier, ahead of his arrival time, walked slowly to the adjacent gabled mansions that housed the Society's club for prominent members and their affluent guests. There were still a number of blocks ahead. Pleasant spring weather, crisp and clear under a starry sky, did not improve the sergeant's mood. The elegance of Gelder Quay, a long, quiet backwater in the inner city, lined on both sides by silver-colored buildings and partly shrouded by majestic elm trees, didn't soothe him either.

"Sergeant?"

"Now what?" de Gier asked the young man in the maroon velvet suit and the flamboyant necktie, stepping under a streetlight ahead. The young man wore a hat, which he took off. "Like my haircut? The barber must still be sweeping his floor. I lost kilos of hair. The suit belongs to my brother Samuel." He pulled de Gier's sleeve. "Where the hell were you? I've been in and out of the club three times, looking for you. Celine is in the roulette room. I had to keep ducking away, she might recognize me even in this outfit."

"The others haven't arrived?"

"They'll be here soon, I came early. Are you going in now?"

"Sure," de Gier said. "I'll do my part. Leave it to the gigolo, that's all I'm good for."

Cardozo ran alongside de Gier, keeping up with the sergeant's long strides. "Do you know that IJsbreker's paintings are in the club's hallway? They didn't bother to sell the loot. There's a million's worth of art inside—Mondrians, Eschers, Appels, anything. Great shit. They just kept it."

"How do you know it's IJsbreker's stuff?" de Gier asked. "We never saw it."

"Got to be," Cardozo panted. "The Peruvian vases are there too, lined up on a long shelf in the hall. I asked the manager. He says the display only came in a few weeks ago. He doesn't know where from. He says the owners put it up."

"Who are the owners?"

"He didn't say, and I couldn't ask too much. Got to be Fernandus, and that baron, de la Faille, the guy who took IJsbreker's place at the bank."

"Hardly conclusive evidence."

"Good enough, Sergeant. We don't work by the book anymore. Shall we take the art too? That would be fun."

De Gier stopped and admired the three tall mansions ahead, reaching up into the sky from the narrow quaysides and the canal in between. He checked his watch. "I'm still early."

"I'm nervous," Cardozo said. "This is different. Nothing to back us up. You think we can do this?"

"Sure," de Gier said. "*You* can do it. I'll be upstairs holding Celine's hand. Smothering her with my charm. Maybe I should knock her down."

"No," Cardozo said.

"Got to knock somebody down," de Gier said. "Where's my black knight? Now the final moment is close. The last goodbye."

"To what?" Cardozo asked.

"To this part of the quest," de Gier said. "I now need to perform a symbolic act. In style. Fight my man. Myself maybe, some form of suicide."

"I'm going crazy too," Cardozo said. "There's quite a crowd inside. City councilmen, that Ronnie Ryder character that the commissaris mentioned, with his dogs and sycophants. Stacks of cash on the table, gambling everywhere, associated hoodlums in suede leather and cowboy boots, a nice selection of lovely ladies. Some show. Posh. A lot of jewels on the ladies. Do we rip them off too?"

"Just take the money," de Gier said. "Do as you're told. We've been through all this, there's a plan. Why are you going crazy?"

Cardozo adjusted his tie. "It's too new for me. There's only the commissaris behind us."

"Maybe that's still too much," de Gier said. "I'm going in."

A Mercedes load of well-dressed, elderly men swooshed through the club's glass revolving doors. De Gier followed.

"Sir?" an athletic black man in an old-fashioned naval officer's uniform asked.

"New member," de Gier said. He was taken to an antique solid-oak table to pay his fee. The hall, with a floor of red and white flagstones, had an Old Masters flavor, with a touch of baroque. The baroque item was a life-size stone angel, dangling from cables under the hallway's arched ceiling. The club's manager, a blond, long-haired gent in a frock coat and striped pants, smoothly accepted de Gier's three new notes.

"Drinks and snacks on the house, sir. If you feel an urge to be connected to a lady, a waiter will take your fee. Feel free to have a good time."

"Oh, yes," de Gier said, "I'll see what I can do for you."

The manager smiled. "All gambling is for cash. In case of trouble, the waiters will take care of things."

"No trouble," de Gier said.

The manager's gold fillings sparkled. "That's good."

De Gier wandered through rooms and corridors, admiring interior decorations. Cream-colored drapes set off niches in the white plaster walls, each niche holding some treasure: a delicate Buddhist statue; a modern sculpture consisting of a bizarre three-dimensional collage of skulls and driftwood; a single semiprecious stone, artfully framed. Oriental rugs graced marble floors. A fountain rained down on a basin where large goldfish with flowing tailfins swam leisurely between waving water plants. Mahogany wainscoting lined gambling rooms where croupiers sang their mantras in French. A tall woman, with black hair cascading down her naked shoulders above a trim satin blue dress, had changed herself to a cherishable object, standing very still with raised arms, one hand holding a tumbler of wine, the other a slice of caviared toast, breathing "Hello" when he passed.

"How're you doing?" de Gier asked. "Seen Celine anywhere?"

The woman unfroze. Her perfume wafted around de Gier. "I could give you a more intense experience. Like to try me out?"

"I would just love to," de Gier said, "but I have to find Celine." The satin woman drifted off, rustling her dress.

"Not helpful," de Gier said. He tried another twisting corridor that ended in a large mirror. De Gier checked his appearance. Good. Perhaps his silk scarf needed adjusting. He did that, but then the image doubled. A tall man, as tall as de Gier, stood next to him, leering into the mirror too. The double adjusted his tie. De Gier smoothed down his curls. The neighbor did likewise.

"Very *nice*," the double said softly. "Are you me? Am I you? Do we reflect? Is your name Baron Bart de la Faille too? Did I split and re-form twice, perhaps? A cloned vision? Was it the better brand of cocaine I just tried, or are we, in bare fact, the other way around, and is what I so fondly consider to be myself a mere projection of another phenomenon I haven't as yet met? Are we frightened or overjoyed?"

"Aha," de Gier said. "There you are. You took your time, but I haven't any right now. Where is Celine?"

"Who," the baron asked, "are you?"

"My name?" de Gier asked. "I'll let you know. I'm busy just now."

"We could penetrate each other's bodies," the baron asked. "Turn each other inside out together." He giggled. "Like gloves. Ever try that? Make a left glove out of a right and vice versa?"

De Gier walked off. He tried another door. Slender arms twined around his neck from behind. "That's the ladies', dear, are you drunk?"

"No," de Gier said, trying to twist free.

"You know who I am?" the female voice whispered.

"Celine?"

"What are you doing here?"

She let go, and he turned around. "I came to see you." She pulled his head down and kissed him full on the mouth. "Hmmm."

"Let's go upstairs," de Gier said.

She kissed him again.

He put his hands on her shoulders. "Upstairs? Let me go and I'll pay the waiter."

"No charge," Celine said. "Be my guest. I'll take care of this." She looked into his eyes. "But can we do it a bit later, please? Let me show you around first. Is this the first time you've been here?"

"Yes," de Gier said, pushing her firmly to a staircase. "Never mind the tour. I can't wait."

"But, Rinus . . ." She half-turned. "What *is* this? I didn't even know you remembered me. You're always so cool."

"Up, up, up." He grabbed her waist, propelled her up the stairs.

"Let go." She leaned back.

"No," de Gier said.

"I'll yell."

He swung her off her feet and held a hand over her mouth. A door swung open, pushed by his foot. He put her down on the bed.

Celine sat up. "Why the passion? What's the hurry? We don't close until four A.M., we have all night."

"Take off your clothes." De Gier smiled. "Please."

"Let's do this later. Why the rush?"

"Because I want you now." De Gier's large brown eyes shone. "Ever since that party at your house. I keep dreaming of you. Take off your clothes."

Celine's face hardened. "I dreamed of you too, but not like this." She reached for the telephone next to the bed. De Gier caught her wrist. "Don't." His arm pulled back.

"Are you going to hit me?"

"I'll have to," de Gier said. "There's no time to be nice. I'm needed downstairs. Don't worry, this will be quick."

"No!" She talked through her hands.

He sat down next to her. "There's a raid planned for a little later on. The colleagues may need my help."

She shook her head.

"I don't want to mess you up." He caressed her shoulder. "I know just where to hit you, not too hard. It won't hurt much. Please let me."

She edged away from him. He put an arm around her and pulled her back. "Stay away from the phone."

She leaned into his arm and dropped her hands. "Please don't. I won't yell." Celine looked up. "There can't be a raid, you're suspended."

"Who told you?"

"De la Faille. I heard that yesterday. There was a special party here to celebrate the commissaris's downfall."

"The baron doesn't know me."

"He knows *of* you. Fernandus threw the party. So how can there be a raid? Were Fernandus and the baron just showing off?"

"No," de Gier said. "I just met the baron. The baron is my man."

"Your man?"

"Bad guy," de Gier said. "I need a bad guy. Do you think the baron looks like me?"

"Bart has piggy eyes." She touched his cheek. "You have beautiful eyes, so warm."

"Same size," de Gier said. "Same mustache. Same type of hair. Does he do judo?"

"Fencing," Celine said. "Bart is good at fencing. All-around sportsman, that's what he says he is. Golf, polo, flies a glider."

"Good. Good." De Gier grinned.

"What do you want to do with him, Rinus? You aren't gay."

De Gier sighed. "Please, Celine, let me put you out."

She turned away. "Undo my zipper."

"No, not that."

"You don't want to?"

"No time."

She looked at her watch. "Isn't it early for a raid? The real stuff happens later, that's when all the big gamblers come in. Tonight there may be a special event. Here, I'll do it myself." She got up and stepped out of her dress. "Want a bath? Shall we push bubbles at each other? We've got nice soap here." She pulled him over to a sunken marble tub in the far corner of the room.

"Later?" de Gier said. "What event?"

"They're going to get Ronnie Ryder for all he's still worth," Celine said. "Ronnie likes me. I've been bringing him luck. If I don't show, he'll probably want to leave. They may come looking for me, but we've still got a few hours. They won't really push him until he's good and drunk. It usually takes a while."

"Aha," de Gier said. "So we wait?"

She nodded. "Yes. Let's have a bath. Would you care for a drink first? You drank bourbon that night. The night I stripped? When you wouldn't look at me?"

De Gier thought.

"Don't you remember? I did it just for you."

"Sure," de Gier said. "That was very nice. Great party."

"Can I phone for a drink?"

He reached for the phone. "Let me do it. What's the number of this room?"

"Seven."

"Room seven," de Gier said. "A bottle of bourbon, two glasses, and ice."

"Take off your jacket and shirt," Celine said. "I love your chest. I saw it once at that judo match at Headquarters. Let me see it again. It'll look more natural when she brings in the drinks."

De Gier obliged.

"The name is Susan," the girl who brought in the drinks said to de Gier. She wore a miniskirt and a clinging T-shirt. "My, don't you have a body! Can I stay? I'm the special tonight. Half-price for the trio."

"No, thanks," de Gier said. "The lady and I are friends. Haven't seen each other for a while. Some other time would be nice."

"Susan might have stayed for free," Celine said. "How foolish of you. She's a hobby whore, likes to wear wet shirts. Didn't you like those long legs? Susan works as a secretary, just comes in one night a week."

"No," de Gier said. "I came for you."

"To knock me out?"

De Gier poured the whiskey. "It'd be better for you if I did."

"But I could be on your side," Celine said. "This place isn't really what I want. The customers are always drunk, they slosh and slobber so."

"Your health," de Gier said. "That's what you get. You're planning to leave?"

"Your health." Celine raised her glass. "Could be."

"Know what you'll do instead?"

"Not yet."

"How's your husband?"

"Unhappy too," Celine said. "He phones. The estate near Marbella is a mess. Some slob owns it, Ten Haaf, dopes up all the time. Guldemeester is the janitor up there, he doesn't like that."

"Does he want to come back?"

"Maybe."

"And you'll be together again?"

"No," Celine said. "It wouldn't work. Come into the bath."

De Gier groaned as he lowered himself into the foam.

"Oh," Celine said. "That's right. Fernandus said you broke your ribs. Do they hurt a lot?"

"Some," de Gier said. "Please, Celine, I can't stay here too long. I'll have to go down in a while. If they knew that you met me here, you might be in worse trouble. If I knock you out, you'll be all right."

She pushed her legs against his. "I'll drown if you knock me out in the bath." She rose from the water, twisting her torso, lifted her long blond hair, allowed it to fall down again. She swayed her hips a little, dipped foam, and covered her breasts. "You like me doing this?"

"Sure," de Gier said. "Your figure is perfect."

She stepped out of the bath and brought his drink. "You trust me now? I could have tried to run away. I won't do that, I'll go down with you and do my tricks on Ronnie, make things more spectacular for you. What's this raid? Are you going to make arrests?"

De Gier left the bath too. "We can't," he said.

"So you *are* suspended. Fernandus and the baron weren't showing off."

"It's not an official raid. We're after the Society's money."

She looked at his clothes lying on the bed, and the pistol, conspicuous on the pale blue shirt. "They let you keep your gun? I've got a gun too." She clipped her pocketbook open and took out a Derringer, pointing it at his chest. "Enough of this now, put up your hands."

De Gier sipped his drink.

She came closer. "This is a .22 Magnum, no safety. All I have to do is pull the trigger. I've learned to handle this thing, it's very effective."

"Did you remember to load it?"

"Of course."

"You probably forgot," de Gier said. "Give it to me. It's empty, I can see from here." He put out his hand. She dropped the gun and he caught it, broke it open, and watched its two cartridges bounce on the bed. He pushed them back into the chambers, snapped the little pistol back together, and gave it back. "You're right."

Celine laughed. "Fool. There's no way to see if this thing is loaded until you open it."

"Tricked you," de Gier said.

"And you let me have it again? What if I shoot you?"

"You won't."

She sat on the bed. "You really weren't afraid? The girls at Headquarters say that you have no nerves. They all adore you. Is it true that you live alone with your cat and that you read a lot and never get involved?"

"How can I live alone if I live with my cat?"

She dropped the derringer into her bag. "Tell me more about the raid. Who's in on it?"

"Eight of us."

"The commissaris too? Does he want to steal the Society's cash?"

"I don't think he'll keep it," de Gier said. "He's gunning for Fernandus. Some old trouble between the two of them. I haven't quite caught on yet, but it doesn't matter. I'm doing my own thing now."

"But you're with the commissaris?"

"So far," de Gier said, "but I don't think he's with me."

She sat down gingerly on his knee. "Shall we fly away?" Her fingertips gently traced his ribs. "I have such a good fantasy with you. You're an angel, just like the angel here in the hall, and you swoop down and pick me up and then we're off, and we never come down again, your wings take us higher and higher and we waft away until we aren't anywhere anymore."

"That's good?" de Gier asked, softly stroking her hair.

"I wouldn't mind not being anywhere. Would you?"

He pointed at the bottle standing on the edge of the bath. She fetched it and came back. "You don't really care for me much, do you? We could have sex. Would that hurt you?"

"Probably," de Gier said.

She poured whiskey. "If you lay on your back and I was very gentle? It's always so quick here, I need more time. Jane says you're slow."

"You discuss my technique?" de Gier asked. "I

thought Constable Jane was shy. She's always shy with me."

"We act a lot," Celine said. "But I do think Jane likes you. So do I. Toine prefers the commissaris. I like him too. Do you know that Toine is with Fernandus now? Isn't that rather a loss? Younger men threaten Toine, but I didn't think she would go for Fernandus. He's all twisted inside."

"The commissaris isn't?"

"Is he?" Celine asked. "You know him best. Guldemeester was always jealous of you. Teacher's pet."

"No," de Gier said.

She pushed him onto his back. "Do you mind? I won't touch your ribs. What do you mean, 'no'? You're not teacher's pet?"

"The commissaris isn't twisted," de Gier said. "And if he is, that's up to him. I don't consider myself his student anymore. Ouch."

"Sorry," Celine said. "Okay now? What if I bend back?"

"Better, go ahead."

"Thanks," Celine said when she disengaged herself. "You were very patient. Did you like it too?"

"Didn't you notice?"

"Yes, but it could have been automatic."

"It wasn't," de Gier said. "Shall we go downstairs?"

She dressed. "You don't still think I'll tell on you?"

De Gier had trouble bending down to pull up his pants. Celine helped. "You'd be in a mess if I did," she said. "There are six waiters and the doorman downstairs, all of them fighters, and the manager throws knives. There's the baron too."

"The all-around sportsman," de Gier said. "I could have the lights turned off at the right moment. There must be a main switch, do you know where it is?"

"I'll show you." She nestled into his arm. "Hold me awhile."

The hug lasted until she stirred.

"But what will you tell them afterward?" de Gier asked.

"I don't know yet."

He rested his chin on her head. "Tell them I turn you on and that you thought I came for you. You don't have to recognize the others in our team, they're supposed to be disguised."

IIII 21 IIII

IN THE CLUB'S LARGEST ROOM, WHERE HALF A DOZEN comfortable couches, upholstered in different materials but all in striking shades of a bright orangy red, were grouped around a roulette table that attracted an enthusiastic crowd, de Gier sat stiffly next to a small gentleman in an old-fashioned but dapper summer suit. The commissaris, hard to recognize under his shock of false white hair, had crossed his legs and was contemplating his highly polished boot. A small hand stroked his full beard, and his pale blue eyes peered at the sergeant through a sparkling lorgnette that he had just, with a delicate gesture, pushed up to the bridge of his thin nose. "Excellent," the commissaris said, tapping de Gier's knee. "That's what I like about working with you, Rinus, you always do so much better than can be expected. So Celine's with us now? You 'turned' her, so to speak?" He glanced at Celine, standing next to Ryder, chattering brightly to the big man, who looked shabby in spite of his white linen jacket and loud checkered pants. Ryder's bulging cheeks dripped with sweat and his bulging eyes stared hungrily at a cluster of thousand-guilder notes, pushed toward him by the croupier's little rake. Ryder's pudgy hands rearranged the money, quickly finding numbered squares. A shiny pendant, a combination of precious stones set in massive gold, dangled from a silk ribbon hung around his neck, as he corrected a choice while the croupier and the crowd waited.

"Rien ne va plus," the croupier sang out. The wheel turned. A small metal ball jumped musically in the sudden hush that pervaded the room. The crowd applauded. Ryder swept up his profits, impassively dispensed by the croupier's magical instrument. Ryder thanked the powers below with a clumsy bow and proposed a toast. Waiters came running with a silver tray.

"To me!" Ryder shouted. "To me!" his cronies shouted, grinning and waving. "To me and all!" Ryder's surprisingly high voice shrilled like a piercing whistle on a lopsided locomotive as he bent down to put an arm around Celine.

"To me and all!" The choir around the pair obediently echoed. The commissaris's and de Gier's glasses were raised too. "Hurrah," the commissaris said.

"Hey-ho," de Gier said softly. "Hey-ho."

"And Celine'll let us know?" the commissaris asked. "Splendid. You really have a way. How do you do it?"

"I was going to knock her out," de Gier said. "I didn't do well at all. There were some risks. She could have gotten away, but I'm not good at hitting women. If she had alarmed the waiters, we would have been in a pretty fix again."

"Not really," the commissaris said. "What can they do? This is a shadowy operation, Rinus. A small bubble. We can prick it, and when we succeed we run away from the foul smell." He touched his flowing beard. "Itchy. The glue prickles. My wife spent most of the afternoon attaching all this hair. I have to bring this off or she'll be most upset. Doesn't like to waste energy, Katrien doesn't."

De Gier had spotted the baron hovering at the other side of the room, and excused himself. Cardozo took his place. "And how did you fare?" the commissaris asked. "Have you picked your waiter?"

"Yes, sir." Cardozo reinserted his multicolored tie, which kept jumping out of his waistcoat. "Your waiter is the fellow with the red sash over there, carrying the smoked salmon. You should try some of that. Do you know they employ slaves here?"

The commissaris observed his waiter, a bowlegged individual with a barrel chest, a low brow, and shaggy tufts sprouting from malformed ears.

"Slaves, Simon?" The commissaris tried to raise his glued-on eyebrows.

"There," Cardozo said. "The Indian lady in the sari. Sayukta. She took me upstairs, we talked for a while."

"Talked?" The commissaris raised his hand, but dropped it again. "Shouldn't scratch. Bah."

"Sayukta's from Calcutta," Cardozo said. "She was born in a park. The rats in the park ate her baby brother, but she learned how to beat them off. Seems like a hard life. Everybody sleeps in the street there, but the parks are worse. And then she got sold to some organization that ships young girls out. The slaves get hired out to brothels, and since they never have proper papers, they're in the power of whoever exploits them. Sayukta's only nineteen. She seems to like me."

"Did you make any promises?" the commissaris asked.

"No, sir, I only said I might perhaps be able to help. She doesn't care for her present occupation."

The commissaris dug his fingers into his sideburns. "You might get her address."

"I have it, sir."

Grijpstra passed the couch, wishing the commissaris a good evening. The adjutant wore a wig too, combed down over his forehead so that the scar of his wound wouldn't show. A walrus mustache drooped down impressively. With his baggy tweed jacket, he could have been British. "Jones is the name," Grijpstra said, pausing briefly. "A parson by trade, representing the lunatic fringe of the Protestant faith. Would they provide attractive indecent minors here? Are we getting close to the kill?"

"Not yet," the commissaris said. "Celine will tell de Gier. Ryder is celebrating now. We want a lot of money on the table. Are our State detectives alert?"

"They're in the poker room now, sir, winning. Trying to get your investment back."

"Karate and Ketchup are gambling too," Cardozo said. "How much did you put in? A thousand for each of us?"

"Never mind mere money," the commissaris said. "It's such a pleasure not having to apply to the administration for funds."

Guests were drifting back into the room, and the croupier came to attention. "I'll play some blackjack," Grijpstra said. "They don't seem to like it when you just eat a lot. Have you sampled the little rolls with mushroom ragout yet? I've had a few, but they're too filling."

"So you sell luxury goods to the Russian elite?" the baron asked de Gier in the poker room. "I believe the more equal comrades do drugs a lot. You have a connection?"

De Gier sucked his cheroot. "I could use a better quality." He winked at the baron. "And some financing, perhaps. So you're a banker?"

De la Faille handed de Gier his card. "Give me a buzz tomorrow, perhaps we shouldn't meet at the bank. Come over to my apartment. Do you sell outboard engines, perhaps? I hear the communist lakes are good for sporty boating, but there's a better market now, with the Iranian army stuck in inundated swamps. Ever been to Iran? I could arrange a passport and a Japanese supply. Officially the trade is banned, but the demand is quite hectic. We could find a way." He touched de Gier's shoulder. "Did you find Celine? You seemed rather in a hurry."

"I had this urge," de Gier said.

"You had met her before?"

De Gier waved about vaguely. "Earlier this evening. I wasn't sure then, but the need suddenly arose."

"You must have found her. You look all relaxed."

"Yes," de Gier said. "So do you. I didn't quite get what you were telling me when we met at the mirror."

The baron shrugged. "Cocaine does that to me. Sudden insight, you know; it's still with me, but I took a downer later on. Drugs are fun, don't you think? Don't know what we ever did without them. To be able to inspire and control the mind at will. Manipulating others is easy enough, merely a matter of applying power at the right time, but the self can be quite silly, jumps around too much, all that intelligence wanting to go astray."

"You were inspired when we met just now?" de Gier asked. "What did you see?"

The baron's hand was still on de Gier's shoulder. "You must have seen it too. Physically, of course, we're very much alike, but I saw more. Mated souls?"

De Gier led the way to the couch. They sat down together.

The baron called a waiter over. "Champagne?"

"Thank you." De Gier took the glass. "No, not mated. Opposed. I think you and I should fight. That's what I saw." He grinned. "A duel to the death."

"But, my dear fellow . . ." The baron stared.

"Didn't you see that?" de Gier asked. "Drawn swords, and we're both riding horses, yours black, mine white, superb stallions. The fog on the field in the early morning. Gold braid on our chests, a single bright-colored feather in our bearskin hats? Going full out at each other. Swishing steel? One of us goes down.''

"No . . ."

"Oh yes," de Gier said. "Any way you like it, of course. Choose your weapons. I'll win anyway. I absolutely have to. I'm the white knight." He suddenly sat up. "Ouch." He felt his chest. "Handicapped, of course. The good always attacks from a weak position, but there should be a happy ending."

"You're on coke too?" the baron asked. "Shouldn't mix it with alcohol too much. What's the happy ending?"

De Gier smiled. "Your corpse."

A waiter came over. "Sir? Mr. Ryder wants to know if the Society can match his bet."

The baron nodded. "Be right with you." He turned to de Gier. "I still don't have your name."

"You'll know it tomorrow." De Gier stood up too.

The baron strode off. He even walks like me, de Gier thought, turning away from the satin woman, who, still unattached, roamed the room behind an all-embracing smile. Karate and Ketchup, dressed in inconspicuous gray suits, played poker. De Gier stumbled and grabbed Karate's shoulder. "Excuse me."

Karate dropped his cards. "I'll pass." He frowned at de Gier. "Get away from me. You drunk?"

"What's the matter?" Ketchup asked Karate. "You couldn't get the ace up your sleeve?"

"Sir?" Karate asked.

"I said," Ketchup said in a loud voice, "that maybe you don't have an ace up your cuff this time."

"Are you," Karate asked ominously, "accusing me of foul play?"

"Are you," de Gier asked Karate, "accusing me of intoxication?"

Two waiters hovered nearby. De Gier walked on.

"Watch those guys," he whispered to a waiter. "Sharpies, you know? Mouthy sharpies?"

The waiter, a small square man with a squint, fluttered an eyelid.

De Gier found Grijpstra in the next room, showing a piece of lobster to another waiter. He poked a finger at his plate, held close under the waiter's nose. "Feces. See? That green stuff inside the shell? That's, eh . . ." Grijpstra dropped his voice. ". . . shit. Lobster droppings. Yagh. Wah."

De Gier wandered on.

Celine stood in the hall. "Where were you? Ryder's going to put up everything he has. The manager is getting more money from the safe."

"Good," de Gier said. "Did you show Cardozo what to do?"

"Yes."

"I could love you," de Gier said.

The commissaris was talking to the roulette croupier. "Now, my man, I've been watching you. You keep tipping that wheel. Shouldn't, you know." The commissaris wagged a finger. "No." He called a waiter. "You there, bring my hat and stick, I'm leaving. I won't make any complaints, of course. In low-class joints like this, foul play can be expected. Thank you." The commissaris pounded his stick on the floor. "Disgusting."

Two tall men, barechested under their leather jackets, with rattling chains on their naked chests, were watching the roulette table, grinning inanely.

The manager came in, escorted by the baron. The manager carried an armful of cash. He put it on the table. "Ronnie," the baron said, "we're ready for you. You sure you want to do this?"

"This is my night," Ryder said, raising his hands. The room had filled up. "Are all of you with me?"

"Yes!" the crowd shouted.

De Gier walked up to Ryder and placed a finger on the big man's nose. "You."

Waiters came closer. There was a clamor elsewhere in the building. The waiters looked over their shoulders. Some shouting penetrated the room.

"You," de Gier said to Ryder. "You, sir, with your loud mouth, you've been irritating me."

The waiters surged forward. The first one, a heavy-set man with no neck, fell over the commissaris's stick. "I'm leaving," the commissaris shrieked. "Foul play."

The lights went out.

A flashlight came on. Four hands, extended from leather sleeves, swept money into linen bags. De Gier hit Ryder on the side of his chin. Ryder fell against a waiter. The shouting in the poker room increased. Cardozo's necktie made a small show of clashing color as the beam of the flashlight touched it. "Where is my waiter?" Cardozo mumbled. "On the floor," the commissaris mumbled. "Pick another."

"Green feces!" Grijpstra shouted. "Yaahg!" A body fell and a tray clanged on the floor. There was another crash in the hall, and a scream.

The lights came on again. "After them," the baron yelled, picking up waiters. De Gier, supporting the commissaris's elbow, reached the hall. The stone angel lay on the floor, without its head. Karate was showing the head to Ketchup. The revolving glass doors still turned. The doorman lay next to the angel's body.

"A doctor!" Grijpstra shouted. "This man is hurt!"

"Phone the police!" Cardozo screamed. "Where's the phone? Can I use the phone?"

"I'm leaving!" the commissaris shouted. Waiters were running toward the revolving doors. De Gier stopped the doors, with two waiters stuck inside.

"Let go of that door!" the manager yelled. De Gier stepped back. The waiters, pushing furiously inside, tumbled out, one into the street, one back into the hallway.

"What's the number?" Cardozo shouted, holding up the phone. "I've forgotten the number."

The baron wrung the telephone from Cardozo's hands and smashed it down.

"You don't want to phone the police?" Cardozo asked. "This is a robbery. Those fellows got away with the loot. I saw them. Black jackets. Chains. Didn't you see them?"

Karate tried to give the angel's head to the manager. The manager shook his head. "As you like," Karate said, "I'm only trying to be helpful." He dropped the head. The manager danced away.

"Clumsy," Ketchup said. "Look what you did. You got him on the toe."

"Sir?" Grijpstra asked the dancing manager. "Your kitchen is serving lobster feces. Do you know that? Yagh."

"After you," de Gier said to the commissaris.

The black doorman staggered away, holding his stomach.

There was a bellow from the roulette room. Ryder came into the hallway, rubbing his chin. "Where's my money?"

"Lost it, old boy," the baron said. "We lost ours too."

"Oh no," Ryder squeaked. "You're responsible for this place. You pay me back, double, I might have won."

"We'll discuss it, old boy."

"And where's the guy who hit me?" Ryder asked.

Guests were leaving the club. Cardozo left with them. "Where's the bathroom?" Grijpstra asked a waiter. "I've got lobster crap all over my hands."

"Miss?" Ketchup asked the satin woman. "Can I have some time with you now?"

Karate stood in front of a group of hostesses, pointing at them in turn. "Eenie, meenie, minie, mo . . ."

"We're closing," the baron shouted. "Sorry, everybody out, please. We'll be closed for the rest of the week, due to refurbishing. 'Bye now. Thank you."

"But we haven't been upstairs yet," Karate protested. "Please? We were gambling all night." He tugged the baron's arm. "We won. Can we copulate some of our winnings away?"

"Out," the baron said.

Guests were shooed to the door. The waiters who had pursued the robbers came back, shaking their heads.

Grijpstra reappeared in the empty hallway, drying his hands with his handkerchief. "Where's the chief cook? I have a complaint."

"Goodbye," the baron said.

Two uniformed policemen came in. "Any trouble?"

"No trouble," the baron said. "Thank you. Closing early tonight."

"What do you mean, no trouble?" Grijpstra asked. "Listen, officers, I'm making a complaint, about the lobster I tried to eat here."

"Please take this man out," the baron said.

"Sir?" the cops said, pointing at the door.

"Oh, very well," Grijpstra said, and left.

When Grijpstra arrived, the commissaris's wife opened the door. "There you are, Adjutant, we were worried about you."

"I'll never eat lobster again," Grijpstra said. "Good evening, ma'am. I'm sorry, I couldn't find a cab, and the night bus was slow. Is everybody here?"

||||| 22 |||||

"PICK HIM UP AT HIS HOUSE?" CARDOZO ASKED.

Adjutant Grijpstra braked for a traffic light. "In the street, I would think. We don't want Huip Fernandus to know. It may take some time. Who knows where those fellows hang out?" The Citroën moved again. "We don't have much time. I have a feeling we should push on. You want to collect that computer later today? What do we want with a computer?"

"Don't know yet," Cardozo said, peering through sheets of rain pushed up by a city bus that passed their car. "Might come in handy. Where's de Gier?"

Grijpstra switched the windshield wipers to double speed. "In bed. The commissaris wants him to rest his ribs. Besides, everybody knows now that the sergeant's suspended."

"De Gier wasn't happy with the raid." Cardozo rolled a cigarette. "Didn't get to do much."

"Except keep Mrs. Guldemeester busy for a while." Grijpstra grinned. "The sergeant didn't want to do that, either. Do you know who brought that stone angel down last night?"

"Karate," Cardozo said. "Cut the wires while I took care of the lights. Karate likes spectacles. He and

Ketchup did well, kept a few waiters out of the way and won a bundle at poker."

"And handed the money over," Grijpstra said. "Surprising. Wicked little devils, but they did pay up. Don't think they kept a penny. Wonder why."

"Honest?" Cardozo asked. "Some of us are honest. You wouldn't have kept any of that Society's money, would you, Adjutant?"

"Bah." Grijpstra shook his head.

"You need money," Cardozo said. "Everybody does."

"Never cared for the stuff." Grijpstra parked the car on the Binnenkant bridge. "Let's hope we see Heul. If we do, you grab him. He may run if he spots me. Do you know what he looks like?"

"Thin?" Cardozo said. "Orange hair? What do you have against money, Adjutant?"

"Money is weight." Grijpstra lit a cigar. "Buys furniture. Furniture clutters the house. Buys gadgets. Gadgets break down. Buys holidays. I hate holidays. Attracts company. I'd rather live alone."

Cardozo puffed on his cigarette. "I rather like money. All that cash yesterday was exciting. Close to a million. We really cleaned that place out. I could have counted it all night. De Gier doesn't like money, either, does he?"

"De Gier is going a little crazy," Grijpstra said. "Keeps babbling about killing that baron. He's been seeing too many movies."

"The sergeant hardly ever sees movies."

Grijpstra gestured. "Or he reads too much. Novels with happy endings. There aren't any happy endings. What really happens is that it all goes on. So he gets the baron, so what? He'll also get a lot of trouble."

"We'll have to get the baron," Cardozo said. "Him and Fernandus. They're the killers we're after."

"No proof."

"The baron shot IJsbreker," Cardozo said. "De la

Faille must have been an officer with some crack outfit in the army, so he's probably a good shot. Set up a rifle in that house over there, in the part occupied by Huip and Heul, second floor. It couldn't have been anywhere else. We're not after proper evidence. The case won't go to court. None of us have any authority now. The authorities are all against us."

"Yes, yes," Grijpstra said as he wiped the fogged-up windshield. "So?"

"So? Last night's raid was illegal, right? If we arrest Heul now, that'll be illegal too. We can only pretend, try to shake the bad guys into tripping themselves up. Aren't we setting them up? For some accident, maybe?"

"De Gier wants a duel," Grijpstra said. "That's crazy. There must be another way."

"Push him or Fernandus into committing some careless crime? Hand them over to Chief Inspector Rood, maybe?"

"Remember that lobster last night?" Grijpstra asked. "That green stuff inside? Sort of pale green? That's the color I'm after for my painting. Mixed it up this morning. I think it's the right shade."

"Hello," Cardozo said, wiping the window with his hand. "That must be Heul. I'll go get him."

Cardozo ran through the rain. Heul, carrying a shopping bag and holding an umbrella, tried to step out of the way. "Heul?" Cardozo asked.

"Yes?"

"Police." A handcuff clicked on Heul's wrist.

"Hey!"

"Hey to you too." Cardozo grabbed Heul's shoulder. The umbrella fell. The other handcuff clicked shut. "Come along." He picked up the umbrella and prodded Heul's back with it. "Forward, buddy. See that Citroën? Keep going."

"Morning," Grijpstra said when Cardozo pushed Heul into the Citroën's backseat. "We meet again.

This time the charge is attempted murder. We'll take you to Headquarters. How have you been?"

Heul stuttered.

"Attempted murder is a nice solid charge," Cardozo said. "We have witnesses who saw you put that tarpaper down. There are other charges too. Receiving stolen property. Remember Carl? Mrs. Jongs made a statement too; she saw you. Nice tight charges."

Grijpstra started the car.

"But . . ." Heul stared at Cardozo. "Shit, man . . ."

"Shhh," Cardozo said. "Yes, Adjutant, what were you saying just now?"

"Last night's soccer game on TV," Grijpstra said. "It's the goalkeeper, I tell you. No good. They should fire the old fogey."

"Hmmm." Cardozo considered the suggestion. "There's luck too, so, okay, he was unlucky. The ball was slippery, maybe. He did manage to catch it, but it slithered into the goal anyway. Can't blame him for that."

"Something with his eyesight," Grijpstra said. "The paper mentioned a medical check. He should be retired."

"Listen," Heul said. "Please. I picked up that tarpaper because it was lying in the road. I pushed it to the side. I'm always cleaning up. Habit, you know?"

"Tell the judge," Cardozo said. "Take the next right, Adjutant, the traffic is blocked ahead."

The alley was blocked too. Grijpstra switched the engine off. "This may take a while, that truck there is loading."

"Oh, no," Heul said. "Oh, shit."

Cardozo turned to the prisoner. "Dumb punk. You really did it now. These charges will stick."

"Listen," Heul said. "Please."

Grijpstra looked at the truck ahead in the narrow

alley. "They've hardly started. I don't know why there's still so much business in town. All this loading. There must be a thousand cartons in that truck." He honked his horn. "They should give the city to the tourists."

"Listen," Heul said. "It wasn't me. Huip told me to lay that tarpaper down, I didn't know what for. He put the Daimler in your way, I wasn't in the car."

"If you had been, you might have gotten hurt," Grijpstra said. He pointed at his scar. "I got hurt, and the sergeant. Judges don't like it when cops get hurt."

"Huip Fernandus," Heul said, "he's your man. I'm nothing. What do you want with me?"

"Got to start somewhere," Cardozo said. "You lost your hat, and our witness saw your hair. She didn't see Huip Fernandus. Mrs. Jongs didn't see him take the paintings and vases from the junkies burglarizing the IJsbreker house—she saw you. Carl helped take stuff downstairs, and who did he give it to?"

"See?" Grijpstra asked.

"Don't you want Huip?" Heul asked.

Grijpstra thought. "Isn't young Fernandus your friend?"

"Ych," Heul said. "You want Huip or not?"

"On what charges?" Cardozo asked. "Because you say so? You're not reliable. You were in it yourself. Shifting the blame."

"Huip will deny the charges, you see," Grijpstra said patiently.

Heul waved his cuffed hands. "Catch him on other charges. Better."

Grijpstra pressed his horn again. A man carrying cartons to the truck came over, dropped his load, and banged on the Citroën's roof. "Quit honking, you're making me nervous."

"Like what charges?" Cardozo asked.

Heul rattled his handcuffs. "Give me a cigarette."

"No," Cardozo said. "I don't like you. What charges?"

"Murder?"

"Huip didn't shoot IJsbreker," Cardozo said. "I don't believe it."

"Huip didn't waste IJsbreker," Heul said. "De la Faille did, I saw that happen. Huip saw it too. If you get Huip, he'll tell you."

Grijpstra had left the car and was arguing with the truckdriver and his mate.

"This is too complicated," Cardozo said. "What's the charge against Huip? Has he murdered someone else?"

"He will," Heul said. "I'll tell you who and how, if you let me go."

Grijpstra came back. "This is interesting, Adjutant," Cardozo said. "Suspect wants to trade."

"You've got nothing on me," Heul said. "So I was Huip's flunky. So I put tarpaper on a street. So I picked up some paintings. You want Huip on real stuff, right?"

"Do I?" Grijpstra asked. "I've got you. Maybe you're enough. The city is short of cells."

"Ryder," Heul said. "Ronnie Ryder. Next Sunday, in a boat, they'll blow him up. If you're there, you can see it happen. Huip will do it by radio, watch Huip push the button."

"Nah," Grijpstra said. He put his arm on the top of the front seat and put the car in reverse. "Move your head to the side, I'm going to back up."

Another truck entered the alley behind the Citroën. Grijpstra switched the engine off again. "Stuck."

"All you have on me," Heul said, "is old stuff. Shaky stuff. It's not a good charge. None of it. Won't hold. But if you see Huip blow up Mr. Ryder . . ."

"Why would Huip do that?" Cardozo asked.

"Some shit," Heul said. "I heard him talk to his father on the phone. Ryder wants money out of the bank or out of the Society or something. Fernandus and de la Faille cleaned him out, and Ryder wants his dough back. He knows about some big deals—coke from Bogotá, heroin from Calcutta, all sorts of shit. He's got them over a barrel. There's a meeting Sunday at the Vinker Lakes to talk it out. They've got speedboats there, Mr. Ryder likes that. He'll take out a boat and then Huip will blow him up. The gas tank will explode. A little plastic bomb that won't leave a trace. Voosh!''

"Voosh," Grijpstra said.

"No more Ronnie Ryder," Heul said. "The engine on the boat blows, and the engine is close to the gas tank. A spark. Huip is good with stuff like that. He wanted to blow up Mrs. Jongs too, but she isn't home now. Burn the house down—it's falling apart anyway, and it's insured. The Society wants to construct a classy building instead, start another club."

"Voosh," Cardozo said.

"Voosh." Heul leaned back. "Give me a cigarette."

Cardozo smoked.

"When exactly will this come about?" Grijpstra asked.

"Sunday, two o'clock. Huip and some expert are fixing the bomb now. Okay? Let me go?

"Who killed the three junkies?" Cardozo asked.

"Huip." Heul's nose dripped, and he tried to get a handkerchief from his pocket. "I wasn't in on that. Nobody told me. I thought the horse was regular—cut, you know? Weak shit. But Huip gave them pure junk supplied by the baron. I didn't like that at all."

Grijpstra sucked his cigar.

"Okay," Heul said. "I'll give you more. I don't want to go to jail, man. I'm too sensitive for jail. Okay?"

"If it's good," Grijpstra said.

"Real good. There's a girl with the Society, from

Calcutta. Calls herself Sayukta. Ruby in her nose. Bare belly. They're going to send her home, but she'll come straight back, carrying four ki's of horse. She doesn't want to, but she'll go, all right.''

''When?''

''Soon.''

''When exactly?''

''I don't know. Very soon. The junk isn't in Calcutta yet. It comes from somewhere else. Nepal. Okay?''

''Okay,'' Grijpstra said. ''For now. If either tip isn't right, we'll get you later. In any way we know of.''

''We know lots of ways these days,'' Cardozo said. ''Quick ways.'' He patted his jacket. ''It's good hunting now. We can do lots of stuff. Not so many regular cops around anymore who'd bother to check. Nice.''

Heul held up his hands. Cardozo unlocked the cuffs. ''Don't forget your umbrella.''

'' 'Bye,'' Heul said. ''Have a good day.'' He scrambled out of the car.

''He thinks we're regular cops,'' Grijpstra said. ''Maybe he thinks we won't dare.''

''We dared last night,'' Cardozo said.

The truck ahead moved away. Grijpstra started the Citroën again. ''Heul's a little guy. Little guys scare easy. Maybe we're getting somewhere now. Pity the Vinker Lakes are out of town, we can't make the arrest.''

Cardozo was pressed back in his seat as the car shot away. ''Ha,'' Grijpstra said. ''If we see it happen, we've got them anyway. We'll bring in the local cops later. Wouldn't do to call them in early. Suspects could notice.''

''Shouldn't we warn Ryder?'' Cardozo asked. ''I mean . . .''

''Yes?''

''I mean he's going to die. He'll blow up in front of us. Can you take that?''

"I've seen Ryder go down once," Grijpstra said. "When de Gier pushed him over. I rather liked seeing him go down."

"This time he'll go up."

"Yes," Grijpstra said. "Where's the computer store you wanted to go to?"

⁄⁄⁄⁄ 23 ⁄⁄⁄⁄

LATER THAT DAY, WHILE GRIJPSTRA WAS HOME painting in the pale green background that would set off his bare-boned ducks, and Cardozo was working with his new computer on the kitchen table that his mother needed to cut cucumbers on, and de Gier was half-asleep on his antique brass bed, the commissaris's wife served tea.

The commissaris came down from his study, yawning and rubbing his eyes, Mrs. Jongs brought a chocolate cake from the oven, and Carl held up his image of Turtle. Turtle himself walked stiffly through the tall weeds in the rear garden on his way to fresh lettuce.

"This is like New York," the commissaris said, sitting down on a cane chair, shielding his eyes from the late-afternoon sun that lit up the back porch. "In the thirties. The Mafia wars. The troops would hole up in safe houses, slobber spaghetti, and gurgle wine."

"What troops?" his wife asked.

"You're my troops," the commissaris said. "I need you all. Last night we won a battle. Now we rest, and later we challenge the enemy again."

Mrs. Jongs tried to whistle, matching notes that could be the opening of a military march. Carl at-

tempted a salute, but his hand missed his head. The
commissaris's wife stamped her slippered feet and
came to attention. "As you were," the commissaris
barked.

"Really, Jan," the commissaris's wife said. "Eat
your cake. Did you deposit that money?"

"I did," the commissaris said. "You should have
seen the teller's face. She needed four colleagues to
get it all sorted."

"Jan." She pinched his cheek. "Carrying a suitcase
full of banknotes around. The streets are alive with
muggers. I should have gone with you."

"I had my cane," the commissaris said. "Good
cake." He held out his plate. "More? Please?"

"Goohood cahake indeeheed," Carl said.

The commissaris's wife rubbed Mrs. Jongs's shriv-
eled shoulder. "You did a great job."

"And did Grijpstra bring good news just now?" the
commissaris's wife asked.

The commissaris picked up Turtle's image. "Yes,
interesting information. I expect Fernandus to contact
me soon. We could stop further trouble, he should see
that by now. He'll just have to give in."

"Oh, dear." She shook her head. "Fernandus will
move too. He's got so much power. Look at you, Jan,
bumbling about on your sore legs. Grijpstra is hurt, de
Gier can't lift an arm without groaning. And look at
us, we can't help you at all."

"I made the cake," Mrs. Jongs said.

The commissaris grinned at Carl. "And you made
another work of most expressive art. The essential
turtle. You must have watched my friend well. Let's
see if Turtle will acknowledge his archetype."

Carl took his construction and carried it into the
garden. The commissaris, his wife, and Mrs. Jongs
watched from the porch. Carl had squatted down
when the shot cracked. The bullet knocked the wire-
and-shingle turtle from Carl's hands. Carl staggered

back. The commissaris stumbled down the garden steps and grabbed hold of Carl. His wife screamed. Mrs. Jongs pointed at a window of a building beyond the rear of the garden and past another garden behind it. "There. Up there."

The commissaris and Carl, arms around each other, climbed the stairs back to the porch. The commissaris's wife pulled them both up. "Quickly, Jan, please."

"Phoo," the commissaris said when he pushed Carl into the house. "No panic, Katrien. Why don't you phone de Gier? Tell him to take a cab. Which window was it, Mrs. Jongs? Could you point it out to me?"

"Stay away from the windows!" the commissaris's wife shouted.

"That's the third floor?" the commissaris asked. "Must be that hotel. There's a hotel there now, on Valerius Street. Do call de Gier, dear."

"He's coming," his wife said, dropping the phone. "He was asleep. What can the sergeant do, Jan?"

"Not too much, I hope," the commissaris said. "Maybe we should have called Grijpstra. Are you all right, Carl?"

"Goohood shot," Carl said. "Meaheant to mihiss me."

The doorbell rang. The commissaris's wife opened the door. "Yes?"

"Voort," the man in the blue blazer and the gray slacks said. "State Detection. Could I see your husband, please?"

"Someone was shooting at us just now," the commissaris's wife said.

"I beg your pardon, ma'am?"

The commissaris came to the door too. "Ah, Voort. Not a good time, I'm afraid. We're under fire here."

Voort stepped back. "I don't quite understand."

The commissaris lit a cigar. "Quite simple. It was a rifle, I'm sure, with a marksman at the trigger, as in the IJsbreker case."

"Call the police," Voort said. "You want me to call them? I have a radio connection from my car."

The commissaris waved the cigar under his nose and sniffed. "Ah, excellent. I don't smoke so much anymore. Rather increases the pleasure. Which police?"

"Is he that stupid fellow who has been bothering you?" the commissaris's wife asked.

"Yes, Katrien."

"Away with you," the commissaris's wife said, poking a finger into Voort's blazer. "Silly man. Shoo." She pushed her husband back and banged the door.

"Now, now, Katrien."

"Really," she said, "shooting at us from the rear, bothering us up front. Won't this ever stop? Mrs. Jongs and I can make some sandbags. Why don't you get your gun? It's upstairs, on your shirts."

"I'm not too good with guns," the commissaris said. "Can't we have more tea?"

The doorbell rang again. The commissaris's wife marched to the door. "Easy now, Katrien," the commissaris said. "Voort is only trying to do a job. No good yelling at the chap."

De Gier came in.

"Ah," the commissaris said. "Very good of you, Rinus. We have a problem here. Someone fired a rifle from the hotel across the garden, third floor. That's on Valerius Street, a hotel. Could you go over there and make inquiries? Here, I'll give you some money."

"Money, sir?"

"Yes," the commissaris said. "Say you're a private detective. Private detectives use money, I believe. Let's see what you can come up with. Mrs. Jongs baked a cake, you can earn yourself a slice."

De Gier looked at the commissaris's wife. "No one got hurt?"

Carl held up his construction. "I was juhust puhutting it down. In the gaharden."

De Gier felt the hole in the turtle's shell. "Would be nice to have the bullet."

"Nobody goes into the garden now," the commissaris's wife said.

"I see, ma'am. I'll be as quick as I can." De Gier took the notes the commissaris was holding out to him. "How are your ribs?" the commissaris's wife asked.

De Gier felt his chest. "I think they're okay now, ma'am, I can take on the foe."

"Don't," the commissaris said.

De Gier was back an hour and a half later. The commissaris's wife let him in. "My husband is upstairs, Rinus, napping again. He's awfully tired these days. I do think the strain is getting too much for him. His legs aren't doing too well, either."

"Yes," de Gier said. "Maybe I should come back tonight?"

"Rinus?" The commissaris stood at the top of the stairs. "Come up, dear fellow. Katrien, do you think we could have a drink?"

Mrs. Jongs brought up a tray, with a tale about lizards. She held up the commissaris's glass against the light. "They lives in there, but I never sees them."

"Thank you, Mrs. Jongs, we won't let them out." The commissaris waited until she had left before he raised his glass. "Here we go, into the unknown again. Exciting, don't you think? We seem to be short of guidelines these days." He drank. "You know, Rinus, I'm learning a lot. About what it's like to be on my own. There was always the State before, but she has left me now."

De Gier replaced his glass. "The State is a she?"

The commissaris nodded. "I think so. Well, Sergeant, what's new?"

"The hotel owner," de Gier said, "let an upstairs

room on the third floor in the rear to a couple, at about three o'clock this afternoon, just for a few hours. The man was tall, handsome, well dressed. He carried a suitcase. Suspect would have been about forty years old. He showed no identification and paid in cash. The lady was younger, attractive, blond hair, not the same class as the man. The hotel owner thought the man to be a company director and the lady a secretary."

"Not a call girl?"

"No," de Gier said. "She seemed unhappy. Call girls put up a show. Female suspect seemed to be in the power of her male companion. A job relationship —she couldn't refuse. The hotel owner didn't hear the shot. There may have been a vacuum cleaner running at the time."

"Ah," the commissaris said.

"The couple arrived in a cab," de Gier said. "Taxi headquarters are close by, so I went over there and gave the radio operator money. He called all cabs, offering a reward to the driver who delivered the couple at the hotel. The man showed up promptly. Cab-drivers are good observers. He described suspects in detail."

"Who?" the commissaris asked.

"The baron and Celine," de Gier said. "I'm positive."

"The baron I believe," the commissaris said. "Why Celine?"

De Gier stretched his legs and looked at his glass.

"Another drink, Sergeant?"

"No, thank you, sir. By now the baron knows who I am. We had some moments together at his club. He had drugged himself then, and I expect that he had a very open mind." De Gier waved a hand. "Maybe this sounds silly, sir."

"No, no. Not at all, Rinus. Let's explore the mystical side of our situation for a bit. Go ahead, if you please."

"Hmmm," de Gier said.

"Go on."

"The baron would be worth fighting." De Gier pulled in his legs and sat up. "A splendid adversary. Did you notice he looks like me?"

"Yes, Sergeant."

"I feel I have prepared for this," de Gier said. "Don't you think the fight would be worthwhile?"

"No," the commissaris said. "Not at all. Leave the baron be, he'll squash himself in the end."

De Gier sat up straighter. "So why bother with Fernandus, sir? You're going all out too. The raid was your show of force. We robbed the club, pushed waiters over, brought the angel down . . . "

"Yes, yes," the commissaris said. "I've been considering that. Childish play, I did rather enjoy it."

De Gier grinned.

"But I wouldn't kill Fernandus," the commissaris said. "I intend to put him in jail, your approach is too medieval. Present society no longer condones death as a penalty; we must allow for our spiritual evolution."

"I'm suspended," de Gier said. He put out his arms and flapped them. "Nice word. Suspension. I feel like I can fly. I'm above it now."

"So was Icarus." The commissaris emptied his glass. "So is Fernandus, or rather, they both think they are. That's why Willem put that angel up in the club's hallway. Pay heed, Rinus. All these symbolic happenings don't come about to be ignored. I think I'll continue as planned. If the baron wants to shoot Carl's turtle, the feat won't impress us. Now why did he take Celine to that hotel?"

"To show her what he's capable of," de Gier said. "To frighten her. The baron suspects that Celine is trying to slip from his grasp. She was with me that night and didn't tip him off, but she hasn't left Fernandus's little band, either."

"We'll let today's assault go." The commissaris pushed his empty glass about. "Heul told Grijpstra and Cardozo today that the Society intends to do away with Ryder. Huip Fernandus will blow up Ryder's speedboat on the Vinker Lakes by making use of some electronic device. I intend to go out there and jump Huip before he can press the button. We'll link the bomb in the boat with the detonator Huip is using, call in the local police at the right time, and have Huip arrested. That way we get to Fernandus via his own son. We'll probably succeed in implicating Fernandus himself as well. Our attack is gaining momentum now, so don't go in for diversions in the meantime. Once we push Fernandus over, the baron will fall too."

The phone rang downstairs. "Jan?" the commissaris's wife called. "It's Fernandus, are you coming down?"

"See?" the commissaris asked.

The commissaris came back. "He's at the café at the corner and wants to speak to me, I'm going over."

De Gier got up. "I'll come along."

"No," the commissaris said. "Go down and eat your cake and try to cheer up Katrien. She has her doubts about what I'm doing. Take my car home and report here tomorrow morning. Thanks for your help so far." He thumped de Gier's belly softly. "We'll win this thing, Rinus. If the gods aren't on our side, we'll manufacture our own and pray for their blessing."

⦚⦚⦚⦚ 24 ⦚⦚⦚⦚

"WHAT WILL IT BE?" FERNANDUS ASKED.

The commissaris looked around the old-fashioned café and greeted the waiter. "Just coffee, please. Separate checks."

"Petty," Fernandus said, holding his index finger and thumb close together. "Real small-minded."

"Yes," the commissaris said brightly, rubbing his hands. "I'm here, Willem. Let's hear the next temptation. Every time we meet, I feel like the protagonist in 'The Temptation of Saint Jan.' Your presence flatters me. I never thought that the denizens of the dark would seek me out—me, a petty official in a small-sized city on a minor planet in an unimportant solar system of a negligible galaxy . . ."

". . . of a piddling universe," Fernandus said.

The waiter brought the coffee, and a gin and tonic for Fernandus. He smiled at the commissaris. "Glad to see you, sir. I read about you in the paper. I wish you strength, we're all with you, sir."

"Thank you," the commissaris said. "I'll survive, Tom. Do you know this man, Mr. Fernandus, the attorney?"

The waiter frowned. "Yes. Friend of yours, sir?"

He looked down at Fernandus. "You're not my friend. My useless son gets his dope from one of the canteens that your Society supports. The miserable monkey has to steal bicycles to support his habit. I kicked him out, but my wife feeds him behind my back." He turned back to the commissaris. "This damned welfare system, sir, and there's so much to do."

"Mr. Fernandus is no friend of mine, Tom." The commissaris frowned too. "I met him here because I won't invite him to my home."

"I see," the waiter said. "Anything else, sir? Piece of apple pie on the house?"

"Why not?" the commissaris asked. "Shouldn't, really." He patted his stomach. "My wife'll have my scalp."

The waiter brought the apple pie.

Fernandus, in an impeccable dark suit and a red silk tie, watched the commissaris eat. "Still hobnobbing with the lower classes, eh? Amazing how habits stick. You used to do that when we were students. Such an unnecessary act, they despise us anyway. Jealousy is a fact of life. What do you think that waiter thinks when he bicycles home and you splash him with mud from your steel-belted radials whizzing under your luxury car? He'd like nothing better than to hang you from the nearest lamppost."

"I like waiters," the commissaris said. "Wouldn't mind being one myself. The profession has possibilities, I think. I read an interesting novel once in which Christ was a waiter, in a railway station restaurant. He changed water into any wine the customer preferred."

"You knocked some of my waiters over, I hear," Fernandus said. "Did that give you pleasure too? Another petty performance. Why go to so much trouble to dent my show? That's all you did." He held his finger close to his thumb again. "Just a little dent, easily repaired."

"It wasn't a lot of trouble at all," the commissaris said. "Easy. Anyone can raid you. You have no defense."

Fernandus waved his glass at the waiter. "No defense? Remember Newton? Every action produces a reaction? I could have popped you this afternoon, or Katrien, or any of those so-called witnesses you're sheltering in your ruin."

"Yes?" the waiter asked.

"Another, please."

"The bar is closed," the waiter said, turning away.

"Bring him a glass of water," the commissaris said. "Poor man is sweating." He ate his last crumbs. "Excellent apple pie, Tom. Your wife made this, I'll bet."

"Yes, sir, she's in the kitchen. Still comes in most days."

"Good," the commissaris said. "Good. Now . . ." He swallowed. ". . . now, Willem, you wouldn't do that. You can't shoot up the home of a chief of detectives, even if I'm not functioning on an official level just now. You could arrange an accident, as you did with Grijpstra and de Gier, but accidents don't fly from the barrel of a rifle. That little incident this afternoon I'll accept as a sick joke. Don't do that again. It upset Katrien."

" 'It upset Katrien,' " Willem said, mimicking the commissaris's high voice. "Do I care about Katrien? I love to play pranks on Katrien. What did she do? Cry? Beg you to give in?"

"No," the commissaris said. "So let's have it, Willem."

"Lay off," Willem said. "I'm tired of this game, you're like a gadfly buzzing about. Buzz off."

The commissaris's eyes twinkled. "What if I do?"

"I talked to your chief," Fernandus said. "He's prepared to reinstate you, not in Homicide, but in something else. I forget what he said now—internal reorganization, I believe. You can keep your rank. Just a few more years and you'll retire anyway."

"And the investigation of Commissaris Voort?"

Fernandus drank his water. "That'll be terminated, of course. Voort came up with a few items that might bother you a bit, but we'll forget about that too."

"We?" the commissaris asked. "You and the Queen?"

"I'm a member of the ruling party," Fernandus said. "I preside over several committees. I whisper into the mayor's ear."

The commissaris brought out a folded handkerchief and shook it out. He carefully blew his nose. "You know what Voort found? Voort found absolutely nothing. He's going back to The Hague. I've produced a lot of nothing during my career, I have no wealth and no important connections. I collect nothing. I'm transparent, you can look right through me. I fade away. Prod me and you stick your finger in thin air. Voort overreached himself constantly. That whole investigation was a mere tumble through clouds. How can he get me if there's nothing there?"

"So now we boast?" Fernandus asked. "Are we starting up our old argument about negativity again? The infinite enters the finite and ultimately there's nothing there and in nothingness everything exists? Wasn't that David Hume? You kept reading those passages to me. But you forgot his conclusions." Fernandus raised a finger. "David Hume, renowned eighteenth-century philosopher who started out as a lawyer and should never have slithered into the unanswerable questions. What did our brilliant thinker come up with in the end?" Fernandus's fist thumped the table. "That he'd rather play backgammon any day than waste any more time on his undeniable conclusion that this creation is empty. He preferred a good time to a logical analysis pointing to the senselessness of life. I quite agree. I'm a better follower of Hume than you are. I provide good times."

"You don't have a good time yourself," the commissaris said. "I refuse to believe it. You repress your true nature. It must burp up all the time. Do you see a psychiatrist at all?"

Fernandus stared, biting his finger.

"See?" the commissaris asked. "What's your complaint? Can't sleep? Short of breath? Feel like you're suffocating at times? You're not really a devil, Willem, you're a good man hiding behind a demonic mask."

"Have you seen your secretary lately?" Fernandus asked.

The commissaris shook his head. "I don't go to the office."

"I see her."

"Good for you."

"Maybe I'll do away with her," Fernandus said. "I do kill people, you know."

"Right," the commissaris said. "My offer still stands. I'm about to grab you, Willem. I may have boasted a little when I spoke to you earlier, but now that I'm in pursuit, I'm surprised how easy it all is. Criminals are always careless. There are so many holes around you that I'm surprised you're still around. Do away with the Society and the Banque du Crédit—I mean total liquidation, with your share of the funds transferred to some needy foreign organization—and confess to some misdeed that will get you into jail for three years. If you do that, I don't go any further. I won't say this again. Refuse and you'll be destroyed. Ruthlessly, I'm afraid. There's no way I can protect you if you won't surrender now."

A spasm, starting at the corners of his mouth, made Fernandus's cheeks tremble. His hands shook. "Tom?" the commissaris called. "Could you bring another glass of water, please?"

Fernandus drank the water. The glass rattled against his teeth.

"Feel better now?" the commissaris asked. "Oh, by the way, I brought you something." He looked through his wallet. "Hope I didn't leave it home . . . no, here it is, you can keep it."

Fernandus pushed the piece of paper away. His hand still shook. "I'll tell you what it is," the commissaris said. "Remember the money that was taken from your club? This is proof that all that cash—a bit more, actually, I included the winnings of my men; after all, we did have a pleasant time at your establishment— now then, this document proves that all the money was transferred to a fund in Calcutta, run by a nun. I hope that organization is honest; we never know, of course, but Katrien thinks it is. The nun, apparently, is concerned with the poor, starving in the streets of her city. She provides housing, food, medical care, and spiritual comfort. I don't know about spiritual comfort, not being religious myself, but I don't think your donation can hurt."

"Listen," Fernandus said, "listen . . ."

"No," the commissaris said. "Your Society was set up to provide help abroad. Now don't bother me any further, Willem. I don't enjoy your company in your present state, and don't blame me if the process of destroying you will be painful to you." He got up. The waiter opened the door. " 'Bye, Tom," the commissaris said, handing him money. "Thank your wife for the pie."

⫴⫴ 25 ⫴⫴

"Jan?" the commissaris's wife whispered. "Jan? Jan?"

He grunted.

"Turn over. You're squeaking. You're having a bad dream."

He turned over. The dream continued. The commissaris sat on Miss Antoinette's lap, or Miss Bakker's lap, they were both the same woman. The woman kissed him and her finger tickled his stomach. "Poor little Jannie," the woman said. She was very beautiful and he reached out to touch her full standing breasts. It was very hot in kindergarten, nobody wore any clothes. "Poor little Jannie," the woman whispered. "Never mind, dear. Nasty Willem is to blame, he told you that I said you could watch the mice, didn't he? And then he told me that you were watching the mice without permission. I'm sorry, I know it now. It was all Willem's fault."

The mice had come out of the terrarium and were dancing around the schoolroom, wearing pointed paper hats. One had Chief Inspector Halba's overbite and another wore a blazer and slacks, like Commissaris Voort. A chief constable mouse tried to climb the woman's leg but she managed to kick it off. Little Willem Fernandus was being whipped in a corner, by Adjutant Grijpstra, who impassively made his leather thong swoosh. De Gier looked out of a window. His eyes twitched every time the whip struck Willem's little pink bottom.

A bell rang and the dream began to shred but the commissaris was still holding on to the woman's breast, which had turned green and very soft, a pasty mass that began to pour over his body and was getting into his mouth. "Lobster feces," a voice boomed. "Please don't consume this substance. We'll speak to the cook."

"Jan? Jan?"

"Yes," the commissaris said.

"Telephone. It's been ringing for a while. Are you going down?"

The telephone had stopped by the time the commissaris got to it, but started up again when he was halfway up the stairs. His leg hurt and he dragged it down the steps once more. "Yes?"

"Sir? De Gier. Could you come over to Wilhelmina Hospital? I can't pick you up. Your car is being dusted for fingerprints right now."

"Anyone hurt?"

"Two," de Gier said. "Heul and Celine. Halba couldn't be reached, but Chief Inspector Rood is here. He'll send over a patrol car."

"I see," the commissaris said. "I see. But I have Carl and Mrs. Jongs here, and Katrien of course."

"I have phoned Grijpstra, sir, he's on his way to you. You want Cardozo too?"

"Yes," the commissaris said. "It'll make Katrien feel better. All right, Rinus, I'll get dressed."

A half hour later the commissaris walked over to the hospital's reception desk and was guided to a room by a young nurse. De Gier opened the door. "Celine just died, sir. Heul's in a deep coma. He won't make it, the doctor says."

"Let's see him."

The thin body on a table gurgled and snored. A young man in a white coat watched the patient. "Heavy overdose, I've seen a lot of them now. The needle was still in his arm. Heroin, I'm sure, but the laboratory will confirm that tomorrow. We're short of staff tonight."

"An addict?" the commissaris asked.

The doctor shook his head. "Not of heroin. I checked his nose and I would say the patient has used a lot of cocaine, but there are no marks on the arms or anywhere else on the body. May have been his first try."

"Where did you find him?" the commissaris asked de Gier.

"In your car, sir, parked in front of my apartment building. About an hour ago. The door lock was broken. Heul was slumped over the wheel."

The commissaris looked at his watch. "Where were you going at three o'clock in the morning?"

"I had a call, sir. The police found Celine in the street, next to a crushed bicycle. She was still alive and mentioned my name. A witness saw her being run down by a black car."

"Mrs. Guldemeester was on her way to you?"

"So it seems." De Gier swayed. "Whoa," the doctor said. "Sit down." He slapped de Gier's face lightly. "Hold it now." The commissaris shook de Gier by the shoulders. "Hello?"

"Yes," de Gier said. "Sorry. I'm here. Rather a lot of blood. Her chest is caved in. According to the witness the car hit her twice. The second time it reversed."

"A lot of internal damage," the doctor said. "Horrible, blood coming from the mouth. I don't understand this very well. What was the lady doing on a bicycle at that time of the night? She was very well dressed. Drunk perhaps? I did smell alcohol."

"I'd like to see her," the commissaris said.

Heul's labored breath was slowing down as de Gier and the commissaris left the room. "Wait here," the commissaris said in the corridor.

Celine's body was in the room next door. The commissaris observed the corpse in silence. The head was twisted to the side, and an arm dangled off the stretcher. Celine's mouth hung open and her eyes stared past the commissaris. "Yes," the commissaris said. "Sure. Could be my fault, you know." He touched his chest and bowed. "Have a good journey."

"Funny," he said when he joined de Gier in the corridor again. "I always think that they've gone somewhere when I see dead bodies. I feel pleased for them. They're out of this. Life's rather a mess, very unreal. All this pain here can't be seriously meant. Whatever comes later must be a lot better. Surely it'll have to be made up to us. A bad break here, and then a holiday somewhere. There's no proof of that, of course."

"Sir?" de Gier said, holding on to a wall.

"Here, hold my arm." The commissaris and de Gier shuffled along. Farther along the corridor, a middle-aged man in a striped suit that bulged around his paunch was making notes on a pad. "Rood?" the commissaris said.

The man looked up. "Hello, sir. Sorry to disturb you about this, but both bodies are known to you, I hear. What do you think happened?"

"A continuation of the IJsbreker case," the commissaris said.

"Which was closed?"

"Yes, Chief Inspector, and reopened by me. Male subject, Heul, was going to implicate others and must have been liquidated before we delved too deeply, and I think the same goes for the lady. A shot was fired into my garden this afternoon intended to hit my pet turtle. We have reason to believe that Celine Gulde-meester was forced somehow to accompany the rifle-man. Perhaps she wanted to tell us about that. She liked de Gier."

"And she was on her way to the sergeant's apart-ment," Rood said. "There is no simpler explanation? An affair? A jealous lover?"

"The suspect I have in mind could be gay," the commissaris said.

Rood pocketed his note pad. "I'd better stay out of this, then. You're in charge of this case."

"I'm off duty," the commissaris said.

Rood shook his head. "You're not, you know. Hav-en't you been told? State Detection could find nothing on you. Me and some others have been exercising pressure on our dimwit chief. You're back in business, sir." He tapped de Gier on the shoulder. "You too, Sergeant. You're feeling okay? Bit pale around the nose? Too much blood for your taste?"

"Just tired," de Gier said. "Forgot to eat tonight. A bit busy."

"I shouldn't be here at all," Chief Inspector Rood said. "Halba's job, really. Seems he doesn't sleep at home much. That's another rotten apple, sir; isn't he due for a transfer? The farther the better."

"I'll be going home," the commissaris said. "Why don't you take care of the report? Would you mind doing that?"

"Overdose and accident, sir?"

"Let's leave it at that for now. No use alerting the papers. Keep it quiet, Chief Inspector."

"Sir," Rood said. "Your car is in the yard."

‖‖ 26 ‖‖

Turtle, hanging from the commissaris's hand, had come out as far as he could, rowing his legs and extending his scaly neck. He peered up at the commissaris's face with hooded eyes. "They thought they got you yesterday, Turtle," the commissaris said. "A good mistake. You think it's my turn now to make a good mistake?" His wife put down his coffee on the little table on the porch. She scratched Turtle's head. "Silly thing. You think he thinks, Jan? Carl's version looks very thoughtful. He's patched him up. Carl's making Noah's Ark now, using the plaster animals from your toy zoo. I said it was all right."

The commissaris stirred his coffee. "My zoo. I used to play a lot with that, trying to figure out what animals could be put together in one cage. I was always short of cages. The lion and the lamb, but that doesn't work so well. Another biblical tale that I could never accept."

"Is that why the lamb is red? You dipped it in paint?"

"And broke off its head," the commissaris said, "but I glued it back on later. Noah's Ark? Very applicable, don't you think? We do have a strangely assorted collection of creatures in the house now."

"You mean Carl and Mrs. Jongs? They get on very well. Mrs. Jongs is cleaning out the hall closet today, throwing out a lot. That's where Carl got the scraps he's using for the ark."

"We'll be adding to our collection today," the commissaris said. "Grijpstra is picking up Miss Antoinette. I think we'll have to place her in safekeeping too. Fernandus was grumbling about her yesterday. I didn't like that."

"Your mistress?" his wife asked. "You want your mistress to stay with us?"

"She isn't my mistress." The commissaris held his wife's hand. "She's my spy, risking her life for our good cause."

"No, Jan, I won't have her here. Such a smart-looking woman, she always makes me feel old and ugly. Don't do this to me."

"Yes," the commissaris said. "I have to. It won't be for long. You're eternally young, Katrien. I can see that clearly. Age has brought out your grace. Just the way you move . . ." He stroked her arm. "And your hair is so beautiful now, pure silver. Young women aren't quite formed, mentally I mean. They make desirable impressions, but the attraction doesn't last."

"That's what I think when I watch you," his wife said. "I like you better than in the early years. Your presence keeps improving."

"Same with all of us," the commissaris said. "If we evolve properly, of course. Fernandus looks much worse now." He looked up. "I thought he was going to have some heart trouble yesterday."

"So how long is Miss Antoinette going to stay, Jan? I may tear her to ribbons. We're incompatible animals if you lock us together."

The commissaris thought.

"Well?"

"You know what you could do?" the commissaris asked. "Link her to Carl. Give her the other room in the attic, they'll be next door. They should be good for each other. Miss Antoinette is always complaining about loneliness, and Carl could use some affection, I think. It may interest her to see what Carl does with his life. They would make a great pair."

"You amuse me," his wife said. "Why don't you grow your hair and wear a long dress and I'll play Beethoven's Fifth on the record player while you arrange the fate of little people?"

"I'll be divine?" the commissaris asked. "What's wrong with arranging a liaison between Miss Antoinette and Carl? I tell you, it'll work out well. Miss Antoinette's lights are lit when she's with handicapped men. I'm a bit of an invalid, too, and Fernandus suffers from evil. Carl is young and handsome, in spite of his affliction."

"Yes, he is," his wife said. "I find him attractive."

"You can't have Carl," the commissaris said. "You have me. Give Carl away. Has Cardozo gone home?"

"Cardozo is very restless." She caressed his shoulders. "A young man picked him up here this afternoon. I think Cardozo called him Izzy. What's Cardozo working on?"

"On our case, I hope." The commissaris stood up. "He asked me if he could bring his computer up here, and I told him yes; I hope you don't mind. He'll also bring a friend, maybe the fellow you mentioned just now. They're going to arrange a demonstration."

She turned to the door. "Not at all, dear. I suppose they'll all stay to dinner. Have you invited Grijpstra and de Gier too? And those two rough young men who swear a lot? And your State Detection friends, the painted horrors?"

"They'll all come later," the commissaris said. "We're having a meeting tonight. Tomorrow we move in for the kill."

"On Sunday?"

"The day of the Lord of Vengeance," the commissaris said.

She looked away.

"What's wrong?"

"Never mind," she said. "Mrs. Jongs and I will bake more cakes."

"What's wrong? Do tell me."

"I don't like it," his wife said, "when you talk about revenge. It hurts me. You should be above all that. You just want to destroy Willem Fernandus, you were talking about him in your sleep again. I've never seen you so upset, thrashing about, kicking me, snoring, mumbling."

"It's got to be done, dear."

"Why?"

"It's my job," the commissaris said triumphantly.

"But you're relieved, Jan, you don't have a job."

"I got it back last night."

"Oh, dear," said the commissaris's wife. "Aren't you clever? I do wish you'd take the trouble to find out what you're really trying to do." She leaned over to kiss him. "You busy little bumbler."

||||| 27 |||||

It was a regular Dutch summer, with heavy rain and fog, but that Sunday afternoon the sun broke out. The commissaris sat quietly in the passenger seat of his Citroën, steered by de Gier on its way to the Vinker Lakes. They had avoided the speedway and were following a country road paved with red bricks and lined on one side with tall poplars, protecting fertile fields. Brown sails topped the dike, moving slowly, cracking when the invisible flat-bottomed vessels that carried them went through the wind. Swans and white ducks moved about in the tall grass, and a cormorant flapped by, struggling with a large eel that had wound itself around its beak.

"So pleasant," the commissaris said. "I wonder why we can't just enjoy ourselves on this planet of plenty, but we keep banging each other in the head. We've raised the defense budget again, I hear."

"We're warriors, too," de Gier said. "We'd get bored if we didn't live in peril."

"Oh, come now, Sergeant, you faint when you see blood."

"Makes it more fun," de Gier said. "The controversy within. Maybe that's why I joined the police, to overcome my fear. I'm going to get him, sir."

"The baron?" the commissaris asked.

De Gier stared straight ahead. "I know you won't let me, but I'll arrange the showdown discreetly. I feel better about it now that he has murdered Celine."

"You can't be sure, Sergeant. All we know is that the killer drove a black car. Does de la Faille drive a black vehicle, perhaps?"

"A black Porsche, sir, Cardozo checked on the computer."

"Yes," the commissaris said. "Very clever, these technical wonders. But if Cardozo and that expert friend of his can break into the police system through a computer that's hooked up to my phone, then anyone else has access to our files too. That's rather frightening, I think."

De Gier cursed as an open sports car overtook the Citroën, blowing its horn. "Ryder, sir. Did you see him? That fat blob? In a Ferrari?"

The commissaris nodded. "Not a sympathetic man, but speeding toward his death. We'll have to prevent that killing, Rinus. I thought about it. It would be tempting to let young Fernandus press his button to strengthen our charge, but there's been enough murder for now. Ridiculous. We've had six corpses so far, all because of a weakening in the Murder Brigade."

"Suicide of the Society," de Gier said. "Who cares? IJsbreker and Heul were criminals, and the junkies wouldn't have lived long anyway. I'm only concerned about Celine. Ryder can go too."

"A capitalist?" the commissaris asked. "Capitalists are still legal and should enjoy our protection."

"Woosh," de Gier said, lifting his hand from the wheel. "There goes Ryder. I grab young Fernandus."

"You grab him *before* the woosh," the commissaris said. "That's an order, Sergeant. Huip could be anywhere when he sets off the bomb, that's my worry, anywhere within sight of the lake. We only have six men out there.''

"Six fishermen," de Gier said. "Grijpstra was all upset about his fishing gear. I saw them getting into the Camaro and the Corvette, with Grijpstra's complete fishing rod collection. You really won over those State detectives; they gave up their free weekend to help us out again. Ketchup and Karate were all gung-ho, of course.''

"Unbridled energy," the commissaris said. "Only useful if we can contain that youthful zest. I'm surprised that you're not losing your adventurous streak, you should be maturing by now. Obtain some distance. I urge you to follow my orders closely.''

De Gier grinned. "I'm still suspended, sir. I haven't received word that I'm on the force again.''

"I give you the word.''

"No, sir, you can't. You haven't been officially reinstated either. The chief inspector's word doesn't count, he's lower in rank than you.''

"Next turn," the commissaris said. "That'll be the Society's motel. I don't want you to be seen. We could hide in the bushes, perhaps, and find some vantage point that'll look out on the motel's marina and the lake, and as close as possible to Huip Fernandus.''

The motel was surrounded by ornamental gardens. De Gier parked next to Ryder's Ferrari. "I'll be off,'' the commissaris said. "Meet you behind the rhododendrons over there.''

De Gier looked in the Ferrari and saw a jacket on the seat. He picked it up. Something rattled. He removed a bunch of keys and a wallet from the jacket's pockets. The uniformed driver of an old-model Rolls-Royce parked farther along was watching. "Friend of mine, Ronnie Ryder,'' de Gier told the driver. "Shouldn't leave his keys and valuables in the car. I'll give them to him. Is this Mr. Fernandus's car?''

"No," the driver said. "All mine. Fernandus has been renting my Rolls by the day."

"I thought Fernandus drove a Daimler."

"Then he should be driving his Daimler," the chauffeur said. "I'm getting mighty tired of Fernandus. Here, sir, my card. I'm available. Pass on the news to your wealthy friends."

"You don't like Willem Fernandus?" de Gier asked pleasantly.

"Can't stand him, sir. He's with his son today, and the son is even worse. I need a change."

"Where were you?" the commissaris asked when de Gier showed up.

"Just checking, sir. Fernandus came with his son today, I thought you'd like to know."

They walked past tennis courts where fresh young ladies in short skirts missed balls, and past a lawn where old men in checkered pants drove about in golf carts. The commissaris muttered.

"Don't care for ball sports, sir?"

"Balls have always infuriated me," the commissaris said, "probably because I could never catch them, except on my head. Here, this might be a good spot." He adjusted his binoculars, aiming them at the motel's terrace. "That's Fernandus, sitting with Ryder and an unknown subject. Here, take these, you have better eyes."

De Gier looked through the glasses. "The young fatso is Huip. I can see his pimples. Yagh, must weigh two hundred pounds and he's as short as his father."

"Can't spot the baron," the commissaris said.

"On the far end, sir, sitting by himself."

"Right." The commissaris grunted. "He does look like a darker version of you. Wavy hair, hooked nose, same posture. You even dress alike."

"The black knight," de Gier said. "Waiting for his rightful fate."

"Are we close enough, you think?" the commissaris asked. "As soon as Ryder takes off in the boat, you'll have to make a dash for the terrace and grab Huip. Get the infernal gadget that'll set off the bomb away from him as soon as you can. Huip won't blow up the boat if it's too close to the terrace. Get hold of his arms and twist them up."

De Gier was looking at the baron.

"Rinus?"

"Yes, sir."

Fernandus and son were chatting and drinking. Ryder ate. A waiter brought a bottle of wine.

"Taking their time," the commissaris said. "I hope we got this thing right and that Heul wasn't trying to impress us."

"Heul is dead," de Gier said. "He got killed because he was seen being arrested by Grijpstra and Cardozo. They didn't want to take any chances when Heul popped up again. They leaned on him and he betrayed his betrayal."

"Possibly," the commissaris said. "In which case they won't try to murder Ryder here." He slapped at a mosquito. "So we're wasting our time. Katrien put a thermos of coffee in the car."

"There's Grijpstra," de Gier said, "on the other shore. He just caught a fish. Man in the cap. And the little fellow farther along must be Cardozo, he's wearing red suspenders."

"You're sure?"

"Not sure," de Gier said. "They're partly hidden in the cattails. Should be them."

"There's still a lot that could go wrong," the commissaris said. "Perhaps I should have taken more precautions. Ah, Ryder is getting up. Look at that speedboat's engine, must be over a hundred horsepower. Huip is getting in."

De Gier whistled softly.

"No," the commissaris said. "That can't be correct. Huip should stay ashore. Now Ryder is getting in too. Are they going out together?''

De Gier dropped his binoculars. "We were misinformed. Huip won't blow himself up. I don't get what they're at."

"Oh, well," the commissaris sighed. "I had to fail somewhere. Too many factors in the equation again. I did try to fit them all in, but I have missed a few here and there. We'll have to rethink our attack most thoroughly next time. Poor Katrien."

De Gier peered through his binoculars. "They're taking off. Your wife, sir?"

"All my guests," the commissaris said. "Katrien wasn't too pleased with Miss Antoinette's arrival this morning. I can't expect her to keep running a hotel. Look, Sergeant, that boat is still increasing speed. Not a good idea. The wake will disturb the canoe over there. Not too thoughtful."

"Bastards," de Gier said. "There are little kids in the canoe. They're turning now, they think the lake belongs to them."

"Don't like it," the commissaris said. "Don't like this at all." He made an impatient gesture. "Surely not."

"What?"

"I was thinking," the commissaris said. "Like in Paris then . . . but Willem wouldn't . . . it doesn't really prove anything . . . although . . .''

The explosion wasn't too loud, but a huge orange ball of fire formed immediately, ballooning up, shot through with burning remnants of the exploding boat. Two bright flaming objects were suspended well above the water where the boat was last seen. De Gier jumped and ran to the terrace. The commissaris limped after him. Startled guests had pushed over their tables and thronged the edge of the dock. Men jumped in boats and started up engines. Waves set up by Ryder's boat lapped against the marina's posts and planks. De Gier ran to the end of the terrace where he had seen de la Faille, but the baron was gone. Fernandus still sat at his table, sipping wine. The commissaris fell into the chair where Ryder had sat. "You . . . you . . ."

"Yes?" Fernandus asked. "Do say it, old chap. You what?"

"Your own son?" the commissaris asked. "But why?"

"Why not?" Fernandus asked.

"But . . ."

Fernandus looked at the lake, where the ball of fire was dying down. "But nothing. You're right, Jan, there's nothing there. You and I are part of it, figments of creative imagination. We can do as we like, and whatever gets in our way and is removable is removed."

"I'll remove you." The commissaris pointed a trembling finger. "You have to go."

"But I'm not removable," Fernandus said. "Neither are you, unfortunately. It wouldn't suit us to do away with one another. You're a powerful official on one side of the line, and I'm an inventive entrepreneur on the other side of whatever divides us. Why don't we shake hands and have a grand old age together?"

"No," the commissaris said. "You'll be destroyed."

"Pity," Fernandus said. "Stupid to the end. You're a coward, Jan, you never dare to think things out."

The baron was at the bar inside the motel. "Hi," de Gier said, taking the next stool. "Why did you blow them up?"

"Oh, hello," de la Faille said. "How did you enjoy the fireworks, Rinus? Do call me Bart."

"Those kids in the canoe might have drowned."

"We do have to take risks," the baron said. "Grand show, wasn't it? Never cared much for either of the victims, although I could put up with Ronnie at times, but a useful purpose will be achieved by Ryder's demise. The other liquidation may be more philosophical, I understand. Uncle is a great man for thinking solutions through. Can't follow him, always. A drink?"

"Bit short of time," de Gier said. "We'll have that duel soon. Okay?"

"No," the baron said.

"Yes," de Gier said. "Soon. To the death. Bare hands."

"I thought I could choose my weapon?"

"Not anymore," de Gier said. " 'Bye. You'll hear from me."

The commissaris read the note left under the windshield wiper of his car. *See you in town, sir. Key's in the ignition.* He looked to the side. Ryder's Ferrari was missing.

He got into the Citroën and drove slowly out of the parking lot. Halfway home, he stopped and limped to the bushes at the side of the road. When he came back he was wiping his lips, holding his other hand on his stomach.

"Jan?" his wife asked when he stumbled into her arms. "Something bad?" She sniffed at his face. "Were you unwell?"

"Willem killed his own son," the commissaris whispered.

She embraced him. "Do you want to lie down? Grijpstra and Cardozo are in your room. Shall I tell them to go away?"

"Tell them to wait," the commissaris said. "I need a bath, won't be long."

⫻⫻⫻ 28 ⫻⫻⫻

THE COMMISSARIS, IN ROBE AND SLIPPERS, GUIDED by his wife, looked old and frail when he shuffled into his study. "Yes," he said softly when he looked around. "Hello, Adjutant, hello, Cardozo. I'm sorry."

Grijpstra sat quietly. Cardozo leaned against a bookcase. "I didn't foresee what happened on the lake," the commissaris said. "It seems logical now. Willem can be quite gruesome. One doesn't like to imagine that sort of thing."

"The others are downstairs," his wife said.

The commissaris turned toward her with an effort. "De Gier came too?"

"Yes."

The commissaris felt his chin. "A showdown, is it? He's calling my bluff."

"De Gier?" his wife asked.

"Yes, dear. But mostly Willem Fernandus, of course. One would like to think that a mishap occurred, that Huip set off the charge by accident, but it didn't go that way. Willem is destroying evidence." He felt for his cigars in the pocket of his robe. "Live evidence. Willem is eliminating his human instruments. First we saw the destruction of the junkies, then Heul's body was dumped in my car. Heul wasn't trustworthy. Willem knew that he would break if we squeezed him too hard. Huip was the next link. We would break Huip too, and Huip would blame his father. There was no love between Willem and his only child. Perhaps Willem wouldn't grant Huip the right of succession; that could be another motive."

"Oh, surely, Jan," his wife said. "It must have been an accident. Don't you think so, Adjutant?"

It became quiet in the room. Voices became audible downstairs.

"Grijpstra?" the commissaris asked.

"No, ma'am," Grijpstra said. "There was no accident. Fernandus knew we were all around him, watching what he'd do next. He pretended to call off Ryder's murder and took Huip's gadget. Then he gave it to the baron. Willem Fernandus trusts only the baron. De la Faille shot IJsbreker and tried to do away with your husband's turtle. He's Fernandus's right hand, like de Gier is your husband's right hand. The others don't matter, they're more like instruments, it seems."

The commissaris opened his tin of cigars and stared at the contents. "I don't like that, Adjutant. We've been working as a group. Your simile is too simple and"—he selected a cigar—"a little nasty perhaps?"

Grijpstra's eyelids fluttered.

"Sir?" Cardozo asked. "I was watching from the shore. I spotted the baron. He left the terrace immediately after the explosion and de Gier went after him. Maybe the sergeant found the detonator in the baron's pocket and we can prove something after all."

The commissaris lit his cigar. "No. This assassination was well planned. De la Faille must have made sure that his device got lost at once. He may have dropped it into the lake. It was probably quite small."

"Now what?" Grijpstra asked. "What do we have

left? Carl could testify that Heul picked up the artworks the junkies took from IJsbreker's house, but
one witness is not enough for us to move ahead. Celine, who saw de la Faille fire a shot at your turtle, is
dead. Huip Fernandus is dead. Nothing now points at
Fernandus, except the baron. Do we wait for Fernandus to kill the baron too?"

The commissaris shook his head. "He won't. De la
Faille is too valuable to Willem, as you pointed out
just now in your lopsided manner. As IJsbreker's re-
placement, de la Faille will run the Society and the
Banque du Crédit; Willem doesn't want to be in the
midst of things."

The commissaris's wife smiled. "But you're so
clever, Jan. You'll come up with something devilish
again, set them against each other somehow."

"Devilish?" the commissaris said. "Katrien . . .
I'm not devilish. I protect the peace . . ."

"Yes, dear, of course." She touched his arm. "I'm
sorry."

"Devilish," the commissaris muttered. "Besides,
there's no time. I don't know what to do."

"Sir?" Cardozo asked.

"No idea," the commissaris said. "Willem won. I
can't go on with this unless I do away with morality
again. All these people in the house." He held his
wife's hand. "Poor thing. Inflicting this inconvenience
on you."

"You're just impatient, dear." She held his hand.
"I don't mind."

"Miss Antoinette too," the commissaris said.
"Maybe I can lodge her with my sister. Where is Miss
Antoinette, anyway?"

"On the porch, dear, helping Carl with that cute ark
he's building. They've smashed some bottles and are
building the sides of glass, so that the animals inside
can be visible."

The commissaris gestured with his cigar. "On the

porch? Perhaps de la Faille is out there with his rifle again. I can't have this, Katrien.''

"Sir?"

"Yes, Cardozo, is your computer connected now?"

"Izzy Sanders is here too," Cardozo said. "Whenever you like, perhaps we can do more than you expected."

"Who *is* this Izzy?" the commissaris's wife asked. "Isn't anybody going to tell me anything?"

The commissaris squeezed her hand. "Izzy used to work for the Banque du Crédit. Cardozo has been very clever indeed." He looked at Cardozo. "I forgot to ask, who paid for all that gear?"

"I did, sir. It wasn't much. It's some phased-out model that Izzy knew about."

"You'd better give me the bill." The commissaris turned back to his wife. "With Izzy's knowledge, we have access to the bank's financial records now. I was hesitant to go that far, but we did have the raid, we may as well go all the way."

"Some sort of spying, dear?"

"More than that, I'm afraid. Well, shall we go downstairs?"

Karate, Ketchup, Sergeant Biersma, and Constable Ramsau got up when the commissaris came into the living room. De Gier stood near the window. A computer was set up on the table. Izzy Sanders sat behind the machine. "Sorry about this afternoon," the commissaris said.

His audience mumbled. "You couldn't have foreseen that," Sergeant Biersma said. "Nobody in his right mind kills his own son."

"Fernandus hasn't been in his right mind as long as I've known him." The commissaris smiled grimly. "If only I had thought a little deeper. We could have rushed the terrace the minute I saw Huip get into that boat."

The mumbling started up again and died down.

"But I didn't think," the commissaris said. "Now we're faced with another infernal gadget. On our side, this time. Izzy? Can you show us?"

"Yes." Izzy worked on the computer's keyboard. The telephone receiver next to the screen crackled. "What's that?" the commissaris's wife asked.

"I'm making a connection with the bank," Izzy said. "Now I'll punch in the codes. Here we are."

The computer's screen lit up. Letters formed. "It wants a command," Izzy said. "Okay." He touched more keys. "I want to see Fernandus's private account. I have to tell it who's asking. Here we go, I'm pretending I'm Fernandus now, these letters represent his ID."

Figures appeared.

"But that's nothing," Sergeant Biersma said. "A few thousand guilders."

"So Fernandus doesn't keep his money in his own account," the commissaris said. "Let's see what the Society owns, Izzy."

More figures appeared.

"That's better," Grijpstra said, "but it still isn't very much. That's probably the takings of a few days. Where does the real money go?"

"We figured that out yesterday," Cardozo said. "We had to go through just about every account in the bank."

Izzy held up a notebook. "I have all the codes. The biggest account is in the name of Ernst Fernandus— about twenty million, plus securities, stocks, bonds, what have you. Here you are."

The screen showed figures and lists.

"But that's a fortune," the commissaris's wife said. "Ernst is a poet who floats around the world in an ancient sailboat. Ernst has no millions."

"Probably not," the commissaris said. "Izzy tells me that Willem can manipulate his brother Ernst's account."

"Maybe Ernst won a lottery, Jan?"

The general mumble rose up again. "Unlikely." "There aren't prizes that big." "A poet!"

"Can we do it now, sir?" Cardozo asked. "We can have the shares sold and all the cash transferred."

"You can do that with the computer?" Grijpstra asked.

Izzy looked up. "Easy. This works like a Teletype too. I can connect with other banks, brokers, anything you like."

"Theft," the commissaris's wife said. "Jan, you can't do that."

He took her hand again. "We did have the raid there, dear, same thing. You didn't mind the raid."

She shook her hand free. "But this is so *sneaky*."

Grijpstra grinned.

"Anything funny, Adjutant?" the commissaris snapped.

Grijpstra put up his hands.

"You mean I am sneaky?"

"Don't get cross with Grijpstra now, dear." The commissaris's wife held his shoulder. "You can be very sneaky at times. Taking money from poor Ernst."

The commissaris put his hand on the computer. "Hold off a minute now. Where could Ernst be? Sailing the seven seas? Who would know?"

"Fleur."

He looked at his wife. "Willem's ex-wife?"

"Fleur," his wife said. "I met her a few months ago, in the street. We had tea together. She mentioned Ernst."

"Would she know where we can find him?"

"I could visit her. She lives close by."

⁗ 29 ⁗

"ERNST?" FLEUR FERNANDUS, NÉE DE LA FAILLE, a plump woman in her sixties, asked. She was dressed according to younger taste and heavily made up. Her bejeweled fingers reminded the commissaris's wife of fat garden worms, splattered with luminous paint. "Ach, Ernst."

The commissaris's wife, in an effort to be polite, complimented Fleur on the elegance of her apartment. "Yes," Fleur said. "Wasn't I lucky that I still had those shares of Willem's bank? Willem always badgered me to have them transferred into his name, but I didn't want to weaken my position. When we divorced, he had to buy me out. Ernst sold his shares much earlier, and was bamboozled royally, but I got a bundle." She shrugged. "Can't expect a business head on the shoulders of a poet."

"Poor Ernst," the commissaris's wife said.

"No money," Fleur said, "but so what? I would have paid him just to have him around." She breathed heavily. "Ernst is such a wonderful man, but of course I had to settle for his greedy brother . . ."

"Ernst is doing well?"

261

". . . and for his brother's retarded son," Fleur finished.

The commissaris's wife fidgeted with her handkerchief.

"Ernst . . ." Fleur clasped her hands together. "Do you know that he asked me to go sailing with him? A hundred years ago? Around the world? And I, like an idiot, refused. We could be living on Mauritius now, and I would have been a nature woman, eating coconuts off trees, splashing about in lagoons, listening to his rhymy wordage." She grinned at her guest. "I have no ear for the stuff, poetry passes me by completely, but I'm good at pretending. I'll bet Ernst's present woman doesn't give half a hoot for his poetry, either."

"Ernst has a woman?"

"Bah." Fleur offered a tray of bonbons. "Have one, they're expensive. Yes. Some native wench who works as a waitress. Ernst was here a month ago, actually looked me up. He sailed in from Mauritius to ask Willem for a loan to buy his girlie a restaurant. Didn't get a penny. Willem tried to interest him in smuggling drugs, but Ernst is too naïve for the real world. I bought him dinner a few times, and clothes so that he could take me out; he dresses rather sloppily."

The commissaris's wife's teeth broke through a thin coating of chocolate. She winced at the oversweet taste. "Not attractive?"

"*Very* attractive," Fleur said. "Sun-bleached jeans, big pectoral muscles, a tattered shirt, straw sandals, unkempt beard. The depth of the sea is in his eyes and he wears a golden earring. Katrien, Ernst is a dream. But I couldn't get him into one of my favorite restaurants looking like that."

"Fleur?"

"I tried to seduce him."

"Fleur?"

Fleur stroked the armrests of her chair. "With money, of course." She kneaded her thighs. "These won't work anymore. I would have liked to keep him here. I wonder if he noticed. Tried to get him to stay here with me, but he'd rather sleep in his boat. Crummy boat."

"Fleur?"

"Yes?"

"I'm sorry to have to tell you this," the commissaris's wife said, "but your son is dead."

"Huip?"

"You only have one son."

"Good," Fleur said. "The hateful monster. I could never stand him; he didn't even have his father's amusing side. Graspy little baby, hurt me a lot, and when he grew up it was even worse. How did he die? Got killed by his cronies? Huip never kept good company. You should have seen the human offal he dragged home from school."

"A boating accident," the commissaris's wife said. "Jan heard about it. I think he even saw it, on the Vinker Lakes earlier today."

"Good," Fleur said. "I always hated those damned lakes. That's where Willem enjoyed himself. Did Willem die too?"

"No, Fleur."

Fleur pushed a large bonbon into her mouth.

"Fleur?"

Fleur swallowed. "So Willem is still out there, making trouble? Why don't you send Jan after him? Jan could catch the miserable sod. Willem isn't all that clever, you know, he does have weak points."

"I think that Jan considers Willem a suspect in a murder case," the commissaris's wife said.

Fleur's eyes bulged. She sucked in her lips. "Hm. He does? Wasn't there something about Jan in the papers? An investigation of some sort? Did your husband turn out badly too?"

"No," the commissaris's wife said. "The other way around. Corrupt officials tried to get him out of the way, but that's all right now, Jan is working again."

"Shouldn't eat these," Fleur said, pushing the bonbons away a little. "Perhaps just one more. Jan should get at Willem's money. Do you know that Willem figures out every night just how much he is worth? To the penny? If it's less than the night before, he has a fit. He would pick up things and throw them."

"At you?"

"No, because I would throw them back." Fleur chewed. "Katrien, tell Jan he should get Willem fined somehow. For nonpayment of taxes—that shouldn't be too hard. Suck his money away, and Willem will be like a deflated scumbag. Jan might work on Willem's drug dealing too, he's been doing that from the day heroin came into the country. Willem was never too normal, but the drugs drove him crazy."

"Does he take drugs, too?"

"No," Fleur said. "It's like his womanizing. I think Willem likes to watch, doesn't get into fun stuff himself."

"Drugs aren't fun."

"No?" Fleur selected another bonbon. "I wonder. They're too expensive for me. They calm you down, I hear. I do get quite nervous."

"Well," said the commissaris's wife, rising and moving toward the door, "nice to see you again, I really love your apartment."

Fleur waddled to the door with her. "Come again."

IIII **30** IIII

Izzy Sanders switched the computer screen on. "Where do you want the money to go, sir?"

"Just a minute." The commissaris took out his note pad. "This is the number of an account. A welfare organization in Calcutta."

Sanders punched in the number. "All of it goes?"

"Yes." The commissaris peered at the screen. "Clean out the accounts of the Society, the bank itself, Willem and Ernst Fernandus, and Baron Bart de la Faille."

"Can I leave something in? It would look better. Zero accounts might draw early attention."

"Now how does this work?" Grijpstra asked. "It's Sunday today."

"I've delayed the commands." Izzy worked his keyboard. "The transactions will take place tomorrow afternoon. With all the bank's computerization, it could take a while before anyone catches on. No human eyes will see this happen."

"Until it's too late?"

"Right," Izzy said. "Shall I leave a few hundred guilders in each account, sir?"

"Fifty guilders will be enough," the commissaris

said. "The more devastating the cleanup, the better. Go ahead, friend. We do appreciate your help."

"There's no risk?" Cardozo asked.

"No." Sanders grinned. "The way I'm working this, it will seem as if the commands were given in the bank's administration, by order of the account holders themselves. I have all the codes."

"And the nun won't give the money back?" Karate asked.

"I'm a Catholic," Ketchup said. "I know nuns. Nuns never give anything back. Finders keepers."

"But she's such a holy nun," said the commissaris's wife.

Sergeant Biersma grunted. "The holier the better. The Lord is the holiest of all, and He never gives anything back, either."

"You know that?" the commissaris asked.

"Yes, sir, I was raised as a member of the Dutch Reformed Protestant Church. We know God at His grimmest."

The computer's keyboard clicked away. Luminous figures flashed on and off.

"There," Sanders said. "Done."

"Grand total?" the commissaris asked.

"Maybe thirty million, sir. I don't know what the shares and bonds will be worth tomorrow. Could be more, the stock market is turning bullish again."

Miss Antoinette's knuckles rapped against the glass door of the porch. Carl held up his ark. The commissaris's wife opened the door and the artwork was shown around. The toy animals inside had been glued together in copulating positions.

"I'll tahake them ouhout again," Carl said. "It's only a johoke."

"They're yours," the commissaris said.

"Then you keeheep the whole thing here, sir. My pleaheasure."

"Why, thank you, dear boy. It's a beautiful piece of

work." The commissaris set the construction on the mantel. "Drinks all around, Katrien?"

The commissaris's stock of liquor was soon depleted, together with all the food in the house, transformed into snacks by his wife and Mrs. Jongs. Ketchup and Karate giggled a lot, patting the computer. Sergeant Biersma and Constable Ramsau swore they would apply for transfers to the Amsterdam Murder Brigade. Grijpstra described his paintings to Miss Antoinette, stressing the importance of background colors. Mrs. Jongs discussed lizards with Carl. Izzy and Cardozo played a war game on the computer, a giveaway from the store that had supplied the equipment, scoring most by hitting ambulances and a platoon of medics. The commissaris found de Gier.

"Hiding?"

"Me?" de Gier asked. "No. Why? I'm just having a quiet drink. Congratulations, sir, you did pull this off well."

"Where's the Ferrari?" the commissaris asked.

De Gier thought. "Ferrari?"

"Ryder's Ferrari that wasn't there when I left the motel. You weren't there, either."

"Oh, *that* Ferrari," de Gier said.

"You won't tell me?"

"Sir," de Gier said. "You've just killed Fernandus."

"I have not."

"He's as good as dead," de Gier said. "He just doesn't know it yet. The baron is in the same position, but I demand the privilege of completing his situation."

"Are you two having a furious little chat?" the commissaris's wife asked. "Would you care for some sausage and mustard? What's the trouble, dear?"

"You tell her, Sergeant," the commissaris snapped.

"Thank you, ma'am." De Gier ate his sausage.

"I'm a white knight. I found my black knight. We will now have a duel."

"Childish," the commissaris said.

"In style," de Gier said. "Just for once I will do something in style. I'm still suspended. I'm flying around. I came down to help your husband out, and now that Cardozo has been good enough to take care of the case, I'll be tootling off and I won't come back until the victory is mine."

"Is he drunk?" the commissaris's wife asked. "Don't drive home, Sergeant. Take a cab." She tapped Mrs. Jongs on the shoulder. "Go and tell Adjutant Grijpstra about your lizards, dear, he wants to paint them. Miss Antoinette? I wonder if you'd do me a favor. Poor Carl is a bit unsteady on his legs; I'm afraid I poured him a rather stiff drink. Would you mind taking him home when the party is over?"

"Rinus," the commissaris said, "please."

De Gier refilled his glass. "Just once," he said dreamily. "Just once. I've heard a lot about it, I've read the exposés, I just want to know what it's like. Good guy kills bad guy."

The guests left, except Mrs. Jongs, who wanted to do the dishes. The commissaris and his wife walked about, picking up ashtrays and glasses. The commissaris's wife smiled; the commissaris frowned.

"Damn de Gier."

"You think he's serious, dear? You think Carl knows what to do with Miss Antoinette?"

"Yes," the commissaris said.

"He won't shy away?"

"Miss Antoinette can be very persistent."

She grabbed hold of him. "You see, it's true. I see it all now. In your office, probably, behind a locked door. Or did you take her to a hotel somewhere? Her apartment, maybe?"

The commissaris dropped a glass. "See what you made me do."

"Answer me, Jan."

"Katrien." He picked up the shards.

"What a fool I've been." She stamped her foot. "The wife is always the last to know. All those evenings you had to work late."

"Hee hee."

"You're *laughing*?"

"You flatter me, Katrien. Me? My teeth come out. See?" He wobbled his lower dentures.

"You don't do it with your plastic teeth, Jan."

"You're like Paul Voort," the commissaris said. "We're in the twentieth century, dear. The Inquisition is over."

"Who is Paul Voort?"

"That nasty man you shooed out of the door. He accused me of theft."

"Ach." She grabbed hold of him again. "You don't steal things."

"I just stole thirty million."

"No, you gave it away."

"And you gave Miss Antoinette away."

"You are jealous." She shook him. "Confess."

"Of Carl," the commissaris said.

"What do you mean, of Carl?"

"*You* like Carl," the commissaris said. "That's why I said he could have Miss Antoinette."

"You're jealous of Carl and me . . ." She held him at arm's length. "Jan!"

"I'm very jealous," the commissaris said. "I realize that now. That's why I destroyed Fernandus."

"You thought that Fernandus and I . . . really, Jan, I'm sixty years old and I haven't seen him in thirty."

"Something else," the commissaris said, "something else again. I haven't thought it all out, but I assure you I never touched Miss Antoinette."

"You're sure now?"

"Sure," the commissaris said. "You can kiss me to make up."

"No, you kiss me."

"That's nice," Mrs. Jongs said from the door. "I never kisses anyone. Bob doesn't like that. It isn't in the price."

⫸ 31 ⫷

Kowsky of the *Courier*, a crablike man with eyes
on stalks, a predatory creature who lived in his own
crack in his own rock, where he rested between quick,
darting attacks, listened to the commissaris with attention.

"You were going to write a piece before on the
Society for Help Abroad," the commissaris said. "I
believe you spent a night at their club, as a guest of
Baron Bart de la Faille. Nothing came of that?"

"Plenty," Kowsky hissed. He sidled a little closer
to the commissaris's desk, leering sideways at Miss
Antoinette, who, neat and modest in her two-piece
suit and lace-trimmed blouse, was pouring coffee.
Kowsky retreated to his chair, holding on to his cup
with his claw. "I'm still gathering material, research-
ing the project."

"Making progress?" The commissaris, trim and
dapper, adjusted his necktie so that it divided his spotless white shirt into symmetrical halves. "I'm sure
you have. Perhaps you'd like some help."

Miss Antoinette watered the begonias on the windowsills, which, responding to their daily portion of
loving care, flowered profusely, brightening the room

with their splashes of glowing red. The leaves of the potted palm fluttered, touched by the morning breeze as Miss Antoinette opened a window. The portrait of the captain of the constabulary smiled down benignly from his golden frame and the glorious past. "Now then," the commissaris said, "perhaps this would be of interest. Reliable informants tell me that the Society is in financial trouble, very likely because of a crisis in the Banque du Crédit. You do know that the Society and the bank are closely linked through their mutual president, the infamous attorney Willem Fernandus. A run on the bank is predicted, which will undoubtedly result in financial failure."

"How come?" Kowsky asked, sucking up coffee.

"You're familiar with the troubles of the Ryder empire?" the commissaris asked. "Ronnie Ryder met with a fatal accident yesterday. His speedboat blew up on the Vinker Lakes. His textile stores, mismanaged and almost bankrupt, were bailed out by the Banque du Crédit, but the bank, by now, is very shaky too. Ryder was known to be an inveterate gambler, losing at roulette in the Society's club."

"Any criminal charges?" Kowsky asked pointing his sharp nose aggressively at the commissaris. "Didn't the manager of the bank commit suicide a while ago?"

"He died by violence," the commissaris said.

"Ryder did away with himself too?"

"Possibly," the commissaris said. "Fernandus's son, Huip, was also in the boat. We could consider the mishap to be a random event. I won't back you up if you mention crime."

"Front-page news," Kowsky said. "Absolutely. Thank you. 'Bye."

Miss Antoinette let him out. The telephone rang. She came back to pick it up. "The chief constable, sir, he wants you to see him right away."

The commissaris nodded. "Tell him to come here,

and I want to see Halba too. Make that sound like an order.'' She passed the message. The commissaris reached over and broke the connection. Miss Antoinette replaced the receiver. ''Do you want me to stay?''

''Please.''

They waited. The door opened. ''What's this?'' the chief constable asked. The commissaris pointed to a chair. ''We'll wait for Halba. Did you tell him to come here?''

''I did not,'' the chief constable said.

The commissaris picked up his phone and dialed, then said, ''Halba. The chief constable and I are waiting for you in my room.''

The chief constable cursed.

''Morning,'' the commissaris said when Halba showed up. ''I'll be brief, so there's no need to sit down. I'm accusing you both, respectively and in ascending order of rank, of incompetence and corruption. I should have come out with this earlier, but I was hampered by the mess that you two helped to bring about. No.'' He raised his hand. ''Shut up. This isn't a discussion. You will, respectively and in ascending order of rank again, apply for early pension and resign. I can't accept a refusal. Should you decide to make a stand, State Detection will uncover, with help from me, a series of misdemeanors that would show you both up personally and further worsen the image of the city's police. If you leave now, I won't take any action, but I can't guarantee that your self-made fate won't trip you up through some other chain of events.'' He stood up. ''Please go. This will be a busy week for me. Hand in your written requests to the administration and leave the building afterward. That'll be all. Miss Antoinette, would you see these men out?''

''Wah,'' the commissaris said, sitting down.

''You're so fierce, sir,'' Miss Antoinette whispered.

"You think they will do all that? Ruin their own careers?"

"They've been ruined for some time," the commissaris said. "They just needed someone to tell them. Would you send in Cardozo?"

Cardozo came in and found the commissaris hopping about on his oriental rug. "Sir?" The commissaris jumped to a geometric design half a yard ahead. "I used to do this for hours when I was a child. This rug was in our living room. I pretended the blue parts were swampy spots where crocodiles and other toothy creatures lived, and the green designs were safe ground, but then I would change it all around, and only the red areas were safe, but not for long again. Reality is like that. Changeable, very. Got to adjust your strategy constantly. Never quite know where you're secure. Educated guesses combined with foolhardy courage . . ."

"Yes?" Cardozo asked. "I just saw the chief constable and Halba in the corridor, sir, arguing with each other like crazy. I yelled good morning at them but they didn't notice me at all. Some internal trouble again?"

"They'll both be leaving us," the commissaris said. "I'm temporarily in charge. The mayor will confirm my position a little later today. I haven't had time to see him yet."

Miss Antoinette walked toward the phone. "Shall I order the mayor to come here too, sir?"

The commissaris smiled. "No, we'll revert to normal tactics now. I'll see him at City Hall." He checked his watch. "As soon as he pleases. Now, Cardozo, there was an Indian lady at the club during the rowdy night we all enjoyed so much. A shapely woman with a red dot on her forehead and a bit of bare belly."

"The one who told me about the Calcutta rats?"

"I forget her name."

"Sayukta, sir. I've seen her since, took her to the zoo."

"Excuse me," Miss Antoinette said, replacing the phone. "The mayor can see you anytime this morning, sir."

The commissaris looked around. "Thank you, dear. Please raise de Gier, he can drive me over. I don't want to have to deal with traffic today. To the zoo, Cardozo? Why the zoo?"

"She wanted to," Cardozo said. "She felt caged herself, and wanted to know she wasn't the only being behind bars."

"I know Sayukta too," Miss Antoinette said. "Willem introduced me to her at the club, we had a bit of a chat. Poor little thing, she was very unhappy."

"Sayukta wants residency here," Cardozo said. "She needs proper papers. Perhaps you could put in a word for her. She'll do anything, even scrub floors."

"I scrubbed Carl's floor this morning," Miss Antoinette said. "He's got a lot of floor, she can help."

"I'll have an apartment too, soon." Cardozo smiled. "Me and Izzy. Maybe Sayukta can come in twice a week. Between the lot of us, we could provide forty hours at minimum wage."

The commissaris gestured impatiently. "Surely we can find her more suitable employment."

"She's quite intelligent," Cardozo said, "Perhaps she could go to school."

"We'll see. So you're friendly with her." The commissaris took out his tin of cigars and put it back in his pocket. "Can you arrange for her to have dinner with us tonight? Are you free, Miss Antoinette? I'd like for a woman to be present. Sayukta must be weary of men, she's only seen us at our worst. I hope you didn't take advantage of her, Simon?"

"No," Cardozo said.

"Of course you did," Miss Antoinette said. "Poor helpless little thing, adrift in a strange country."

"I did not," Cardozo said. "That's Halba's approach."

"Halba doesn't work here anymore," the commissaris said. "What was that just now about you and Izzy sharing an apartment? I thought the fellow was an AWOL Israeli soldier."

"My mother took care of that trouble, sir. Izzy will have his Dutch passport again. Mr. Rosenblatt won't oppose the application."

"The Israeli consul?" the commissaris asked. "I thought he was a fanatic." He mused. "On the right side, of course."

"My mother spoke to the consul, sir."

The commissaris thought. "I see. Your mother. And she's letting you go? You're allowed to live apart from her?"

"She'll still have my brother, Samuel," Cardozo said. "The unemployed genius who can't cook for himself or do his own laundry."

"Genius," the commissaris said. "You're a bit of a genius too. I don't know what I would have done without your help. That reminds me, Cardozo, how much for the computer?"

Cardozo mentioned the amount. "But it's ours, sir. Izzy and mine. We'll have some fun. Izzy'll teach me all the secrets."

"No, it was used in my private investigation. Maybe it'll be helpful on some future occasion." The commissaris brought out his checkbook.

Cardozo got up and walked to the door. "No, really, sir."

"You're sure? Let me pay one-third."

"No, sir. Where do you want to have dinner?"

"Any restaurant of Sayukta's choice."

"She doesn't know about restaurants, sir."

"Up to you, then. See you tonight. Let's hope she can be trusted." The commissaris turned toward Miss

Antoinette. "What do you think? What I have in mind is rather risky."

"I thought I was your spy," Miss Antoinette said.

The commissaris shook his head. "Willem must have seen through your playacting by now."

Miss Antoinette pushed out a moist lower lip. "Playacting, sir?"

The commissaris walked back to his rug. "I see. So you liked Willem. A loving old man. No, I can't use you now. Besides, Carl may not like it."

"Carl?" Cardozo asked. "That's right. Why were you scrubbing Carl's floor?"

Miss Antoinette hid behind a mysterious smile.

"Yes," the commissaris said, "you were only supposed to take him home last night. Did you like Carl's place? Grijpstra and de Gier were very impressed. An indoor allegorical garden. I'd like to see that collective work of art myself."

"We'll invite you to dinner, sir, but I'd like to clean up a bit more first. Oh, Cardozo, my apartment is available now. Would you and Izzy be interested? You can take over the lease."

"Proceeding as planned," the commissaris said, and skipped back to his desk.

"Your legs don't hurt today?" Cardozo asked.

"What legs?"

"Your rheumatism?"

"Oh," the commissaris said. "Right. That's mostly psychosomatic, Cardozo. I keep telling my wife. It's all of you frustrating me. I can see the world as it should be, but then it never is, and you interfere with my continuous attempts at improving conditions." The commissaris's thin lips tightened. He muttered at a potted palm.

"I'll get de Gier," Miss Antoinette said. "Can't raise him on the phone."

"Did he say 'bunch of dimwits'?" Cardozo asked in the corridor. "Did you hear that too?"

"Arrogant little man," Miss Antoinette said. "But what do I care? I finally found myself the ideal lover."

"Carl?"

"Yes," Miss Antoinette said. "Carl. A true artist. You're all too practical for me. Shallow thinkers. You're out for results. Carl explained that to me last night. There are never results. And nothing matters much, isn't that a relief? I always thought things mattered, and it made me so afraid."

"De Gier talks like that too," Cardozo said.

"Bah. De Gier."

"All women like de Gier," Cardozo said. "You do too."

Miss Antoinette smiled dreamily. "I won't have to share Carl. I just love his sculptures. They're so sexy, don't you think?"

"And Carl himself?"

"Very sexy, and he can't get away." She touched Cardozo's arm. "You guys get away. De Gier took Carl and me to Carl's loft last night, in a sports car. You should have seen him roar off. Disgusting. Carl won't roar off, I'll have to drive him about, he'll be dependent on me. I'll inspire him and we'll be happy forever." Miss Antoinette danced away, swinging her hips.

Cardozo waited at the elevator. Grijpstra joined him. "Do you know," Cardozo asked, "that some women want to cripple us?"

"No," Grijpstra said.

"You don't agree?"

"No," Grijpstra said. "Not *some* women. *All* women want to cripple us. We're objects to be possessed."

"That's bad."

"Not bad." Grijpstra pushed Cardozo into the elevator. "It's true. The truth can't be classified, but it can be used."

"How?" Cardozo asked.

The elevator stopped at the first floor and Grijpstra rushed off. Cardozo ran along. "How, Adjutant?"

"If ever I find out I might just let you know," Grijpstra said. "Meanwhile, I'll live alone. Leave me alone too, Cardozo, I've got work to do."

"Where?"

"At the airport."

"What?"

"A trap," Grijpstra said. "I'm setting up a trap. You'll hear in due course."

⦚⦚⦚⦚ 32 ⦚⦚⦚⦚

THE NEXT DAY'S *Courier* outdid itself in a display of subtle venom without making any outright statements. A front-page article pointed at possible instability of the Banque du Crédit. The second page discussed the woes of the Ryder clothing stores, brought about, possibly, by the luxurious life-style and gambling of its president and main shareholder. Ryder's accidental death, already reported on, was covered in more detail, and a photograph showed the remnants of his boat, studied by State Police officers in uniform. The Society for Help Abroad was linked (the word "separately" appeared various times) to a shuffle at Police Headquarters. The commissaris, reading the article to Grijpstra and de Gier, rustled the paper. "I didn't tell him that. Kowsky must have other informants in this building."

"Good," Grijpstra said. "I like the photographs that illustrate that article. Halba and the chief constable at the club's bar, cavorting with half-naked women. Kowsky must have kept that snapshot up his sleeve. Probably smuggled a photographer in."

"Kowsky has a minicamera himself," de Gier said. "He showed it to me once. Shall we get busy, sir?"

The commissaris put his paper down. "Yes. Use all your contacts. I'll work on the Tax Inspection Office. You two can raid the club later this week; I'll assign a chief inspector. The warrant will be for gambling without a license. We'll make it official this time."

"Chief Inspector Rood, sir?"

"No. Someone else. Make as many arrests as you can, and see if we can make them implicate Fernandus and de la Faille. I'll work on the Central Bank too, see if they'll send inspectors down. We'll push from all sides and do as much damage as we can."

"Will the mayor help?" Grijpstra asked.

The commissaris nodded. "Yes. He wants me to go slow, but I'll ignore that advice, I think." He rubbed his hands. "To work."

So they worked. The bank came down and was closed behind sealed doors. Warrants for the arrests of Fernandus and the baron were issued, based on statements provided by the Society's manager and waiters, and several employees of the Banque du Crédit, but Fernandus could not be located. De la Faille's trail led as far as the Belgian border.

"Now what?" Grijpstra asked when he saw the commissaris later that week.

"Wait," the commissaris said.

"Any news yet from Calcutta?" Cardozo asked. The commissaris read a Teletype message. "*Supply from Nepal due soon. Courier ready. Will inform you of flight number and date.*"

"We're ready too," the commissaris said. "This is from our narcotics commissioner out there. Where's de Gier?"

"Gone," Grijpstra said solemnly.

The telephone rang. "I'm not here," the commissaris said. He placed his elbows on his desk and dropped his chin on his clasped hands. "Gone?"

"It's the chief of the Tax Inspection Office, sir,"

Miss Antoinette said, covering the receiver with her hand.

The commissaris waved impatiently. "This is more urgent, dear. I'm out to everybody." He looked straight ahead. "Gone?"

Grijpstra harrumphed.

"Harrumph?" Cardozo asked. "What sort of answer is that? Where is the sergeant?"

"No sergeant," Grijpstra said placidly. "I don't think de Gier cares for his title anymore. He said he wouldn't come down. He's suspended in thin air."

"Adjutant," the commissaris said, "de Gier's been reinstated. I had an envelope placed on his desk. His salary will be paid in full with apologies and all. What more does he want?"

"More." Grijpstra flicked dust off his knee. "The white knight didn't open his envelope."

"The white knight?" Cardozo asked. "But that's silly. He wasn't serious, was he? The sergeant likes to hold on to a joke."

"No joke."

"So where is he?" the commissaris asked. "You're closer to de Gier than anyone else. Did he leave the city? Where is his cat?"

"At my house," Grijpstra said. "He brought it last night, in a Ferrari. I've got his furniture too, it came in a truck. I don't want de Gier's furniture. And he didn't just leave the city, he left the country."

"So why did you take his furniture? Or did you leave it in the street?"

"I took it, sir."

"And what about de Gier's apartment?"

"I don't know. For rent, I suppose."

"Evidently he isn't planning to come back," the commissaris said. "He could always get a job here. De Gier's always offered jobs. Has he got money, Adjutant?"

"Savings."

"Savings?" the commissaris repeated. "He always complains about his overdraft."

"Not for the last year, sir." Grijpstra smiled grimly. "He hasn't bought any new clothes for a year. He stayed home for his holidays. Refused to pay for my coffee. Hardly went out."

"The stock market," Cardozo said. "I've seen him looking at the *Financial Times* in the canteen."

"And at maps," Grijpstra said.

"What maps?"

"Maps of New Guinea, sir."

"No," the commissaris said. "That fantasy too? But that goes back years. When that Papuan suspect got away, he sent a postcard later, I believe."

"What Papuan?" Cardozo asked.

"A good man," the commissaris said, "who managed to get away. Grijpstra can tell you. This is serious." He picked up a pencil and tapped it on his desk.

"Well, de Gier was suspended, sir," Grijpstra said. "And he's free anyway. If he goes, he goes."

"Surely." The commissaris let the pencil slide from his hand. "But do we want him to kill the baron? That's not a good start. He might get hurt, too, his ribs haven't healed."

"He's in pain," Cardozo said. "It hurts him when he breathes deeply. I could see that. De Gier was very careful how he moved."

"You don't want him to duel with the baron, sir?" Grijpstra asked.

The commissaris played with his pencil. "No."

The telephone rang again. Miss Antoinette answered. "State Police, sir, about the accident on the Vinker Lakes."

"Good luck to them," the commissaris said.

"He isn't here," Miss Antoinette said into the telephone.

Cardozo flattened his hair with both hands. "The

baron's probably in Spain, at Ten Haaf's estate in Marbella, where Guldemeester is working now.''

''Are we sure?'' the commissaris asked. ''We know by now that Ten Haaf was financially interested in the Banque du Crédit and the Society; he must have dropped some money in the crash. And Fernandus and the baron probably own part of the estate in Marbella. If the baron went to cash in his share, he may not be received very well.''

''Ten Haaf is a helpless junkie now,'' Grijpstra said. ''He used to be big in local crime, but since his retirement, he's changed into a slob. He's happy to have any of his cronies visit. He runs some sort of recreation center for what he calls the Mob. I think the baron would be welcome in Marbella.''

''Another godfather, eh?'' the commissaris asked. ''A nest of crime up in the mountains? Weary warriors are given a rest. Do I see it all now? Is de Gier going to fight the bad guys in their lair? Racing up in Ryder's Ferrari? In style?''

''In style,'' Cardozo said. ''That's what he kept saying. I see it too, sir. He has spelled it all out to me, many a time. Police work is too limited; he stayed on only because of you; you were teaching him and so forth, but eventually he would break away and continue his quest on his own.''

''De Gier's forty-two,'' Grijpstra said. ''Quite a difficult age. I was wondering, when I got into my forties, whether I shouldn't make a change.''

''Coffee, everyone?'' Miss Antoinette asked. ''Here you are. De Gier is a romantic, Constable Jane is always saying that.''

''What's a romantic, dear?'' The commissaris sipped his coffee. ''You mean he's a bit crazy?''

''Like Carl.'' Miss Antoinette smiled. ''Carl says you've got to do things differently. Figure out how everybody does it and then do it otherwise. De Gier is like that too, but he isn't as courageous as Carl. Carl doesn't want an example. De Gier has you."

"Me," the commissaris said. "How could he imitate me? I live a perfectly ordinary life."

"Your mind," Grijpstra said.

"What about my mind?"

"Well," Grijpstra said. "Perhaps I could explain, but I'll probably annoy you. I've been annoying you lately. Never mind, sir."

"Go on," Cardozo said. "Annoy the commissaris. You always annoy everybody else."

"Please annoy me," the commissaris said. "You'll have to, I'm afraid. I have to understand de Gier's motivation before I do anything."

"What can you do?" Cardozo asked. "If de Gier hasn't opened his envelope, he's on perpetual unpaid leave. If he doesn't come back, he's not under your orders."

The telephone rang. "The mayor, sir," Miss Antoinette said. The commissaris waved a limp hand. "He's not here," said Miss Antoinette.

Grijpstra stripped a cigar out of its plastic cover, bit off its end, spat, and missed the ashtray. "Yagh," said Miss Antoinette.

Grijpstra grinned and lit his cigar. "Very well. You were de Gier's example, sir. He saw you as a teacher. They call that a guru these days. You were out of reach. You lived on your cloud. In de Gier's eyes, you were—"

"Detached?" the commissaris said. "I don't like that word."

"But why don't you like it?" Grijpstra asked. "Because you'd like to be detached, right? Who wouldn't? But who is?" Grijpstra made wavy movements with his hands and feet, lost his balance, and flopped back in his chair. Cardozo laughed. "Right," Grijpstra said. "We fall back. De Gier claimed you never fell back, sir, that you somehow managed to stay aloft, high up, so high that you could choose your angles from which to swoop down on suspects—or on us."

"But he does that," Cardozo said. "The commissaris does that."

"You still have some faith in me?" the commissaris asked. "That's nice, Cardozo. The adjutant evidently doesn't."

"No," Grijpstra said. "I do."

"You still have faith in me?"

"Some," Grijpstra said. "Some reasonable faith. De Gier's faith was more. Unreasonable, I always thought. I told him that many a time. I said you would disappoint him. And that he wouldn't be able to stand the disappointment. It would break him, I said. He would go crazy."

"Carl is crazy," Miss Antoinette said. "But not all the way. He's also responsible. Do you know that Carl has no debts? I thought all men had debts, that's why they're so boring. They're stuck, having to pay off their debts."

"I see," the commissaris said. He shook his head. "Would you mind blowing your smoke a bit more to the side, Adjutant, please? It isn't twelve o'clock yet." He touched the tin of cigars on his desk.

"Yes." Grijpstra blew smoke at the ceiling. "So then you came down to fight your private enemy, Willem Fernandus. You came down rather heavily. De Gier saw that. You were personally involved. Gurus are never involved. I told de Gier that would happen."

"Willem hates you too," Miss Antoinette said. "You hate Willem, don't you sir?"

"Ah," Cardozo said. "So that's what it was. I was wondering too. I even dreamed about it. One of my horrible insect dreams, they always tear away at each other and their legs are stuck in glue. They sometimes fight in my mouth, and I can't spit them out."

The commissaris started to pick up his coffee cup,

but it slipped from his hand and rattled back on the saucer. "I see."

"You do?" Grijpstra asked. "You see foolish de Gier racing his silly tin roller skate up a molehill to challenge a useless moron to a dumb duel?"

"Unfor . . ." The commissaris cleared his throat. "Excuse me. Unfortunate, very. We have to stop him. De Gier'll probably beat the baron, in spite of his sore ribs. He's clever enough."

"And sneaky," Cardozo said.

"Which he learned from me," the commissaris said. "But de Gier still has sore ribs. I hope he took his gun."

"No," Grijpstra said. "I checked. The sergeant-at-arms has de Gier's gun."

"Oh, dear," the commissaris said. "Just when things were going well. What do you suggest we do, Adjutant? Fly out to Marbella? We may be too late. De Gier's driving a fast car, and there are no speed limits on the Belgian and French freeways."

"No, I don't think we can stop de Gier," Grijpstra said, picking up the ragged end of his cigar and placing it carefully in the ashtray. "I'm sneaky too, sir"—he grinned—"but on my own. My sneakiness is mine. I didn't pick it up anywhere. A phone is quicker than a plane. Miss Antoinette? Could you find out the number of the Ten Haaf estate in Marbella?"

Miss Antoinette picked up the telephone.

"I don't quite see . . ." the commissaris said. "Isn't that dangerous, Grijpstra? Warning them off?"

"Yes," Grijpstra said. "I wouldn't do that." He got up, picked up the silver thermos flask, and refilled everybody's cup. Miss Antoinette gave him a slip of paper. Grijpstra grinned. "That's the number? Very well. Please dial it and ask for Guldemeester."

"Oh, dear," the commissaris said. "I hope you know what you're doing, Adjutant."

Grijpstra took over the phone. "Hello? Grijpstra here. Can you hear me? What's all the noise?"

"You have a cordless phone? I can hardly hear you. Could you phone back? Yes, I'm at my office." He put the phone down. "Miss Antoinette? Could you ask the girls downstairs to pass the call here when Guldemeester phones back?"

They waited. In a few moments the telephone rang.

"Yes," Grijpstra said. "That's better. You're at the house now? Very well. Listen, I'm phoning about Celine. You've heard, haven't you? Read it in the papers? Right. But it wasn't an accident. Listen, I'm sorry about Celine, just wanted to tell you." Grijpstra held his hand over the mouthpiece. "You see, Guldemeester still loves her, de Gier told me that. Thinks he loves her, anyway. Celine said—" He took off his hand. "What's that? Yes. No accident. Sure I'm sure."

"Yes. I could tell you, but perhaps you don't want to know. Listen, something else. You know about the changes here? Chief constable and Halba gone? You get the *Courier* there? Okay, then you know . . .

"Yes. Quite a bit of change. The commissaris is in charge now for the time being . . .

"You don't like it there?

"I see. I could ask the commissaris. Can't guarantee anything, of course."

Grijpstra coughed. "Sorry. My cigar. Terrible weather here. All the windows closed. Yeah, I'm alone. Why?

"Celine's accident? You sure you want to know? You may not like it . . .

"Okay. It's like this. The Society—you were wrong there, you know—bunch of assholes, they abused Celine. She didn't like it there . . . Abused how?

"Well, I don't have the details, but that's what she said. No, not to me, but we've got ways of hearing things . . .

"Yes, we had someone there. Anyway, your wife didn't like her job at the club. Wanted out, but they wouldn't let her, see. Bunch of killers too, you should have known that . . .

"Of course. The junkies, IJsbreker and so forth, and now this Ronnie Ryder too, you must have seen that in the paper. And Heul. Remember Heul? They shot him full of smack and dumped him in the commissaris's car . . .

"Yes. A mess. Celine found out, and she was going to tell us . . .

"Sure. They ran her down. Twice. Hit her from the side and then reversed the car and ran over her. She was still alive when we found her. Lots of internal damage . . .

"Yes. she told us who . . .

"Want to know? I can tell you . . .

"You're ready? Okay, but listen, be careful. The baron . . .

Grijpstra waited, holding the phone.

"Yes. Absolutely. No doubt in my mind . . .

"You'll get him?

"Yes, I thought he was with you in Marbella now. Wanted to warn you . . .

"Well, listen. I heard that you wanted to come back to us, and if the baron finds out, you'll be in danger . . .

"Don't mention it. Want some advice?

"Okay, here's what you do. Take him for a walk. I know Marbella, spent a holiday there. Didn't like it. Bad place. There are paths there with steep cliffs . . .

"Okay, now remember. The baron fell. Slipped. You didn't see him slip. He was there, and then he wasn't. Stick to that. Just tell one story. Keep it short. I don't have to tell you that. You've been in the business a long time yourself . . .

"Right. Good luck . . . No, that's all right. My

pleasure. We've worked together for years. Just thought I'd let you know. 'Bye now. 'Bye.''

Grijpstra replaced the receiver.

"Shit," Cardozo said. "Grijpstra . . ."

The commissaris checked his watch. "Eleven-fifty." He took a cigar from his tin and lit it.

"Good for you," Miss Antoinette said, touching Grijpstra's arm.

"Yes," the commissaris said. "Good for you, Grijpstra. I don't think I could have done that."

Grijpstra got up. "Yes, sir, you could."

"Maybe . . . but it would have taken me some time."

Grijpstra stood near the door. "It took me some time too, sir. I've thought about it ever since de Gier said good-bye at nine o'clock this morning. By the way, he sends his best wishes to all of you. I was only supposed to tell you tomorrow, to give him a bit of a start."

"And he'll go from there to New Guinea?" the commissaris asked.

"From Barcelona, sir, by freighter. He's not in a hurry. The trip will give him time to reflect on his future."

"Oh, dear," the commissaris said. "I hope he'll make it. Ten Haaf may have a bunch of bodyguards up there."

"He'll make it, sir. I'll be in my office if you need me." Grijpstra closed the door with some force. The bang made the commissaris shiver.

‖‖‖ 33 ‖‖‖

THE LARGE LIGHT-GRAY ROOM OVERLOOKING THE
arrival hall of Amsterdam Airport, set off with glass
walls that allowed the inhabitants to look out but no
one to look in, became tense with suppressed emo-
tion. A high-ranking customs officer in a pale green
uniform paced up and down. A State Police colonel,
resplendent in his sky blue tunic decorated with silver
braid, walked from window to window, peering out.
Grijpstra and Cardozo watched TV screens that kept
flashing off and on, showing different parts of another
hall where the public milled about, waiting for arriving
passengers. Portable two-way radios murmured terse
messages. Blown-up color photographs of a young Indian woman in an orange sari, smiling innocently into
the camera, lay on the room's tables and desks. The
commissaris, hands behind his back, stood quietly in
a corner.

"Could you describe suspect again?" the State Police colonel asked, looking over his shoulder. "Pity
we don't have a photograph. Sly fellow indeed. Quite
a feat, shying away from cameras all his life. You are
sure suspect really exists?"

"My size," the commissaris said. "My age. Silver

curly hair, a fringe, shiny bald in the center. Side-burns, silvery too, thick. Sunburned. Likes to wear flashy rings. Dresses well. Spectacles like mine."

"A neat elderly gent?" the colonel asked. "Like yourself?"

"Yes," the commissaris said. "But Fernandus wears darker suits and he has more hair. He's fatter too."

"And you're sure he's around?" the customs officer asked.

"I don't know anything for sure," the commissaris said. "I've never been able to grasp the absolute. It's very likely that he's here."

"Fernandus is here," Grijpstra said. "What was her name again? Suyuki? Brings in five ki's of the finest Nepalese heroin on Fernandus's orders. Fernandus is broke and a fugitive from justice. We're told that suspect has an insane need of money. We've carefully set this up. Suspect's got to be here."

"Where?" Cardozo asked, peering at his TV screen. "If he's here, he should be visible by now."

"He'll probably appear at the very last moment," the commissaris said.

The Air India flight's arrival was announced on the PA system. There was a flutter of bright-colored saris in the welcomers' section of the hall. Men with very white eyeballs and dark mustaches ran about, children pressed themselves against the barriers.

"You better go down, sir," the colonel said to the commissaris. "You're the only one who can properly identify suspect."

The commissaris left. "The commissaris will be visible enough," Grijpstra said to Cardozo. "Good thing he always wears those light shantung suits. His white hair will shine too, and his skull."

"Hello?" the colonel said into his radio. "The commissaris has gone down. Watch him. Also watch out for a young Indian woman in a bright orange long

dress. She carries a maroon bag. Whoever takes the
bag from her is the suspect. Over and out." He turned
to the customs officer. "Your people have been in-
structed?"

"They'll let her through," the customs officer said.
He pointed. "There she is."

"The Indian lady is coming through," the colonel
whispered into his radio. "Attention. Coming through
now."

"Wow!" Cardozo shouted. "Look. Who is who?
Two of them!"

"What?" the colonel asked.

"Where?" the customs officer shouted.

"Here," Grijpstra said, tapping his screen. "Two
of them. One of them just came out of the toilet. I
spotted him."

"Where?"

"What?"

"Two commissarises," Cardozo said.

"Goddamn," the colonel muttered. "And there are
my men, all confused, of course. Why wasn't I told
they were twins? What *is* this nonsense?"

"They are both approaching the gate," Grijpstra
said.

"Goddamn twins," the colonel said. "Where are
these silvery curls? The dark suit? The sideburns?
They're both about bald, both in shantung suits."

Grijpstra and Cardozo rushed off. One of the two
look-alikes grabbed Sayukta's bag and was immediately lost in the crowd. The commissaris was seen to
pursue Fernandus, not too successfully; people kept
getting in his way, Cardozo and Grijpstra appeared on
the screens, running toward the hall's exits.

"We'd better go down too," the colonel said.

They found the commissaris standing in the hall,
deep in thought.

"Suspect got away?" the colonel asked. "Why
didn't you tell me you and suspect are twins?"

"Cousins," the commissaris said. "Twice removed."

"Very smart," the customs officer said. "Suspect dressed up like you. But he still carries the bag." The colonel called over his plain-clothes assistants. "A maroon bag, damn it. Man carrying a maroon bag. Looks like the commissaris here. Go on. Off with you." He spoke into his portophone. "Suspect in shantung suit, sparse gray hair, small build, carrying a maroon bag, probably has left the building by now. On his way to the parking lot."

"No," the commissaris said. "No, I don't think Fernandus has a car. Probably wants a taxi now. Let's go outside. There will be a line."

They walked outside. An orderly line of passengers had formed near the taxi stand. "Indian," the commissaris said. "Maybe he is that Indian. I lost Willem near the toilets. He could be an Indian now. An Indian with a large suitcase, big enough to hold the bag. That man over there, maybe. Apprehend him."

"Now really, sir," the colonel said. "The man in the black coat, with the long dark hair?"

The commissaris went back into the hall and reappeared, accompanied by Grijpstra and Cardozo.

"But that's an Indian," the colonel said. "Suspect isn't a magician, is he? Where did he get the wig and the coat?"

"And the large suitcase?" the customs officer asked.

"In the toilets somewhere," the commissaris muttered. "Grijpstra, grab him from the left. Cardozo, take him from the right. That's Fernandus. Quickly now, he's getting to the front of the line."

"Impossible," the colonel said.

The Indian gentleman glanced over his shoulder. The commissaris waved. "Willem, hello." The Indian stepped out of the line, ran to the front, pushed an old lady aside, and tried to scramble into a cab. Grijpstra and Cardozo ran after him and pulled him back, pointed guns at his head, yanked at his wrists. The suitcase fell. Handcuffs clicked shut.

"This way," the colonel shouted, sprinting toward the struggling suspect, who was protesting his rough treatment in singsong English.

"That's an Indian," the customs officer said. "I know Indians, I see them all the time. We've made a dreadful mistake."

The commissaris lifted off the Indian's hair. "Nice try, Willem."

Bystanders gaped. "On your way," the colonel shouted. "On your way. Nothing to see here. Move along, move along, your taxis are waiting." The customs officer picked up Fernandus's suitcase. "The bag is in there," the commissaris said. The colonel bent over and lifted packages wrapped in transparent plastic from the bag inside the suitcase.

The commissaris prodded Fernandus's stomach. "You lost weight. You look better now. Trying to imitate me, Willem. Too late for that now."

"The hell," Fernandus hissed. "The hell."

"Shall we go?" the commissaris asked "You've lost, Willem, can't think of all the reasons now. We'll do that later."

⫸ 34 ⫷

HARD RAIN HIT THE CITY AGAIN ON THE DAY MISS
Antoinette and Carl got married, beating down on the
shiny tarmac of the long narrow Overtoom, splashing
up against buildings and cars, trying to drench the
commissaris's wife and Mrs. Jongs, who shared the
same umbrella. Cardozo pushed the commissaris up
the long steep stairs. "That's all right, Sergeant," the
commissaris kept saying. "I'm not totally decrepit
yet." "Easy now, sir," Cardozo kept saying. Grijpstra walked behind them, holding a large parcel. Ketchup and Karate carried clinking bottles in brown
paper bags.

"Very nice," everyone said when they finally
reached the top floor. The front part of Carl's loft had
been changed into a semblance of a normal apartment,
but behind a row of man-sized rubber trees, Carl's
wonderland started, and the commissaris wandered
about, studying the profusion of Carl's thoughts, realized in different materials in a number of odd styles.
Carl's father still read the *Financial Times* and his
mother swooped down from the ceiling, pointing her
long beak filled with double rows of fanglike teeth. "I
didn't invihite them," Carl said. "They're tohoo bu-

husy." He served as a guide, explaining the various objects.

"You'll have your exhibition soon," the commissaris said. "You may sell a lot of these. Don't you mind?"

"We'll have some room," Antoinette said. "And you'll make more, won't you, Carl? Will you make me too?"

"Another bihird of preyhey," Carl said, putting his arm around his wife, "that gohobbles me up."

"Presents," said the commissaris's wife. The presents were practical, in accordance with a list of useful household items provided by the bride. "Ah, a parsley mill," Antoinette said, clapping her hands. "Just what we need Carl, for your salads. Ah, freezer trays, look Carl, for your soup. You know," she said to Mrs. Jongs, "Carl lives on soup. He used to make a bucket of soup a week, he'd throw in anything that he found on sale. Dreadful taste."

"Alwahays different," Carl said.

"I'm making gourmet soups now," Antoinette said.

"Bob eats soup too," Mrs. Jongs said. "But then the lizards gets into the pot and he chokes." She had brought an electric coffee grinder. Ketchup and Karate opened bottles.

They all drank to the happy couple and then to Grijpstra's painting. "What a striking green background," the commissaris said. "Makes your ducks come out very well. Just like they're swimming out of the weeds. Are those real weeds?"

"Dried," Grijpstra said. "I fished them out of the canal at Prince's Island. Took forever to steam the smell out."

Carl hung the painting, helped by Grijpstra. Meanwhile they discussed art, agreeing that anything can be done, in all dimensions, combining incompatibles, and that colors should never match. "And music," Grijpstra said. "I think music should fit in, but I don't dare to do that yet. Like these ducks here. Next time I make ducks I'll use real bones, glue them on the canvas and make them movable maybe, you pull something and they scratch against each other."

Carl agreed that scratching was the ultimate sound. "You plahay druhums, I heahear?"

"Yeh, drums," Grijpstra said. They walked back together to the kitchen part of the loft and Grijpstra scratched pots with a wooden spoon. "Hear? But that isn't the sound of skeleton ducks. I can find it if I try. It was easier when de Gier was still around. He played a good flute, and I'd scratch around his notes."

"There was a postcard from de Gier," the commissaris said to his wife. "From the eastern part of New Guinea. He must be moving around."

"Never mind de Gier," his wife said, "I don't want you to go there too."

"De Gier sent me a picture of a Papuan drum," Grijpstra told Cardozo. "Huge. A hollowed-out tree. I'd like to play that."

"From Port Moresby?" Cardozo asked. "I had a postcard too."

"No, inland. There's a river, he said he went up by boat."

"Don't worry, Katrien," the commissaris said. "Grijpstra wants to go as well. Bit of a holiday, maybe. Maybe later."

"Your vermouth, ma'am," Karate said.

Mrs. Jongs drank sherry. Grijpstra tapped Carl's father's wooden head with his spoon. "That's a good sound."

"Becauhause there's nobody hohome," Carl said. "When he's hohome it souhounds bad."

"We're home," Antoinette said. "Isn't it nice to be home together, Carl?"

"Greahate change," Carl said. He explained to Karate that he drove a car now, Antoinette's car, nothing to it. He had learned to drive and gotten his license. They went to a party and Antoinette drank too much, so he had to drive them home. As he walked to the car, a patrol car came by. The cops jumped out. They'd seen him swaying across the pavement. "So I saihaid, 'I'm spahastic.' And the cops apologized. They were very sorry. Never mind. It hadn't happened. A mistake. Go ahead. Good night, sir. 'Bye now."

"You weren't drunk," Karate said.

"Vehery druhunk," Carl said.

The telephone rang. Antoinette picked it up. "One moment, please, he's here." She gave the phone to the commissaris.

"Are you on call?" his wife asked.

"Yes, Katrien. Hello?"

He listened. "Yes, all right."

"You have to go?" his wife asked.

"Yes, dear, I'll see you at home."

"I'll take you," Cardozo said.

"No, thank you, Sergeant, I'd better go alone." He turned to his wife. "It's Willem."

"No." She held his hand. "No. Willem is in jail. That's over, don't go to see him."

"He's in the hospital," the commissaris said. "I've known about Willem's illness since last week."

"Under guard?" Grijpstra asked. "They shouldn't let him out of jail. He'll escape, sir. Think of something, impersonate a doctor, we'll have to go after him again."

"Leukemia," the commissaris said. "He wouldn't go far. I spoke to Dr. Peters in the hospital. He said Fernandus wasn't doing very well."

"Fernandus will fake anything," Grijpstra said. "Let me go with you. We can take care of this."

"We'll take Fernandus for a walk?" the commissaris asked. "Please, Adjutant. The baron didn't survive his walk. Let's leave this to nature."

"Shall I go with you?" Antoinette said. "I rather like Mr. Fernandus."

"Noho," Carl said.

"Sometimes," Mrs. Jongs said, "it's better they dies, but they don't dies easy."

"You're only going to gloat," said the commissaris's wife. "Don't do that, Jan. Leave Willem be. It's a happy ending for you, I don't want you to be happy that way."

"Nothing ever ends," the commissaris muttered. "What do you know? You can be pretty silly, Katrien."

"I'm sorry," she said. "But you were after him so much. You never really go after anyone, but this time . . . sitting in the garden talking to yourself . . . up at all hours . . . cursing and swearing in your bath . . . I don't want to see you like that, please."

"Maybe you should go, then, sir," Grijpstra said. "You hunted him and now you've got to be in at the kill. It's only fair. He sees that too. That's why he's asking you to come over."

"The cancer is killing him," the commissaris said. "Leukemia is blood cancer."

"No," Karate said, "that's only afterward. You got to die of something. It's like my father—he died of cancer too, but that wasn't it really. He was an engine driver and he made some mistake and he got fired. Couldn't drive his engine no more. Nothing to do. People ask him, 'What are you?' and he says he is nothing. Once you're nothing you got to go, so you got to get sick."

"My father's done nothing all his life," Ketchup said.

"Sure," Karate said. "But now take that away. Tell him he's got to work. He's got to give up doing nothing, right? And doing nothing is all of his life? So he'll break his back or catch his death of cold."

* * *

The commissaris drove himself over. He waited at the hospital's reception counter until a nurse came to take him up. The nurse smiled sadly at the forlorn little figure waiting in the hall. "You must be his brother," she said. "Please follow me, sir. What a remarkable likeness."

⁗ 35 ⁗

"BUT I'M DYING," FERNANDUS SAID, SITTING UP against his clean, fluffy cushions. "Don't look so nervous, Jan. There's no gun under the sheets. You won. You said you were going to destroy me, and by Jove, you did."

"You believe in Jove now?" the commissaris asked, wondering who would have sent Fernandus the red roses on his night table.

"The nurse brought them in," Fernandus said. "They have lots of flowers here. Nobody would send me flowers."

The commissaris acknowledged the information with a careful smile. Fernandus nodded too. "I could always read your thoughts. Conforming thoughts. The obvious again. You think like the majority. Not amazing at all, the way our lives turned out."

"Can I smoke here?" the commissaris asked.

"Sure. Got a cigar for me?"

The commissaris brought out his tin, holding it close to his chest.

"No," Fernandus said. "I don't believe this. Go on, give me a cigar. You're still punishing me? Thanks. A light too, if you please."

The commissaris looked about the bright room. "No guard?"

"No." Fernandus held the tip of his cigar under his nose and sniffed. "You could buy a better brand. Leave the tin anyway, I'll be gone tomorrow afternoon. At four sharp, they say, got the word today, that's why I called you."

"Back to jail?" The commissaris felt his leg. "If you're dying, they might let you do it here."

"They'll kill me here." Fernandus grinned. "Pain in your legs? Good. Is your trouble getting worse?"

The commissaris got up. "You enervate me, Willem. Mind if I cut this short? Is there anything in particular you want to say?"

Fernandus struggled weakly into a more upright position. "Sit down, Jan, I've got pains too, the pleasure is mutual, you can laugh at me. I've got leukemia, did they tell you that?" He held up a finger. "Listen. I looked it up. Acute forms are fatal within weeks or months. Symptoms include weakness, fatigue, anemia, and hemorrhaging. Leukemia is invariably fatal. This is goodbye. Say goodbye in style."

"Goodbye," the commissaris said. He sat down.

"You don't want to know about the euthanasia?" Fernandus asked.

"So you'll be killed at four o'clock tomorrow," the commissaris said. "What do you want me to say? That I'm sorry to hear it?"

Fernandus kept sliding back. "Help me up."

"Maybe you're more comfortable lying flat."

"I'm not." Fernandus grimaced. "Go on. Thanks. A little higher. Push that pillow down. Mind my cigar. So how do you feel about our little war now, eh? I hear you got the baron killed and that Guldemeester has been arrested. Did you mess that up?" He shrugged. "It doesn't always quite work the way we set it up. They fell down together and Guldemeester broke his legs. Or was that the way you planned it?

Exterminate everyone who ever associated with me? Stamp out the vermin?"

"Who told you about that happening?" the commissaris asked.

Fernandus pointed at the phone next to the flowers. "Ten Haaf."

The commissaris shook his head. "That was a forced move. De la Faille would have shown up in Holland again; the police are patient."

"Yes." Fernandus nodded at the nurse who came in. "We could have some tea. Thank you, dear, you're looking even prettier today." He looked at his visitor. "So now you're the official again, using proper methods? I took that away from you for a while. Dropped the rules. You should be grateful. You could prove yourself." He reached over and touched the commissaris's knee. "You think you did well?"

The commissaris smiled. "Yes. All things considered."

"No," Fernandus said. "Your motivation was wrong. Do you know that now?"

"Wait," the commissaris said. "Before I forget. What happened to Ryder's car? Did Ten Haaf mention the Ferrari?"

"Ten Haaf's got the Ferrari." Fernandus raised a shoulder. "That's an unimportant detail, Jan. Your man left the car. Your fellow came too late." He lifted an eyebrow. "What was the matter with that sergeant? He couldn't arrest the baron in Spain, or had you arranged for a foreign warrant? Was there time for that?"

"Never mind," the commissaris said.

"But I do." Fernandus thumped his bed. "Must have been something personal too. Like you and me. Your man used a stolen car. Is he still with the police?"

"Rinus is in New Guinea now," the commissaris said, reaching out too, but withdrawing his hand before it could touch Fernandus's leg. "That part of our conflict worked out rather well. I've been wanting de Gier to strike out on his own for a while now, but he kept clinging to his routine."

"Or to you," Fernandus said. "Halba . . ." He grinned. "What a lout. You got him to resign, I hear. Stupid ass. Halba said you have a dedicated staff—sort of groupies, you're a father to them."

The commissaris accepted a cup of tea from the tray the nurse was holding.

"You've been drinking?" Fernandus asked after the nurse had left. He sniffed. "Whiskey?" He looked at his watch. "You drink at your office?"

"A wedding party," the commissaris said. "My secretary got married."

"*The* secretary?" Fernandus's eyes gleamed.

"Yes."

"Whom did she marry?"

The commissaris put down his tea. "I'll be right back."

He came back some twenty minutes later.

"A long leak?" Fernandus asked.

The commissaris sat down again. "I spoke to Dr. Peters."

"Oh." Fernandus nodded. "Let's have another cigar. I say, do me a favor and look in that closet. There's a bottle there, the guard bought it for me before he was sent back."

The commissaris fetched the bottle. "Pour it in the cups," Fernandus said. He waved both hands. "Don't be an idiot now. We go back forever, Jan, and this is it. You saw the doctor, so you must believe me now."

The commissaris muttered while he poured the whiskey.

"Did you say 'shit'?" Fernandus asked. "You don't want to face me? Here's shit in your eye."

The commissaris raised his cup. "Your health." He lowered the cup again. "Sorry."

"Not your health either," Fernandus said. "I want you to suffer. Here's to the pain in your leg." He drank. "Do you know why I asked you to come?"

"Sure," the commissaris said. "To brag. Save your last breath, Willem." He raised his hands. "No, really, shut up. I'll drink your liquor, but I've had enough of your claptrap by now." He drank too. "Sixty years of wrong views. I know your side of the argument. I'm the weak one who refused to experiment. We agree there are no absolute morals . . ."

"We do," Fernandus said. "In theory you always saw that, but you were conventional, you took the easy way out. Sold your soul to the opinion of the majority. Waved the flag, sang the national anthem."

"And why not?" The commissaris looked over the rim of his cup. "This isn't a bad country. You betrayed it."

"I never betrayed myself," Fernandus said. "I maneuvered along with whoever happened to be in power, always covering my exits. I'm for me, like everybody else is for everybody else, it's a nasty truth and I faced up to it. I had a good time. You didn't."

The commissaris winked. "Always covered your exits, eh? So how come I caught you at the taxi stand?"

Fernandus held up his cup. "You betrayed our mutual views. And you and I are the same. You're my weak side, my eternal embarrassment, my shame. Of all those eager watchdogs, you were the only one who could foresee what I might do." Fernandus smacked his lips. "I hoped—it's true, even if you don't believe me—I hoped that you'd let me go, to continue the game. But you had to get rid of me, you ass. Couldn't face the truth."

The commissaris refilled the cups. "The truth . . . what if there isn't any?"

Fernandus sighed pleasurably. "Good buzz. Hits the painkiller just right." He looked at his cigar. "You thought I'd die of lung cancer, I'm sure. I had stopped smoking, then I started again because of you. I thought about that later. Did you know they suspected lung cancer, the doctors?"

"No." The commissaris balanced his cup on the palm of his hand. "Why should I know that? I have been avoiding you. I asked you a question. What if there isn't any truth? What if even our supposition that there's no truth isn't true? Wouldn't we have to make up our own truth then?"

"But I did," Fernandus said loudly. "*You* didn't. You accepted the made-up truth of present unevolved society. I hypothesized that nothing matters and that therefore I could make myself matter and that I should do anything to bring about the best possible time for me. I succeeded at doing that. Most of my life I had everything that my own gods would hand me on a platter." Fernandus giggled. "Including your secretary. Now whom did she marry?"

"The junkie," the commissaris said, "who is no junkie and whom you failed to kill. A most courageous and talented artist. Carl."

Fernandus studied the swirling contents of his cup. "The unbalanced boy who stutters?"

"Yes."

Fernandus drank. "Yes, I didn't figure that out very well, you can't blame me for that. You always had the power of the state behind you, and I could only rely on my own weak crew. I was handicapped. Even so, I did pretty well."

"You didn't get my secretary," the commissaris said. "She was my spy. You never knew that."

Fernandus held up his cup again. "But I did, I saw through your gambit at once. I never trusted Toine."

He grinned. "But what a chance! She had to play along a bit and I stretched that out as far as her imagination would go. I reconstructed Miss Bakker . . . heh heh."

"Yes," the commissaris said. "You sure you can drink this much? The alcohol might conk you out."

"I'll be all right."

"Sure," the commissaris said. "You'll be fine. Tomorrow you die and nobody cares. Your wife has become a fat slobbering sow. Your son waits for you in hell. The baron, your trusted right hand, will turn into a festering demon who'll spread himself all over your ghost. Heul and the junkies you overdosed in that garbage boat changed into cancerous cells that are now sucking your marrow."

"Whoa," Fernandus shouted. "Save your poetry, Jan. What brings on this petty rage? Getting sozzled already?"

"A bit." The commissaris nodded. "Just a bit. I'd better not get drunk. If I do, Katrien will be furious."

Fernandus imitated the commissaris's voice. " 'Katrien will be furious.' Here you are, sixty years old, head of the municipal police, a knight in the Order of the Queen, and you live in peril of your dragon lady."

The commissaris frowned. "Katrien wanted to come too. Be grateful she didn't."

"I would have told her about Miss Bakker," Fernandus said, slurring the edges of his words. "That's where it all started. It's so simple, looking back. That's what's nice about approaching death. Suddenly the worn-out memory becomes quite clear. Listen"— he gestured, careful not to spill his whiskey—"listen, Jan. You and I were both born of middle-aged, flat-chested mothers, that's the key to our desire. Absence of good breasts. We both tried to make Miss Bakker our mother. You succeeded because you were good at being cute. I got you off her lap. I deprived you of motherly love, of big breasts to lean your cute little head against, and to feel a bit, I saw you do that."

"No," the commissaris said. "Right. Let's assume you're right. It would have made no difference if I had stayed on Miss Bakker's lap or not. Now listen to this. I agree, we keep going back to that basic supposition, I agree that there's nothing at all. No morals. No good or evil. We made it up ourselves. We, humanity." He waved his cup wildly.

"Careful," Fernandus said.

"So there's this big empty universe," the commissaris said. "With some minute specks of matter floating around, and we're on a speck. But the speck is nothing, either. So we can do as we like. We can be friendly or unfriendly. Maybe we're clever, you and I . . ."

"Very clever," Fernandus said. "But what's the good of intelligence if it isn't used? You never used yours. You toed all these lines. On the tips of your toes, tongue hanging out, conforming, pleasing essentially powerless authorities like the Queen. Bah! Never daring to do anything at all on your own, refusing the good gifts. You never even had a proper car."

"I have a very nice car," the commissaris said, "serves me well, thank you, and a comfortable house, and a turtle, and a coffee pot, I've got everything. Now hold off for a minute. So maybe I'm clever. I can manipulate the others, make them do what I like. Abuse them. What good does that do?"

"There's no good," Fernandus said. "There's only our own selection of self-made values."

"Please," the commissaris said. "Don't interrupt all the time. I have manipulated people, I still do, but for their own . . ." He hesitated.

"Good," Fernandus finished. "There you go again. There is no good. There's pleasure and there's non-pleasure. There's tension and a nice free feeling.

There's frustration and indulgence. I always went for pleasure. Whose pleasure, eh?''

"Your own," the commissaris said. "Look where you are now."

Fernandus patted his cushion. "I'm comfortable. I arranged for my own painless death tomorrow. I don't want well-wishers around when I die. Just a scientist in a nice clean coat, holding a clean needle with fast poison. I won't even feel death, for I'll be put to sleep first. Nice sleep, Jan. You're an old man too. You know how good it is to nap." He smiled. "Drift away slowly, the bright colors around you fading into all sorts of subtle soft shades. The sounds dying out, and suddenly you drift free, that's what it will be like."

"And then?"

Fernandus shook his head. "Then nothing. I'm looking forward to that. My body is old now, I'm getting rid of a faulty instrument, and my mind can go too. I had fun with it, but it's getting slow. It didn't get me out of the damned airport. The hell with my mind." He pounded the mattress. "And the hell with you."

"No," the commissaris said. "I'll go to heaven." He sighed. "Maybe you did right after all, Willem. Hell could be exciting. Heaven will be dull. Hell is probably like your club and I'd be forever looking at half-naked women and eating caviar on toast."

"You're serious?" Fernandus asked. "I also think hell will be like the Society's club, or like the motel at the lakeside. I wouldn't mind that. Being young again. I'll swim. I used to enjoy that."

"In boiling tar," the commissaris said. "And I'll be on an aromatic cloud. You hurt and I float in boredom." He emptied the bottle into the cup. "I hope the angels will send me down to relieve your pain."

"I'd pull you into the tar too," Fernandus said. "You'd be very welcome."

The commissaris got up. "You did that during our

final adventure. I lost a lot of face. My men thought I
was this detached eternal father who could be shaken
by nothing earthly at all. Now they're bad-mouthing
what's left of my image. De Gier broke away. Grijpstra gets cleverer by the day. Cardozo sees through my
veils. Katrien . . .'' The commissaris groaned.

"I'm sorry," Fernandus whispered.

The commissaris didn't hear.

Fernandus whispered louder.

"You're sorry?" the commissaris asked. "You?"

"I'm human," Fernandus said. "You're right. I
lose. I see that now. You'd better go."

The commissaris got up.

Fernandus stirred weakly. "Help me up again, Jan,
the pillows keep slipping down."

"You should rest," the commissaris said.

"I'll sit up," Fernandus said, glancing at the phone.
"I'd better receive death properly."

"That'll be tomorrow," the commissaris said.
" 'Bye."

The commissaris walked slowly to the elevator. He
wasn't too drunk. The bottle had only been half full,
and Fernandus had drunk half of that. But he wasn't
sober, either. My judgment is impaired, the commissaris thought, remembering a lecture on alcoholism.
Drunks have impaired judgment. Should I forgive Willem? the commissaris thought. Do I accept his humanity after all? Or am I too mellow now?

He crossed the hospital's parking lot, on his way to
his car. Why had Fernandus wanted to sit up? Why
had he glanced at the phone? Whom did he want to
contact so urgently?

No, the commissaris thought, taking time to admire
an ominous dark gray cloud filling in a piece of blue
sky. Sure, policemen habitually go for the lowest motive when they analyze a suspect's activity, but Fernandus was no longer a suspect. And, under present
circumstances, he himself should no longer act as a

cop. Cops are human too, they forgive and forget. Hadn't Fernandus admitted to his humanity after all? Even said he was sorry?

The commissaris put his hand on the Citroën's door. Then he let go of the handle again and turned around. Behind him the hospital stared silently, through its many window eyes.

Perhaps, the commissaris thought. Yes, perhaps. There had been a case in Rotterdam where a high-ranking police officer, out of uniform, driving home after a party where he had been manipulated by a colleague into overindulging, was arrested by officers trailing him in a patrol car. The Rotterdam commissaris had lost his job, the officers who made the arrest were promoted ahead of time. The colleague had taken the ex-commissaris's position. A clear motive in that case.

Again?

Why not? the commissaris thought sadly. Criminals never have too many choices as to how they will materialize their petty schemes.

The commissaris walked away from the Citroën and crossed the parking lot, in spite of the sudden downpour released by the ominous cloud. He reached the avenue that passed by the hospital. There was a tram shelter and he sat on its hard bench. A coincidence, no doubt, but there was a patrol car across the road, partly hidden behind a parked truck. Two cops were staring at the hospital's parking lot.

The commissaris stood up and located Fernandus's window in the large building behind him. He thought he saw a pajama-clad figure, partly hidden by curtains. He waved, but Fernandus wouldn't be able to see him through the dirty glass of the shelter's wall.

A tram came riding up, harshly clanging its bell. The commissaris stepped outside, shivering as cold raindrops hit him sharply in the neck. The rain was coming down so hard that drops ricocheted from the pavement, lashing at his hands and cheeks. He shivered, thinking of his warm dry car. Well, he would pick it up later. The commissaris boarded the tram.

"What are you doing out of bed?" a nurse asked Fernandus. "Here, let me help you." She was too late. Fernandus had fallen over already. She frowned as she pulled the muttering patient up. Such a nice little gentleman. Such horribly foul language.